D0407764

MERCY CREEK

ALSO AVAILABLE BY M.E. BROWNING

The Jo Wyatt Mysteries

Shadow Ridge

(writing as Micki Browning)

Beached

Adrift

MERCY CREEK

A JO WYATT MYSTERY

M. E. Browning

NEW YORK

This is a work of fiction. All of the names, characters, organizations, places, and events portrayed in this novel are either products of the author's imagination or are used fictitiously. Any resemblance to real or actual events, locales, or persons, living or dead, is entirely coincidental.

Published in the United States by Crooked Lane Books, an imprint of The Quick Brown Fox & Company LLC.

Crooked Lane Books and its logo are trademarks of The Quick Brown Fox & Company LLC.

Library of Congress Catalog-in-Publication data available upon request.

ISBN (hardcover): 978-1-64385-762-6
ISBN (ebook): 978-1-64385-763-3

Cover design by Nicole Lecht

Printed in the United States.

www.crookedlanebooks.com

Crooked Lane Books
34 West 27th St., 10th Floor
New York, NY 10001

First Edition: October 2021

10 9 8 7 6 5 4 3 2 1

For David who inspires me to fly,
and Mandy for teaching me how to stick the landing.

1

Everyone had a story from that night. Some saw a man, others saw a girl, still others saw nothing at all but didn't want to squander the opportunity to be part of something larger than themselves. To varying degrees, they were all wrong. Only two people knew the full truth.

That Saturday, visitors to the county fair clustered in the dappled shade cast by carnival rides and rested on hay bales scattered like afterthoughts between games of chance and food booths, the soles of their shoes sticky with ice cream drips and spilled sodas.

Detective Jo Wyatt stepped into the shadow of the Hall of Mirrors to watch the crowd. She grabbed the collar of her uniform and pumped it a few times in a futile attempt to push cooler air between her ballistic vest and sweat-sodden T-shirt.

The Echo Valley Fair marked the end of summer, but even now, as the relentless Colorado sun dipped, heat rose in waves around bare ankles and stroller wheels as families retreated toward the parking lots. An older crowd began to creep in, prowling the midway. The beer garden overflowed.

Within minutes the sun dropped behind the valley walls and the fairground lights flickered to life, their wan orange glow a beacon to moths confused by the strobing brightness of rides and games. Calliope music and the midway's technopop collided in a crazed mishmash of notes so loud they echoed in Jo's chest. She raised the volume of her radio.

The day shift officers had clocked out, having handled nothing more pressing than a man locked out of his car and an allegation of unfair judging flung by the second-place winner of the bake-off.

Jo gauged the teeming crowd of unfamiliar faces. Tonight would be different.

* * *

Carnival music was creepy, Lena decided. Each ride had its own weird tune and it all seemed to crash against her with equal force, following her no matter where she went.

The guys in the booths were louder than they had been earlier, more aggressive, calling out, trying to get her to part with her tickets. Some of the guys roamed, jumping out at people, flicking cards and making jokes she didn't understand while smiling at her older sister.

Marisa tossed her hair. Smiled back. Sometimes they let her play for free.

"Let's go back to the livestock pavilion," Lena said.

"Quit being such a baby." Marisa glanced over her shoulder at the guy running the shooting gallery booth and tossed her hair. Again.

Lena rolled her eyes and wondered how long it would be before her sister ditched her.

"Hold up a sec." Marisa tugged at the hem of her skintight skirt and flopped down on a hay bale.

She'd been wearing pants when they'd left the house. The big purse she always carried probably hid an entire wardrobe Momma knew nothing about. Lena wondered if the missing key to Grandma's car was tucked in there too.

Marisa unzipped one of her boots and pulled up her thin sock.

Lena pointed. "What happened to the bottom of your boot?"

Her sister ran her finger along the arch. "I painted it red."

"Why?"

"It makes them more valuable."

"Since when does coloring the bottom of your shoes make them more valuable?"

Marisa's eyes lit up in a way that happened whenever she spoke about clothes or how she was going to hit it big in Hollywood someday. "In Paris there's this guy who designs shoes and all of them have red soles. He's the only one allowed to do that. It's his thing."

"But he didn't make those boots."

"All the famous women wear his shoes." She waved to someone in the crowd.

"You're not famous and you bought them at Payless."

"What do you know about fashion?"

"I know enough not to paint the bottom of my boots to make them look like someone else made them."

Marisa shoved her foot into her boot and yanked the zipper closed. "You bought your boots from the co-op." She handed Lena her cell phone.

"You should have bought yours there, too." Lena dutifully pointed the lens at her sister.

"Take a couple this time." Marisa leaned back on her hands and arched her back, her hair nearly brushing the hay bale, and the expression on her face pouty like the girls in the magazines she was always looking at.

Lena snapped several photos and held out the phone. "All those high heels are good for is punching holes in the ground."

"Oh, Lena." Marisa's voice dropped as if she was sharing a secret. "If you ever looked up from your animals long enough, you'd see there's so much more to the world." Her thumbs rapidly tapped the tiny keyboard of her phone.

In the center of the midway, a carnival guy held a long-handled mallet and called out to people as they passed by. He was older—somewhere in his twenties—and wore a tank top. Green and blue tattoos covered his arms, and his biceps bulged as he pointed the oversized hammer at the tower behind him. It looked like a giant thermometer with numbers running along one edge and *High Striker* spelled out on the other.

"Come on, men. There's no easier way to impress the ladies." He grabbed the mallet and tapped the plate. "You just have to find the proper motivation if you want to get it up . . ." He pointed with his chin to the top of the game and paused dramatically. "There." He craned his neck and leered at Marisa. Lena wondered if he was looking up her sister's skirt. "What happens later is up to you."

Never breaking eye contact, he took a mighty swing. The puck raced up the tower, setting off a rainbow of lights and whistles before it smashed into the bell at the top. He winked in their direction. "Score."

Twenty minutes later, Marisa was gone.

* * *

Lena gave up looking for her sister and returned to the livestock pavilion. Marisa could keep her music and crowds and stupid friends.

Only a few people still wandered around the dimly lit livestock pavilion. The fireworks would start soon, and most people headed for the excitement outside, a world away from the comforting sound of animals snuffling and pawing at their bedding.

Marisa was probably hanging out near the river with her friends, drinking beer. Maybe smoking a cigarette or even a joint. Doing things she didn't think her baby sister knew about.

Lena walked through an aisle stacked with poultry and rabbit cages. The pens holding goats, swine, and sheep took up the middle. At the back of the pavilion stretched a long row of three-sided cattle stalls. The smells of straw, grain, and animals replaced the gross smell of deep-fried candy bars and churros that had clogged her throat on the midway.

Near the end of the row, Lena stopped.

"Hey there, Bluebell." Technically, he was number twenty-four, like his ear tag said. Her father didn't believe in naming livestock, but to her, he'd always be Bluebell—even after she sold him at the auction to be slaughtered. Just because that was his fate didn't mean he shouldn't have a name to be remembered by. She remembered them all.

She patted his hip and slid her hand along his spine so he wouldn't shy as she moved into the stall. She double-checked the halter, pausing to scratch his forehead. A piece of straw swirled in his water bucket and she fished it out. The cold water cooled her hot skin.

"You did good today. Sorry I won't be spending the night with you, but Papa got called out to Dawson's ranch to stitch up some mare."

He swished his tail and it struck the rail with a metallic ring.

"Don't get yourself all riled. I'll be back tomorrow before you know it."

If she hadn't been showing Bluebell this afternoon, she'd have gone with her father. Her sutures had really improved this summer and were almost as neat as his. No one would guess they'd been made by an eleven-year-old. If nothing else, she could have helped keep the horse calm.

Instead, she'd go home with Marisa and spend the night at Momma's. She wondered if Marisa would show up before the 4-H leader called lights out in the pavilion or if Lena would have to walk to her mom's house by herself in the dark.

She reached down and jiggled the feed pan to smooth out the grain that Bluebell had pushed to the edges.

"That's some cow."

The male voice startled them both, and Bluebell stomped his rear hoof. Lena peered over the Hereford's withers. At first all she saw were the tattoos. An ugly monster head with a gaping mouth and snake tongue seemed to snap at her. It was the carny from the High Striker standing at the edge of the stall.

"It's a steer," she stuttered. "And my sister isn't here."

"Not your sister I wanted to talk to." He swayed a bit as he moved into the stall, like when her mother drank too much wine and tried to hide it.

Lena ducked under Bluebell's throat and came up on the other side. She looked around the pavilion, now empty of people.

"Suspect they're all out waiting on the fireworks," he said.

The first boom echoed through the space. Several sheep bleated their disapproval and Bluebell jerked against his halter.

"Shhhh, now." Lena reached her hand down and scratched his chest. "All that racket's just some stupid fireworks."

"Nothing to worry about," the man added. He had the same look in his eyes that Papa's border collie got right before he cut off the escape route of a runaway cow.

A bigger boom thundered through the pavilion. Halter clips clanged against the rails as uneasy cattle shuffled in their stalls. Her own legs shook as she sidled toward Bluebell's rear.

He matched her steps. "What's a little thing like you doing in here all by yourself?"

"My father will be back any minute." Her voice shook.

He smiled, baring his teeth. "I'll be sure to introduce myself when he arrives."

A series of explosions, sharp as gunfire, erupted outside. Somewhere a cow lowed. Several more joined in, their voices pitiful with fear.

"You're upsetting my steer. You need to leave."

"Oh, your cow's just fine. I think it's you that's scared."

He spoke with the same low voice that Lena used with injured animals. The one she used right before she did something she knew would hurt but had to be done.

"You're a pretty little thing," he crooned. "Nice and quiet."

Her tongue stuck to the roof of her mouth. She stood frozen. A warm trickle started down her leg, and the wet spot expanded on her jeans.

He edged closer. "I like them quiet."

* * *

Jo ran.

The suspect veered off the sidewalk and slid down the hillside toward the creek.

She plunged off the side of the embankment, sliding through dirt and duff, closing the distance. She keyed her shoulder mic. "Entering the creek, heading west toward the Animas. I need someone on the River Trail."

Narrow-leaf cottonwood and willows shimmered silver in the moonlight and wove a thicket of branches along the water, herding the suspect toward the cobbled stream bed.

Jo splashed into the ankle-deep water. Close enough now to almost touch.

Her lungs burned. With a final burst of speed, she lunged. Shoved his shoulder while he was mid-stride.

The man sprawled into the creek. Rolled onto his feet with a bellow. A knife in his hand.

Without thinking, she'd drawn her gun. "Drop it!"

Flashlight beams sliced the foliage. Snapping branches and crashing footsteps marked the other officers' progress as they neared. Estes shouted Jo's name. Her eyes never left the man standing just feet away.

"Over here!" She focused on the man's shoulder, watching for the twitch that would telegraph his intentions. "You need to drop the knife. Now." Her voice rose above the burble of the stream. "Or things are going to get a whole lot worse for you tonight."

She shifted her weight to her front leg and carefully shuffled her rear foot until she found firmer footing and settled into a more stable shooting stance. "Drop the knife." She aimed center mass. Drew a deep breath, willed her heart to slow.

The knife splashed into the creek near the bank.

"On your right." Estes broke through the brush beside her.

"Get down on your knees," Jo ordered. "Hands behind your head."

"It's my friend's truck," the man said.

Jo holstered her gun and moved forward while Estes covered her. She gripped his fingers and bowed the suspect backward, keeping him off balance while she searched him for weapons, then cuffed him.

"Not according to the owner." She double-locked the cuffs while Estes radioed dispatch they had one in custody.

An explosion above the treetops made Jo flinch. Fireworks slashed the darkness and burst into balls of purple and green and dazzling white that sparkled briefly, then disappeared.

2

The sun had the blinding intensity of a beautiful day, and Tilda Marquet slapped the car visor down. It was no use. Even wearing sunglasses, the morning glare burned her retinas, and she saw little more than the silhouettes of the dead bugs on her windshield.

"One more month." She muttered the words like a mantra.

The hospital disappeared from her rearview mirror and she joined the line of traffic headed toward town, constantly veering over the road's center line to avoid the packs of Sunday morning cyclists riding along the shoulder.

A minivan roared past her, despite oncoming traffic. Another person who didn't know how to drive beyond his hood. She slowed slightly to let the driver merge in front of her. Maybe people would be more careful if they saw what came through the ER.

Last night it had been Lara's and Jim's kid. Probably texting from the time he left the fairgrounds until he hit the bar ditch and plowed his parent's pickup through ten yards of wire fencing. Deputies found the truck on its roof. Medics finally located Jake up the road, hopping around on one leg, trying to round up the escaped cattle. One look at his shallow breathing when he arrived at the ER had told her that in addition to his mangled knee, he'd cracked a couple of ribs too.

Ranch kids. They were a tough lot.

She drove the remaining ten miles on autopilot. It was seven thirty when she walked into her townhouse. Upstairs, she opened her eldest daughter's door. A twinge of jealousy tightened Tilda's lips as she stared at the racks of new clothes, the stacked boxes of shoes and piles of purses. She imagined this was what a Hollywood starlet's dressing room looked like, a mountain of options. Options Tilda no longer had—in truth had never known.

One rack created a wall that hid the bed from the doorway, but the three-way mirror that dominated Marisa's makeup table reflected her daughter still sleeping, her breathing even and untroubled. Tilda shut the door with enough force to wake a normal person, but Marisa slept like the dead. Always had. Sometimes Tilda wished she'd had normal girls. Or maybe boys. Weren't they supposed to be easier?

She passed the closed door of her own bedroom and descended the stairs.

The siren song of chardonnay drew Tilda into the kitchen, and she pulled a bottle from the fridge. To the world it was seven thirty in the morning. For her it was the end of another in a long line of twelve-hour graveyard shifts and she couldn't wait to rotate back to days. She poured herself a glass. The bottle clanked loudly against the counter, but the door to the den was closed. It didn't matter anyway. Lena would have left for the fairgrounds an hour ago.

"One more month," she muttered and took a long pull, then topped off the glass and settled into her recliner in the living room.

* * *

Tilda swatted at the vibration on her thigh, then blinked the sleep from her eyes and dug the cell phone from the pocket of her scrubs. She glanced at the blurred screen and groaned.

"Hey, Chuck." It came out as a croak and she cleared her throat.

The 4-H leader spoke, but his words didn't make sense. She struggled into a seated position and the recliner's footrest snapped down with finality.

"Sorry, I'm going to need you to repeat that," she said.

"Lena." He sounded annoyed, or busy. Maybe both. "Just because the judging's over doesn't mean she can shirk her duties today."

Tilda bristled. Lena was the responsible one. Hell, when she was Lena's age, Sunday mornings were all about cartoons, not hustling to take care of a half-ton cow. "You woke me from a dead sleep, so maybe dial down the outrage and tell me what this is about."

"She's late."

Good God. He woke her up for this? "I'm sure she's apologized for being late. Knowing Lena, she'll more than make up the time."

"No, I mean she's late as in she's not here."

"What do you mean she isn't there?"

"Never showed up. I'm hoping you can light a fire under her. The gates open in about a half hour."

She leaned forward to look at the clock on the DVD player and a ray of light through the window blinded her. "Give me ten minutes."

* * *

A woman who enjoyed sleep as much as she did should never have become a nurse. Or had children.

Tilda carried her wineglass to the sink. Figures, the one time she doesn't bother to open the den door is the one time Lena decides to be a normal kid and sleep in.

"One more month," she muttered before raising her voice. "Lena. Wake up, you're late."

A lawn mower fired up outside.

"Galena Patrice Flores! You better be out of that bed by the time I get to the door."

She rinsed the glass and flipped it upside down on the dish rack. Marisa had left a note on the counter. Short and sweet. She'd left to meet her girlfriends for breakfast and a shopping trip to Farmington. Not *could* she go. No. Marisa didn't ask for permission anymore. Another consequence of Tilda working graveyards. Free-range kids.

The noise of the mower made it impossible to hear if Lena was up. Tilda dropped Marisa's note onto the counter. "Lena!"

It wasn't even her weekend to have Lena. Not that it mattered. Whatever Lucero wanted, he got—everyone else be damned. Well, he was going to get more than he bargained for when she got hold of him. This no-notice bullshit had to stop. An unexpected emergency her ass. Probably a tryst with some dark-haired bimbo who didn't know any better—but who'd learn. They all did, eventually. She sure had.

The tile beneath Tilda's feet alternated hot and cold as she passed through the shadows that stretched between windows. At the door she hesitated, her hand on the knob. The growl of the mower grew louder. Too loud. It filled her head with the buzzing of a thousand bees and a shiver raced across her scalp as if they were all trying to escape at once. She jerked her hand back.

Only one other time had she ever had such a visceral awareness. A feeling she couldn't explain of a knowledge she had no way of knowing. But she knew. Knew the moment she entered the den that nothing would ever be the same again.

The buzzing grew. A pounding of her pulse in her ears. So loud she closed her eyes against it. Drew a deep breath. Yanked open the door.

Empty.

* * *

"Lena!"

The twisted wrought iron banister dug into Tilda's palm as she pulled herself up the stairs. Willed her feet to move faster.

Marisa's door stood open. Tilda raced into the bedroom. Threw off the bedsheets, opened the closet. Peeked behind racks.

She spun, her eyes darting around the room. Lena was small, she could be anywhere. Tilda fell to her knees, raised the bed skirt. Nothing but discarded shoes and fashion magazines.

Inside the bathroom, she flung open the shower curtain as if playing a demented game of hide-and-seek. A shampoo bottle teetered and fell against another bottle on the shower ledge, and an avalanche of conditioners, hair masks, and other toiletries crashed onto the tile floor. No Lena.

She tore through her own bedroom. The master bath. Not a single clue to her daughter's whereabouts.

The garage? Tilda descended the steps two at a time and tripped near the bottom. Reflexively, her hand shot out. Her body weight drove her into the wall, and she felt the tendons in her wrist stretch. She rested her forehead against the painted surface and cradled her wrist tight against her chest. Forced herself to breathe.

Think.

The buzzing lost its ferocity. She bit her lip. Stood there until her heart settled. Her mind cleared.

This was stupid. There had to be a simple explanation. No need to get so worked up.

The door to the garage creaked when she pushed it open. The obvious answer was Lena had gone with her sister. For two steps she managed to believe it. Never mind that Lena hated shopping—almost as much as Marisa despised having her younger sister tagging along when she was out with her friends.

Her mother's old Crown Victoria filled the one-car garage. Tilda squeezed along the passenger side, the mirror pressing into her gut. In a month the car would be Marisa's to drive. Now, she cupped her hands between her face and the window and peered into the dark interior, searching for her other daughter. Empty.

Lucero must have swung by the house and picked her up. It would be just like him to change plans without telling her. She yanked the drawstrings of her scrubs tight around her waist.

Except he would have taken her straight to the fairgrounds. He'd always been a strict disciplinarian. Plus, there was her steer to take care of. No way would he let Lena skip out on that.

Friends? She wrapped her arms around herself. Did Lena have friends? She had to have someone; she was quiet, not a hermit. Tears pricked Tilda's eyes. From the moment she'd been born, Lena had belonged to Lucero. And Tilda hated him for it.

With nowhere else to search, she returned to the den. As an ER nurse, she knew how to handle an emergency. Knew to take one task at a time. Get the job done. But that was with other people. This was Lena.

For a long moment she stood motionless on the threshold of the den. Light fought through the closed blinds and painted the room with stripes. Outside, the mower died, and in the silence, she whispered a prayer to a god she didn't believe existed. Already the heat of the day warmed the space. The daybed Lena used when she visited was neatly made, the decorative pillows precisely placed as if they'd never been moved. The first of the James Herriot books lay splayed upside down on the desk. Tilda ran her finger along the broken spine. How many times could Lena read the same story?

Would she have taken the book to the fairgrounds to pass the time? Tilda's smile faded. She understood Marisa, but her youngest daughter was different, and Tilda didn't know where to look. Didn't know what thoughts ran through Lena's mind. The only thing she knew for certain was that the backpack Lena always carried was missing.

Hope, fragile as a butterfly, fluttered to life, and Tilda clung to it.

Lena never went anywhere without her backpack. She called it her emergency kit. The canvas rucksack contained a set of tools and first aid supplies Lucero had given her after she started shadowing him on his vet rounds. Naturally, Lena would have taken it when she left for the fairgrounds.

Relief flooded Tilda's body and her shoulders sagged. It was a normal morning after all—Lena'd just gotten off to a late start. Chuck would be calling any minute to say she'd arrived.

Outside, another motor—smaller this time—sputtered, but didn't catch. It took her neighbor two more pulls before the motor caught and settled into a high-pitched whine.

A pebble crashed against the window blind, setting it asway, and a blade of sunshine sliced across her face.

The buzzing in her head returned. Tilda crept closer to the window, never taking her eyes off the fluttering blind. Mustering her courage, she grabbed the shade and pulled it away from the casing.

Her neighbor used an edger along the sidewalk. The tool bit into the lawn, screeching and bucking when it hit concrete.

And Tilda saw it all through the window that wasn't supposed to be open.

3

Jo heard the screams while she was falling, and then there was nothing but the rush of cold water that shocked the breath from her lungs. Her feet found the bottom of the dunk tank and she stood, slicking the hair back from her face. At least she was awake now.

"That's for eating my last rope of licorice," Squint MacAllister said. Normally reserved, his face bore the trace of a smile.

"I replaced it with a whole bucket." She reset the lever that held the bench of the dunk tank in place.

"Conveniently while I was on vacation."

The fairground gates had reopened at nine. Not even fifteen minutes later and the old uniform shirt and patrol shorts she wore were soaked—courtesy of her partner.

She clambered onto her perch. Last night's shift was overtime, this morning's gig was to raise money for the Boys and Girls Club of Echo Valley. It was the only reason she had been able to drag herself out of bed after a night that had included two felony arrests, a hit-and-run in the parking lot, and an all-out brawl at the beer garden after the taps ran dry.

A fresh round of screams from the nearby Tilt-a-Whirl morphed into little-girl giggles. She needed coffee.

Unlike the crowd last night, this morning's crowd held plenty of familiar faces, and a small crowd gathered to watch the detectives.

Squint tossed a second softball into the air while he waited for her to get settled. Ever the gentleman.

"Not a bad arm, for an old guy," Jo taunted.

He tipped his Stetson back slightly and wound up his long limbs. "This one's for filling my car with balloons."

"It was your birthday."

The ball hit the target with a crack and she dropped gracelessly into the tank.

Time to change tactics. Back on the bench, she'd just opened her mouth when he let loose another line drive.

He waited until she finished snorting the water out of her nose, and then said, "That one was solely for fun."

"Who needs children when I've got you?" She twined her fingers through the metal grating above the water line.

"It's not the same."

"No?"

His cell phone rang. He peeked at the caller ID and handed the remaining ball to the dispatcher manning the line of kids and parents, all eager to throw the ball themselves.

Squint had been her training officer when she'd first joined the ranks of the Echo Valley Police Department thirteen years ago. They'd teamed up again when she made detective a couple of years back. She knew his every expression; the tells no one else would have noticed. He'd stiffened just slightly, giving his full attention to the call, almost as if by listening hard enough, he could solve the problem before it was fully articulated. She climbed from the cage and grabbed her towel.

Deputy Corbett from the sheriff's department was waiting in the wings for his turn in the tank, and she called him over. "Sorry, looks like I've got a call-out."

"No worries."

She grabbed her shoes and backpack. The sun burned a bright spot in the cloudless sky, but the air seemed suddenly cooler. Under her dripping uniform, Jo shivered.

Squint ended the call and they ducked behind the tank. Straw clung to Jo's bare feet.

"Dickinson's out on a missing child case," he said.

Every day during the five days the fair was in town at least one child got separated from his family. Usually, after a tense ten-minute search, an officer would find the wayward one by the petting zoo or cotton candy trailer. The only problem was Dickinson wasn't working the fair.

"Where's he at?" Jo asked.

"Tilda Marquet's place."

"Marisa?"

Squint shook his head. "No."

* * *

On a map, Echo Valley appeared as a small dot not far above New Mexico's northern border in the southwest corner of Colorado. The city was urban enough to have its own craft brewery, but rural enough that bears rummaged through the trash at night. Tilda Marquet lived in one of the valley's newer developments, an orderly hierarchy of townhomes, houses, and extravagant faux chateaux where value was determined by how high up the mountain one climbed and how many pines framed the view.

Other than her college years, Jo had spent her entire life in the valley, and it hadn't taken her long to learn that policing a small community often meant knowing the people involved in the calls. Sometimes that worked to her advantage. She could only wait and see how it would unfold with Tilda.

Jo and Squint walked up the center of the shared driveway between Tilda's Pathfinder and her neighbor's pickup truck. The curtain in an upstairs window of the adjoining townhome flicked open. An older bald man watched their progress. Squint touched his fingers to the brim of his hat. The man stared, unmoving.

Officer Elijah Dickinson opened the door of Tilda's townhouse before the detectives reached the porch. He glanced over his shoulder and stepped outside, pulling the door softly closed behind him.

"Are you okay?" Jo asked.

Eli rubbed his hand across the back of his neck. "It's been an interesting morning."

Missing person calls always started at the patrol level. The assigned officer would talk to the reporting party, get the basics. If the missing person was an adult and there was no indication of foul play, there wasn't much the police could do. Adults had the right to pick up stakes and not tell anyone their plans. If the missing person was a teenager over sixteen, cops had a couple more options. But when the missing person was an at-risk adult or a child, the protocols were different. Timelines were shortened. Detectives were called.

Eli continued. "For starters, Ms. Marquet—"

The door opened. "Jessup, thank God you're here." Tilda buried her face against Squint's chest.

Few people knew Squint's given name; even fewer used it. And if Jo didn't know better, she'd say her partner was intentionally avoiding eye contact with her.

Tilda tilted her head to look up at Squint and noticed Jo. "What's she doing here?"

Squint gently disengaged. "Let's go inside," he said.

Tilda squared her shoulders, but her face remained pinched. "Of course." She still wore her ER scrubs and looked as if she'd been awake for a week. "Please, come in." She leaned on Squint and motioned the others forward.

Dickinson led the way. Jo had never been inside one of these townhomes, but it appeared to share the same layout as nearly every other townhome in the valley. Narrow hallway with requisite door into the garage on the left, staircase on the right. Based on a smudge on the wall, someone had come down too fast and used the wall as a backstop. Probably Marisa.

Family photos lined the hallway. Tilda with a laughing baby girl in a collection that chronicled the mundane milestones of the firstborn. The baby grew into a toddler before any of the photos showed a sibling.

"That's Marisa," Tilda said, pointing.

Up close, Jo detected alcohol on the woman's breath. Was this what Dickinson had tried to warn them about?

Tilda pointed to another frame. "She's seven or eight in that photo."

Marisa's resemblance to her mother was uncanny. It was her eyes, a light gray that dared you to look away. Next to her sister, the younger daughter faded into the background. A few years later, she disappeared almost completely—at least in the photos. The few candids there were of Lena almost always had an animal in the frame rather than another person.

"Marisa was four when Lena was born." Tilda's voice held an edge, as if she too noticed the imbalance of photos. "Lena wasn't even a year old when her father and I divorced. She moved in with him after she turned six."

"Was that her choice or yours?" Jo asked.

"Hers." Tilda stepped forward, but there was no way around Jo and Dickinson in the small space.

"Could she be with Lucero now?" Jo pressed.

"We only speak when we absolutely have to." Tilda jerked the hem of her scrub shirt as if to remove a twelve-hour shift's worth of wrinkles in a single tug. "When's the last time you spoke to your ex?"

"Last night."

"Oh, that's right. Cameron's a sergeant now. I'd heard you didn't get it. Must be awkward."

Jo ignored the dig, but if ever there was a time to reach out to an ex, it was when your daughter was missing.

"Tilda." Squint stepped between the women. "We'll need his phone number."

"It won't do you any good. I've been trying to reach him all morning. I can't get through."

Dickinson broke in. "He lives in Coyote Canyon. Cell service out there is spotty. I've left a message. Estes is on his way out there now."

"I can promise you she's not there," Tilda said. "Whether he's there or not."

Custody issues between divorced parents accounted for more than a few missing children. "How can you be so sure?" Jo asked.

Tilda made a production of answering to Squint. "She was supposed to be at the fairgrounds this morning at seven to take care of her steer and muck the stall before the gates opened."

Jo hadn't expected a warm welcome, but when a person calls the police because their child is missing, she hadn't expected to be stonewalled, either.

They came upon a solitary nail in the wall, and Tilda raised a hand to her mouth. Squint placed his hand on her back. "Let's sit down and start at the beginning."

The hallway opened into a great room consisting of living and dining space that butted up against the kitchen. A breakfast bar with a sink on one side and bar stools on the other helped divide the space. Blackened bananas and an unopened box of cereal sat on the counter. An upside-down wineglass drained in the rack.

Tilda noticed her scrutiny. "Marisa doesn't eat breakfast. The cereal was for Lena." She stomped on the trashcan pedal and dropped the bananas in the garbage. "I don't know what to do first when Lena comes home. Hug her or ground her."

"Has she ever run away?" Squint asked.

"She's eleven, Jessup." In the silence, Tilda's shoulders drooped. "No. She's never gone anywhere without permission."

Squint guided her to the couch and then chose the club chair next to her and balanced his hat on the arm.

Jo pulled a notepad from her bag. She was the on-call detective this weekend, but Squint obviously had a better rapport with Tilda. They'd worked together long enough that there was no need to discuss who would take the lead on the interview. He'd ask the questions, she'd capture the answers. Hopefully they'd uncover a benign reason why an eleven-year-old girl wasn't where she was supposed to be.

"I couldn't wait to get home this morning." Tilda perched on the edge of the cushion and raked her nails through her hair. "Last night was crazy, what with the fair in town, and then Jake—Lara and Jim's kid—crashed through the front fence of Johansen's ranch out by Mercy Creek. It finally quieted down around four, and I left the hospital at seven. When I got home, Marisa was asleep."

"And Lena?" Squint prodded.

She raised her hands to her face and rubbed her eyes. "Lena left before I got home." She dropped her hands. "I fell asleep. Next thing I know Chuck Ellison, the 4-H leader, is on the phone asking me to light a fire under Lena because she hadn't shown up yet."

The scratch of Jo's pen was the only noise while the officers let the silence push Tilda to tell the story her way.

Despite the early hour, the air conditioner kicked on, and Tilda jumped. "I haven't wanted a cigarette this bad in years." She clutched her hands in her lap, and the knuckles whitened. "What now? How do we find my baby?"

As far as relating information, Tilda's statement was stingy.

"Where was Lena last night before you left for work?" Squint asked.

"The fair. She practically lives there when it's in town. Every year she enters some animal. Lena's steer won the blue in market beef. I was sleeping, but a couple hours later she called to let me know her steer was named reserve grand champion, or something."

Squint leaned forward. "Did she come home after that?"

"She wasn't supposed to come home at all. Kids with livestock can spend the night at the fairgrounds as long as they have a parent or guardian with them. A lot of the 4-H kids treat it like a big slumber party. Her father," she iced the word, "was supposed to spend the night with her."

"He didn't?" Squint asked.

"Lucero sent me a text as I was getting ready to leave for work that he got called out to a ranch over in Cortez to tend some horse or cow or God knows what. Stuck me with figuring out new arrangements. I had to ask Marisa to watch her sister last night."

"Did they stay the night?"

"Oh, hell no." Tilda laughed. "Lena's the ranch girl, not Marisa. They would have come home right after the fireworks."

Jo looked up from her notes. "Would have? Did you confirm that they did?"

The merriment fell from Tilda's face. "Marisa was gone by the time Chuck called." She slid her feet out of her Crocs and folded her legs under her on the couch.

"So we don't know if Lena came home last night," Jo said aloud and made another note on the to-do list side of her pad.

Tilda leaned forward and made a show of reading the badge attached to Jo's belt. "Of course she came home, *Detective*." Tilda said. "She was with her sister."

"We just need to verify what we can, so we know how best to proceed," Squint said. "Where is Marisa now?"

"She left a note saying she was meeting up with friends and driving to Farmington to shop for school clothes. You know teenage girls. They'll be gone all day. Hell, Lena will be home before Marisa even gets back." She looked at Jo. "And before you ask, I've been trying to reach Marisa for the last hour."

Curled up on the couch, Tilda looked lost in her own home. Jo remembered that look. Had seen it for the first time years ago. And its reappearance set off alarm bells. "We're going to do everything we possibly can to find Lena and bring her home."

"Of course you are. It's your job now, isn't it?"

Dickinson handed Jo a large photograph. A little girl with serious brown eyes that seemed too large for her heart-shaped face stared out of the school photo. A faint scar ran across her forehead. Her lips were parted, not in a smile, exactly, rather a look of curiosity that revealed a small gap between her front teeth. A thick brown braid hung over her shoulder. She wore a sage green T-shirt under bib overalls that had been almost completely cropped from the picture.

Where would a little girl go?

"There's more," Dickinson said quietly.

The last of Tilda's reserve crumbled. Tears filled her eyes. "Times are tough. I make decent money, but." She lifted her chin. "Money's tight. You know what it's like working graveyards. You can't sleep when it's too hot."

No danger of that. It had to be in the sixties in the house.

"The girls know to keep things buttoned up, keep the energy bill in check." Tears rolled down Tilda's cheeks, but she made no move to wipe them away. "Lena sleeps in the den on the weekends she stays. She was there last night. This morning when I checked, the window was wide open. She'd never have opened the window. Especially not at night, not on a ground floor, not when I'm not home."

Both detectives focused on Dickinson.

He shook his head. "No signs of forced entry, but I waited for you before processing the room."

Jo's to-do list crawled all the way down the page. They'd have to find and interview Lucero and Marisa. Talk to the 4-H leader, see if anyone had been annoying the kids at the fair. In the meantime, they'd canvass the neighborhood, retrace the path Lena would most likely have taken to the fairgrounds. Dickinson had already released an initial broadcast. She'd update the watch commander. Process the bedroom for possible evidence.

It was crucial that she create a timeline—determine the window of opportunity when Lena could have disappeared. Right now, that stretched all the way back to last night. With any luck, Lena's disappearance was merely a communication snafu and she was either with her father or at a friend's house. But they had to nail it down. If she'd run away or, worse, been abducted, time was their enemy.

Jo tucked the photo of Lena in her folio, but it was Lucero's face in the forefront of her mind.

Lucero and Tilda.

Had she ever really known either of them?

4

With a twist of the base, the silky filaments of the powder brush disappeared into the handle, and Jo tossed the brush into the tackle box that served as her print kit. Black powder smudged the windowsill of the den. More dusted the glass itself. She clicked on her flashlight and held it at an oblique angle, hoping to see a ridge or swirl emerge in relief. Nothing.

Squint stepped into the room holding an evidence bag with Lena's toothbrush. "Anything?"

Jo shook her head and repositioned the flashlight.

"Nothing usable, or nothing?" He placed the package next to his open camera case and another evidence bag holding Lena's hairbrush.

"I pulled some prints throughout the room, but not a single print where I'd hoped to find one." Jo clicked off the light. "Nothing on the headboard, nothing on the interior doorknob. Nothing on the windowsill. Not a single finger or palm print."

"Wiped?"

Jo turned her gloves inside out as she pulled them off. "I'll need to ask Tilda when she last cleaned, but nobody's that good a housekeeper. Especially someone who works graves. The only print I pulled around the window was where Tilda said she'd touched the blind when she looked outside.

"That's not good."

"No."

Jo's radio blared, and she lowered the volume. Dispatcher Dakota Kaplan's southern drawl repeated the BOLO for Galena Patrice Flores. Gender, age, hair color, height, weight. Important information, but only a thumbnail description that revealed none of the quirks that captured a little girl's personality.

"Any word from Lucero or Marisa?" Jo asked.

"Not yet."

She took another long look at the room. "Nothing adds up."

"Talk me through it."

In their two years of being partners, this had become their habit. Bouncing thoughts back and forth helped clarify murky circumstances, especially at the start of an investigation when the path it would take wasn't yet known. Squint tended to focus on the facts at hand. Jo dwelled on what seemed to be missing.

"The biggest mystery?" Jo pointed to the window. "Someone opened it, so where are the prints? If it was Lena, why would she wipe the sill clean? And knowing how her mom feels about the subject, wouldn't she have shut it before leaving the house?"

"Unless she wasn't allowed to," Squint said.

They both remained silent for a moment. The clock had started on their investigation, but there was frustratingly little they could do but speculate until they spoke with Marisa and Lucero.

"If Lena was abducted," Jo said, "it makes sense to grab her backpack, but why make the bed?"

"She could have made it before she left." Squint opened up a larger bag and placed the smaller bags inside. "It's also possible she didn't get into it last night. Or someone else made it."

"No way to tell if anyone boosted themselves into the room from the outside." A French drain ran alongside the house, grass grew beyond the gravel, and the cedar siding all conspired to hide any evidence that someone had lurked outside. "What if she ran away?" Jo asked.

Squint knelt beside a Pelican case and picked up his digital camera. "Lena's awful young to be a runaway." He detached the flash and capped the lens. "And besides, she sounds too responsible."

"I was five when I told my mom I was going to run away. She helped me pack a suitcase and told me I wasn't allowed to cross any streets." Jo tucked the flashlight in her back pocket. "I walked around the block three times before I got tired and came home."

"I'm betting your mother was hoping for a couple more laps."

"Let me know when you want help packing up your desk."

He closed the latches on the camera case and they snapped sharp and overloud in the small room. "The waiting is always the worst."

A sick feeling entered Jo's stomach. A little girl was missing, and there was no good reason for her to be gone. "We can't wait," Jo said.

"Wait for what?" Tilda stood in the doorway. Her hair had come out of its ponytail, and her eyes were bloodshot from lack of sleep.

Jo dipped her head toward the window. "Tilda, can you tell me the last time you cleaned this windowsill?"

A sudden flush colored Tilda's face. She clenched her fists and moved toward Jo. "Goddamn you, Jo Wyatt!"

Squint rose.

Tilda tried to step around Squint, but he blocked her. "You've never once stopped judging me." She jabbed her finger at Jo. "How about finding my daughter rather than worrying about my fucking windows."

"I'm not judging you," Jo said. "I need to know."

"Tilda." Squint lowered his voice. "It's important."

"Why?" Tilda spun away from Squint and momentarily buried her face in her hands. "Goddammit," she whispered, then turned back. Slower this time. "I don't know." She raised her eyes toward the ceiling and blinked back tears. "How many flies were there?"

Jo stepped around them both. "I'll brief the sergeant."

* * *

Outside, Jo hid from the sun on Tilda's small stoop. She ended the call and tapped the phone against her chin a couple of times while she thought.

The front door opened and Squint joined her.

"How's Tilda?" Jo asked.

"The more time that passes, the more worried she becomes." He settled his hat on his head.

"Yeah. Me too."

He studied her. "Want to tell me what's going on between you two?"

"She doesn't care for me."

"Don't need to be a detective to figure that out. Any particular reason?"

"None that are valid," Jo said.

Squint crossed his arms and leaned against the cedar siding. "You sure about that?"

Jo glanced at the door. "Now's not the time to explore either of our relationships with Tilda."

"Fair enough." He removed a small notebook from the breast pocket of his shirt. "Marisa just checked in. The girls left the fairgrounds right after the fireworks. She figures they were home around twenty-two hundred. Lena went to bed almost immediately. Said she was tired and had to get up early. Marisa stayed up another two hours or so checking her social media, listening to music." He lowered the pad a bit. "I'm assuming that's normal behavior for teens?"

"Don't look at me. You're the one with kids."

"Boys. And they stopped being teens about a decade ago." He flipped the page. "This morning, Marisa left the house to meet her friends around zero eight. Lena had planned to leave by six thirty. Marisa didn't hear any noise from the den to suggest Lena was still home, but she never thought to check, either."

Jo opened an app on her cell phone. "Sunrise was at six thirty-six, so it would have been plenty light already. Did Marisa give any idea what route they took home?"

"They came out the backside of the fairgrounds and dropped onto the river trail." When he finished giving her the details, he added, "Did you get in touch with the sarge?"

"Pieretti didn't want to jump the gun on anything before confirming Lena wasn't with Lucero or Marisa. So now we're in a holding pattern until we hear from Dad."

"How do you want to proceed?" he asked.

"Start a neighborhood canvass. If this is more than a misunderstanding, it'd be nice to have that done. Now that we know how they came home, I'll retrace the path the girls took from the fairgrounds. See if anything along the way gives me concern. Then I can interview the 4-H leader."

"I can handle the canvass," he said. "Dickinson should be back any minute with the fliers. When everything is done here, we can rally at the fairgrounds. I'll give you a ride back."

"I'll take the houses between here and the entry road on my way to the fairgrounds. No sense you having all the fun. Besides, the neighbor in the window didn't seem to like you. I want to find out what that's all about."

* * *

Canvassing sucked. It was the police equivalent of brushing one's teeth. A mindless task that was critical to the health of the investigation. An assignment that, if not done methodically, resulted in holes where you didn't want them that took more effort to fix later than if it had been done right from the start.

Jo began with Tilda's neighbor, duly noting the address of the townhouse and the license plate of his truck in her notebook. Over the years, she'd come to recognize that a person's reaction to meeting the police could be very revealing. The neighbor had mad-dogged them. And it was time to find out why.

The Echo Valley Police Department had a whopping forty-four employees, of whom six were civilian office workers. Of the sworn personnel, three were command staff, three wore detective badges, and two worked in the schools as resource officers. That left thirty officers to cover three shifts, seven days a week. By the time the two lieutenants and five sergeants were sifted out of the mix, actual boots on the ground typically belonged to a mere three officers. Factor in days off, sick time, and hunting season—and Jo and her partner had a lot of doors to knock on.

And Glowering Guy wasn't answering his.

She knocked again. Music played inside the townhouse. Some country song, heavy on the twang. Maybe he'd gone out. Perhaps his definition of a perfect Sunday didn't include talking to the police.

She stepped off the porch and craned her neck. The window he'd shadowed earlier loomed empty.

Jo worked her way down the street, peering into vehicles in case Lena had crawled inside one. She recorded the license plate of every car, every address, and whether or not anyone answered the door. So far, zero for four. Not surprising. If you wanted to talk to someone at home, visit a ranch or a farm. You might have to track them down in the field, but they'd be home. In town, people left their houses to go to work. Even those who didn't eke their living from the land still enjoyed the great outdoors, and on the weekend, there were trails to hike, rapids to shoot, bikes to ride, and beer to drink.

By the time she finished speaking to the woman at the last house, she'd tucked eight of her business cards into door jambs, made a whopping two contacts, received consent to do cursory searches of both houses and still didn't know any more information regarding Lena's whereabouts.

She looked back toward Tilda's townhouse. The neighbor's car hadn't moved. There could be any number of reasons he'd watched the two detectives walk up Tilda's driveway—and as many reasons why he hadn't opened the door when she'd knocked.

But what if one of those reasons was that he had a secret?

5

From inside the townhouse, Tilda listened to the car as it approached. The change of the engine as it settled into an idle in front of the driveway. The door that creaked open and the giggles of girls switching seats. They squealed their goodbyes and see-you-laters and what-about-tonights before the car door finally slammed shut. The motor whined as it picked up speed and took the girls home to where they were supposed to be.

In the time between the car door slamming and the front door opening, Tilda rewound the day. She imagined her daughters together shopping for school clothes. Laughing as they carried the loot they'd bought into the house. Marisa's bags would overflow. Mostly accessories, each item fulfilling some photo shoot need.

The majority of the bags Lena carried would belong to Marisa. Her own bag might contain a new pair of dungarees, maybe another set of overalls, a T-shirt or two, a flannel shirt that could double as a jacket. All basic necessities that would cause Marisa to question whether they were really sisters.

Lately, Lena had been hounding Tilda for a new pair of muck boots to replace the ones she'd nearly outgrown. Tilda had been so tired working graves, she kept putting Lena off, hoping her ex would pony up for the boots. It wasn't like Lena was mucking stalls in the townhouse. It'd be nice to think maybe Lena had persuaded her sister and the girls had stopped at the co-op on the way home.

Tilda closed her eyes and held the image for as long as hope allowed, until the door opened and Marisa entered. Alone.

"So how long is she grounded for?" Marisa breezed past the kitchen island where Tilda stood and tossed her bags on the couch. "Wait till I show you the dress I found. It'll coordinate perfectly with the Steve Madden sandals they just sent me. Megan wanted it, but they only had the one. The dress, not the sandals. I didn't have the heart to tell her she'd never be able to squeeze into it."

Tilda swallowed the lump in her throat. Her eldest daughter glowed. It was a trick of the light that followed Marisa wherever she went. Some energy that welled up inside her. The same energy the casting agent had noticed when she had plucked Marisa from a crowd of wannabe extras. A week later, the production crew had landed in the valley and filmed an opening scene for a pilot that never aired. Even though Marisa had never even spoken a line, by the end of the shoot, she was convinced she and her mother needed to pick up stakes and move to Hollywood.

Maybe they all should have gone. Maybe if they had, Marisa wouldn't be standing alone in the middle of the living room. Maybe. Maybe. Maybe.

"What do you think?" She pressed the sundress against her body and struck a pose, as if already seeing herself on some beach, looking out at the surf through large-framed glasses, wishing she was old enough to drink champagne.

"Momma?" Marisa's eyes demanded her attention.

"She's—" Tilda cleared her throat. Tried again. "She's not back yet, baby."

"What time is she getting home?"

"The police were here all morning." She took a deep breath. "They'll be back in a bit."

Tilda watched her daughter's face as she deciphered the message in the words Tilda couldn't speak.

Finally, Marisa's shoulders slumped. "Why aren't we doing something?"

"We are doing something. Something important." Tilda added another name to the short list in front of her. The relatives were easy. Only Tilda's mother was still alive. "Who is Lena friends with?"

"Bluebell."

Tilda swallowed her retort. "Please be serious. You must know some of them."

"I am serious. When's the last time she brought home a friend with less than four legs?" Marisa circled the kitchen island. "What about her teacher from last year? Wouldn't she know who Lena hung out with?"

"Yes. Of course. I should have thought of that." She reached out as Marisa made another lap. Tilda drew her into a hug. "Thank you."

Marisa squirmed out of her arms. "This is lame. We're wasting time. We should be using the media to find her."

"Detective MacAllister asked us to make a list of Lena's friends. That's what we're doing."

"And where is this Detective MacAllister right now?"

"For heaven's sake, Marisa. He's trying to find your sister." Her words were whip fast.

Marisa's eyes welled. "I'm sorry, Momma." She doubled over the island and buried her head in her crossed arms. "I'm so sorry. I should have checked on her this morning. If I had only—"

"Marisa Chantel Flores, not another word." Tilda draped herself around her daughter's thin shoulders. Placed her cheek against the back of her head. Squeezed. "Lena is fine. Any minute we're going to talk to one of her friends who knows exactly where she is. We'll look back on this someday and laugh. Look at me, Marisa." She shook her daughter. "Look at me."

Marisa stood, pressing her palms against her eyes. "But what if—"

"No what ifs." She pulled her daughter's hands away from her face. "It was Mrs. Leister, wasn't it?"

"That was my homeroom teacher last year." Marisa ran her sleeve under her nose. "Wasn't it Hall or Ball or something?"

"Beale. Mrs. Beale." Tilda picked up the pen and added the name to the notepad. "What about kids from 4-H?"

"Dad would know that. What's he doing?"

"The police are trying to track him down. They want to talk to him."

"Track him down?" Marisa said. "You mean like arrest him?"

"Why on earth would you think that?" Something long buried unwound in her gut like a snake.

Marisa opened the refrigerator and rummaged through the deli drawer. "When's the last time you ate something? I bet you haven't eaten since yesterday."

Tilda stood frozen. Ink from the nib of the pen blotted on the page. "Honey. Is there something I need to know about your father?"

"We have some of the cheddar you like so much. I can make you a grilled cheese." She dropped the plastic bag back into the drawer, but still faced away. “Or I can make smoothies for us. That wouldn’t be as fattening.”

A shaky line scored the page, and Tilda laid the pen tight against the edge of the pad, the clip placed to the outside so it couldn’t roll away and lose itself in the shadow she’d locked away so long ago. “Marisa?”

“I’m sorry, Momma. I didn’t mean anything. It’s just that he was supposed to have Lena last night. That’s all.” She finally turned around and her eyes filled with tears. “If he doesn’t have her, where is she?” Marisa took a step forward, hesitated, and then threw herself at her mother, burrowing her face against Tilda’s shoulder.

Tilda wrapped her arms around Marisa and inhaled the complicated scent of her daughter. Layers of shampoo, and conditioner, and serums, and lord knows what else that somehow created a perfume of influence.

“I don’t know, baby.” She tightened her hold around her daughter. Wondered if she’d ever be able to let her go again. “I don’t know.”

6

Distance in Echo Valley often depended on the mode of transportation used to cover it. As the crow flew, the fairgrounds were slightly more than a mile from Tilda's house. By car, the circuitous route stretched nearly five miles. An eleven-year-old girl had limited options, but traveling by foot opened up some shortcuts.

The road from the development wound its way down the hill to the college. Jo walked along the right edge, pausing frequently to examine bits of trash, or to toe the foliage to make certain nothing hid beneath the leaves.

At the college, Jo took the shortest route across the quad, banking that a young girl on her way to feed her steer wouldn't dilly-dally along the way. Other than a group playing Frisbee golf, the campus appeared empty.

Echo Valley College stood on an ancient river terrace that was once part of the original valley floor until the river continued to carve another three hundred feet out of the sandstone. A series of switchbacks linked the edge of the mesa to downtown and was a popular path when school was in session.

Jo dropped onto the trail. From the overlook, the valley spread out before her, ringed by buttes, hogbacks, peaks, and mountains. Little poofs of dust rose around her boots and clung to the hem of her pants as she wove past pinyons and scrub trees. The buzz and thrum of morning had faded with the rising sun and growing heat and quieted all but the most enthusiastic birds. The trail terminated at the base of the hill next to a house and a rock path kept hikers and students from encroaching on the yard.

It seemed a safe bet that Lena would retrace the same route she'd traveled the night before, and after a short walk, Jo arrived at the river trail.

The water level of the Animas River rose and fell with the seasons, and the past winter had been brutal. Even now, the last brushstrokes of white still clung to the peaks, and snowmelt sluiced through the valley on its way to New Mexico and beyond.

Lena should have been walking this path around seven that morning. There would have been the typical early morning joggers, people on bikes, the occasional transient. It wasn't a dangerous walk, but it still provided plenty of opportunity for something bad to happen to an eleven-year-old girl by herself.

Armed with a flier, Jo headed upstream. The fair was the draw today, and the river trail wasn't as crowded as normal. Some did a double-take when they saw her, but whether it was because of her slacks and button-down ensemble on a blistering day, or the pancake holster on her hip and the array of equipment clipped around her belt, she couldn't tell. Either way, she wished she was still wearing her patrol shorts from the dunk tank. Jo greeted everyone she encountered and showed them the flier with Lena's photo, but no one yet had responded with new information.

The trail crossed the river. At the peak of the footbridge Jo paused and leaned against the rail. Slightly north of the bridge was a small island, and beyond that was an elevation change in the river that created a spillway. The drop was only a few feet, but the crush of water that tumbled off the edge was still strong enough to trap a child against the bottom. From her vantage, it was impossible to see past the curtain of water. Jo hoped against hope that Lena hadn't somehow fallen victim to the river.

Away from the pour-over, the frothed water lost its energy and butted against the tiny tuft of land in the middle of the river, dividing, swirling, and gently eddying around the island before rejoining again downriver. It was a rite of passage to swim to the island. Older kids dragged coolers behind them, or used the tiny island as a way station when they tubed down the river. Some summers you could wade to it. But not this year.

A flash of white fluttered in the current, caught in the weeds along the island's shore. She took out her phone and used the camera to zoom in on the item. It rose and fell in the water, too small to be a plastic bag.

Jo shaded her eyes and looked upriver. Two teens had floated to the bank above the spillway to avoid the drop and were pulling their tubes out of the river. She retraced her steps and cut across the grass.

"Hey there." Jo hid her concern under a smile. "I wonder if you could help me with something."

The guy held his tether and threw his tube into the water, but the girl brightened. "What's up?"

"I'm looking for a missing girl." Jo stashed her phone and drew out the photocopy of Lena. "Hopefully, it's a simple miscommunication, but have either of you seen her?"

The guy barely glanced at the photo, but the girl pushed her sunglasses onto her head and studied the page.

"I'm sorry," she said. "I don't recognize her."

"Maybe you can help me with something else. I was up on the bridge and saw something on the island that may be related to a case I'm working and I'm not exactly dressed for a swim. If one of you could float over to the island and take a peek, I'd appreciate it."

"Sure," the girl said. "Where am I looking?"

"This side of the point." Jo pointed. "It looks like some kind of white fabric that's caught in the eddy. It's probably just trash, but better safe, you know?"

The guy tugged the girl's arm. "Come on, Kara. We don't have time for this."

The girl glared at her companion. "Don't be such a dick."

"Suit yourself." He waded into the water and sat in his tube, then pushed off. "I'll meet you around the bend."

"Whatever." For a second, she watched him float downstream. "Tyler's my brother." She laughed. "I didn't want you to think I'd fall for someone like that."

"You know it's his job as a brother to drive you crazy."

Jo was an only child, but no one knew her better than Aiden Teague—part brother and part something Jo found hard to explain. Growing up, she'd spent so much time with Aiden at his family's Lupine Ledge Ranch that his father once joked he was going to claim her as another dependent. Fifty acres offered an irresistible draw and plenty of opportunity for mischief to two kids who'd become so close they occasionally wanted to kill each other. Almost succeeded once. Even as adults, the pranks they pulled on each other made her glad her job came with health insurance.

"I'm counting down the days until he leaves for college." Kara laughed.

College. Jo and Aiden had originally planned to attend the same university, but life had intervened with scholarships to different parts of the state. In the days leading to Aiden's departure, he'd asked her on a date. It took him asking twice more before she believed he wasn't screwing with her.

She'd worn a dress with heels that pinched her feet. He'd picked her up in his truck, reeking of a cologne she'd never smelled before. Dinner was an excruciating exercise in awkwardness, ending when he knocked over his water. The peppercorn between her teeth was a bonus. They squandered an entire week avoiding each other. But the morning he was supposed to leave for college, Jo knew she couldn't let him leave without saying goodbye, and as soon as it was light, she slipped from the house.

Outside, his truck blocked the driveway with him asleep in the cab. He woke when she climbed in the passenger side. Without a word, they drove to the lake. Their shoulders touched—first in the cab, then later as they sat side by side along the shore, silence making sense of their worlds in a way no words could. When he stood, she did too. She had to tilt her head for him to kiss her. They held hands the entire way back to the house, his thumb caressing her knuckles. When Aiden drove away, Jo took an involuntary step toward the receding truck as if some external force pushed her to follow him. In the vacuum, she was left disoriented—and terrified by how much of her life was entwined with his.

Jo blinked away the image of Aiden. "You might be surprised how much you'll miss your brother when he's not around." She refocused on the task at hand. "Thanks for the help. If you can tell what it is, great, but please don't touch it."

"No worries. Back in a flash."

Kara climbed into her tube far enough above the island to let the current carry her back. All the while the girl floated, Jo kept hoping she was wrong about what she'd seen from the bridge. That the scrap really was a trash bag. A discarded wrapper. Nothing to worry about.

Kara grounded the tube, and leaned over the scrap. A puzzled expression clouded her face.

Jo's mind jumped forward. She'd need to radio for another officer. Collect the item. Photos. Check for more evidence. Notify Dickinson and Squint. Bring in the chain of command, call out search and rescue.

The girl pushed away from the island and paddled back toward Jo.

In the shallows, Kara flipped the tube on edge and stood. She glanced at the flier still in Jo's hand and just as quickly looked away. "I think it's a pair of girl's underwear."

7

School Resource Officer Pamela Asher trudged through the shallows of the Animas River towing a cooler. Several people clustered on the footbridge and tracked her progress with their cell phones.

Jo took the line from the SRO's outstretched hand and passed her a towel. "Sorry to send you into such cold water."

"Not any colder than the hose water them firefighters used to fill the dunk tank. 'Sides, I've got plenty of bioprene to keep me warm. You'd be a popsicle before making it halfway to the island."

Pam had the kind of body she liked to call *fully inflated*. She said her kids at the schools liked her that way. Made her soft to hug even though she wore her vest.

"You know Lena?" Jo asked.

Pam had worked for the Echo Valley Police Department for twenty-two years—seven years longer than any other woman had ever managed. The last ten years she'd been assigned to the valley's schools, rotating her schedule to spend time in each of the elementary, middle, and high schools.

"Good kid. Quiet." Pam dropped the towel on her head and started scrubbing her hair. "A bit of a loner, but not because she isn't friendly, she's just shy. Should have seen that little girl's face, though, on career day when one of the County Search and Rescue gals brought in a tracking dog. Thought she'd died and gone to heaven." She pulled the towel off her head and her short hair stuck out at all angles. "I did not just say that."

Everett Cloud, the reporter for the *Valley Courier*, stood among the crowd on the bridge and trained his camera on Jo.

Fundamentally, cops and reporters chased the same goal: the truth. But sit them down with a beer and ask them what stood in their way? The reporter wouldn't think twice before blurting out *the police*. The cop would order another beer, give the tab to the reporter, and move to another table, because anything the officer said would end up misquoted on the front page.

Jo shifted to put her back to the reporter and reeled in the cooler. "You ever get vibes from Lena that her shyness was caused by an unhappy home life?"

"Never once. She loves her daddy. Wants to be a vet just like him. Course, she's going into the sixth grade this year. Who knows what she'll want to be after middle school."

"How's she feel about her mom?"

Pam paused blotting. "Can't say I ever recall her speaking about her momma. Or that sister of hers either."

"Marisa?"

"Miz Influencer herself." Pam wrung out the towel and slung it over her shoulder. "That could be the source of her shyness. Everyone knows Marisa. Lena doesn't have that kind of a spotlight on her."

"Jealousy?"

"Can't say I'm close enough to the family to know that. Never once had to counsel Lena—unlike her sister. Lordy, that girl is single-minded. If she needs a picture, she thinks she can do whatever she wants to get it. Should have seen the fuss she made when I told her I was going to confiscate her cell phone if she didn't shape up."

Jo glanced over her shoulder at the bridge. "You can do that?"

"Naw. But for about a day and a half, she behaved." Pam laughed.

Jo knelt by the cooler and tilted the lid. Inside was her camera, a pair of panties temporarily consigned to a plastic bag, and a crumpled set of latex gloves.

The possibility of the underwear belonging to Galena Flores was a long shot, but the fact remained, to be caught at the point of the island, the underwear had to have entered the river upstream. And only a little further upstream was the very place Lena was supposed to have been this morning. Taken together, it added a sinister element to the case that Jo couldn't overlook but fervently hoped wasn't true.

The fundamentals of the investigation hadn't changed: find the girl. But in lieu of actionable information, it was always prudent to treat a disappearance as an abduction. Lena's age, an opened window, girl's panties, a missing father. There were too many what ifs. Time was valuable—and even now it was slipping away at an uncomfortable pace.

Since finding the underwear, there had been a significant reshuffling and expansion of tasks. Having an officer in the dunk tank made one assignment a lot easier to delegate, and Pam responded from the fairgrounds to act as the designated swimmer and evidence collector. Estes and his trainee dropped off Jo's car, so she had her own set of wheels and then remained the only two officers handling calls for service on patrol.

Squint had taken over the fairgrounds, interviewing the 4-H leader and poking around the livestock pavilion. With a bit of luck, there would be security cameras. With even better luck, they'd be operational. Detective Sergeant Pieretti was on his way in and would brief the new chief—who was probably thrilled to have a potentially high-profile case before his feet were fully wet. Regardless, the request to the sheriff for search and rescue would have to come from Chief Prather.

Despite all the pieces in play, nothing would make Jo happier than to learn Lena was with her father and they'd all been chasing their tails.

On the bridge, Everett Cloud broke away from the crowd and followed the footpath toward the officers' location. He greeted Pam. "Officer Asher."

Jo slammed the cooler lid shut and adopted her best *I'm-too-busy-to-talk-to-you-now* face, which was her go-to expression with the reporter ever since he'd thrown her under the bus in an article last winter. It never worked, but it made her feel better.

He nodded to Jo but didn't smile. "I understand you're investigating a missing child. Is what you're doing here connected to the investigation?"

As a reporter, he should know better than to ask a two-part question. It allowed her to answer the one she wanted. "A flier has already been faxed to your office. Eleven-year-old Galena Flores has been reported missing by her family. Anything you can do to get the word out would be greatly appreciated. Now, if you'll excuse me."

"I understand you've recovered a pair of girl's underwear. Do they belong to the missing girl?"

He spoke softly and slowly, and not for the first time she wondered if he modulated his voice to lull people into trusting him or if that was how he really spoke.

He mistook her silence as encouragement to keep talking. "I spoke with a gentleman who said you'd asked him for help identifying something curious on the point."

Tyler. Kara's assessment of her brother suddenly seemed a lot more accurate. "You got played. No gentleman's been near the island."

"Maybe not, but his sister was."

Jo's phone rang and saved her from saying something she'd regret. The screen read *Unknown*, but even without a name, she recognized the number.

She held up a finger. "Sorry, I've got to take this. The watch commander will be able to answer any further questions." She connected the call and walked a few steps away from the riverbank. "Mr. Flores."

"Are you going to arrest me?"

She stopped mid-step and slowly placed her foot on the ground. "Should I?"

"You tell me. There's a note on my door to contact Detective Wyatt, and you just called me Mr. Flores. Considering our past history, I'm sure you can understand my concern."

In the background she heard Pam address the reporter. "Now, Mr. Cloud, you know better than to try to eavesdrop on police business. Detective Wyatt already told you to take your questions to the watch commander. He's at the station. You know the way."

Actually, the watch commander was up at the fairgrounds with Squint, but Jo had no intention of redirecting him. She focused on Lucero. "Are you at the house?"

"What's this about, Jo?"

"I need to talk to you about your daughter."

"Got to be more specific than that. I've got two of them."

Was he yanking her chain, or did he not know? "Did you get Tilda's messages?"

"Look, I know it was my weekend. But I had to head out to Dawson's ranch for one of his mares last night. I didn't have time to swing into town to pick Lena up."

She made a mental note of Dawson's ranch. "I'm not calling you regarding your custody arrangements. Is Lena with you?"

"Can you cut to the chase? I'm a busy man." The reception crackled. Was he at the house? "I've still got two more ranches to call on this afternoon, and I already told you Lena was with her mother."

"Actually, no, you didn't, and that wasn't the question." Why was he being so evasive?

"I don't have anything to say to you."

"Lena didn't show up at the fairgrounds this morning. So let me ask you again, is Lena with you?"

"What do you mean she's not at the fairgrounds?"

During a normal conversation his reaction to her question would have told Jo everything she needed to know, but they hadn't had a normal conversation since high school.

"Lucero. This is your daughter we're talking about, so can you please put aside your feelings about me and answer my question?"

"Lena's not with me."

Dammit. "Are you home?"

"I'm home, but I can come to you."

Everett Cloud idly slapped his reporter notebook against his free hand while he waited for Jo to finish.

"Sit tight," she said. "I'm en route."

8

Lucero lived fifteen miles west of Echo Valley's city limits in Coyote Canyon. Jo barreled down the two-lane road that rose and fell with the hills and swept through sharp curves that made the route popular with cyclists during warmer months and hazardous for drivers during winter. She'd never been to his ranch. She knew him when he lived down the street from her. He'd been a grade ahead of her, but that had never been an issue when they were kids. That seemed so long ago now.

The entry gate looked new, and a *Flores Large Animal Veterinary* sign hung from the header rail. The gravel driveway forked: to the right, barns, hay sheds, and equipment garages sprouted at regular intervals; to the left sat his house.

He knew she was coming and she parked by an ATV and climbed the steps to the front entrance. When there was no answer at the door, she headed toward the barn.

From the outside, the barn appeared larger than most but with less character. A typical pitched roof sat atop utilitarian yellow siding, and a timber portico protected an opened roll-up door wide enough to allow a tractor access via the concrete center aisle.

Jo entered and stepped to the side to avoid being silhouetted by the outside light while her eyes adjusted to the gloom. Even in the shadows, the heat choked her throat. A series of ventilation fans hummed throughout the barn but failed to cool the hay- and horse-scented air.

Her sight returned. Shelves lined the wall behind her. A barn cat, still as a gargoyle, stared down at her from one of the upper shelves.

"Lucero?"

"Back here."

His voice came from the far end of the barn and was deeper than she remembered.

Fifteen stalls, plus a wash-down and farrier bays, took up one side of the building. The opposite wall held the business end of the barn, with four closed doors and another entryway. If she had to guess, a tack room, office, and surgery hid behind three of the doors. The fourth room was secured by a metal door with an electronic lock. Probably his medical stockroom.

"Heard you pull in," Lucero said as she approached. "Figured you had enough sense to know I can't drop everything just because you want to talk to me."

An interesting statement considering he'd been willing to drive to town.

Jo stopped next to a rolling table covered with various surgical implements. This last portion of the barn was an open space that currently held an equine chute occupied by a buckskin pressed firmly between the side rails. A surgical drape covered the rear half of its body, and Lucero wore a disposable jumpsuit, surgical mask, hairnet, and headlamp. If it weren't for the fact that he was wrist deep into an incision in the horse's side, he could have been working a homicide scene.

He glanced toward Jo, stopping just short of blinding her with the headlamp. "So where did you find her?"

Jo dragged her eyes away from the surgery and studied the man behind the mask. She remembered him as taller. What other tricks of memory would she discover about this man who, as a teen, had been one of her good friends?

"Lucero. I don't think you've grasped the severity of what's going on. Lena is missing. I know she was supposed to be at the fairgrounds last night, but is there any way she could be here at the ranch?"

"She was with her mother last night." He slowly extracted his hand and then swabbed the wound.

Jo bit her tongue. "Tilda's the one who called us."

"Then Lena must be at the fairgrounds." He trained his headlamp on a plastic package. "Open the suture kit for me. My hands are slippery."

Still the same bossypants he'd been as a teenager, and she hated that she'd spread the kit on the table before realizing she'd fallen into the same pattern as when she'd thought he could do no wrong.

"We've got officers up there now, and there's no sign of your daughter at the fairgrounds. She's not with Marisa, either. So before this escalates further, I need to make sure she didn't come home without telling you."

Lucero selected a tool that looked like a pair of needle-nose pliers and grabbed a pre-threaded curved needle. The tip of his tools disappeared beneath the animal's skin as he started to suture a deeper layer. The horse didn't move. Must be a hell of a local anesthesia.

"Lena wouldn't do that," he said.

Would he be this obstinate with Squint, or was he acting this way because he was talking to her? "I just need to do a walk-through of the property. Make sure she isn't in the house."

He straightened to his full height. "I don't think so."

She shook her head. "I need to look for Lena."

"No."

The ventilation fan above them struggled, the blades slicing the heavy air.

Finally she asked, "What are you hiding, Lucero?"

He flinched. "Why is it that every time there's trouble in my life, you're there?"

Fine, if he wanted to ask twenty questions, she had a few of her own. "Where were you last night?"

He set down the needle, and his fingers lingered over the scalpel.

Jo's hand dropped to her gun.

He scowled and his headlamp dipped. "You going to arrest me for something I didn't do?"

"Not unless you're stupid enough to give me a reason," she said.

"Didn't need a reason last time." He laughed, an ugly sound, and the horse pulled against its halter.

The moment lengthened. The scalpel gleamed on the table between them, but it was far from being the only weapon within Lucero's reach in the barn. Not that Lucero would need a single one of them. He'd been a wrestler in high school. Stocky and strong. Knew how to break a control hold.

"I didn't arrest you," Jo said.

"No." Lucero picked up the needle again, then turned back to his patient. "You had your father do it."

She changed gears but didn't let her guard down. "Don't jeopardize your daughter's safety because of something that happened between us in high school."

"That *something* damn near ruined my life."

"Every minute you waste puts her at greater risk."

"Jesus Christ, Jo." He snipped the thread and tossed the instrument on the table. It landed with a clatter and the horse startled. "Even now, you can't bring yourself to apologize."

Her patience broke. "You want an apology, talk to Tilda."

His face reddened. "Get off my property."

She drew a deep breath. Forced herself to keep her voice measured. "I'm doing everything I can to find your daughter. The best-case scenario is that she's inside your house sleeping." Her voice slowed down even further. Did he remember that tell? Recognize the danger sign? "This doesn't end because you say so. If I leave before I have a chance to see that she's not here, I'll be back with a search warrant, a whole lot of backup, and we'll be looking for a lot more than a child."

The beam of his headlamp hit her full in the face and he advanced. Through slitted eyes, she saw his bloodied hands, spattered jumpsuit.

She shifted her balance to the balls of her feet, flexed her knees, but otherwise held her ground. "I've got a pair of girl's underwear in my car that I want to compare to the type your daughter wears."

He lowered his foot as if the barn floor had turned to ice. "Underwear."

She blinked away the after image of his light. "Panties."

The color appeared to drain from his face, but her vision still saw everything in grayscale and she couldn't be sure. Guilt or concern? Once she would have known how to read her friend. Maybe she'd been wrong about that, too.

After several breaths, he pushed away from the stall, leaving a bloodied handprint. "I need ten minutes to finish with the mare." His voice was thick and he cleared his throat. "Then I'll show you anything you need to see."

9

Jo waited until she cleared the canyon before hitting the speed dial for Squint and putting the call on speaker. He'd barely said hello before she said, "We need to call in the cavalry."

His sigh drifted across the line. "Those were not the words I was hoping to hear."

"Worse yet, Lucero has no idea where Lena might be." Jo braked for a curve, then accelerated through the apex.

"How was Lucero?"

"He's not a big fan of police. Ordered me off the property before I convinced him it was in his best interest to allow me to take a gander around his place."

"Not the response I would have expected from the father of a missing child."

"I'll give you the full run-down when we meet at the station," Jo said. "Did you learn anything at the fairgrounds?"

"I really miss being a kid."

Jo had a difficult time envisioning Squint as a child. And when she did, he always held an official Red Ryder, carbine action, two-hundred-shot, range model air rifle with a compass in the stock, picking off prairie dogs on the back forty of his family's ranch.

Unaware of her internal musing, Squint continued. "The 4-H leader confirmed he saw Lena and Marisa hanging out together on the midway. He knew Lena wasn't spending the night so he assumed they were on their way home."

"I wonder if someone followed them home."

"I'm hopeful surveillance may tell us. There are security cameras in all the exhibit halls, the livestock pavilion, parking lots, along the midway, and the entrance gate."

"I sense a *but* coming."

"But, not all of the feeds were operational," he said.

Two turkey vultures picked at something alongside the road, and she swerved slightly. "Let me guess."

"The livestock pavilion and one of the parking lot cams were dead."

"Anything on the outside of the pavilion?"

"It's from a poor angle, but I've reviewed all of today's footage through noon. There's no sign of Lena coming in from the front and none of the other kids in the pavilion saw her this morning. Recordings prior to midnight are already archived, but I've put in a request for Friday and Saturday's activity."

"ETA on the turnaround?"

"Best case, tomorrow when someone from IT is back in the office."

Jo passed the etched flagstone *Welcome to Echo Valley* sign that greeted travelers as they entered the city, and she slowed for a traffic light. "Speaking of bosses, you talk to Pieretti yet?"

"He's downstairs setting up the chief's conference room."

The light turned and Jo made a left. "The chief's already okayed setting up a command post?"

"I don't know that the chief's given his blessing. I suspect Pieretti wants to put his best face forward and make a good impression."

"Sounds like dating. Wait till the chief finds out he farts in the weight room when he does squats."

She could practically hear Squint shake his head. "I think it's more in line with proving small-town cops are as conscientious as those from larger agencies," he said.

"I would have thought that was self-evident." She hit her turn signal and made a right into the historic section of downtown. "I'm a couple blocks away. I'll start the backgrounds on the parents after I arrive."

"Way ahead of you. But I won't be able to get a copy of the divorce and custody agreements until the courts open tomorrow."

"Anything interesting pop up?"

"Just the case involving you," he said.

* * *

The faint outline of three bullet holes marred the wall next to the public entrance of the Echo Valley Police Department, invisible to all but those who knew where to look. And Jo always looked. In an odd way, the divots usually left her feeling triumphant. Walls didn't bleed, and that night, neither did any officers. The scales of justice had remained balanced. Today, the slant of the sun threw the ghostly impressions in ominous relief. Jo glanced over her shoulder before pushing through the glass door, a collection of evidence bags in hand.

Squint's words followed her into the empty lobby. Lucero. Tilda. Jo. That case had haunted her since she was a teenager.

On the other side of the customer service window, Sarah flipped through a stack of police reports. For nearly two decades, she'd greeted the people who wandered into the lobby for help and handled all the records needs of the department. About eight years ago, she started training her daughter, Sarah, to replace her, but as the department grew, so too did the need for two records techs. In order to keep them straight, officers had dubbed them Simply Sarah and Young Sarah. But make no mistake—if someone said *Sarah*, everyone knew it meant the elder of the two clerks.

Sarah looked pointedly at the bags Jo held. "I don't suppose you have a little girl hiding in all those bags."

"I'm afraid not," Jo said.

"That poor child's mother must be worried sick." Sarah triggered the electronic door release leading into the secured part of the station.

"Thanks." Jo reached for the door.

"Good grief, child. Come here."

Jo backtracked. "What?"

"I'm not one to judge, but your sergeant might be curious why you have hay all over your backside." Sarah made a circle with her finger. "Turn around." She reached through the sliding window and brushed off Jo's back. "I'll let you get the rest."

"It's not what you think."

"Sounds to me like you have a guilty conscience." Sarah flipped through a police report until she found the page she wanted. "Is there a special someone I need to meet?"

Heat rushed to Jo's face as she juggled the bags and swiped at the back of her trousers with her free hand. "The divorce has only been final five months."

Sarah inked the bottom of a stamp and slammed it down on the paper. "And?"

"Right now, I'm more interested in finding a little girl."

* * *

The PD building had started life as a fire station, and multiple renovations had resulted in a maze of oddly shaped offices. Jo wove her way to the stairs that led to the detective bureau—a designation far grander than the actual space it occupied.

Near the upper landing, she detected the distinctive whiff of bacon, and she picked up her pace. Inside the office, Squint sat behind his computer, but it was the greasy bag from Heifer & Hog on her desk that captured her attention.

"Oh, thank God." She dropped the evidence bags on the chair next to her desk.

He wiped the corner of his mouth with a napkin. "Your Dr Pepper's in the fridge."

She darted into the tiny dinette adjacent to the office to wash her hands. "You're the best."

"You owe me five-fifty."

"And just like that, you blew it." She returned with her soda and a crumpled paper towel. "Pieretti still downstairs?"

"Should be up any moment."

She slid a pile of paperwork to the side and tore at the bag. No sense putting off the inevitable. "You read the reports?"

The two detectives' desks were pushed together so they faced each other—which might have proved beneficial for large projects if the desks weren't at different heights.

He neatly folded his sandwich wrapper into a tight square. "I did. Tough decision for you to make as a sixteen-year-old."

Jo unwrapped her BLT. "Not really." She bit into the sandwich and closed her eyes. "Thank you."

"So what happened between you and Tilda?"

Jo spoke around a mouthful. "I could ask you the same thing."

"You could, but then you'd be avoiding my question."

That was the thing about talking with other cops, Squint especially. He knew all the dodges. She'd never kept anything from her partner. Never wanted to. But this was different.

"It's all in the reports," Jo said.

"I get the distinct impression there's a whole lot left unsaid."

"My dad was never known for going into a lot of detail." She sipped her soda. "Lucero's family moved into the neighborhood when he was in grade school. He was a year ahead of me, but we spent a fair amount of time together. I was a junior in high school when Tilda Marquet moved to the valley. She took a shine to Lucero."

"I can see where that would present a problem."

"Wrong already." A chunk of avocado fell out of the sandwich and she stuffed it back in. "Lucero came to me for advice. Even then, Tilda was a beauty. He thought she was out of his league. I encouraged him to ask her out. They dated." She took another mammoth bite.

"Never figured you for a matchmaker."

"They're divorced."

"Good thing you had a fallback plan."

"One day Tilda came to see me—she knew my dad was a cop. Her wrist was bruised and her shoulder was all scraped up. She told me she'd tried to break up with Lucero, but he exploded, grabbed her and pushed her down. Lucero had a temper. I'd seen it. She left, but before I could tell Dad, she called and begged me not to say anything."

"And?"

Jo scowled. "I thought you said you read the report? Dad arrested him." Her father had joined the department before Jo had been born. Growing up, it had been both a blessing and a curse, but from an early age, Jo knew she wanted to follow in her father's footsteps. By high school she had a working knowledge of the criminal statutes. She'd had no choice but to tell her father.

Squint thumbed through a neat stack of paper. "The case was dismissed in the furtherance of justice."

"Tilda recanted. Told the prosecutor she'd fallen off a horse. Claimed I was jealous and wanted to break them up."

"I do not understand teenage girls."

"No one does," Jo said. "Her injuries were consistent enough with a riding accident that the DA's office dropped the charges. But Lucero had already lost out on a scholarship he desperately needed. He blamed me. Needless to say, our friendship took a hit—which I suspect was Tilda's goal all along. It wasn't much later, I heard she was pregnant. Lucero's father sold their house to scrape together tuition money and packed Lucero off to school in Fort Collins. Tilda followed and they got married."

"And lived happily ever after."

"Not if you do the math. Either Tilda wasn't pregnant or something happened and they lost the child. Marisa came along later. And as Tilda said, Lena was barely a toddler when they split."

Footsteps on the stairs interrupted them. Pieretti. It always sounded like he was carrying something heavy. He entered the detective bay and commandeered the empty chair next to Squint's desk. "Please tell me you found our missing at her father's place."

From a span and control perspective, Sergeant Kip Pieretti had it easy with only two detectives to wrangle—especially considering one of them was Squint. If she had to guess, odds were she was the one responsible for his perennially harried expression.

"I wish I could," Jo said.

"So what do we really have here? Lost kid? Runaway? Abduction? What?"

"That's the sixty-four-thousand-dollar question." Jo took a slug of soda. "There's too many unanswered questions to treat this as anything but worst-case scenario."

Pieretti took off his glasses and wiped them with his shirttail. "Any good news?"

Jo nodded. "The panties we fished out of the Animas didn't match any that Lena had at her father's. I sent a photo of the underwear to Dickinson while he was still at the mother's. No match there, either."

"Tell me more about the parents."

Squint took over. "Lucero Flores and Tilda Marquet. Acrimonious divorce. We'll get the custody agreement tomorrow, but they both reported they have split custody of the girls. Marisa lives with mom. Lena with Dad.

The database reports numerous weapons registered under Lucero's name, mostly long guns, a couple of handguns. No record of anything registered to Tilda. Other than a couple of traffic stops, neither has a criminal history." He glanced at Jo before continuing. "Lucero was arrested as a teen after Tilda filed a domestic violence complaint, but the DA declined to prosecute and the case went nowhere."

Pieretti replaced his glasses. They immediately slid down his nose and he looked over the top of the lenses. "Do the parents have alibis?"

"Tilda worked a graveyard shift in the ER last night, which checks out," Jo said. "Lucero's a large animal vet and claims he had an emergency call-out. That's not confirmed yet."

"Suspicions?" the sergeant asked.

Both detectives remained quiet a long moment. Finally Squint spoke. "Tilda was distraught. My first impression is she didn't have anything to do with her daughter's disappearance."

Pieretti turned to Jo. "And dad?"

Jo rolled the bottom of her soda bottle in little circles. "I don't think he had any involvement."

Squint leaned back in his chair and folded his hands in his lap. It struck Jo as a subtle rebuke.

"I did a cursory search across the property," she continued. "Right now we don't know if we have a lost eleven-year-old in the forest, or if this is an abduction and she was snatched from the townhouse or while on her way to the fairgrounds."

"Speaking of the fair." Pieretti allowed the question to hang.

"Summit Amusements—home of over-the-top rides." Squint held up a stapled report. "I was able to get a list of employees from security, but I'll have to go through HR to get anything more than names. I had the guys working the fairground detail help ID as many of the workers as possible before the fair shut down and they headed to their next stop—which, by the way, is Pueblo."

"Neighborhood suspects?"

"The creepy guy next door to Tilda's gave us stink-eye when we arrived." As a cop, Jo had been on the receiving end of plenty of odd looks, but something about Tilda's neighbor raised her hackles. "I'm pretty sure he was home when I tried to contact him, but he didn't answer."

“Nothing that comes up in a proximity search,” Squint said. “But I’ll check property records tomorrow with the county clerk to get owner info. Records is running registrations on the license plates we collected from the canvass. We’ll run locals on those names after we get the printouts.”

Jo glanced at her wrist. “Sarge, no offense, but we’re burning daylight. A hasty team is going to have an easier time of it if we can get the chief to put a call in to the sheriff for authorization before dark.”

“To search what?” Pieretti asked. “You already covered the route she would have taken to the fairgrounds.”

“The townhouse backs up against Sage Gulch. That’s a lot of open territory.”

“In the opposite direction from the fairgrounds.”

“She’s eleven, Sarge. Do you want to be the one to tell her parents we didn’t do everything possible to find their daughter?”

He wiped his already clean glasses a second time and sighed. “I’ll make the call.”

After the sergeant disappeared into his office, Squint leaned forward. “Any reason you didn’t mention Lucero’s reluctance to let you search his place?”

Jo picked up the other half of her sandwich and took a large bite while she decided how to answer. Finally she settled on the truth. “Pieretti asked if I suspected Lucero. I don’t.”

“Being innocent once doesn’t make him innocent now.”

It was so much more complicated than that. By the time Jo had returned to school for her senior year, interest in the drama had waned. Tilda had a reputation for being possessive and insecure, and then one of the sophomores got pregnant, and any lingering interest in Jo evaporated. But the whole thing had left Jo conflicted. Tilda’s behavior perplexed her—but even more disconcerting was how thoroughly Tilda had duped her. Sure, Jo had only been acting on what Tilda had told her, but if she had seen through the lie, Lucero wouldn’t have gone to jail or lost out on his scholarship. They’d never be friends again, but finding Lena was a way to make up for the harm she’d caused him all those years ago.

“Being a liar then doesn’t make Tilda a liar now, either,” Jo said. “But of the two of them, she’s the one who’s filed a false report.”

"That's not technically true. Your father arrested Lucero based on your statement and physical evidence. Tilda never lied to a police officer."

"Seriously?" Jo dropped her sandwich. The top slice of bread shifted, dragging the neat layers into a confused mess. "Why are you covering for her?" She tried to read her partner's expression, but he wore the bland façade he donned when speaking with a suspect. A sense of loss dragged down her shoulders. "Or are you asking me if I made it up?"

Before Squint could respond, Pieretti reappeared next to their desks, his cell phone still pressed against his ear. "Yes. Thank you, Chief." He disconnected. "He's making the call now." He glanced back and forth between the two detectives, his head cocked like a puppy that detected sound thrumming at an unfamiliar frequency. "Did I miss something?"

"Nope," Jo answered.

"Uh-huh. Well, whatever it is, put it aside." He slid the phone into the case on his waist. "As long as patrol can spare him, Dickinson will respond with the team since he's already up on the details."

Jo pulled the sandwich wrapper aside and opened her notebook. "Sarah already faxed the BOLO to the media." All told, about a dozen outlets were linked to the speed dial, but only the *Valley Courier* and a single local TV channel were in the valley itself. "If this doesn't resolve tonight, we need to think about a press conference tomorrow. Try to get the bigger networks on board."

"You volunteering?" Pieretti asked.

"Not a chance. Bad enough Everett Cloud was taking photos while Pam and I were at the river. I'd expect one of his scintillating articles in the morning edition."

Squint opened his computer browser and clicked through some pages. "There's already a blurb reporting Lena missing. No details yet."

"They can't report what we don't have. I figure we only have another day—two at the most—before they start building their own story."

Pieretti rubbed his eyes and his glasses jostled up and down. "Have we notified Crime Stoppers?"

"We?" Jo raised an eyebrow.

"In the royal sense. Which really means one of you."

"We have," Squint confirmed.

"Okay, then. I'll keep tabs on the search team. We need to nail down dad's story."

"On it." Jo flipped to a sheet. "He said he was called out to Dawson's ranch. I'll head out that way. If this is an abduction, we should put a tap on Tilda's phone line. Lucero's too."

"Either of them have the means to pay a ransom?"

"Depends on the size and scope of the demand," Jo answered. "One's an ER nurse, the other a vet. We won't know until we run financials, but they both have access to drugs—which could be as valuable."

"And the FBI?" Squint asked.

Pieretti's lips thinned slightly. "The chief wants us to hold off for a bit."

Jo jiggled her mouse to wake up her computer. "He knows he's in Echo Valley now, right? We don't have three hundred officers and our own helicopter."

The sheriff and police departments shared a central records system that contained all the contacts, citations, reports, and whatnot each agency generated. She typed Dawson into a search field and hit Send. A list of Dawsons appeared on the screen. She scanned the column of first names until she found Clyde, and then clicked again.

"The chief's confident we have the necessary resources to find an eleven-year-old girl."

"He said that?" She jotted the address and phone number in her notebook. Like most properties with acreage, the ranch was outside city limits.

"Not in so many words," the sergeant admitted.

She leaned back. The new chief had only been with the department a couple of weeks, and everyone was still on their best behavior while trying to figure him out. The reviews were mixed. Jo's interaction with him so far was limited to exchanging good mornings in the hallway. "What were his words?"

Pieretti opened his mouth, but then shook his head and headed toward his office. "Let me know what you learn at Dawson's ranch."

10

The trip to Dawson's ranch was a bust. Jo spoke to Mrs. Dawson—or more accurately listened to the woman's ten-minute diatribe regarding judging malfeasance at this year's fair. When the lecture veered into the merits of Crisco over butter-based pie crusts, Jo politely interrupted and wheedled Clyde's cell phone number from her.

"But it won't do you any good. He's fishing up in the high country. There's no cell service."

Which, Jo bet, was probably the point of the trip.

Since then, she'd visited a list of Lena's friends, trying to ferret out any tidbit of information to help create a profile of Lena and determine if there was any possibility she'd left her home voluntarily. The portrait of Lena that emerged painted her as a quiet child with an inquisitive mind who loved the outdoors, bonded with every animal she'd ever met, had few close friends but lots of classmates who liked her, and was afraid of the dark.

That last snippet concerned Jo. Plenty of young children worried about monsters under the bed or creatures in the closet, but those fears diminished with age. What caused fear in older children tended to be threats that emerged from the shadows, and often had a name.

Now, Jo stood within a cluster of trucks and SUVs parked in the small dirt lot at the trailhead while Officer Eli Dickinson and subdued members of the search and rescue team stowed their gear.

In less than an hour, she and Squint would update Tilda on the day's progress. The only problem was that, while they'd ticked off a lot of tasks, they really hadn't made any headway.

Eli closed the trunk of his patrol car. Dust coated the lower half of his navy blue uniform pants, and he'd donned his PD ball cap to keep the sun off his face. Even so, he sported a new shade of burn on his face and arms.

Jo returned to her own car and grabbed a small bottle of aloe vera lotion from her backpack and tossed it to Eli. "You're going to need this."

Pete Vasquez, the field team leader, swung his backpack off his shoulder and crammed the bag between two plastic bins of emergency equipment in the cab of his truck. Rappel ropes, extra helmets, and tarps obscured the floor. "I was hoping to get the stand-down message."

"Nothing would have pleased me more." Even as dusk approached, the blistering heat hadn't abated. Jo's once crisp blouse clung to her body. Tomorrow she'd ditch the dress clothes in favor of a more practical uniform for tromping around search areas. She sipped from her water bottle. A shadowy image of Lena alone, hurt, and thirsty rose up. "Did you see anything along the trails to suggest Lena had been up this way?"

He unwound the bandana from his neck and dragged it across his forehead, then propped his sunglasses on top of his head. "The area's pretty heavily trafficked. Even with the fair in town, we encountered plenty of hikers, more than a few bikers. Some recent hoof marks." He stuffed the cloth in the back pocket of his cargo pants. "Lots of overlapping prints. Nothing definitive. But we were moving at a decent clip."

Jo knew the area well. With access so close to town, it was a favorite spot for morning runs, lunchtime hikes, and unwinding after work. The main draw was a meadow loop trail with plenty of scenic vistas and easy terrain that made it a favorite with families. Mountain bikers bombed the steep, technical single-track trails that radiated off the loop. Plus there were pathways connected to adjoining trail systems. All told, the area consisted of more than twenty-two miles of loops, switchbacks, and opportunities for a child to get confused and lost.

"Any chance of getting a dog?" Jo asked.

"I tried to get one today, but Millie and Artemis were working an overdue hiker call above Silverton. They're on their way back and will deploy whenever you're ready. The earlier the better, so the dog can start working before the heat mucks up the scent and the trails get crowded. With any luck, Artemis will help us figure out where we should be looking."

“Thanks.” A yawn snuck up on Jo, and she flared her nostrils trying to stifle it. It didn’t work. “Sorry. It’s not the company.” She stretched her neck. “I wish I had better info for you guys. There’s a good chance I had you chasing your tails today.”

“You don’t know that.”

That was the problem. Too much remained unknown. An investigation was always its messiest in the beginning. Like a jigsaw puzzle right after its pieces were spilled onto a table, everything was chaotic. The responding officers began the sorting process, often constructing the framework and making educated guesses about the big picture. But in larger cases, the intricacies were left to the detectives to piece together. With so many possibilities, initial impressions were often wrong. Hell, in this case, even something seemingly as simple as what clothes Lena had been wearing when she disappeared was impossible to report with certainty. Lucero had no idea what items his daughter had packed, and Marisa hadn’t seen Lena since walking home from the fairgrounds.

Jo swirled the water around in her bottle. “If Artemis leads back this way, can you rally your team for a Type II search and follow?”

Pete smiled and the lines surrounding his eyes deepened. “I’ve already got a team on standby.”

Today’s Type I search was a down and dirty “hasty” search that focused on checking ridge lines, cliffs, ditches—any place Lena might have fallen and injured or trapped herself. A Type II search, on the other hand, was a methodical slog that involved multiple teams and utilized mantracking skills—skills that achieved the best results in areas less traveled. Artemis used scent rather than visual clues. Using both tracking and trailing methods upped the odds of success.

“I collected several scent articles from Lena’s laundry basket at her dad’s place—he’s got primary custody—in case we field more than one canine team.”

She pulled out her phone and addressed Eli. “Did you get the photos of the boot prints I sent you earlier? The dad was positive they belonged to Lena and there’s a strong chance she’s wearing the same boots. Pretty much everybody we spoke to agrees she rarely wears anything else.”

Eli nodded. “We made sure everyone on the team had a copy.”

"Based on the tread wear, Lena pronates," Pete said. "And the stride length will be particularly helpful if we end up taking a closer look tomorrow."

Swing shift had been called in early to help with the typical calls for service. Officers already tired from working the fair found themselves donning their uniform again.

"I need to run back to the station to prep some info for the graveyard guys before heading back up here to bring Mom up to speed with what we've done today. Anything you need from me before I head out?" Jo asked.

Eli jumped in. "Don't worry. If something crops up, I got it. I'll be back at the station after the SAR debrief."

Jo crushed her bottle. Eleven hours into the investigation and they hadn't even turned over all the pieces yet. With no real insight into what had happened, this was a feeble attempt to cobble disparate hypotheses together to see if they hinted at the bigger picture.

And right now, nothing fit.

11

Thank God.

Tilda flung open the door but instead of her daughter, Jessup and Jo stood on her doorstep, their faces in shadow cast by the streetlight at the end of the block. Lena had been gone twelve hours. Seven hundred twenty minutes. Too many seconds to calculate while they stood on her doorstep, their stillness impossible to read.

Her hand tightened on the knob, her knees nearly buckling. "Lena?" Her voice cracked.

Jo must have registered the underlying question. Her arm came up. Conciliatory. "We haven't found her, yet. We just wanted to let you know where we are with the investigation. What's next. Talk to Marisa."

Tilda slumped against the doorframe. There was still hope.

Twelve hours—seven hundred twenty-*one* minutes—a lifetime when your baby was missing. Each minute—

A light touch on her arm startled her. She shrugged off Jo's hand, but the concern in the detective's eyes lingered, even as she stepped back to allow Jessup to move forward and shepherd them all into the living room.

"Tell me what you know." Her heart ached. A physical pain unlike any she knew how to treat. "Tell me everything."

Jessup waited until she took her place on the couch and then chose the chair next to her. He'd taken his hat off the minute he crossed the threshold. Leaning forward, he ran the brim through his fingers. Straw. A summer weight, similar to the hat he'd worn at the hospital where she'd learned to recognize his pain. She put her hand on his thigh. "Rip the Band-Aid off, Jessup."

And he did. His voice held steady even as he used terms such as uncertain, unknown, pending. Hope. They were the same words she'd spoken to him when she'd worked the ward and it was him pressing her for information regarding his wife. Had he, too, only heard every third word?

Her cell phone rang. She checked the screen and declined the call.

"We need to ask for your permission, Tilda."

His voice was gentle. The voice he'd used to speak to his wife, even though she couldn't hear him at the end. It wasn't the voice he'd used with Tilda then. That voice had been tinged with frustration at his inability to control his situation. Anger at his wife's prognosis. Helplessness. This voice held compassion. She didn't want to look beneath the surface of it. The enormity of it would swallow her. "You need medical records."

"Lena's dental records as well," Jessup said. "And since she hasn't returned, there are a few more things we should collect."

"You think Lena's . . ." The word formed in her mind, but she couldn't voice it. No parent should have to ask if their child was dead.

"No," Jo answered.

"Then why the hell aren't you out looking for her?" Tilda pinched the bridge of her nose, trying to short-circuit the headache that throbbed behind her eyes. This time yesterday, she was in the ER, introducing herself to patients who had come in earlier in the day. She'd signed up for an overtime shift later in the week. Yesterday she'd been a nurse in a place where nothing much happened. Marisa complained about how boring her life was in the valley. Children came home when they were supposed to. Kids joined 4-H. Did chores. All that dissolved with a phone call. Now, nothing would be the same until Lena returned home. "I'd like to help search." *Do something.*

"That's really not a good idea," he said. "We need you to be available, here."

Tilda sighed. "Out of the way, you mean."

Jessup smiled and something inside her cracked open. "I may not always be able to tell you everything, but I won't lie."

Her phone rang. Sienna. Again. She turned off the ringer and put the phone face down on the table. "No lies." She studied the hands in her lap. "Not about Lena."

"Do you have a house phone, or do you only use your mobile?" he asked.

Jo opened her notebook. Playing the secretary seemed out of character. In high school, she had always done her own thing, never much caring about what the group thought. Only happy when she was covered in dirt or nose deep in a book. Maybe she'd learned life was easier some days when you just met expectations.

"Cell phone." There hadn't been as much overtime lately. She didn't need the expense of another line. Especially with an ex who didn't understand the financial needs of the girls.

"You're going to start receiving a lot of calls once people learn Lena's missing. Not all of them will be from friends. With your permission, we'd like to install a landline tomorrow. You'll be able to forward your number to it, but it will allow us to record the contacts if necessary. We'd also like you to keep a log of who called and when."

A call log. Her mouth went dry. "Are you expecting a ransom request?"

"At this point anything is possible," Jessup warned. "There will be people wanting to help, media asking for insider information, others who could try to take advantage of you. You don't have to talk to anyone."

She nodded. Like the damn bobblehead dog in the back window of her mother's car, it seemed like nodding was all she was doing lately.

Jessup stopped fiddling with the brim of his hat. She'd watched him enough in the hospital and she braced herself.

"We'd like you to take a polygraph."

She stopped nodding. "You're kidding, right?" She was a suspect? This had to be Jo's doing. Jessup would never . . .

"Everyone is a suspect until they're ruled out," he said.

"And Lucero? This never would have happened if he hadn't—"

"He'll be asked to take one as well," Jessup said. "We'll schedule them back to back, so the media can't make a big deal about one parent taking the test if the other one doesn't."

"That makes it sound like I don't have to take it."

"We can't compel you to take one, no."

"But you think I should?"

She looked between the two detectives. Finally Jo spoke. "We can't make that decision for you, Tilda. The choice is yours."

"But if I don't everyone will think I'm guilty," she said, then added, "even though I don't have anything to hide." The ceiling fan above them whirred. "Let me know what Lucero says."

"Of course," Jessup said. "I also need to ask if you're seeing someone?"

There had been a time Tilda had wanted him to ask her that question. Wanted someone to love her like he had loved his wife. This evening, the question meant something completely different. Something sinister. "So you *do* think someone snatched Lena."

"We haven't been able to rule it out."

Tilda caught Jo staring at her. She tucked her feet onto the couch. Made herself a smaller target. "No one serious. Echo Valley isn't exactly teeming with prospects."

"Anyone take a shine to Lena?"

"Never got to a point where I wanted to introduce anyone to the girls."

"Did they know you had daughters?" Jo asked.

"Of course." The lie flowed easily. It was hard enough to score a date as a thirty-something single woman. Throw in kids and it became damn near impossible.

"Any conversations that, in hindsight, raised red flags?"

Had there been? Her dates usually followed a pattern. Drinks at the Hitching Post if she felt like a cowboy. Valhalla when she was looking for a biker. Both bars had a revolving door of tumbleweeds who blew through town. Enough drinks, and dinner became an afterthought. The cowboys at least had trucks. No one asked if she had kids.

"Lucero's been dating one of the dealers over at the casino. I don't know if it's serious, but if it is, she might not be too happy to raise a kid that isn't hers."

Jo clicked her pen. "Do you know her name?"

"Misty Trujillo."

"I'll need the names of the men you've recently dated as well," Jo said.

Tilda worried the bottom of her shirt. She was back to nodding again, but she had no intention of admitting she didn't know or remember most of their names. Jo already thought she was trash, she couldn't bear Jessup thinking it too. "What about the Amber Alert?"

Jessup answered. "We've shared information with the media, but an Amber Alert requires specific information that we don't have."

"Good God! What more do you need? My daughter is missing!" The thread caught on a callus and a portion of the hem unraveled.

"We don't know for certain Lena's been kidnapped. An Amber Alert requires car details, suspect description, information we don't have."

"She sure as hell didn't run away." Why would she? She had her animals, her family. *Lucero.* She sprang from the couch and for a second the room tilted before she regained her balance. Both officers stood too. To hell with them, they could watch her pace. Her heart pulsed loud in her ears. Why had Marisa been so suspicious of her father? Evasive when pressed? Had it been fear Tilda had seen in her daughter's eyes or concern? The roar grew louder. If Lucero had done anything to hurt her child, she'd kill him.

She strode to the hallway and stopped. Marisa sat on the stairs, her thin arms wrapped around her knees, her long hair pulled over one shoulder. How long had she been there?

Tilda struggled to keep her voice level. "Go upstairs, baby doll. I'll fill you in when we're done."

"I should be part of this. She's my sister."

"Please, not now, Marisa."

"But I can help. That man mentioned the media may call. I'd be good at that."

"I said, not now." She watched her daughter's face crumple.

Her daughter stood. Graceful. Poised. "I'm here when you need me, Momma."

She rubbed her temple, partly to shield Marisa's view of the color rising to her cheeks. "I know, honey. Now go on." She stopped herself before she said she'd tuck her daughter in. "Please."

Marisa opened her mouth as if to say something more and then decided against it. Her gaze flickered past Tilda's shoulder and then she disappeared toward her room.

Tilda spun. The two detectives waited for her. Jo's eyes locked on where Marisa had just stood.

"Is there anything else you can think of that's important for us to know?" Jo asked, her voice pitched low as if to draw Tilda back from a dangerous ledge.

The question was intentionally open-ended. But did they really want to know that Lena's left eye was slightly more green than her right one? Or that she used a rosemary shampoo, and after her bath her skin smelled woodsy, like the scent released from walking on a shaded trail on a hot day. That she was kind? Did either one of them care that Lena's feet weren't ticklish, but if you lightly brushed the nape of her neck when her hair was braided, she'd squeal and goose bumps would speckle her arms?

Tilda raked her nails through her hair. "She's got freckles across her nose," she said, finally. "The gap between her front teeth leaves a funny impression when she bites into an apple. She hates banana cream pie, but loves bananas." The words tumbled from her mouth, gaining speed. "When she eats trail mix, she picks out all the nuts first and then eats the M&Ms and raisins at the same time because she thinks it's like eating Raisinets. When she reads, she looks up every word she doesn't understand in a beat-up pocket dictionary she always has in her backpack. There's a cowlick in the front of her head that creates a poof in her bangs that Marisa always teases her about." More words. Faster. "She sings off key and for years wondered how Little Miss Muffet could eat a curb. The first word she spoke was Dada, and it broke my heart." Her voice quavered.

Jessup removed a neatly folded handkerchief from his pocket and handed it to her. An embroidered monogram graced the corner. She turned it over and over but didn't unfold the fabric. He cupped her elbow and guided her back to the living room.

Jo walked into the kitchen and returned with a glass of water.

"I don't want water." Her voice shook.

"I know. You want your daughter." Jo set the glass on the coffee table. "I'd like to talk to Marisa." The words gave Tilda a modicum of control, but Jo wasn't asking permission.

"I'll call her downstairs."

"It would be better if I could speak to her alone," Jo said.

"You mean without me being there." She didn't expect a response and she wasn't disappointed. "Jessup, do you mind speaking with Marisa? I'd like to talk to Jo."

Some silent communication passed between the two detectives before Jessup agreed. Jo scribbled a brief note, tore out the page and extended it to her partner.

He took the page without reading it. "Holler if you need anything."

She wasn't sure who he was talking to.

Jo settled into the club chair. She wore the studied nonchalance of a person about to receive a tetanus shot. Deceptively relaxed, poised to spring. Tilda let her stew.

Jo hadn't changed much since high school. Her nose had a slight bend to it that indicated it had been broken. If today was any indication, she still hadn't learned how to fix her hair in anything more elaborate than a ponytail. The biggest difference was something inscrutable behind her eyes, as if they'd seen too much and she was wary of giving too much of herself away.

She waited for Jo to break first. But for a woman who was all business a moment ago, she acted like she had all the time in the world now.

"I think Lucero had something to do with Lena's disappearance." As soon as the words were out of Tilda's mouth, she realized how absurd it was to have this conversation with Jo Wyatt.

"Why do you think that?"

"Mother's intuition? I don't know." Another lie.

"Have you seen any bruises, unexplained injuries?"

"No."

"Any behavioral changes? Loss of appetite, withdrawal?"

Had she missed something? "She lives with her father."

Jo cocked her head slightly. "I need something actionable."

"Earlier, I told Marisa that you were trying to locate her father. She immediately thought you were going to arrest him."

"Did you ask her why she would think such a thing?"

Was there condescension in Jo's voice? "I'm not stupid." Her own words sounded chilly. "When I asked her, she tried to play it off, but it was obvious something was wrong. She was hiding something. Like she knew he'd done something to Lena. Something bad." Tilda drew a deep breath and before she lost her nerve, she blurted, "What if he hurt Lena like he hurt me?"

Maybe it was the lighting, but the detective seemed to age as the words hung in the space between them.

"What do you mean like he hurt you?"

Tilda snapped. "You know damn well what I mean."

"I'm a police officer now, Tilda." Jo spoke slowly, a sure sign she was pissed. "If Lucero has hurt you or the girls, I want to know about it. If you think he is somehow responsible for Lena's disappearance, I want to know about that too."

"Why do you think I'm telling you all this?"

"That's a good question." Jo took out her cell phone and tapped a message. Probably to Jessup so he could ask Marisa about it. "You obviously have a better relationship with Detective MacAllister. Exactly why are you telling me?"

"You know our history."

"Detective MacAllister has read the reports."

The news took Tilda by surprise. It had all happened so long ago, she'd thought any record of that godawful time would have been buried beneath years of more recent reports. Like medical records that didn't get passed from one practitioner to another. Duly recorded but rarely referenced.

This was ridiculous. "You believed me, once."

"That was a long time ago."

"You know the truth." God, the woman was infuriating. Possibly even more so now that she wore a badge. "You knew it then—and you know it sitting here now."

"The only thing I know for certain is that you lied."

"I didn't lie."

Jo's left eyebrow shot up—something Tilda hadn't seen since high school. It was every bit as irritating now as it was then.

"You're going to have to be more specific, because you either lied to me when you told me Lucero hurt you, or to my father when you said I made everything up."

"Didn't they teach you in cop school that it's not uncommon for women to take back their statements regarding domestic abuse?"

"They did. But as a kid, I didn't know that. I believed every word you told me, even though Lucero was my friend. Why'd you change your story?"

"None of your business."

"Were you pregnant?"

Tilda felt the color crawl up her neck, and she had an overwhelming desire to slap the smug right off Jo's face.

"Fuck you."

Jo smiled the uninhibited, genuine smile of their high school days, the one that lit up her entire face. "You needed that."

The change in Jo's demeanor put Tilda on guard.

"Now that that's out of your system. Let me explain something to you." All Jo's lightheartedness vanished. She leaned forward, invading Tilda's space, forcing her to lean back until the sofa cushions had no more give. "Lena is the one who needs my help and I'm working for her. If the investigation leads me to believe you had something to do with her disappearance, I will do everything in my power to build a case against you."

Tilda opened her mouth, but Jo plunged on. "If I uncover anything to make me believe Lucero had something to do with Lena's disappearance, I will do the same. But believe me when I say that I'm going to do everything in my power to find Galena and bring her home, and I will never lose sight of the fact that her return is more important than any investigation."

Tilda had forgotten how brutally honest Jo could be. That idealistic sense of righteousness that made her insufferable, even as a gawky teen. How many *Jo stories* had Tilda suffered through while dating Lucero? Listening to him prattle on about their shared experiences. The ass-whooping she'd saved him from after his family first moved to the valley. Had Lucero fallen in love with Jo then, or had his feelings grown over time? She doubted he knew. Jo certainly didn't. There was only one person she'd drop everything for and that was Aiden Teague. To her, Lucero was just one of the boys.

By comparison, Tilda was Lucero's consolation prize. The woman who never quite measured up. Jo was opinionated, reckless, and too trusting of those she considered friends. In a more charitable light, the things Tilda most hated about Jo also made her confident, courageous, and loyal. But she wasn't inclined toward charity when it involved Jo Wyatt.

"I work for Lena," Jo repeated. She leaned back in the club chair and reopened her notebook, all business again. "Do you have a problem with that?"

Tilda shook her head. "Not at all." But that, too, was a lie.

12

The stars broke through the darkness and painted the sky with a brush-stroke of glitter.

Squint unlocked the passenger side of his detective car. "So?"

"The text I sent you pretty much summed it up." Jo kicked his rear tire. "Tilda believes Lucero had something to do with Lena's disappearance. She even trotted out the incident in high school. Claimed it established Lucero's propensity for violence."

"I see."

"That makes one of us." She looked up at the sky again. The Lucero she'd known as a child had loved animals and wouldn't hurt anyone. Or so she'd thought. And yet she'd believed Tilda. The man she'd spoken to in the stable was someone different. Someone who'd put her on guard.

Squint removed his hat and bounced it against his leg. "There could be something to it."

"Marisa say something?"

"Not about her father. Nothing to suggest Lena wanted to hurt herself, either." He leaned his back against the side of the car and worked the brim of his hat lightly through his hands. "Marisa is quite the entrepreneur. Not only does she get companies to send her things to shill on her social media sites, but then she turns around and sells the items to other girls at school. She claims she had several hundred dollars stashed in her room."

A star detached and streaked across the sky. Jo automatically made a wish. "And it's gone?"

"Well, she says it is."

"You sound hesitant," Jo said.

"Not about the money. Unless Tilda took it without telling Marisa, the most logical assumption is that Lena took it."

"Don't forget the open window."

"True, but Marisa kept the cash in a makeup bag stuffed in a boot in a box in her closet and under a pile of clothes the likes of which I've never seen."

"You had boys," Jo reminded him.

"It seems unlikely that someone would know where the cash was and not disturb or take anything else in the house. Plus, she doesn't know exactly when it went missing. The last time she added money to the stash was about a week ago."

"So she thinks Lena took it."

"She wouldn't say one way or the other," Squint said. "Only that it was gone."

The curtains in the front bedroom were sheer enough that Marisa's shadowy outline could be seen moving about her room.

"Does Tilda know about this?" Jo asked.

"Tilda's aware of the merchandise, but Marisa never told her about the side gig at the high school or that she's been socking away her pennies—"

"Literally."

"—so she didn't know how to broach the theft."

"How much was stolen?"

"About eight hundred. She makes deposits in thousand-dollar increments. So far, she's squirreled away more than twelve grand."

"That's a lot of pennies." Heck, it was almost as much as Jo had put away, and she was saving for a down payment on a home. "Could she be lying about the theft?"

"Always a possibility, but to what end?"

Jo couldn't answer and countered with her own question. "What did she have to say about her father?"

"Nothing bad. But the question clearly made her uncomfortable."

"Not surprising. She's a fifteen-year-old child who is being asked questions about her father's behavior that could land him in a whole lot of trouble."

A sliver of light suddenly divided them, and their heads tilted up in unison. Marisa stood at the window peering down at them. She raised her hand in a weak wave and the curtain fell back into place. The light snapped off.

"Did you get the impression Marisa was being abused?" Jo asked.

"No, but that would certainly account for her reticence."

"Which means we could have an eleven-year-old on the lam because she's trying to avoid her father." So much for wishing on a star.

13

Sleep proved elusive, and finally after a few fitful hours, Jo quit chasing it. She bypassed her office clothes and dressed for the day in a police department polo shirt, 5.11 cargo pants, and patrol boots. Her duty belt hung around her waist and the radio dug into her side. Rather than head to the station, she detoured and parked her Explorer a few doors down from Tilda's townhome, then killed the engine.

A neighborhood at four o'clock in the morning held secrets. Sometimes darkness hid teenagers sneaking back into their homes. Moonless nights brought out prowlers casing targets and raccoons in search of trash. Who else showed up remained to be seen.

She stepped from the car and eased her door shut. The engine ticked as it cooled. Keeping to the shadows, she tucked next to a scruffy-barked oak across the street from the townhouse and waited. The front porch light blazed like a beacon to call Lena home. The rest of the townhouse was dark. Hopefully Tilda had been able to sleep—at least a little. The coming days were going to be difficult.

Slowly, the night noises resumed, surrounding her with the scrape and scratch of wildlife and the hum of insects, all punctuated by the occasional car traveling through the valley in the distance.

Today was going to be busy. Another search, another stab at contacting Dawson to confirm Lucero's whereabouts, and Child Protective Services to see if either parent had ever found themselves sideways with the agency. Then there were the requests: court documents, employee lists, medical and dental records, DMV returns on the registered owners of plates collected during the canvass. Putting the trash company on alert to check the commercial dumpsters before they were dumped into the trucks.

Steal some time to talk to Squint. Tilda's bombshell, Marisa's theft. She wanted to plumb that with him further. Maybe they both had blind spots.

The front door of the townhome opened and Tilda stepped quietly onto the porch. Despite the warmth of the night, she rubbed her arms as if she were cold while she looked up and down the street.

"Lena?"

By the time the voice drifted across the street only the desperation remained audible. Tilda hugged herself tighter. Pain radiated off of her in waves and lapped at Jo's feet.

With a final glance in both directions, Tilda retreated into the house.

In the distance, lightning played over the mesa. Echo Valley always seemed a breath away from disaster. Wildfires threatened to burn it down. Summer monsoons triggered flooding and mudslides. Autumn winds blasted through the canyons and plucked at people's nerves. Soon the snows would be upon them.

All in all, paradise had a deceptively dangerous side. Unlike a disaster that brought people together, a missing child was a personal hell. Sure, people would rally, they'd pass out fliers, host a pancake breakfast fund-raiser, but at night most people would return to their own house, hug their child a little bit longer than normal, and thank God it wasn't their kid who hadn't come home.

Headlights raked the landscape of the corner lot as a car turned onto Tilda's street and continued up the wrong side of the roadway. Jo melted behind the tree. The boxy sedan lurched and dipped in concert with the newspapers flung from the driver's seat. At Tilda's place, the car rolled to a stop and the driver dimmed his headlights. A diagonal Volvo emblem crossed the front grill. Dull red light glowed low in the car. It distorted the driver's face with misplaced shadows.

The driver struck a match and touched the flame to his cigarette, then tossed the match onto the ground outside his window. Resting his elbow on the doorframe, he stared toward the townhouse while he smoked, the tip of the cigarette flaring with each drag. Once he dipped his head to peer through the windshield at the upper story, then resumed his vigil. Finally, he flicked the lit butt from the car to join the spent match.

The Volvo rolled forward and when it cleared the apron of the driveway, the driver stomped on the accelerator and resumed his halting progress of delivering the morning edition.

Jo keyed the mic on her radio. "David-three to any available unit in the area of Quail Ridge."

"Sam-three, couple blocks away."

Great. Sergeant Cameron Finch, affectionately known as her ex.

"I need you to stop a dark, older model Volvo currently southbound in the 200 block of Ptarmigan Place. No cite. I just need a driver ID. I'll explain further off air." No sense alerting anyone who might be scanning.

"You got PC?"

She glared at the radio. Did he really think she'd stop a car without probable cause? "Inoperable brake light." Not to mention driving on the wrong side of the road, littering, and showing too much interest in a house where a little girl went missing. "I'm in my POV, I'll pull in behind you."

The Volvo disappeared around the corner and Jo came out of hiding. She pulled a latex glove from her pocket and stooped to collect the cigarette butt and match, and then climbed into her car. Headlights off, she pulled up to the end of the block. In the predawn hours, the roar of the approaching patrol car carried through her open window. She hung back until Cameron positioned himself behind the Volvo, then she closed the gap as he called the stop out over the air. The driver pulled over immediately.

Jo approached on the passenger side while Cameron greeted the driver. The back seat was full of banded and bagged newspapers that cascaded onto the floorboard. A gooseneck map light drew power from the cigarette lighter socket. Similar to the lights hardwired into patrol cars, it was outfitted with a red lens that protected night vision. He'd DIY'd a barrier that kept the newspapers on the front seat from sliding onto the floorboard where they'd get lost in a collection of food wrappers and coffee cups.

When the driver reached for the glove box, Jo focused her light on it. He gave her the once over and dug out his paperwork. His face was like the end cut of a loaf of bread: rounded at the crown and square through the jaw. Bland features superimposed on pasty skin.

When Cameron had the driver's license and registration, they both returned to the patrol car.

"So, whattya got?" He passed her the documentation.

Even at zero dark thirty, he was bright-eyed. Cameron was magnetic in a way that had once attracted her. But either he'd flipped or she had, or maybe they'd each turned slightly, and what had once kept them close now pushed them apart.

"Not sure." She tucked her flashlight under her arm. "Either he chose the worst possible place for a smoke break, or he has a suspicious interest in the house that our missing disappeared from." She keyed her mic and gave the dispatcher the name and birthdate of the driver.

Dakota Kaplan answered, her southern drawl unhurried. "David-three. Your subject Tingler is clear and valid. Currently on probation in El Paso County."

"Copy." Jo flicked the front of the license. "Well, that make things easier. Twenty-one years old and already on probation."

"You mean a name like Tingler wasn't enough?"

"I prefer something that stands up in court." Jo took her time approaching Aaron Tingler's window. "Good morning, Mr. Tingler."

His hair was nearly shaved along the sides and longer on top, waved into place with a fair amount of gel.

"I'm not on probation anymore," he said.

"Excuse me?" Her voice carried in the early morning quiet.

Tingler sucked his teeth. "Your dispatcher said I was on probation. I'm not. That ended two weeks ago. Go ahead and check. I'll wait." He tapped a beat against the steering wheel to a song only he heard.

"Echo, David-three." She ran the beam of her flashlight throughout the passenger compartment looking for a scanner while dispatch replied, and then she continued. "Can you reconfirm probation status? Subject claims he's fulfilled his requirement."

Dispatch keyed the mic and Dakota's fingers tapped the keyboard in the background. "David-three, my error. Probation status on your subject expired August tenth."

It was the rare day her friend made a mistake on the air. Jo would have to give her grief, later. "Copy."

Aaron's face broke out in a wide grin and he wagged his phone. "There's an app for everything now. So tell me, officer . . ."

"Detective Wyatt."

"What a strange first name. I'm curious. Why would Detective Wyatt be interested in who I am? Looking to score a date? I'd be happy to oblige."

"I like to know a bit about my dates before going out with them." Jo plastered a smile across her face. "Like why you were on probation."

"Let's see, I like running stadiums, thirty-two-ounce steaks, and am searching for the perfect partner in crime. But you look a bit old for me." His forehead creased with mock concern. "Or are you just tired?"

"How long have you been working for the *Courier*?"

"Not much for foreplay, are you? Look, I'm on the clock. How about you buy me a cup of coffee when I'm through and we get to know each other. Or we can skip the coffee and cut to the chase."

"How about I write you a ticket, instead."

"For a taillight? That's just the kind of chicken shit thing that gives cops a bad name."

"A broken taillight is an equipment violation. Get it fixed and nothing goes on your record."

"You do you."

"Now, driving on the wrong side of the roadway?" Jo continued. "That's a different story. Depending on your driving record, a moving violation could have some serious repercussions. At the very least, it'll probably raise your insurance rates, but if you've got other points, it could result in losing your license."

"I was delivering newspapers." Some of the cockiness left his voice. "No one else was around."

"I don't recall newspaper delivery being an exception to the rules of the road."

"You always so bitchy?"

She glanced across the top of the roof. Cameron grinned back but thankfully remained quiet.

"I'm not normally up this early. But in all fairness, while I'm explaining things, I should also inform you that throwing a lighted cigarette or match from a vehicle is a class two misdemeanor. Tossing a match *and* cigarette? Well, that's two separate counts—and each count is punishable by three to twelve months in jail and up to a thousand dollar fine. Thank goodness neither one sparked a fire. That would have opened up a whole new can of worms."

"How do you know about that?"

"Oh, you know. Cops are never around when you need us, but darned if we aren't Johnny-on-the-spot when you don't," Jo said.

"I didn't do anything. Just stopped for a smoke. Why you busting my balls?"

"It's what she does when she's bored," Cameron said from the opposite side of the car.

Jo ignored him. "You know who lives there?"

"I deliver their paper. Of course I do."

That was a surprise. She thought the *Courier* would only provide their drivers with a list of addresses. Something else to follow up with the paper.

"You know anyone personally?"

"No." He propped his elbow on the armrest and rested the side of his head against the tip of his fingers. "What do you want?"

"I started this conversation by asking you a couple of very simple questions."

He raised his eyes in a manner that would make a teenager proud. "It's been so long ago now, I don't remember what they were."

"Fortunately, I do," Jo said. "Why were you on probation?"

"Theft."

Evasive and honest at the same time. Kudos. "That covers a lot of territory: petty, auto, robbery, burglary, what?"

He narrowed his eyes. "Burglary."

"How long have you worked for the paper?"

"I don't know." He sucked his teeth again. "Six weeks?"

"I'll just assume you received permission from your probation officer before you changed jurisdictions. Who's your PO?"

"Did you miss the part about me not having one?"

"I'll give you that one." It was easy enough to learn once she was back at the station. "Where you living now?"

All his earlier playfulness was gone. "You've got my license."

"I'm going to go out on a limb and speculate you're not commuting from Colorado Springs."

"I'm staying with family while I finish college."

Jo glanced at the registration again. The address on the registration was local, and the registered owner shared the same last name. "Whose car is it?"

"My dad's. He's helping me get back on my feet."

No need to give him grief over that. She was doing the same thing. "I appreciate your cooperation this morning, Mr. Tingler."

The cockiness returned, and his hooded eyes leisurely traced a path across her body that started at her boots and paused at her breasts. "I can be very cooperative."

"I'm sure you can." Considering she was wearing a ballistic vest, his over-the-top power play fell woefully short. "Sit tight, I'll be back in a moment with your citation."

"You're writing me a ticket?"

"Taillight. When you get it fixed, stop by the station and I'll sign it off." She backtracked toward the patrol car.

"You're cold," he said loud enough for her to hear.

At the patrol car she asked to use Cameron's cite book.

He pried it from its place wedged on the dashboard. "You do look kinda tired."

She yanked it out of his hand. "And you wonder why we're no longer married?"

He laughed. "You worried he's going to pull a Casper?"

"I don't think he's going to disappear, but I don't want to spook him. He's in the system and I can always follow up with his family. If he turns out to be something more than a paper delivery guy with a nicotine addiction, I'm hoping he'll come to me instead of me having to track him down."

"I was starting to think you were going to haul him in on the misdemeanor."

"More interested in his DNA—which, in case it becomes relevant, I now have, courtesy of his cigarette." She finished scratching out the citation and clicked her pen closed. "Besides, that really would be chicken shit."

14

Tilda rubbed the back of her hand across her face. The grit under her lids dug in and scratched her eyes. At some point she'd have to sleep, but the prospect frightened her. She'd been awake for twenty-two hours. Not the longest she'd ever had her eyes open, but considering she'd only slept about an hour after her shift, she was feeling the burn.

She sat on the floor, the tiles cool through her thin cotton shorts, Jessup's handkerchief stuffed into her pocket. She'd towel-dried her hair, but the moisture from the ends soaked into her burgundy T-shirt in an expanding blot, dark as blood. She wouldn't have showered at all if Marisa hadn't commented about her scrubs. But that had been hours ago.

The laptop emitted a ghoulish glow that tinted everything on the coffee table slightly blue. She typed missing children into the browser search bar. *About 1,060,000,000 results (0.84 seconds).* She counted the zeros. Not one million as she'd first read. *Millions.* Children who had run away or been snatched or lost their way. Children who were already statistics on the internet and whose parents were using up the resources she needed for her child. The only child who mattered. Lena.

She reached for her wineglass. The surface of the chardonnay appeared stippled in the glow, as if a storm were somehow trapped inside the bowl. Only when the glass chattered against her teeth did she realize her hand was shaking. She sipped, holding the oaky taste in her mouth until it warmed and coated her tongue.

Darkness amplified everything, and she concentrated on the individual sounds. The whirring of the laptop. The clank of a cube dropping from the automatic ice maker. The crickets beyond the walls. Upstairs Marisa turned in her bed. Tilda listened for Lena. Surely, as a mother, she should sense her daughter. Know if she were hurt or scared. Tilda swallowed. They were of the same tissue and blood. Shouldn't that mean something? And if so, why did she only feel empty?

The second sip went down easier. It sanded the sharp edges of the cheap stuff she bought at the grocery store. The bottles from the bottom shelf. One more sip for courage and she confronted the returns on her laptop screen.

The National Center for Missing & Exploited Children sat at the top of the list. Below that were current news stories. The Polly Klaas Foundation was next. Then Wikipedia. Statistics. Photos. Alerts. Missing children from today. This year. Last year. New developments. Cold cases. She took another sip and kept scanning. Missing children in America, by state. International Centres. Then there were the acronyms—FBI, DOJ, OJP NCJRS—as if the use of letters somehow mitigated the fear of needing the help of an agency large enough to be known by its initials.

A photograph derailed her scrolling. A little girl. The image was obviously a school photo with its ubiquitous mottled blue background. The girl appeared to be in first, maybe second grade. She had short, blond hair and droopy eyes that sagged as if the photographer had taken the photo mid-blink and didn't care enough to take another. The teaser blurb was incomplete. *After a three-hour standoff, police shot and killed an Albuquerque man who had abducted his daughter and was attempting to flee the state. The girl . . .* The sentence dissolved in ellipses that demanded a click as payment for more information.

Tilda scrolled through seven pages of returns, too frightened to click on any single entry.

How long had Lena been gone? Was she even now crying for her mother or father?

Dawn would be breaking soon. She clenched her fists and wondered when she'd grabbed the handkerchief from her pocket. She smoothed the crumpled cotton across her thigh and lightly traced the delicate letters.

She scrambled to her feet. The cloth fell to the floor, and the wineglass teetered. The graceful swirls didn't belong to Jessup. The initials belonged to his dead wife—and damned if she'd think about ghosts tonight. The closer she got to the front door, the narrower the hall became until the walls were so close she could hardly touch the doorknob. This time would be different. This time, Lena would answer.

Outside, the porch light pushed back the last bit of darkness. She tried to peer into it. Beyond it. She'd never once thought of the valley as a sinister place. Lena loved it. Marisa hated it. But Tilda rarely wasted brain cells even thinking about it. Echo Valley had been her parents' choice. As a teenager, she'd just been along for the ride. In the valley, she'd met Lucero. At the time, she thought she'd gotten the best part of the deal. High school had been followed by a stint in Fort Collins while Lucero earned his DVM degree. Then they'd returned to the valley as Mr. and Mrs., a kid in tow, living the dream, too stupid to realize some dreams only lasted as long as you stayed asleep.

She should have listened to Marisa when she'd launched her campaign to move to California. Strange to think Marisa had been the same age Lena was now. They were so different. Marisa had that damn brush with Hollywood that convinced her she was the next Hannah Montana or something. But her excitement had been infectious and Tilda started to think maybe her eldest daughter was right—not about becoming a child star, lord knows they all had their problems—but that California might be a good place for a do-over. A place where she'd find a man who appreciated her for herself and not just a quick toss. A man who would love not only her, but her two girls. A man unlike Lucero.

She leaned against the railing. A splinter dug into her bare forearm.

Lena had been all of six years old when she'd decided life could not move forward without a dog of her own. That had been a hard no. It wasn't like Tilda's paycheck could cover another mouth, even one that ate kibble from a bag. During the blowout that followed, Lena chirped that her dad would let her have one. Without stopping to think, Tilda had countered that maybe Lena should live with her father—knowing full well her ex wasn't about to be saddled with a kid. Turns out she was wrong. After a year had rolled around, she'd figured he'd be tired of playing daddy to an elementary age kid. Wrong again.

Then came the court paperwork. Motions to modify custody. Friends assured her the courts always awarded primary custody to the mother. Strike three. She should have anticipated the child support modification.

An early morning mosquito buzzed past her ear, and she waved it away.

Around the same time, Marisa discovered social media. The little stinker had filched Tilda's credit card from her wallet, then ordered her first outfit from H&M. The Saturday it arrived, Marisa dragged Lena outside and staged a photo shoot in the backyard, making sure the price tags were hidden. Once they finished, Marisa had brushed the dirt from the clothes, packaged them up, and sent them back. Then she did it again. And again. It was actually kind of genius. By the time Tilda caught on to the charges, her daughter had already amassed an impressive following on two social media sites.

Tilda had no idea what an influencer even was until vendors started sending products to her daughter to review and model. After that, she was on board. It saved a boatload of money on school clothes and helped stretch the paychecks. But if anything, Marisa's success only increased her desire to leave the valley. Tilda considered it. Who wouldn't? It was a chance to start over with her girls at her side, but Lucero, ever the spiteful bastard, refused to budge on custody. And here she stayed.

Lucero should have let them go. Then they wouldn't be in this fucking mess. Lena would be safe. Marisa would be happy chasing her dream of making it big in Hollywood. At the very least Tilda would be swimming in a larger dating pool.

She wrapped her arms around herself. Somewhere in Sage Gulch a coyote howled, a lonely cry that made Tilda tilt her head back.

The horrible, fucked up, soul-slicing truth was that Lena had disappeared from *her* home. The same home Lena had voluntarily abandoned when she was six.

"Lena!" Her voice ricocheted though the neighborhood, startling two mourning doves into flight.

She held her breath. Waiting. Not even the coyote answered.

Morning twilight brightened the sky from the bottom up and the ridge above her materialized from the blackness. Jo would be back soon with a search dog.

The newspaper delivery guy had tossed the paper onto the lawn again. Any moment the sprinklers would pop up like prairie dogs in a field and reduce the morning edition to pulp. She left it. The only news she wanted wouldn't come from a scrap of newsprint.

She retreated from the porch. Back to her laptop. A collage of photos scrolled across the screen. Mostly of Marisa. Tilda drained the wineglass, then tapped the computer back to life and backtracked two pages.

The girl with droopy eyes stared out from the screen. Pain shot through Tilda's chest and radiated outward. She flattened her palm against her sternum, digging her fingertips in with enough pressure to feel the ribs over her heart. The girl looked nothing like Lena. She wasn't anything like Lena. The acidic taste of warm wine clogged her throat. But she couldn't turn away from the droopy-eyed girl who was nothing—not a goddamn thing—like her own daughter.

15

Artemis sat quietly in the meeting room dressed for work in a bright orange search and rescue vest emblazoned with the county seal, a small beacon similar to the one Jo clipped to her clothes when she went for a run, and a harness with a short lead attached.

"Morning, everyone." Jo dropped her backpack on an empty chair. "May I?" Jo called out to Millie Tillerson, Artemis's handler.

"Of course," Millie answered from across the room. "She's missed you."

Jo squatted down and dug her hands into the German shepherd's thick ruff and gave the dog a good shake. "Hey there, Artie. You ready to find us a little girl today?"

Artemis pushed her head into Jo's chest and nearly bowled her over.

Eli slathered sunscreen on his bare arms. "Morning, Sunshine."

Pete Vasquez scrawled team assignments at the front of the room on one whiteboard. "Sign-in sheet's on the front table."

Various topo maps, aerial shots of the mesa, and trail maps were already taped to another board. The industrial-sized electric percolator in the back of the room gurgled, and the comforting scent of coffee filled the room. A stack of paper cups and a canister of powdered cream shared the table with a Motorola charging bank—each of its six slots full with a radio or an extra battery.

"Coffee should be ready any second. The night crew should be in any minute. Day shift is scheduled for zero six thirty. We'll be out the door by seven."

The lure of caffeine drew Jo to the urn where Millie prepped her travel mug. A mushroom cloud of powder billowed up from her cup. Jo leaned in for a quick hug. "Thanks for coming out so early. I know you had a late night."

In her early fifties, Millie was sleek as a kestrel, nimble as a peregrine, and had a raucous laugh that put the scream of a red-tailed hawk to shame. Jo prided herself on being fit, but hiking with Millie was like target shooting with a handgun against someone firing a rifle. You might be a crack shot, but you were still competing for second place.

"It's going to be another scorcher. The more ground we can cover before noon the better." Millie checked her watch. "By the time we get going, we'll have a solid four or five hours before Artemis is going to need a break. It won't be so bad if the trail takes us along the river, she can always cool off in the water, but if we're up on the mesa, it's going to feel like a furnace."

"Eli is point for the PD today. Squint and I are running down other leads, but I wanted to accompany you to the townhouse. See if Artemis picks up on anything that changes my priorities."

"That's the PLS?"

Jo nodded.

Emergency services personnel might not have a secret handshake, but they certainly spoke a language peppered with acronyms, lingo, and jargon that confused the uninitiated. SAR rolled off the tongue quicker than search and rescue. PLS referred to the point last seen. The shorthand kept radio traffic concise and misunderstandings low. But the beauty of operating under a formal incident command system was that ICS could expand from a two-person patrol call into a multijurisdictional major event where operations, planning, finance, and logistics all had their own staff and responsibilities—and as the incident wound down, so too did incident command.

This morning, the command post was a stuffy room at the county extension building. It could as easily have been the tailgate of Pete's truck. But this room afforded a coffee pot and air-conditioning while he plotted out his search strategy before the rest of the team arrived.

Pete moved to the map board. A bird's eye view of Tilda's townhouse showed its location in relation to both Sage Gulch and downtown. Jo had a similar printout in her office, only from a lower elevation that showed the immediate neighborhood. She used it as a checklist for which residents had already been contacted.

More team members straggled in—volunteers mostly, an equal number of men and women all working under the umbrella of the county sheriff.

"Detective Wyatt," Pete said. "Since you're here, do you want to kick things off?"

Grabbing her coffee, Jo moved to the front of the room. Unlike the night crew, the men and women in front of her were hearing about Lena for the first time. "Thank you all for helping the PD out with this case. Galena Flores is a healthy eleven-year-old girl who walked home from the fairgrounds Saturday night with her sister. They arrived at the residence around twenty-two hundred—which is the last confirmed contact we have of her. She was supposed to return to the fairgrounds Sunday morning. The plan was for her to walk back, which would have placed her on the road and river trail about this time of day yesterday. Only she never showed up. PD got the call around zero eight thirty and Officer Eli Dickinson responded."

Eli waved his hand, but everyone in the room probably already knew him.

"Due to the age of the child, the response escalated fairly quickly. There was a delay while we tracked down one of the parents, but during that time, officers completed an initial neighborhood canvass, with negative results," Jo said.

Several of the SAR group jotted notes while Jo continued to brief the details that would help them with their search.

"As for Lena. She's shy, but comfortable outdoors, hasn't met an animal she didn't want to adopt, and frequently hikes with her father. According to him, and depending on the terrain, they'd average a bit more than two miles an hour. Plus, they've done the Cross Creek Loop before, so that's what—seven miles?"

"Seven point four," one of the team members said without looking up from his pad.

"We don't have a great deal more than that," Jo said. "Eli will be out with you today. With a bit of luck, Millie and Artemis will winnow down the potential number of search areas." Otherwise, every hour would only increase the amount of ground the searchers would have to cover—a possibility Jo had to plan for, like it or not.

Millie slid out of her chair. "The game plan is a quick run through the house, then move outside for a perimeter search. The heat index isn't doing us any favors, which is why Artemis and I are heading out while you all finish briefing. As soon as I know something, I'll check in with a report."

Pete nodded. "Give us some good news."

* * *

When most people think of a tracking dog, they envision a bloodhound, nose to the ground, ears dragging, baying when it finds the trail. No other breed has a better schnozz to do scent work, but most of the working breeds, like German shepherds, made good search dogs, and Jo would put Artemis up against a hound any day. German shepherds had intelligence and drive on their side, and Artemis was making short work of the bottom level of Tilda's townhouse.

The trio formed a caravan: Artemis in the lead, Millie sandwiched in the center, and Jo trailing far enough behind to stay out of the way. Tilda swayed at the crossroad of the hallway and great room and appeared lost.

"We've already searched inside," Tilda said.

It was a common observation, but Millie explained the protocol as if it were the first time she'd ever heard it. "I don't want to overlook the possibility that your daughter was injured and unable to respond or had holed up in a cubby someplace. Kids can be pretty ingenious, and it wouldn't be the first time Artemis found a child where others had already searched."

Artemis paused at a media cabinet but quickly resumed her search, circling the kitchen island, giving cursory attention to the cabinets before passing Tilda and moving down the hall.

Tilda looked skeptical. "There has to be all kinds of scents in here, and Lena's would be all over the place."

Millie's eyes never left her dog. "Artemis is trained to scent discriminate. If Lena is here, Artemis will find her."

The shepherd paused next to the landing of the stairs and focused on the garage door, her nose running along the sill, then returned to Millie. Artemis circled her handler once before trotting back to the door.

"May I go into the garage?" Millie asked.

Tilda nodded. Artemis shot through the door before Millie found the light switch.

"Sorry, I've been meaning to get the light fixed," Tilda said. "You can open the door if you like."

"No worries, I've got a flashlight," Millie said.

Jo held the door so light from the hallway seeped in and bounced the beam of her flashlight off the ceiling, filling the space with a soft glow.

An older model Crown Victoria took up most of the space in the single-car garage. Artemis made a lap around the car, disappearing down the driver side, and reemerging from under the rear end.

Tilda moved closer. "Do you need me to open the garage door? Move anything?"

In a wilderness scenario, dog teams always had a spotter. The handler had one responsibility, watching the dog. That meant everything else fell to the support person—radio communications, compass and map work, and keeping an eye out for potentially dangerous situations—which included distractions.

Right now, that job fell to Jo. "Is this the same car your mom had when we were in high school?"

"One and the same." Tilda craned her neck to see around Jo and then gave up. "I tried to get her to trade it in once. She wouldn't. Now she's in Evergreen Manor."

The name of the locked facility explained it all. A mother with Alzheimer's and now a missing child. How much more could Tilda take before she broke? Jo chose her words carefully. "That must be difficult. I'm sorry."

Tilda narrowed her eyes slightly as if trying to detect a note of sarcasm that wasn't there. "Marisa turns sixteen in a couple of months. It'll become hers."

Jo had difficulty envisioning the teen zipping around town in a full-size sedan that was once the choice of police agencies across the nation. Her father used to park his squad car in the driveway when he came home for his meal break. He'd let her play with the lights and occasionally even allow her to hit the siren. Now they just looked like tired undercover cars for officers who didn't care if they were made or not.

Artemis doubled back to the front passenger door, her nose traveling the crease of the jamb.

"When's the last time Lena was in the car?" Millie asked.

Tilda's brow knit. "A couple days ago? I usually drive the beast when I take Lena back to her father's. Otherwise the battery dies."

Millie tried the door handle, then shined the light through the window.

"Let me get the keys," Tilda said.

"No need. I can see it's empty." Millie reached down and scratched Artemis behind the ear. "May we go upstairs?"

"Give me a minute to make sure Marisa is awake." Tilda used the railing to help pull herself up the stairs. "Marisa. Wake up, honey."

Jo lowered her voice and leaned closer to Millie. "I'm anxious to get outside."

"Me too. It won't take but a moment to run through the upstairs."

A door clicked closed upstairs and Tilda reappeared. "Marisa will be down in a minute."

A minute stretched into ten before Marisa padded downstairs, dressed in a cropped top pajama set, carrying a massive tote, and trailing a cloud of perfume.

Marisa caught Jo eyeballing the bag. "It's a Tory Burch bag from this year's collection. Genuine leather, plenty of room. Perfect as a stylish weekender for special getaways. If you like it, I can probably score one for you."

Even if it was proper to accept gifts, her idea of a special getaway usually involved steep inclines, a road bike, and plenty of sweat. A riding buddy was optional. "Thanks, but I usually just carry a backpack."

"Retro." Marisa yawned. "Nice."

Artemis pressed between her handler and Jo and sniffed the teen. Marisa drew back and shifted the bag to her other shoulder. "Does he bite?"

Millie grabbed Artemis's harness and pulled her back slightly and gave the signal to sit. "Actually, he's a she. This is Artemis, and no, she doesn't bite. But she's working right now or I'd let you say hi."

Jo knew better. Marisa's perfume made Jo's eyes water. She could only imagine what it was doing to the hundreds of millions of scent receptors in Artemis's nose.

"Is it even light out?" Marisa glided down the hallway until all that was left of her was a cloying scent of something Jo probably couldn't pronounce.

"May we?" Jo asked.

Tilda stepped out of the way but didn't say anything.

Artemis took the lead and the search train chugged up the stairs.

* * *

Outside, the day was already hot—even though it was early enough that most people were still on their first cup of coffee. In the morning light, Jo was optimistic. Today they'd find Lena. How could they not? The orange-clad search and rescue volunteers all shared a single goal.

At the corner of the side yard, Millie presented the baggie with the scent article to her dog. Artemis nudged it and then looked up.

"Go fishing," Millie said enthusiastically.

Artemis traveled faster along the grassy corridor between Tilda's building and the neighboring duplex than she had in the house, and she passed the den window without breaking stride.

Millie called her back. "Artemis, check here."

The shepherd dutifully returned, nosing Jo in passing. Millie patted the sill, and Artemis planted her front paws on the ledge but quickly lost interest and continued down the grass alley. Artemis rounded the rear corner of Tilda's backyard with Millie and Jo trotting behind her.

Each townhome in the community had a small private yard. In this block, the fences were backed by a retaining wall that held back the wild vegetation of the hillside and created a two-foot difference in elevation. Artemis plunged into the scrub, her bright orange vest a blur as she swept back and forth.

Jo scrambled higher up the incline and paralleled the K9 team. From her vantage, she had a clear view into both yards. An abundance of colorful potted plants surrounded a garden bench in Tilda's yard and a bistro table sat on the patio. It offered a stark contrast to her neighbor's dirt and weed lawn and the dented hibachi grill on the stained slab.

Breaking out of the vegetation, Artemis glanced up the hillside but followed the line of the duplex, searching for a scent to follow. Nose alternating between ground and air, the shepherd cleared the far side of the duplex.

Jo slid down the hillside and caught up to the team in the front. The morning sun promised to be relentless, and she lowered her sunglasses as she raised her gaze to the neighbor's window. Despite the empty driveway, she half expected Glowering Man to appear like an apparition. Creepy and ominous. She still needed to talk to him and was disappointed when the window remained vacant.

Artemis sat by Millie's side—a disappointing sign that the work here was done. All told, the search inside and around the duplex had taken less than a half hour—and that was with the ten-minute delay while they waited for Marisa to come downstairs.

"Well, this didn't work out like I'd hoped," Jo said.

"This heat is a beast," Millie said. "It's so still the scent cone probably traveled straight up—and that's assuming we have any scent left at all. I'll head back to the command post and check in with Pete, grab my spotter, and then run Artemis down by the river trail. The air's heavier down there. We may get lucky and Artemis will pick up on the rising scent as the earth warms. I just wish we'd been available yesterday evening."

"I'm sure the hiker appreciated you being in Silverton."

"After he got over the initial fright of a German shepherd crashing through the brush and sticking her nose in his face, yeah, he was pretty grateful." Millie reached down and scratched behind Artemis's ear before tilting her head to look at Jo. "I know you're worried. But lost children tend to keep moving until they get too tired to walk. If Lena's still in the area, she'll leave us a fresh scent trail. So go do whatever it is you need to do. The day's young, and we got this."

16

Unlike her sergeant, the new chief didn't make a lot of noise when he climbed the stairs to the detective bureau. Jo was mid-bite into her breakfast burrito and staring at the computer monitor when he strode into the detective bureau. She scrambled to her feet.

"Chief."

"We pay people around here to eat?" The lines feathering from his eyes nearly hid the fact that his smile didn't quite reach them.

A chile took its time sliding down her throat, and she dissolved into a coughing fit. She reached for her coffee, aware that her opportunity to make a good impression was dwindling. Instead, she pointed at the burrito. "Have you eaten at El Tecolote yet?"

"No. I'm not much for spicy food." He patted his belly. Since he'd been hired, the chief had made a point of wearing his uniform rather than a business suit. Just one of the guys, despite the array of stars on his collar.

He pointed to the chair next to her desk. "May I?"

Aaron Tingler's name blinked in her computer search bar, but he'd have to wait. "Of course." She grabbed the loop on top of her backpack and stowed it under her desk.

"I've talked to a lot of people since I was sworn in as chief. When I introduced myself to the district attorney, I learned you'd had a lot to do with that particular changing of the guard. I don't know many officers keen to unseat a district attorney. Takes courage."

This seemed a fine moment to hold her tongue, and she waited for him to continue.

"I read your personnel file too. Why aren't you a sergeant?"

His posture gave nothing away. He'd asked a deceptively simple question—which, as chief, he knew she was incapable of answering. Her job was to test for the position. Someone higher up the food chain made the final choice. "I don't think I'm the person to answer that question, sir."

"Medals for valor aren't handed out like candy. Tell me about the incident."

Her eyes fell on the stack of registrations from the canvass that needed her attention. "Right place, right time, I suppose."

He cocked his elbows on the chair arms and steepled his fingers in front of his chin. "I don't subscribe to false modesty, Detective. The citation describes a rather harrowing encounter."

She kept her face neutral. If he already knew the details, why was he wasting her time with questions? Especially when there was a far more pressing matter at hand. "Chief, I'm not trying to be flippant." But she also didn't want to answer. The question stirred up memories she'd worked hard to put to rest. "I was in the right place to notice a traffic violation."

The driver had refused to yield until he came to a dark spot in the road north of town. That little deviation from the norm had put her on alert. Probably saved her life.

"As I approached, I heard a sound coming from the trunk." A hollow thump, thump, that had spiked her adrenaline and had her reaching for her gun. "About that time, the car door opened so fast it bounced back and hit the driver as he rolled out of the car. He shot once. I shot three rounds." Failsafe drills taught officers to deliver two rounds to the chest, one to the head. She'd managed to land two out of three rounds. Then the fight was on.

"Turns out he was wanted for murder out of Albuquerque. Had a woman in the trunk."

Bound and gagged. Helpless. The duct tape across her mouth pulsed in and out as she struggled to breathe until Jo ripped it off. Then the screams. Screams Jo still occasionally heard.

"I'd shot him in the chest. He bled out at the scene."

Lips pursed, the chief nodded methodically, like someone who didn't really care about what he was hearing, but couldn't wait to get back to what he wanted to say. "Before I put a stake in the ground here in Echo

Valley, I wanted to make certain I knew what challenges I'd be facing. The thirty-thousand-foot view, so to speak. What do you suppose I discovered?"

He'd torn open her wound again. She let it bleed while considering this next inane question, no longer caring if she impressed him. But if the man wanted to test her, she'd oblige with a broadside of staff-level issues no sergeant would ever implement but that she'd learned for last year's promotional exam. Let him draw his own damn conclusions about her promotability.

"I would imagine you learned that Echo Valley is a wonderful place to live but its police agency is plagued by the type of issues that have always challenged rural agencies. Recruitment and retention issues, budgetary shortfalls—especially when it comes to convincing a community that doesn't have a particularly high crime rate that training and equipment are still essential needs. That if we had a person who knew how to pursue and administer grants we could defray the costs of those very same needs. And while it's not yet rampant, we're seeing an increase of forged prescriptions for opioids. Meth has a foothold in the community—especially in the county, which increases property crimes in the city. We're a whistle stop on a thoroughfare between Albuquerque and Denver that sees a lot of trafficking, yet we don't have the staffing to join an interdiction team."

There was probably more he'd discovered, but for a man who didn't like spicy food, he'd evidently overlooked that come autumn, so many places roasted the season's chile harvest that the whole town smelled like it had just been pepper sprayed. "Did I miss anything?" It came out like a challenge. Perhaps it was.

Squint's voice carried from the bottom of the stairs as he greeted someone. She almost sighed with relief when she heard his tread on the steps. Anything to save her from this godawful conversation.

The chief stood. "I also learned I had a detective who was almost disciplined for being insubordinate and that this same detective was the focus of a news article that cast the department in a rather unflattering light." He lifted her coffee mug from the desk and tilted it to read the side. "Communities must respect their police forces before they'll support them. Discord doesn't engender that trust."

Heat rose to her face. No doubt his administrative assistant, Harriet Landeau, had been happy to fill in the blanks for the new chief. How long was she going to have to pay for an article she had nothing to do with?

"Seems this agency has never promoted a woman to sergeant," the chief continued. "I wanted to address the elephant in the room. Ensure we don't have a problem."

The burrito in her stomach no longer seemed such a great idea. "I'm not really sure what question you're asking me to answer. But let me assure you, I've wanted to work for this department for as long as I remember. I wouldn't do anything to jeopardize it."

He set down her mug, positioning the handle exactly as she'd had it. "Good, because I'm going to promote you."

She froze. Her mind kept turning over and over like an engine that couldn't quite catch. How long had she waited to hear those words? Then in a rush of heat, she realized he wasn't offering her the job, simply the opportunity.

"Thank you, Chief. I appreciate your confidence in me and of course, I'm looking forward to the next opening, although I suspect it won't be for some time."

"That's where you're wrong."

Jo ran through the department roster. No one had put in a resignation. No one was out injured. The population hadn't swelled to the point where the agency was getting more people. "I didn't realize there was an opening."

"I've been here long enough now to recognize the need for some changes. Everything's still on the table, but one thing's for certain. Going forward, patrol will have another sergeant. You."

She caught her breath. "Me." But then the thought triggered an alarm. "Without a test?"

"I plan to announce it before the next council meeting. There's a supervisory course being offered in Grand Junction during the last week of September. I've already had Harriet reserve your slot."

Sergeant. Jo had once pinned her father's sergeant's badge to her own uniform shirt to experience the extra weight of responsibility that went with the job. Decide if she really wanted it. The next day, she'd ordered a book on police supervision and started studying. Worked her ass off to make sure she tested well. Dreamed of hearing the news that she'd been selected.

The screensaver kicked on and the word of the day scrolled across her computer monitor.

"With all due respect, sir." That phrase always seemed to act as a warning. A red flag that maybe she should take a breath, reconsider her next words.

"Congratulations, Sergeant Wyatt." He stuck out his hand.

She shook her head. "I don't know what to say."

His eyebrow shot up. "Yes? Thank you? When do I start?"

"Thank you, of course," she stuttered. "But I'm not sure handing me stripes is a good idea." The words tasted like sawdust and she almost choked on them.

He dropped his hand. "Then it's a good thing that I'm the chief and it's my decision to make."

"You just caught me by surprise. May I have a bit of time to think about it before I give you my answer?"

He pursed his lips again—an expression Jo had seen as a child whenever she'd annoyed her mother. It hadn't boded well then, and she didn't imagine it was any better coming from the man who signed her paychecks.

"I didn't expect it to be a difficult decision, Detective." Did he emphasize her rank? "I'll need an answer by Friday or we'll need to cancel the training slot."

"Thank you, sir."

Squint tapped the back of his knuckles against the doorframe. "Good morning, Chief. Am I interrupting?"

The chief's expression lightened. Just one of the boys again. "Not at all. I was telling Detective Wyatt I'd like a team briefing on the missing girl case later this morning. Determine if we have enough boots on the ground. Say, eleven?"

"We could give you the rundown now," Jo said. With so much to do, the last thing they needed was a meeting in the center of the day unless it involved a whole new slate of state or federal resources.

"Eleven should give you enough time to find her." He jockeyed around Squint to get to the door and then called back over his shoulder. "Earn the community's trust with some results."

Squint dropped a file on his desk. "I've seen that look before. What'd I miss?"

"You mean my I-should-have-ordered-a-margarita-to-wash-down-my-breakfast-burrito look? Or . . ." She lifted her mug and held it next to her face. "My I-have-neither-the-time-nor-the-crayons-to-explain-this-to-you look?"

"The look that lulls people into underestimating you."

"Huh. I didn't know I had that look." Jo rocked back in her chair. If he'd heard anything, his expression didn't give it away. "Among other things, the chief asked me why I wasn't a sergeant. Brought up Everett Cloud's newspaper article. Asked me if we had a problem."

"'We' as in the department, or you?"

"Unclear. There's more, but that was the gist. I'll bend your ear about the rest after we find a certain little girl."

"You okay?"

That was never a casual question between the two of them.

"For now." She rummaged in her backpack and let her hair hide her face from his scrutiny. "All I know is I don't trust a man who turns up his nose at El Tecolote's breakfast burritos." She lobbed a foil-wrapped missile to Squint. "Complete with fire salsa. What's in the file?" Anything to avoid dwelling on the fact that she might have just committed career suicide.

"The list of carnival workers supplied by Summit Amusement security and the field contact info our guys working the fair detail were able to collect. Guess how many match?"

She reclaimed her abandoned burrito and tipped more salsa onto the edge. "At least we got some names. Where do you peg our chances of getting an accurate list from their HR department?"

"Based on the transient nature of the business and the number of H-2B visa holders they employ from Mexico, I'm not hopeful. But I've already sent the email request. And while you were out playing with puppies, I cross-referenced and started running the ones we got DOBs on."

"Speaking of puppies. The good news is Artemis wasn't the least bit interested in the den window, so chances are Lena wasn't dragged through it. Bad news, though, is Artemis didn't pick up on anything that points us in a definitive direction, either."

"As soon as the courthouse opens, I'll make the run for records," Squint said. "You?"

She rescued a napkin from the depth of her drawer and wiped her mouth. "Set up the helpline number. Track down Dawson. Nail down Lucero's story that he was at the ranch."

"Or not."

"Wherever the truth takes me." She crumpled the wrapper. "On the way back, I want to stop at the *Courier* office. See if I can get any info on one of their delivery guys."

"Just how early did you get going today?"

"Early enough to have a conversation with a paper boy, play with a puppy, procure breakfast, have a tête-à-tête with the chief, ruin any chance I ever had to promote, and most importantly make my partner look like a lop."

"I'm going to really enjoy breaking this case for you."

"We good?" Until she spoke the words, she didn't realize how much rode on his answer.

"We always were. Plus, you remembered fire salsa."

"Excellent. You owe me four bucks."

17

The field was just beginning to flower the delicate clusters of purple that signaled the alfalfa's beauty and worth had peaked for the season's final cutting. The scent of freshly mown hay swirled around Jo and erased the years since Aiden Teague had taught her how to drive his family's beat-up International tractor on the Lupine Ledge Ranch. She'd been equal parts thrilled and terrified pulling a swather, looking over her shoulder at the windrows forming behind her, the tingle that raced through her when Aiden's hand brushed hers on the steering wheel as he'd helped adjust the course.

Today, she stood on the headland of a different field. A dusty orange Kubota bore down on her, shunting aside sliced and crimped grass to dry under the relentless sun.

Near the end of the row, the driver idled the engine. "Help you?"

"Mr. Dawson? I'm Detective Jo Wyatt with the Echo Valley Police Department. Do you have a moment?"

He cast a glance first at the sky, then the uncut field, before turning off the tractor and lowering his bulk from the open cab. "When the missus told me an officer named Joe wanted to talk to me, I have to admit, you weren't exactly what I pictured."

"Well, I'm sorry to disappoint you, Mr. Dawson."

"I should always be this disappointed. You J.C.'s girl?" He wiped his hand against his coveralls and stuck it out to shake.

"Guilty as charged." Joseph Charles Wyatt. She never knew if that was a helpful fact to admit. Her father had deep roots in the valley and a storied history as a sergeant before an injury had ended his career.

"Wondered as much when I read about that hullabaloo with the old district attorney's wife. What brings a city officer out to talk to the likes of me?"

Jo sidestepped so he wasn't staring into the sun. "I was given your name as a possible witness and was hoping you could help me out."

"Witness or suspect? Though can't say I've had much fun lately, so that must mean I've been minding my manners."

"I'm only here to fill in the pieces of a puzzle. I assure you, you're not in any trouble. But I was hoping to talk to you a bit about Saturday."

"This past Saturday?" he asked. Jo nodded, and he continued. "Well, that's easy enough. Me and the missus spent most of the day at the fair. She'd entered some of her baked goods in the various whatnots they judge. For the first time in years, she didn't win a blue—which, let me tell you, did not sit well with her."

That was an understatement. "And the evening?" Lucero had notified Tilda around six thirty that he was on his way to the ranch.

"I thought maybe a date would cheer her up, so we headed on over to the Stockyard's for a steak. Even ordered dessert." He leaned toward Jo and lowered his voice. "Word to the wise. Don't order chokecherry pie if that happens to be the same kind of pie your better half entered at the fair. Made for an early night."

She was careful not to belie the importance of her next question. "What time was that?"

"Must have been about seven."

The familiar flurry always tickled her belly first. That first flush of excitement that maybe she was about to find the crack she could drive a chisel into. Work it until secrets started to spill out and finally break the whole case open. This time, though, the thrill was tempered by something darker. A lump that weighed her down while all around her the world went still.

"A little after seven," he corrected himself. "We only missed the first few minutes of *Bonanza*," he said. "Nothing soothes the missus's ruffled feathers quite like Lorne Greene. I'd be jealous if I weren't so darned grateful. Of course, he's dead now, so that helps. Although for a while, I did have some pretty thick sideburns."

The prickle of sweat beaded her hairline, but despite the heat, her fingers had gone cold. "Did you have any visitors that evening?"

He laughed. "The missus wasn't much up for company, no."

The iciness spread from her fingertips and wound around her arms. "I know this is a strange question, but are any of your horses injured?"

"These days, I've just got the one." He removed his ball cap and wiped his sleeve across his forehead. "She's old, but fit as a fiddle."

A crow swooped past them and alighted in the top branches of a lonely sycamore along the driveway. The tree pulled double duty as a fence post, and years-old barbed wire cut deep into the bleached gray trunk. The dirt driveway twisted between the fields and circled in front of a gable barn. One side of the roof drooped, a thread-worn tarp pegged over a rotted section.

"Do you stable anyone else's horses here?"

He shook his head. "You sure you have the right Dawson?"

"How about your son? He own any horses?"

"Nah." Clyde smoothed back his peppered hair and replaced the cap. Sweat curls clung to his neck. "Kurt says there's nothing a horse can do that an ATV can't do better. 'Sides, he's living in town now."

His emphasis on *town* left little doubt that if he'd been chewing, he'd have spit a stream of tobacco juice to punctuate the word.

"Any chance you know Lucero Flores?"

"The vet? Sure. In fact, I ran into him just yesterday morning at Columbine Lake. But it's been ages since Destiny's done something stupid enough to need a house call. The few head of cattle I run usually don't get themselves into trouble I can't handle myself."

Heat rose from the road in shimmers that bent and reimagined the landscape and carried the stench of a bloated animal rotting in the nearby bar ditch. She blinked and the truth came into focus. "I didn't peg him for a fisherman."

"Well, I was fishing up by Butch's Fishcamp. He was hiking. Although by the looks of his knapsack, you'd have thought he was about find a place to set up camp."

"Your wife said—"

"Oh, I know where you're going with this one. She told you I was in the high country." He waved away the statement with an embarrassed chuckle. "Truth is, if I told her I was just over the hill at Columbine Lake, she'd have wanted to come along. I love the missus dearly, but fishing requires quiet, and, well, that's just not something she stocks in her pantry."

"What time do you think this was?"

He stroked his chin. "The trout were still biting, so it couldn't have been much after eight. Sometime before it got too hot."

"One final question. You mentioned Lucero had a knapsack?" She stressed the last word as if she wasn't sure what he meant.

"One of them waxed canvas backpacks no one uses anymore."

"Gotcha. Thank you, Mr. Dawson. I appreciate your time."

"You seem mighty interested in the doc. Something I need to be aware of?"

"His daughter, Lena, is missing and he'd mentioned that he'd seen you. I just needed to confirm you'd run into each other."

And why he'd lied about it.

18

Jo slid into the chief's conference room with seconds to spare, which, based on the number of people seated around the table, was a couple of minutes too late.

"Glad you could join us, Detective Wyatt." Chief Prather pointed toward an empty chair.

Second in size only to the briefing room, the chief's conference room served double duty as an incident command post when emergencies arose.

She set her notebook on the table next to Squint. "I think it's time to call in the FBI."

The chief tapped his pen against his unopened leather folio. "Let's park that for now. I'm confident we can find a little girl. I've raised three children. Trust me when I say kids are like dogs, they'll come home when they're hungry."

Jo dropped gracelessly into the chair. She opened her mouth, but Squint cut her off. "We're not convinced she ran away."

The chief sat at the head of the mammoth table, his admin assistant, Harriet Landeau, to his left taking notes. "A change of heart, Detective MacAllister? I got a different impression when we spoke in the hallway. Regardless, everything I've heard up to this point indicates that's exactly what she did. An opened window alone is not evidence of anything other than someone forgetting to shut it. According to the records, there's never been a child kidnapping in Echo Valley."

It was faulty logic. Using that reasoning, there'd never be a female sergeant either—but he'd just offered her the job.

"Chief—"

"Don't worry, Detective, as the lead on the case, I've saved you for last, so you can speak uninterrupted."

Last? What the hell? She didn't dare look at Squint. Sergeant Pieretti shook his head ever so slightly at her in warning.

The chief opened his folio and signaled Harriet. She gathered the stack of papers in front of her and slid the top sheet to Captain Fitzgerald and then circled the table to distribute the remaining pages.

"Where I came from," the chief said, "we did things differently."

Everyone studied the handout. Of course he'd done things differently. He came from an urban agency with a beach. Echo Valley was a small jurisdiction ringed by mountains.

"Starting today," the chief continued, "we're going to have a daily press conference to update the community on our efforts to bring Galena home. She may have run away, but of course, we can't overlook other possibilities. I've outlined the information I'll need by fifteen hundred hours each day so we can hit the evening news."

The list covered three quarters of the page. Minutiae mostly. Busy work that would pull them away from actually working Lena's case—not to mention the rest of their caseload.

Pieretti held up the sheet.

The chief stopped him. "We need to leverage the moment. I'm a new face in the valley. This is the perfect opportunity for people to get to know me and for me to reassure them that we take every case seriously. Manage the optics, so to speak. That way, if the case does go south, it looks like we've been on it since day one."

Jo stiffened. "We have been," she said. "And we do take our cases seriously. In fact—"

"We'll get to you in a few minutes, Detective." The chief turned to the striped side of the table. "What have we done with the media so far?"

She fought the urge to throw down her pen. Under the table Squint pressed the toe of his boot against hers. She risked a quick glance around the table. Captain Rodney Fitzgerald sat ramrod straight in his chair. Sergeant Begay had missile lock on the chief and looked like he wanted to fire. Young Sarah's eyes were round, but she quickly lowered her face. The expressions on the sheriff's office and search and rescue representatives were blank—because they weren't there. So much for interagency collaboration.

"The initial news release went out yesterday afternoon," Sergeant Begay answered.

Jo hung in through his explanation of the patrol-updated dedicated media newsline, but when the sergeant shifted to the list of outlets included in the fax machine's media speed dial, she tapped out. Half-listening, she was in the middle of prioritizing her to-do list when Everett Cloud's name broke through the static like the piercing squelch of an officer broadcasting on his portable radio while standing too close to an open patrol car.

"Other than Cloud," the sergeant added, "only Mindy Delgado, the reporter for KEV-TV, called in requesting additional information."

"Let's go wider," the chief said.

"Wider?"

Sergeant Begay rarely blinked. It made his gaze uncomfortably intense, and most people caught in his crosshairs squirmed. Not the chief.

"You know, Denver. Some of the other large metro areas. Let's put Echo Valley on the map. Show the rest of the state how it's done."

Color her crazy, but Jo doubted Denver needed their example.

Pieretti broke in. "Point of order. We're actually part of the New Mexico news market."

In truth, Echo Valley suffered from a bit of an identity crisis. Its position in the southwest corner of the Centennial State made its residents Coloradans, but the closest major city was Albuquerque, and more people were familiar with the goings-on of their southern neighbors than the political events of their own state. It really annoyed the Bronco fans.

Captain Fitzgerald took over. If he disagreed with the chief's direction, he'd save that for a conversation behind closed doors. Now, he flipped to a fresh page and pointed his pen toward the detectives. "Jo, as lead, we'll need you behind the podium. Squint, too, if you're free. At least one of the parents needs to be there. Both would be better. I'll contact the sheriff and the county SAR coordinator—"

Chief Prather put his hand flat on the table close to the captain. "Just the parents for now, Rod." Never lifting his hand, he pointed at Jo. "Detective Wyatt, I want you to prep Tina for a news conference."

"Tilda, sir."

"I'm sure she'll appreciate tips from another woman in this situation. You know, things like stick to the script, please come home, don't smile. The basics." He shifted his attention to the sergeants again. "In the meantime, I want drones up in the air. Show we're on the cutting edge of technology usage. Give us something that demonstrates we're moving forward. We do have drones, don't we?"

Pieretti reached behind his chair and grabbed a poster-size tube leaning against the wall. He unrolled a laminated map of the city across the center of the conference table and weighted one edge with a stapler. "Search and rescue guys have been flying one over the mesa." He pointed to the area on the map for the chief's benefit, "but drones are of limited use when they encounter trees. Most of the area within the current parameters is thickly canopied." He circled another part of the map. "The drone's camera can't penetrate the summer foliage to see a person on the ground."

"In addition to the drones, SAR ran a hasty team across the mesa yesterday, and a slower Type II search last night. Both were a bust," Pieretti said. "Jo was out to the house with a K9 search team this morning before things heated up. Nothing useful out of that either. The K9 team redeployed along the river trail. Other teams are up at the fairgrounds."

"Anything else?" The chief's pen had yet to blot his paper, but Harriet had been scratching away at her notebook at a furious rate.

"I'll defer to Jo and Squint for the latest," Pieretti said.

"Alright then, Detective MacAllister?"

Jo pulled her chair closer to the table. She hadn't had a chance to talk to Squint since she'd been out at the ranch. Maybe he'd managed to uncover something actionable in his records search.

"The fair tore down last night. Their next stop is Pueblo and I would imagine they've already arrived. The corporate offices are in Houston, and HR faxed over an employee list with names and DOBs of current employees on this route. Sarah is in the process of running them."

"The other Sarah," the younger record tech said as she made a note. "I'm cross-referencing the plat records against the canvass vehicle owners." Her head popped up. "Sorry, Squint. I didn't mean to interrupt."

"I appreciate the clarification, Sarah," he said. "I'll be able to pick up Friday and Saturday's surveillance video this afternoon. We have an eyewitness who spotted the sisters leaving the livestock pavilion Saturday night, which corroborates Marisa's statement they were together at the fair. But so far, there's no sign of Lena on any of the Sunday morning feeds."

The chief double tapped his pen. "Don't forget to check for doorbell cameras and the registrant database."

If Squint was annoyed by the chief's micromanagement, he didn't show it, but then again, on the reaction continuum, he usually landed somewhere between unflappable and bemused. Jo nudged his boot under the table, anyway—more for her own benefit. Their former chief had had his quirks, but at least he'd trusted his people to get the job done.

"We haven't forgotten. The closest sexual offender registrant lives north of the fairground," Squint answered.

A knock on the door caused Squint to pause and the elder Sarah peeked into the room. "You may want to turn on channel twelve."

Jo's stomach sank. "Why?"

"Tilda Marquet is holding a news conference."

19

"I don't know if this is a good idea, Marisa." Tilda wiped her hands across her slacks. She should have chosen a skirt. Already sweat formed under her waistband.

"I promise you, Momma, this is the best thing we can do to find Lena. The more people who know she's missing, the more people there'll be to help look for her. It's called leveraging."

"Are you ready, Ms. Marquet?"

Tilda jumped, then focused on the reporter. Missy? No, Mindy. "Almost."

More reporters stood on the driveway, glancing up from their phones to gauge if it was time to spring into action. Marisa had moved the car earlier to clear a space for the equipment. Now a cluster of cameras and microphones waited. Were they on? There weren't any telltale red lights. Maybe that was only on the cameras. Or something she only thought should be there and not something that actually was. It wasn't as if she had much experience. Would give anything not to be gaining it now.

"When you're ready." Mindy's voice had an artificial cadence. It was meant to calm Tilda down, but instead it only increased her desire to flee. "After you say your piece, the reporters may want to ask you some questions. When you're all through, I'll shoot my lede in front of the house. The others may do the same, or just take it back to the studio."

Marisa nudged her head against Tilda's shoulder. "I'll be right next to you, Momma. Don't worry. I'm not going anywhere."

"Yes." She cleared her throat. "Yes, let's get this over with," she said louder.

Mindy gestured to her camerawoman as the trio approached the microphones. The others scrambled into their places.

"Remember, just look at me. Pretend the camera isn't even there," Mindy said. "Speak from the heart, you'll be fine."

Look. Pretend. Her hand rubbed her chest. How could she speak from a heart that had been ground into pieces so fine it felt as if her whole chest was filled with sand?

The reporter peeled away and took her place in the group.

Marisa flipped her hair over her shoulder, smoothing it effortlessly into place. She stood erect. Composed. She'd chosen a skirt and paired it with a fluttery blouse and strappy sandals that looked fresh from their box. Tilda picked at her own frumpy polyester blouse. She should have paid more attention to her makeup. It was always the pretty ones who got the most help. The most attention. She needed that. For Lena.

Tilda stopped in front of the microphones. The spindly stalks knotted together like a horror movie bouquet, ready to swallow her words. The cameras faced them. Large round empty eyes full of accusation. *How could a mother lose her daughter? What kind of a mother did that? Where were you?*

Marisa nudged her. "Not at the cameras."

"Ms. Marquet?"

Mindy again. In the sun, her lemon-yellow sheath dress was too cheerful. Too bright.

"Sorry. Are we ready?" Tilda's throat tightened. Mindy gave her an encouraging nod. The dark-haired man next to her held a simple notepad and had the most compassionate eyes she'd ever seen. Mindy be damned. This was the man she'd speak to.

"Good morning," Tilda said before tilting her head back for a second and pressing her lips together. "Actually, no. It's not a good morning. It's horrible. My name is Tilda Marquet, and my baby's gone." It came out in a rush of breath and now she was having trouble breathing, and the microphones were too close, the camera too hungry, the sun too hot, and if she didn't calm herself down, she wouldn't get through this and Lena would never come home. Oh God, her daughter had to come home. She tightened her fingers around the photo of Lena. Gulped.

"She disappeared yesterday morning on her way to the fairgrounds. The police have all the information, but not a single answer about where she could be. Not one. The only thing I know is Galena's not home yet. So I'm asking you for help. Any information you may have is valuable. Did you see her? If you know about anything . . . suspicious."

Tears welled in her eyes. The only thing Lena was to these people was a story. And Tilda was about to ruin it. "I don't want to hold a photograph of Galena. I want to hold my daughter. Feel her hug me back." She bowed her head. Tears dripped onto her blouse. The goddamn ugly blouse she knew she'd never wear again. She ran her hand under her nose. Wiped away the snot. "I'm sorry. This was a mistake." She lifted her face. "I can't do this."

Marisa placed her hand on Tilda's elbow, drew her a step away from the mics and gently pried the photo from her hands. She tipped her forehead against Tilda's. "I've got this."

Her teenaged daughter turned toward the cameras and held up the photo of Lena.

"This is my sister, Galena Flores. In a few weeks, she'll be in sixth grade and she's really smart. Probably smarter than me. She wants to be a veterinarian when she grows up. And you should see her with animals. They love her." She paused, demanding their attention. "We all do."

Behind her daughter, Tilda watched the faces of the reporters perk up as Marisa spun the story they wanted to hear.

"I tease her all the time about being annoying, but she's actually pretty sweet. That's why I don't understand why this is happening."

Marisa reached back for her mother's hand. Squeezed. "It's been so scary since Lena disappeared, not knowing where she's at, what she's doing. As you can see"—she gestured toward Tilda—"it's really hard to stand here. But we need your help. We need you to help us find my sister." Marisa's voice caught. "We miss her so much."

Mindy tipped the microphone toward herself. "If you could speak to Lena, what would you tell her?"

"Please come home."

A male reporter asked. "Do you think she ran away?"

Marisa hesitated. One beat. Two beats. Three.

Tilda stepped forward. "No. Definitely not."

"What do you think happened?"

"Perhaps you should ask her father that." The words whiplashed into the sunshine, too fast to take back and quickly overpowered by the hiss and crack of the reporters' questions.

Only the man with the notepad stayed quiet, although now she saw a phone tucked under his tablet. She focused on his stillness while all the other reporters waved their arms trying to get her attention. His eyes still held that same sense of understanding. No judgment. Lena wasn't just a story. Not to him.

Marisa stepped in front of Tilda, shielding her from the cameras. The reporters quieted. "The police are setting up a helpline. Any information you have about Galena could be exactly the bit that we need to help us find her. That's all we have for now. I want to—*we*"—Marisa snaked her arm around Tilda's waist—"want to thank you for your help."

Tilda scraped aside the hair plastered to her forehead, and tucked it behind her ear. Her blouse clung to her, and she'd kill for something cold and wet. It didn't even have to be alcoholic, just something to alleviate the dryness that choked her.

The reporters bombarded them with more questions, and she flinched as each one hit her.

"Do you want me to take questions?" Marisa asked. Everything about her glowed.

"The police didn't give us a helpline number."

Marisa leaned close and whispered, "But they have to now."

In the glare of the sun, Marisa's shadow eclipsed her own. In that instant, Tilda hated her eldest daughter. Hated her for her ability to enchant reporters and followers and casting agents. For stealing the limelight from Lena. Most of all she hated her daughter for doing the very things she, as Lena's mother, should have been able to do and couldn't. She shook off her daughter's hand. "We're done."

The reporters had encircled them, and she crashed into the reporter with the notebook.

He caught her elbow and held it until she regained her balance.

"I'm sorry," he said. "I just wanted to give you this before I left." He handed her a business card. "I know how difficult this was. I'm going to do what I can to get the word out about your daughter."

"Thank you, Mr. . . ." She flipped the card.

"Cloud. Everett Cloud. I'm with the *Valley Courier*." He pointed to his card. "If I can be of help, you have my cell phone number."

His voice was as gentle as his eyes. If they'd met in a bar, he'd be the one she tried to ditch.

"Mr. Cloud, would you like to come inside?"

20

Jo pushed the AV cart into the department's small conference room and plugged in the television. "Sorry to keep you waiting. Thank you for coming to the station to speak with me."

Six people could fit around the table, and Lucero had chosen to sit at the end. His face sagged as if pulled down by the weight of the stubble that shadowed his cheeks. The scent of his cologne overwhelmed the small room, and she wondered if it was an attempt to hide the fact that he hadn't showered.

"Like I had a choice," he said.

"You do have a choice, Lucero." Jo selected a remote, grabbed her notebook off the lower shelf of the cart, and squeezed around the far side of the table so there was nothing to block his path to the doorway. Two pinhole cameras recorded their interactions, and Sergeant Pieretti watched in real time in a tiny room down the hall. No way was she giving a defense attorney a reason to toss the interview. "You're not under arrest, the door is closed for our privacy, but you can leave any time you choose, and I can't compel you to answer my questions."

He sat up, drawing his crossed arms to his chest. One corner of the white *Visitor* sticker affixed to his shirt had already curled. "Get to the point, Jo."

"I want to find your daughter."

The fingers of his right hand drummed against his bicep. "Is this where you try to convince me we're friends?"

"It's not my job to be your friend, Lucero. And your anger with me isn't going to help your daughter. Can we agree this is about Lena?"

"She's still missing."

"That's why you're here. You have joint custody of Lena, but she predominately lives with you. When we spoke yesterday, I asked you the kind of questions I needed to know in that moment. Now I need to ask more questions. Her routines, likes, dislikes, fears. Things that you as a father may—or may not—know. Some will be about you. Some about Tilda. You may wonder how some of my questions are relevant, but they are, Lucero. Every question I ask is meant to get us closer to finding Lena. I need your help to do that."

He said nothing.

"You don't have to like me," she said. "But I'm asking you to trust me."

"Why should I do that?"

She canted her head to the side. "Because I'm very good at what I do."

He rested his chin on his thumb, and his index finger pushed the flesh of his cheek upward. Jo let him search her face for as long as he needed.

"Am I a suspect?" he finally asked.

"Today, you're here as a source of information. If you had no involvement in Lena's disappearance, the investigation will clearly indicate that. But there's only one way I can assess your truthfulness and credibility—and that's with your full cooperation. No hiding anything. No lies."

Still cradling his chin, he dropped his index finger and rubbed it across his chin. "What do you need to know?"

She opened her portfolio and drew out her pen. Taking notes served a couple of purposes. It slowed down the interview, which gave her more time to consider his behavior, learn his speech patterns, determine if his tics revealed stress. Discover how much of the boy she knew was still present in the stranger she faced today. She started with easy questions; biographical information, his job, how he liked living in the valley, and duly documented his every response so she didn't draw undue attention to any one question.

"What about hobbies?"

"Hobbies?"

"You know, what do you do to blow off steam?" she clarified.

"Work keeps me occupied."

"You mentioned yesterday that you and Lena like to hike, together."

"When time allows," he said. "The practice has really taken off. Haven't had the chance to hike in several weeks."

"So how do you deal with stress? Fish? Cycle? Run?"

"Are you asking if I have anger management problems?"

She jiggled the pen between her two fingers. "Do you?"

"I work harder when I'm stressed."

"What does Lena do while you're working?"

"A lot of times she goes with me." He raised his chin and a gleam entered his eyes. "You should see her with animals—any kind, doesn't matter. I don't know if it's her voice or touch, but I've never once seen an animal snap or shy away from her. She's a natural."

"Sounds like she follows in her father's footsteps."

He gave her a sharp look. "I have book learning. She's got something that can't be taught."

"When doesn't she go with you?"

"I don't wake her when I get a late call-out. Usually, I'm back before she realizes I'm gone. If she needs anything, she knows to go to the neighbor."

"Which one?" she asked.

"Elaine Jenkins—owns the place north of us."

Now was as good a time as any. "Tell me about Tilda."

He shifted in his seat. "She's my ex for a reason."

"And what reason is that?"

"I don't like her very much."

"Do you think she had anything to do with Lena's disappearance?"

"Tilda and I have had more than our share of disagreements, but she's always been a good mother to my children."

Jo wrote *my children* in her notebook. "I'm going to ask you a few questions that we've already asked Tilda as a matter of procedure, so please don't read too much into it."

"Go on."

"Will you take a polygraph?"

"I'm not sure I trust the technology."

"That wasn't the question."

"No."

She wrote down his answer. "It's my understanding Lena doesn't have a mobile phone. Is that correct?"

"Correct."

She knew the answer to this next question, but asked it anyway. "So when she calls her friends in 4-H, she uses the house phone?"

"We don't have a landline. She uses my cell."

"Will you sign a release for your phone records so we can see who she called in the past two months?"

He fidgeted. "It's my business phone, too. My client files are confidential. I'd rather not."

Jo didn't want to spook him, and she changed direction. "Why'd Lena want to live with you and not Tilda?"

His swagger returned. "Just because a woman's a good mother doesn't mean the father isn't better."

"True. What about Marisa?"

"Marisa?"

"Your eldest daughter."

"I know who she is, Jo. What are you asking?"

"Did you ever think about requesting custody of both girls?"

"Marisa's her mother's daughter."

"Considering your opinion of Tilda, that doesn't seem to be a ringing endorsement of your eldest child."

"You're twisting my words." He got a faraway look while he thought. "Marisa's just such a girl."

"As is Lena."

"Night and day. Lena's a ranch kid through and through. Tough. Doesn't mind getting dirty. Isn't squeamish. Does what she's told. No backtalk. I don't have to worry about her chores getting done, or her being late because she has to try on four different outfits to get ready. I understand Lena. Marisa talks a different language. She's a smart girl, but she cares too much what others think about her. Always fussing."

"Do you think she had anything to do with Lena's disappearance?"

He laughed and the years fell away and Jo caught a glimpse of the friend she once had.

"Sorry," he said. "I'm trying to picture Marisa in jail. I can't imagine she'd ever risk having to wear orange all the time. They're sisters. They have their differences, but they'd do anything for each other."

"How do you discipline the girls when they step out of line?"

He stretched and draped his arm across the back of his chair. "Discipline is a mother's job."

"Not when you have joint custody. Surely, there are times Lena gets on your nerves. She's an eleven-year-old girl. It happens. So what then?"

"I haven't needed to spank Lena since she was six."

"Is that when she got the scar on her forehead?"

His face registered surprise. "Tilda told you about that?"

It was the year Lena had moved in with Lucero. She tapped the notebook with her pen. "So what happened?"

The chair squeaked as he repositioned himself. "I was collecting a semen sample from a stud I used to own. Told Lena to stay put while I paraded him past the tease mare. He starts stomping and screaming to get the mare's attention. Turned into a handful. Lena wanted a closer look and got knocked down for her curiosity."

She waited for more, but he was done talking. "You left out the part about spanking your daughter."

"That stallion could have killed her." He fumbled around for words. "I swatted her. Hard enough she banged up against the gate post and dug a divot out of her forehead that took a dozen stitches to close up."

He dipped his head and plucked at the lapel of his shirt. "The thing is, I was mad at myself, not her." He looked up. "She was six. She shouldn't have been anywhere near that horse. I'm around blood all day . . . When I saw her face . . . It's different when it's coming from your kid. That was the last time I raised a hand to my daughter."

"Did you know Tilda held a news conference earlier today?" Jo asked.

Lucero shook his head. "She didn't talk to me about it."

"No, I don't imagine she did." Jo dropped her pen and picked up the remote. A click later and reporter Mindy Delgado flashed onto the television screen.

"A frantic search is underway at this very moment as police comb the area for a missing eleven-year-old girl from Echo Valley. Galena Patrice Flores vanished early Sunday morning while presumably walking along the river trail on her way to the Echo Valley Fairgrounds. The family is working with local authorities, but so far, leads are scarce. I'm here now with her mother, Tilda Marquet, and Galena's sister, Marisa."

The report cut to Tilda and Marisa positioned so the porch in the background framed them, the white picket railing acting as an ironic warning that not all dreams come true. Dark circles ringed Tilda's eyes. She'd changed into dark slacks and an ill-fitting top. Rouge brightened her cheeks, but the color threw her paleness into starker relief. She clutched a photo of Lena in front of her so tightly her knuckles whitened, and Jo knew it was to keep from shaking. In contrast, Marisa stood poised in a floral summer blouse and plain skirt, her hair swept to one side. Makeup as subdued as her demeanor.

"I know my daughter is missing," Lucero said. "Here's a thought, instead of grilling me, maybe you should be out looking for her."

"There are currently teams in three separate locations searching for your daughter."

Marisa finished speaking, and Tilda made the plea for Lena to come home.

Jo pointed toward the television. "You're going to want to hear this next part."

Out of the frame, a male voice posed a question. "What do you think happened?"

In a flash, Tilda's face hardened. "Perhaps you should ask her father that."

Lucero sucked in a breath. Then his chair hit the wall behind him and he was on his feet. "What the hell does she mean by that?"

Jo paused the recording. "Please sit down, Lucero."

"I thought you said I wasn't a suspect."

"I said I was gathering information. That's what I'm doing. Sit." She gestured to the chair. "Please."

He strode to the door.

"If you didn't have anything to do with Lena's disappearance you have nothing to worry about from me." Jo slid her pen into its slot and closed her portfolio. "If you did? This won't be the last time we speak."

"Go to hell." He grabbed the door handle.

"You're not under arrest, and no one's going to stop you from leaving. But what kind of a detective do you think I'd be if I didn't follow up on one parent's suspicions? Now's your chance to disagree. Tell me why she's wrong. Or tell me why she's right and we can figure out a way to do the right thing by Lena."

His hand remained on the knob, but he bowed his head. "You're not going to believe a word I say."

"Why would Tilda suggest you have insight into what happened to your daughter?"

"I don't know."

"Think harder. This is important."

He turned and leaned his back against the door. She edged her chair away from the table to give herself some reaction time in the event he wanted to do something stupid, but otherwise maintained her same demeanor. Hopefully, he'd mirror it.

"She was always a liar," he said.

"Tilda said you were supposed to spend Saturday night at the fairgrounds with Lena, but at the last minute you changed your plans. Where'd you go?"

He paced between the door and his vacant chair. "You asked me the same damn question, yesterday. The answer hasn't changed. I had an emergency call-out."

She opened her portfolio again. "That's right. Dawson's ranch. A mare, wasn't it?"

"Yeah. A mare."

She scratched out a note. "What was wrong with it?"

He stopped pacing. "The mare? Are you kidding me? What the hell difference does it make?"

She raised her eyebrow, her pen poised above the pad.

"It tried to clear a fence it shouldn't have. Can we get back to figuring out why my ex would lie to you?"

"Tell me about the rest of your evening."

He resumed pacing. "I stitched it up. Went home. Showered. Slept."

"Anyone with you?" Jo asked.

"No."

"Anyone at the house?"

Lucero's eyes narrowed. "Where are you going with this?"

"Yes or no, please."

"No."

"Let me make sure I got this straight. You texted Tilda about the call-out, saddled her with making alternate arrangements while you went to

Dawson's Ranch, patched up a horse, went home to your empty house, and called it a night. Did I miss anything?"

"I didn't saddle her with anything. She's Lena's mother."

"Duly noted. Otherwise, how'd I do?"

He glanced at his watch. "Yeah. That sounds about right."

"About right isn't good enough. What did I misunderstand?"

"No, I mean, yeah. That sounds right."

"Okay, now I'm really confused, because here's the thing. You never went to Dawson's ranch."

"Sorry, I thought you said Gleeson. I was at Gleeson's ranch."

"Gleeson's. You sure?"

He crossed his arms.

She was about to lose him. She drew a piece of paper with an image on it from under the pad. "This is a copy of the photo I took of your text to Tilda." She slid the paper across the table. "I'm still confused. Since you weren't where you said you'd be, exactly where were you?"

Lucero planted his fists, knuckles down, on the table and leaned toward her. "It had nothing to do with Lena."

"Then you need to let me check that out, or frankly, it looks damn suspicious. Maybe you'd be more comfortable telling me what you were doing at Columbine Lake Sunday morning?"

He threw open the door with enough force it crumpled the doorstop. "We're done."

Jo sprang from her seat and followed Lucero through the lobby and out the front door. "I can't help you if you don't tell me the truth."

He rounded on Jo, so close she could smell the sourness of his breath, and her hand snapped up to block him from getting closer. "Don't pretend you want to help me."

"What are you hiding, Lucero?" she whispered.

The lobby door squeaked behind her, and Sergeant Pieretti stepped beside her. "Is there a problem here?"

Lucero's eyes never left Jo's face as he stepped back, hocked, and spit on the sidewalk.

Pieretti moved toward Lucero, and Jo placed her hand on his arm. "We're good, Sarge."

Lucero stomped toward a massive blue pickup nosed into the visitor's stall, opened the door, and stood on the running board. "I'd never do anything to hurt my daughter." He slammed the door. A second later the engine roared and he disappeared down the road.

"You okay?" Pieretti asked.

Jo pulled out her cell phone and nodded as she hit the speed dial. Squint answered immediately.

"Elvis has left the building. And based on his current mood, I'm betting he's not going to be too keen to find you guys waiting at his ranch to execute a search warrant."

21

Don't pretend you want to help me.

Lucero's accusation followed Jo into the station and dogged her heels as she returned to the conference room.

It was a comforting fairy tale that monsters were easy to recognize and lived in lands far away. In reality, they preyed much closer to home. Statistically, most children went missing in the company of a family member.

The DVD player's tray opened, and she retrieved the recording of Tilda's news conference.

Love and hate drove people to unimaginable acts. And from what Jo had seen, neither Tilda nor Lucero had yet cooled their passions in their dealings with each other. They were miles away from the apathy most divorced couples reached.

But their anger was with each other, not with Lena.

She clicked the jewel case closed and gathered her notebook.

Lucero had overreacted at least once before. Even he'd admitted it, and that mishap with Lena had required a dozen stitches to fix. From Jo's own interactions with him, it was obvious his temper hadn't improved any—although to be fair, she could be the one engendering that reaction.

Timing skewed in his favor. Marisa had said she was with Lena from the time she arrived at the fair until they got home. Lucero would have had to collect his daughter sometime after 2200 hours Saturday and before she arrived at the fairgrounds on Sunday. It was possible, and in a way it made sense to snatch Lena from her mother's place to divert suspicion.

The most damning issue was the deception about his whereabouts—and whether his motivation was innocuous, malicious, or something in between. Regardless, it was one thing to decline comment, quite another to lie.

He'd visited Columbine Lake. And now, so must the police. They'd need boats. Divers. A dog trained for water recovery. Searchers along the shoreline, more on the trails. Mounted patrol if they could get them. Still more at Lucero's house. His property.

She needed to find Pieretti. He had the pull to get that particular ball rolling. She was halfway up the stairs when the younger Sarah called out goodnight to someone else on the ground floor. Lucero's interview had taken longer than she thought, and the *Valley Courier* office closed at 1700. So much for knocking out a quick stop at the paper to learn more about Aaron Tingler.

Pieretti hadn't made it upstairs yet, but Jo found a large interdepartmental envelope balanced across the top of her and Squint's computer monitors—Sarah's way of alerting the detectives that something important had come in. Even though it might be addressed to only one of them, whoever returned to the office first would take a peek.

Jo unwound the string holding it closed and upended it over her desk, knocking over a pile of messages from the tip line. A large external hard drive slid out, partially dragging a sheet of paper along with it.

The memo was from the city IT tech—the only person Jo had ever met whose messages routinely included footnotes. This particular memo lacked annotation but did describe the contents of the hard drive. True to form, the woman had gone out of her way to make sure the detectives knew what to look for and where to find it.

Jo connected the drive and opened it on her computer. She found the index document and printed two copies—one for her and one for Squint. The master sheet identified all the cameras on the fairgrounds property, their operational status, and area of focus.

The sheer number of files made her eyes water. Although there were fifteen cameras across the property, only thirteen were operational: two inside the exhibit halls, three more for the parking lots, one each for the concessions building and maintenance yard, one monitored the rodeo arena, three covered the midway, one recorded the entry gate, and the final camera overlooked the rear fence line. She did the math. Three days' worth of video, divided by eight-hour increments multiplied by thirteen cameras reminded her why she'd always hated word problems in math class.

The clomp on the stairs signaled the return of Sergeant Pieretti, and she hit him with her thoughts before he cleared the threshold. "Lucero's lack of candor means we need to shift search teams to Columbine Lake—both water and the shore."

"Agreed. I'm off to the fairgrounds now. The chief gave the okay to set up a command post, and there's no sense making the SAR guys relocate their operations center."

She plucked her radio out of the charging dock. "Do we have a dedicated radio channel yet?"

"Tactical two."

She adjusted the settings. "And the FBI?"

"Local field office notified and on standby if the chief deems we need help."

"Will he?"

Pieretti pushed his glasses up. "We'll have to wait and see. For now, we're keeping the command post minimally staffed. Captain Fitzgerald is incident commander. I'm the investigative coordinator. Pete's representing search and rescue. Briefings will be at zero six and eighteen hundred. Make them when you can, I'll cover when you or Squint need to be elsewhere. Daily activity logs are mandatory."

She flipped to a blank page of her legal pad. Every hour of this investigation seemed to necessitate a new page to accommodate shifting priorities. Aaron Tingler moved down the list, Lucero moved up. Search warrants, records checks, interviews. She waved toward her monitor. "Surveillance came in."

"Excellent." He leaned over her shoulder and whistled. "That's a lot of surveillance."

All the footage would eventually have to be reviewed, but short of search and rescue saving the day or what Squint might find at Lucero's ranch, these videos were possibly the best clues they had.

"According to the 4-H leader, Lena spent most of the day in the pavilion. Unfortunately, that's one of the areas that doesn't have a working camera." Jo flipped her pen between her fingers. "He also told Squint he'd spotted the girls on the midway sometime during the evening. I figured I'd start there. See if someone had taken undue interest in Lena."

"Lord, I hope not."

He disappeared into his office and reemerged carrying his go-bag. "Where are you with your paperwork?"

"Yesterday's initial and evidence reports are done. Haven't touched a thing from today, yet." She held up the pile of slips. "Messages are starting to come in to the tip line. Sarah put a note on each one as to the nature of the tip." Jo read them aloud as she flipped through them. "I hope you find her. Hope you find her. This is such a sad case. A psychic offering to help. Try looking at the commune in Delta. More of the same."

"Knock out your follow-ups, then go home. The surveillance will be here tomorrow," Pieretti said.

She rocked back in her chair. "Is that an order?"

"A strong suggestion." His glasses had slipped again, and he looked over the rim. "The brass is already tallying the overtime, and I'd like to keep my stripes."

An aspect of supervision she didn't look forward to enforcing. "I'm more than happy to take comp time."

"For which I'm eternally grateful," he said, "but that doesn't change the fact that you need sleep. I'll see you at six."

Cop shows got a lot of things wrong—racking a gun right before needing to shoot, chasing suspects while wearing high heels, and instantaneous lab results. But the most egregious error was the lack of paperwork anyone did. Ever. Everything she'd touched the last few days required a follow-up. Her case file had stickie notes all over it, but it was organized. Still, it needed to be done, or she'd end up forgetting something—and a sloppy report wouldn't help anyone. With a last glance at the video files, she opened up the reporting program, flipped back through her notes, and started typing.

22

The beauty of a suggestion was that it implied a modicum of choice. And with the follow-ups submitted and the equivalent of a week's worth of coffee in Jo's system, sleep was out of the question. That left the surveillance videos.

The organization of the files was straightforward. Each video was titled with the date, start time, and camera location. The midway cameras were further broken down by section: food, games, and rides.

Nostalgia aside, fairs were money-making endeavors. Admission and craft entry fees benefited the county. Ticket sales to the demolition derby, amateur rodeo, pancake breakfasts, and livestock sales supported local charities. But the carnival company raked in the real money with their midway attractions. At some point, everyone had to walk through the stuffed animal and balloon-lined gauntlet of games.

Jo selected the video that started at 1601 hours on Saturday and settled in.

The angle of the camera from atop a light pole gave her a bird's-eye perspective she hadn't had while working the fair on foot. The black and white video captured a corridor with games on both sides. Some, like the rope ladder climb, basketball toss, and Skee-Ball, operated in the open. Other games required booths, many with panels that swung up and locked open during the day, and dropped down and secured at night. Those games were easy to identify in the video as most had their names painted in wild fonts on the panels. The towering ring-the-bell game marked the crossroads where all the radiating avenues converged. Hay bales filled in space and served the dual purpose of providing seating and blocking access to the back of the booths.

She fast-forwarded to 1900 hours. By this time Lucero had sent his text to Tilda and she'd arranged for Marisa to watch over Lena. In theory, the two sisters had rendezvoused in the pavilion where Lena had planned on meeting her father. Whether that had actually occurred remained to be determined.

The crowds ebbed and flowed. Jo increased the playback speed and her eyes darted across the screen, seeking Lena or Marisa in the throng.

The tape neared 2000 hours before the sisters flounced into the frame—or rather, Marisa did—and Jo logged the time on her tablet. Lena trailed slightly, using her sister's body to block some of the more aggressive game hawkers.

Lena looked as if she'd just stepped out of the show ring. Her tightly braided hair started on one side of her head and swooped to the other side à la Elsa from *Frozen*, and she wore a yoked shirt with rolled-up sleeves, blue jeans, and boots. The only thing missing was a curry comb sticking out of her back pocket. The crowd parted and Jo clicked a screenshot of the girls. Without knowing more about the clothes Lena had packed, this could be the outfit she was wearing when she disappeared.

Marisa's look was decidedly more adult. Her long hair loosely spiraled around her face and down her back. She wore a gingham shirt knotted at the waist, a skirt that made Daisy Dukes look modest, and a pair of heeled boots.

Every few feet or so, Marisa stopped and exchanged hugs, air kisses, or conversation with someone she knew, while her younger sister looked around, obviously bored. Occasionally Marisa stepped up to a booth, but Jo never saw her hand over a ticket, even though she played several games.

The sisters drew closer to the camera and claimed one of the empty hay bales. After adjusting her shoe, Marisa handed her phone to Lena and struck a pose, then another, and another. After the last photo, she reclaimed the phone and hunched over it. The two-handed grip suggested she was typing, and Jo added a reminder to her to-do list to review Marisa's social media feeds along with those of the 4-H leader and other club members.

Marisa stood first and resumed dispensing favors like a queen: a brisk nod, an enthusiastic wave, the occasional frosty smile. Suddenly, her body stiffened. Jo followed her gaze to the shooting gallery.

Lena tugged on her sister's sleeve and pointed toward the livestock pavilion. Marisa said something, but Lena widened her stance and crossed her arms. What followed was classic sibling negotiations complete with head shakes and a foot stomp. Marisa dug into her purse and removed a string of carnival tickets and thrust it at her sister. Lena's shoulders drooped, but she took it and walked dejectedly out of the frame in the direction of the food concessions.

After she disappeared, Marisa set her sights on the shooting gallery.

Jo tapped her pen against the pad. Marisa had claimed to be with her sister all evening. Granted, a short trip to grab something to eat might not register as a separation to a teen, but it registered as an inconsistency to an investigator.

The booth stood near the end of the corridor, and the level of detail diminished with each step Marisa took away from the camera. At her approach, a girl at the booth waved, then snaked her arm around the waist of a young man. The shape of the logo on his T-shirt looked like the Echo Valley College football logo. Based on the way he strained the fabric of the tee, it was a safe bet he was one of the players.

Marisa gave the girl a perfunctory hug, her attention already on Mr. Football. A full volley of coy smiles and hair twisting followed—which seemed designed to please one half of the couple and infuriate the other.

"The plot thickens." Her pen scratched across the tablet as the teen drama continued to unfold.

Marisa leaned close to the guy's ear as he aimed the game rifle, and then, with a final hair toss, left the booth. The girl immediately rounded on the guy, but his focus was still trained on Marisa, who walked toward the camera with a twisted grin on her face. Slow down the replay and add an explosion behind her and it'd make a great film trailer.

Marisa walked out of the frame. With her attention on the arguing couple, Jo almost missed Lena reentering the arcade alley carrying two drinks. A family had claimed the hay bale the sisters had sat on earlier. Lena turned a slow circle and then chose another hay bale to stand upon, rising on her tiptoes to gain more height. The moment felt oddly intimate, and heartbreaking. Finally, she stepped down and continued her search on foot, peeking around people and into the corners, behind the booths. Her posture changed by degrees as she reached the conclusion her sister had abandoned her. She dumped the drinks in a trashcan, and as dusk deepened into night, she headed toward the livestock pavilion.

Jo paused the tape, noted the time, and stood to stretch. Caffeine was no substitute for exercise. It had been three days since she'd run or cycled or anything, and she was starting to feel sluggish. She needed to carve out some time, but not tonight.

Tonight, she refilled her mug from the cold carafe and microwaved the stale coffee back to life. The out-of-balance carousel plate clicked with each rotation while she considered the remaining files. Lena had probably headed straight for the pavilion. Marisa could be anywhere.

Jo rescued a small carton from the depths of the fridge and tipped some creamer into her coffee. White specks swirled to the top. She sniffed it and carried it back to her desk to see if her hunch about Lena proved true.

Each of the videos had a time stamp, but it was impossible to tell if they were in sync. The distance between cameras precluded a person from stepping out of one video and immediately into the next. Still, it only took a couple of minutes before Lena was once again in view. By this time, most people were heading out of the pavilion, their faces already tipped skyward in anticipation of the fireworks display. Parents wrangling kids. The occasional stroller. Duos and trios. Lena passed them all, and no one followed her inside.

Jo backed up the footage. The same mass exodus played out at the door farther away. The camera angle only partially captured the north door, but a single man slipped past the exiting crowd. She replayed the snippet twice more, taking screenshots, but between the angle and the outgoing crowd, the only thing she could confirm was that the man was wearing a light-colored tank top.

A few minutes later, exploding fireworks alternately washed out and brightened the video. By this time, Jo had been ankle deep in Mercy Creek, putting handcuffs on a suspected auto thief. And in hindsight, she hoped she hadn't been blind to a graver danger.

She pulled Saturday night's duty roster from the case file and traced her finger down the list. Everyone assigned to the fairgrounds detail had assisted on her call in some capacity: the chase, setting a containment perimeter, the arrest, or the crime scene. It was certainly possible that someone could have noted the shift of fairgrounds personnel and taken advantage of the PD's distraction.

The coffee had gone cold again, and the tang of the creamer was more pronounced. She'd been so busy watching the front of the pavilion, she'd forgotten about the two openings in the rear. And Marisa was still MIA.

She scrolled through the files and found Saturday evening's file. A service alley stretched between the fence and the back of the livestock pavilion and ended at the maintenance shed, an oversized garage that sheltered the various heavy equipment, tools, and fencing panels needed for the upkeep and support of the events.

Movement on the rear service road was minimal: carnival workers looking for a place for a quick smoke or walking through to the area where their personal trailers were located; kids who'd mucked out stalls in the pavilion and were getting rid of the evidence; the occasional service truck with its bed full of trash bags; a patrol car skirting the traffic on the main road.

She sped through sections when no one was visible, anxious to get to the time when Lena was inside the building. Dusk darkened the video before a person entered the frame who she recognized.

Marisa.

She had her back to the camera and this time the teen had accessorized her outfit with the arm of Mr. Football draped over her shoulders. They walked toward a section of shrubs that lined the fence. Prince Charming gave a quick look around and Jo saw his face clearly for the first time.

"No way."

Aaron Tingler shrugged the backpack he was carrying off his shoulder and dug out a beer. He twisted the cap off and handed it to Marisa and then retrieved one for himself. They clinked the longnecks and chugged.

Tingler downed his and tossed the bottle into the shrubs. He held the branches of a larger shrub aside for Marisa, and then stepped in after her. The foliage snapped back into place. So much for his statement about not knowing anyone at the house.

On the far side of the fence, the land sloped down to the river trail. From there, they could follow the trail north or south, or abandon it altogether and pick their way to the river itself. If she had to bet, she'd put her money on the river. The romantic draw of the river and raging hormones made the risk of turning an ankle worth it. Besides, Lena was still at the fair, and Marisa was supposed to be watching her.

But considering Tingler, was Marisa truly a willing participant in whatever followed?

The time stamp on this footage confirmed they must have hooked up shortly after Marisa ditched Lena.

Darkness deepened before the bushes shook again. Tingler popped onto the service path and hurried out of view.

"That didn't take long." Jo tapped her pen against the blotter while she waited. "Come on, Marisa, where are you?"

The service path remained empty. Once more, splashes of light flickered across the screen. By now, most people were up front watching the fireworks show or were hotfooting it toward the parking lot, trying to reach their cars before the closing crush.

Finally, Marisa reappeared. A little less steady, her shirt no longer knotted. Head down, shoulders hunched. And in a blink, she disappeared into the livestock pavilion.

Jo's heart sank. She'd experienced Aaron Tingler's brand of charm during the traffic stop, but she'd been wearing a vest and gun at the time. Marisa might think herself worldly, but it didn't change the fact she was a fifteen-year-old girl wearing a short skirt and a ton of attitude. The age of consent in Colorado was seventeen. But like many states, Colorado had a Romeo and Juliet law that essentially decriminalized sex if the participants were close in age and the act was consensual. But was it?

The fireworks neared their conclusion, and any minute the two sisters would be spotted in front of the pavilion by the witness Squint had interviewed.

Jo was reaching for the mouse when a man exited the pavilion from the north door. A bright firework exploded and bathed the service road in flickering brightness. The man wore a tank top and his arms were covered in tattoos.

Excitement tickled her belly. "Well, hello again, Mr. Mystery Man." She clicked a screenshot. The image opened on her screen. There was something familiar about him, but the faces she'd encountered in the footage and those she'd seen in person working the fair melded. Without the crowd surrounding him, she captured the full length of his body. An object protruded slightly from the front pocket of his jeans, but when she expanded the photo, it blurred too much to determine what it was.

The phone on her desk rang, and she picked up without moving her eyes from the screen.

"Detective Wyatt."

"Hey, hold on a sec," Dakota Kaplan said.

Jo glanced at the caller ID to see if Dakota was calling as a dispatcher or friend.

The dispatcher returned to the line. "Sorry about that. I'm assigned to the command post for the foreseeable future."

"No prob. What's going on?"

"The deputy in charge of the sector four search team just requested Doc Ingersleben and wanted you notified."

Jo closed her eyes. There was only one reason to call out the coroner. "I'm en route."

23

Tilda hadn't adjusted to having an officer in the house, and she jumped to answer the knock at the door. Officer Dickinson held up his hand. "I've got it."

Was this what it felt like to have a butler? If so, it was highly overrated. Maybe she'd like it better if she lived in a palace—or at the very least a bigger house. The officer was courteous and doing his best to be unobtrusive, but most butlers didn't wear a blue uniform and a gun.

Indistinct voices grew louder. "Tilda, honey? This officer says I can't come in. I've told him he must be mistaken."

Tilda sighed. "Let her in."

"I cannot believe I had to hear about this on the news." Sienna Walker-Castaneda huffed down the hallway holding a casserole dish. She paused next to Tilda long enough to bestow an air kiss, and then swept into the kitchen. "This was in my freezer, so don't refreeze it." She opened the refrigerator and started rearranging things to create space and slid the dish on the shelf. "I forget who made it for me, but I'm glad someone's finally going to eat it."

Tilda sank into her recliner again. "What is it?"

"Lasagna, maybe? Something Italian. Good comfort food. You'll love it." Sienna gave Dickinson the once over. "Do you mind? This is a private conversation."

He made eye contact with Tilda, and she gave him a tired nod. He opened the back slider and stepped outside. "I'll be right here if the phone rings or someone else comes to the door." He left the slider cracked slightly.

Sienna moved as if to shut it the rest of the way.

"Leave it," Tilda said.

"Yes, ma'am." Sienna placed her tote on the counter next to a ream of fliers and extracted a bottle of wine. "Looks like I got here just in time." She retrieved the opener from the utensil drawer. A quick slash removed the maroon foil and she stabbed the cork and twisted. "Bernie had this in his cellar. It's got a fancy crest on the label, so I'm guessing it's good."

Definitely better than anything Tilda had in her cabinet. "It's Bernie, now?"

"Only when he's not around. But honestly, Bernard? It makes him sound like he's a hundred years old." She pointed the corkscrew at Tilda and the rock on her ring finger caught the light. "Don't say it."

"Wouldn't dream of it. Is he in town?" She drained the last swallow from her current glass and held it out toward Sienna, too tired to brave the whirlwind in the kitchen.

"Is he ever?" Sienna poured past the point of propriety, which tonight was a good thing. "Some emergency session involving midterms or endangered species or heaven forbid, some committee member got a hangnail." She handed the glass back. "Drink. I'll be back in a jiff, then you can tell me all the stuff that isn't on television."

In the swoosh of her wake, Tilda saw only the image of Sienna's husband: Congressman Bernard W. Castaneda, the representative from Colorado's Third Congressional District. Well known, well respected, just the kind of guy who might be able to light a fire under the police department.

"I think Lucero had something to do with Lena's disappearance."

Sienna jerked, splashing red wine onto the counter where it puddled like blood. "Lucero? No way." Something more than disbelief tinged Sienna's words.

Tilda chided herself. A native of the valley, Sienna had known Lucero even longer than Tilda had. Probably as long as Jo.

Sienna grabbed Tilda's favorite dish towel and dabbed at the splash, then with a final angry swipe threw the towel into the sink. "I don't believe it."

"Believe what you want. It doesn't change the facts."

She joined Tilda in the living room. "And just what are the facts?" Sienna kicked off her shoes and curled up on the edge of the couch, placing her glass on the end table. "What the hell is going on?"

It usually didn't take much to sway Sienna's thinking, but over the years, Tilda had learned that Sienna often needed a bit of time to process information. "I should go check on Marisa before she hits the sack."

"Marisa's fine. You can't drop a bombshell like that and walk away."

Tilda nearly dropped her glass on the table in her haste to stand. For the past two days, people had been telling her what to do, what to think, who to speak to. She'd had enough.

Sienna jumped to her feet. "Oh, sweetie. I didn't think. Of course. Go." She gathered Tilda into a bear hug and then held her at arm's length. "I'm an idiot. Please, please. Forgive me?"

Perfume hung in the air between them. Something expensive. Far more delicate than the Lady Stetson Sienna had worn in high school. Still as cloying.

"I'll be back in a minute," Tilda said.

Sienna nodded. Subdued. Silent. The surest sign her feelings were hurt. "Give Marisa a hug from me."

They'd been friends since forever and Tilda forced a smile. Sienna was just being Sienna. "I'm on edge. Sorry."

The concern lifted from her friend's eyes. "Tell her I took her advice and bought a Burberry trench the last time I went to DC with Bernie." She loosened her grip on Tilda's arms. "She's got a bright future, that one." Her eyes widened. "Not that Lena doesn't."

The smoldering feeling in Tilda's gut flashed into a full-blown, lose-your-shit inferno and she itched to slap Sienna. Throw something. Howl. The cop on the patio materialized from the darkness and peered through the door.

"I won't be long." Tilda turned her back on them both. At the base of the stairs, Tilda remembered her wine. Almost went back for it, but wasn't ready to make nice with her friend. Maybe this was how Lucero had felt right before he'd hit her.

The steps ahead of her rose higher than they ever had and she grabbed the banister to pull herself along. Sienna. The woman thrived on drama. Always had. Even in high school, it was as if she drew energy from confusion. Relished when people smarter than her didn't know what to do any more than she did. People thought education was the great equalizer but they were wrong; chaos was.

A dull light seeped from beneath Marisa's door. With a guilty start she realized she didn't know if her daughter had eaten dinner. She leaned her forehead against the doorframe as her throat closed. She had to do better. She had two daughters. They both needed her.

There was soft clicking on the other side of the door. Tilda knocked softly. When she didn't get an answer, she slipped inside her daughter's room. Three unopened boxes sat next to the wall. No doubt items for her next photo shoot. Tilda eased around the clothes rack and stood beside her daughter's bed. Marisa faced away, her body curled like a question mark and her breaths not yet slow enough for sleep. The screen of her mobile phone glowed through the sheet and her laptop was closed on the nightstand. If Tilda reached over, she had no doubt it'd be warm to the touch.

Tilda stroked her daughter's hair off her face and kissed her forehead. "I love you more than you know."

She snapped the light off and closed the door behind her. A moment later the soft click of the laptop keyboard resumed.

Downstairs, Tilda paused at the end of the hallway. The television played a commercial, but thankfully Sienna had muted the volume. She still claimed the corner of the couch, but now she held her phone in both hands, thumbs tapping a message.

Tilda entered the room. "Say hi to Bernard for me."

Twin lines formed between her brows and replaced her smile. She tucked the phone into her back pocket. "How's Marisa?"

"Asleep."

She dragged the throw pillow onto her lap. "I topped off your glass."

Code for *I'm sorry.* "Thanks." Tilda flopped into the recliner.

"Look, if you don't want to talk, I understand."

When she'd first met Sienna, she'd thought her plain and poor. Ironic considering there was only one person in the room who could afford Burberry, and she was married to a man who adored his wife. It felt dirty to ask, but Tilda wasn't above exploiting any opportunity in order to find her daughter—whether that was stoking Jo's anger, revealing Lucero's vulnerability, or soliciting Bernard's pull. As the press conference proved, the squeaky wheel got greased, and political pressure made everything squeak. Which meant she had to convince Sienna that Lucero wasn't the prince she thought he was.

"I never told you about what happened between me and Lucero in high school," Tilda said.

"Lucero did."

"Really?" Tilda's wineglass stopped halfway to her lips. "When?"

Sienna plucked absently at the fringe edging the pillow. "About a year ago, maybe? I ran into him at Hank's Diner."

"You never told me."

"You have a nasty habit of biting the head off of anyone who brings up his name," Sienna said.

Tilda couldn't argue. "What did he say?"

Sienna shifted. Reached for her glass. "That you made the whole thing up and Jo went along with it to punish him for making a nasty crack about Aiden Teague."

"Ah, high school. Fun times." It didn't surprise her in the least that Lucero had lied about hurting her, but this was the first she'd heard that Aiden was somehow involved. "Did you believe him?"

"I didn't bring *him* a casserole and two bottles of wine." A piece of fringe from the pillow she clutched came off in her fingers. "Why do you think he had something to do with Lena?"

"Lucero is a violent man. I didn't lie about what happened in high school—at least not until I took it all back."

"Why?"

"Why, what?"

"Why'd you take it back if it was the truth?"

If. "I loved him."

"But if he hurt you—"

"He did hurt me, Sienna. And Marisa said something that makes me think he's hurt Lena, too."

"He loves that little girl."

"He loved me too, once," Tilda said. "He hasn't changed. I see it. That anger. It's always there, ready to come out."

Near the end of their senior year, they'd fallen into a pattern: one day trying to make mature decisions about putting their relationship on hold through college, the next day giving in to their hormones with Shakespearean-level angst and declarations of never-ending love.

It had been his turn that day. They should break up. She'd snapped. Said something nasty. The words were gone, but she'd never forget the change that came over his face. The way his lips pulled back, baring his teeth like an animal about to attack. How his hand tightened around the wrench he held a second before he winged it past her head. The thunk of metal against wood when it hit the barn wall behind her. Then he'd grabbed her around her wrist, slapped her across the face, and threw her to the ground. The pain was immediate. The humiliation came later.

Sienna touched her arm. "Are you okay?"

The room came back into focus. She jumped up to refill her glass and the floor tilted slightly. "Will you ask Bernard to help me?"

"Help you how?"

"I need his influence. No one's taking this seriously. Certainly not the police—Jo hates me. She won't listen to anything I have to say against Lucero."

"She doesn't hate you."

"It took a fucking press conference to get a tip line." Tilda slammed the bottle down on the counter.

"Do you have anything concrete against Lucero? I mean, I know you think he's done something, but do the police?"

"He refuses to take a polygraph. Why would he do that unless he has something to hide?"

"He's always been incredibly private. You of all people know that."

"Fuck his privacy."

The A/C kicked on. A puff of warmth blasted through the vent followed by a wave of arctic air. Sienna pulled out her phone and glanced at the screen. Her lips curved ever so slightly and she tapped a reply, then gave Tilda her full attention. "Maybe there's some other reason."

"More important than his daughter?" She snorted. "The bastard won't sign a release for his phone records, either."

Sienna tucked her own phone away. "Why do they need his records? Didn't Lena have her own phone?"

"He carried on about getting her one after I told him I couldn't afford to add her to my account. If he didn't, she may have used his phone. Called . . . someone. God, Sienna, what if she set up a meet with some pervert she met on the internet or something?" She planted her elbows on the counter and held her head.

"You and I both know Lena wouldn't do that."

The banner for the ten o'clock news swooshed across the screen. Sienna clicked the remote and raised the volume.

The story cut to the reporter, all shiny hair and bright teeth. Her mouth moved, but all Tilda heard was a buzz. "Turn it off," she demanded.

Sienna stared at the television. "You have to admit, Marisa did an amazing job."

"I said, turn it off." She lurched around the island and snatched the remote off the coffee table. Mashed button after button.

"Here." Sienna rose. "Let me." She took the remote and the screen went dark. Looking into Tilda's eyes, she spoke softly. "I saw Lena at the fairgrounds, Saturday. She was in the ring, showing Bluebell."

The words were meant to be comforting, Tilda was adult enough to know that. But it hurt. Hurt that Sienna had seen her daughter more recently than she had.

"She was the littlest kid in the ring. Parading that steer around like it was a puppy. Keeping his head up. Setting his feet properly. Wielding her show stick like a pro. She got that confidence from Lucero."

"He's—"

"Not the monster you think he is."

24

Five months after the divorce and Jo was still sleeping in her old bedroom in the home she'd grown up in. She dropped her backpack by the nightstand. At least she'd retired the air mattress she'd slept on when she first moved out of her house—the home she'd found, but that her ex kept, along with the master bedroom furniture. She'd taken the pieces from the guest room and tried not to dwell on the irony. The rest of her life was packed away in boxes in the garage, waiting for the day she'd find her own place to buy.

Until then, well, here she was. Stalled.

She removed her stud earrings and dropped them on the Wedgwood blue saucer on her dresser and then ran her finger over the raised cream-colored leaves that twined along the edge. The matching teacup and saucer set was one of the few extravagances her mother had ever allowed herself, and she'd sipped her tea from it every morning. Jo was eleven when she broke the cup.

Lena's age.

The day's events had followed Jo home. Normally by this stage in an investigation, things were supposed to start making sense. Instead, she found herself digging through a mound of lies: a father who lied about his alibi, a sister who lied about who she was with, the paper delivery guy who'd lied about personally knowing the occupants of Tilda's townhouse—and in an unrelated twist might have sexually assaulted Marisa. Then there was the unidentified man whose exit from the livestock pavilion suspiciously followed on the heels of Marisa's entry. And while it wasn't a part of the investigation, the offer of the promotion muddied everything.

She fished the small key from her rear pocket and placed it next to her earrings. Dust from the mesa clung to her clothes. She kicked out of her boots and exchanged her dirty clothes for a pair of shorts and a T-shirt. Only one thing currently under her control could improve this night, and she tiptoed toward the kitchen.

Joseph Charles Wyatt snored gently in his recliner in the living room. He'd taken to parking himself in his favorite chair and listening to the police scanner on the nights she was late coming home. It was the surest sign of their recent and fragile detente.

She'd wanted to talk to him. Settle something that bothered her. Maybe it was just as well he was sleeping. Some dirt was best left unturned.

The fireplace was dark on such a hot night, but a James Cagney movie played low on the television and bathed her father in flickering shades of gray. More salt than pepper sprinkled his close-cropped hair these days. A crooked nose dominated his face. The chiseled cheeks of his youth were now gaunt. Her namesake, the man she'd once wanted to emulate, had grown old.

The day she'd been sworn in as an Echo Valley police officer, she'd dressed in an empty locker room and tucked two photos into the lining of her ballistic vest. After raising her hand and vowing to protect the public trust, her father accepted her badge from the chief and stabbed the pin through the fabric of her shirt. He'd leaned close and warned her that if she wore it well, the badge would bring her nothing but heartache.

Before she could question him, well-wishers surrounded her spouting *chip off the old block*, or speculating whether the city would survive with two Wyatts in uniform.

Only Aiden had given her a gift—a small silver handcuff key. "For your pocket, Jo-elle, not your key ring," he'd whispered into her ear before kissing her cheek. It wasn't until later she discovered he'd had it engraved with words so tiny she'd almost missed them. *Never give up.*

She eased the freezer door open, but it squeaked anyway. In the ambient light, she found the container.

Where was Aiden now? It was a question she'd grown accustomed to asking herself over the years. She hadn't heard from him in a couple of months, which meant he was undercover again. Unable to wear the St. Michael medallion she'd given him as a graduation present when he'd completed DEA basic agent training at Quantico. Over the years, she'd offered up many names while in the nave of All Saints in the Valley. His was the only one she whispered every time.

The kitchen light flashed on, spiking her pulse and exposing her spoon-deep in contemplation with a pint of Phish Food ice cream.

"I'd have bet this would be a bourbon night." Her father stood by the switch. "Must be worse than I thought."

He'd been right about the heartache. Every cop encountered people in pain, in crisis, in denial of the twist fate had given them, but in a small town, she often knew the people by name. She'd learned to compartmentalize. Distance herself. But distance had been impossible after Dakota's earlier dispatch. From the time Jo left the office until she arrived at the search site, all she could think about was how to break the news to Tilda when there was no gentle way to tell a parent their child was dead.

"Definitely had better days." Jo raised the spoon to her mouth. "Searchers called out the coroner. I thought they'd found Lena."

"I heard. Figured you could use some company."

It was a rare offer. J. C. Wyatt wasn't the kind of man to dispense fatherly advice, and when he did it usually ran along the line of *suck it up*, or *you might want to try something different next time*. She pushed her skepticism aside. He'd provided the opportunity. It was time to turn some dirt. "What do you remember from when you arrested Lucero Flores?"

The look he gave her mirrored the one he'd given her the day she'd first brought the whole mess to his attention. "Never thought he'd be the one to drive you to ice cream."

"Not the first time I've gone on a bender with Ben and Jerry. But for the record, tonight's jag was primarily over a foot."

"A lot of hullabaloo over a bear paw."

When it came to gossip, quilting bees couldn't hold a candle to a group of retired policemen who routinely met for breakfast at Hank's Diner.

"Thank God. But to be honest, this wasn't an issue of someone not knowing about the similarities between bear paws and human hands and feet." Jo jabbed her spoon into the dark chocolate ice cream, probing for the marshmallow ribbon. "The bones had been there too long to have been Lena, but I'd have called Doc Ing, too."

The skeletal remains of a cub's paw had been discovered in a recess that protected them from being scattered by other animals. The claw phalanges had been removed, which in southwest Colorado meant they were probably currently adorning someone's neck. The remaining bones formed a convincing display of a human foot. And even though the size was wrong to be Lena, it was a relief when Doc Ingersleben concluded the subtle V-shaped groove at the end of the toes marked the bones as belonging to the genus *Ursus* and not an unknown victim.

But it also meant Lena was still missing.

"I caught that Marquet girl on the news tonight." He nudged Jo out of the way to get to the cabinet next to the refrigerator and pulled down the industrial-size tub of Folgers. "Didn't have much good to say about the department."

She didn't know if he meant the mother or the daughter, but the answer was the same. "We haven't found Lena." *Yet.*

"Don't imagine the new chief was too keen on being left out."

"That he was not. He countered with a call for volunteers for tomorrow's search." Her father's ability to avoid questions was legendary and she asked again. "So what about Lucero?"

"Not much to tell," he said. "You read the report."

"Kinda sparse on details."

He dug the plastic coffee scoop out of the grounds. "He was guilty."

"But how did you know that?" The caffeine that had carried her through most of the surveillance videos had worn off hours ago, and her words were sharper than she intended.

His forehead furrowed. "You told me he was."

"I was seventeen, Dad. I didn't have a badge, and I suck at telling when people are lying to me."

"Don't be stupid. You're as good a judge of character as any I've seen." He jammed a paper filter into the basket. "Didn't need to be a doctor to see that girl had been tuned up, no matter what she said about a horse. 'Sides, he lied."

"How so?"

"His knuckles were swollen. Claimed he was working on his truck, the wrench slipped and he'd smashed his hand. Except the boy didn't know a carburetor from a crankshaft and admitted that he and that girl were having problems."

"Her name is Tilda. And why wasn't that in the report?"

He wagged the coffee scoop at her. "Don't you be taking that tone with me. I'm not one of your trainees. I did my job. Took photos, arrested him—despite all her backpedaling. But you've been on the job long enough to know there's no use putting a lot of energy in a nowhere case."

"If it was such a crap case, why'd you even bother arresting him?"

"How many times you ever come running to me to tattle on a friend?" He shoved the coffee tub back on the shelf. "None. That's how many."

"I think he may be responsible for his daughter's disappearance."

"Course he is."

She scraped the soft part around the edge and then extended the pint to her father. "I don't have the evidence."

"Then find it." He waved off the container. "Whatever happened to plain vanilla?"

"Not everything is that simple."

He slammed the coffee basket closed. "You going to take the position?"

Eating an entire pint of rich ice cream had been a mistake. Her heart worked overtime to compensate. "What position?"

"You up for more than one? Sergeant."

And there it was. The real reason he wanted to talk. "Who blabbed?"

He crossed his arms. "So, it's true."

"Can't help but think the chief is setting me up for failure by handing me stripes. I'd rather compete for them."

"That's not an answer."

Maybe she was more like her father than she'd like to believe.

"He hands you stripes and you'll be trying to justify his decision for the rest of your career." His face screwed up. "You'll be known as an affirmative action promotion who didn't deserve it."

She scraped the last bit of caramel from the carton and dumped it in the trash. "The chief gave me until Friday to make up my mind."

"You're not doing yourself any favors dragging out your answer."

"No." Fallout be damned. The decision could wait. Lena couldn't. "I've got briefing at zero six. I'll try to be quiet when I get up."

25

The sun climbed the cloudless sky. Not a single breath rippled the mirror of water reflecting the peaks and wooded shores that sheltered Butch's Fishcamp on the other side of Columbine Lake.

By comparison, the boat ramp parking area bustled with activity. Horse and boat trailers, emergency services vehicles, unmarked detective cars, two news vans, and the personal vehicles belonging to searchers packed the lot.

Jo manned the check-in table. Like arsonists watching their fires, sometimes abductors volunteered to help search—either to revel in the moment or to obstruct the investigation by wrangling their way to a specific sector to destroy evidence or steer searchers in the wrong direction.

She straightened her stack of fliers and added them to Sarah's, weighting them with a rock. "Our work here is done."

"*My* work is done. You're fifteen minutes away from the press briefing." Sarah clipped the sign-in sheets together. "You want me to take these back to the office and put them on your desk, or do you want to keep them with you?"

"If you don't mind taking them, that'd be great."

"You got it," Sarah said.

The morning had unfolded as planned. Between 0730 and 0830 hours, Jo and the younger Sarah had checked in sixty-two volunteer searchers—none of whom pinged on Jo's radar. Each person provided their identification, signed waivers, and then proceeded to the search and rescue coordinator at the next table for assignment to a specific sector. At 0830 the chief thanked everyone for their help and then broke them into their teams for further instructions. By 0900 everyone hit the trails.

In the aftermath, command staff jawed next to the detectives' cars. Fire and rescue personnel clustered by the canopied first aid station. The media gaggle regrouped after shooting their B-rolls and set up their equipment near the podium. Most of the media faces she knew, but she'd never met the reporters who'd arrived in the two satellite vans covered with Albuquerque news channel logos.

The only person she didn't see was the Animas County sheriff. An elected official, he wasn't one to miss many photo ops. But determining the lineup for a press conference was above Jo's pay grade.

Jo wandered down to the water's edge to stretch out muscles that had sat too long. A small jon boat traversed a section of the lake. Despite the outboard motor, one of the four people aboard manned oars, intentionally slowing the pace. A water search dog stretched out on the squared flat bow, its paws hanging over the edge, its nose extended toward the water. The handler rested his hand on the dog's harness, watching for an alert that signaled his dog had detected the scent of gases and oils released by a decomposing body.

During the 0600 law enforcement briefing, the SAR leader had reduced the picturesque lake to search terms: 150,000 acre-feet of water, more than 170,000 acres of surface area. The surrounding terrain was divided into sectors that alternated between gentle trails and steep inclines.

The only vehicle access to the lake was via a county road carved into the hillside that skirted the north side of the lake. The entrance road dropped down to the water and dead ended at the boat ramp parking lot. A brown sign prohibiting motor vehicles marked the start of the dirt trail that wound its way around to the south side of the lake and Butch's Fishcamp—which was neither a camp nor a hole-in-the-wall fish-fry like its name suggested. Merely a place that rewarded early morning anglers in search of solitude and the occasional trout.

Already teams on foot scoured the shoreline in an effort to locate clues that would narrow the boat teams' search parameters. Additional searchers canvassed the area where Lucero was last seen hiking. Mounted patrol combed the more rugged terrain.

Until they were needed elsewhere, the public safety dive team from San Juan, New Mexico, was off on the other side of the lake conducting a surface search. Jo offered a quick prayer the divers wouldn't need to get wet.

Everett Cloud slid down the small embankment toward her. Short of jumping in the lake, there was no way to avoid him.

"Maybe between the two of us, our prayers will work." He spoke softly despite the commotion behind them.

"What makes you think I was praying?"

"The way you tilted your head back." He tipped his own head back. "And right before you opened your eyes, you bowed your head. Like you were centering yourself." He cleared his throat, unable to meet her eyes. "I'm sorry. I'm a reporter. I imagine it's like being a cop. We see things and assign meaning to it."

"Remind me never to play poker with you." She pointed to the patrol captain. "Captain Fitzgerald is the media liaison. I'm sure he can answer your questions."

"I just wanted to wish you luck in your investigation, Detective Wyatt."

"Thank you, Mr. Cloud. By the way, that was a nice photograph you took at the press conference that ran in the paper today." And it was. He'd captured Marisa and Tilda together, their foreheads touching and eyes closed in a powerful moment of fear and hope and love.

"Everett," he said. "Please call me Everett."

The water had smoothed out again. "If you'll excuse me, I should head toward the briefing."

"I interviewed Ms. Marquet yesterday," he said, causing Jo to stop. "She's convinced her husband abducted their daughter. Is that why the focus has shifted to this area? Mr. Flores's ranch and practice is just on the other side of that hill." He pointed with his chin.

"Is that so?" Her PR mask fell into place, and she suppressed the urge to hip check him into the lake. Served her right for dropping her guard around a reporter.

The department hadn't outed Lucero—or anyone else—as a suspect in an abduction. Too many things had to be confirmed first, including that Lena had actually been abducted. By the time police agencies touted someone as a person of interest, they'd already amassed a pretty thick file to back up their declaration. Lucero's file was growing but still thin. An announcement that he was a suspect would not only be premature but detrimental to the investigation.

"Our goal is, first and foremost, to find Lena," she said. "Yesterday, we searched the mesa behind her mother's home as that was the last place Lena had been seen. This is the closest recreational area to her father's residence, which makes this an obvious second choice."

"And Mr. Flores?"

"Last I checked, he wasn't missing. Captain Fitzgerald will be taking all the media questions in a few minutes. Excuse me, Mr. Cloud."

She scrambled up the incline. The climb hadn't winded her, but she breathed through her nose like a bull, equally annoyed with Everett Cloud and her chief. With the volunteer registration complete, she shouldn't be here. The brass had cast themselves in all the speaking roles. Jo had been chosen as an extra, someone to stand behind the stars and look earnest, while the clock still ticked and the pile of leads on her desk grew cold.

A familiar car pulled into the lot, and Squint parked near the entrance. Great, now they were both out of commission.

He stood in the vee of his driver door and peered beyond the roof. When he spotted her in the crowd, he signaled.

Briefing started in five minutes, but she veered toward him anyway. His demeanor wasn't excited enough to have found Lena, but the fact that he wasn't walking toward the briefing meant something else had cropped up.

She drew near the passenger side of the car. "What's up?"

"Thought you might like an excuse to go back to work."

"You have no idea," she said.

"Then why are you glaring at me?"

She twisted her mouth. "Let's just say it's been a cloudy morning."

He glanced toward the media vans. "Raining reporters again?"

"Just one. Let me go tell Pieretti before they start."

"No need." He leaned his elbow on the roof of the car. "Unlike you, he takes my calls and we have his blessing."

"Sorry about that." Jo pulled the phone out of her belt holster and raised the volume. "So, what fun have you planned for us?"

"I thought you'd enjoy going with me to chat with Sebastian Vescent."

She snapped the phone back in place. "Who?"

"The man you so aptly dubbed Glowering Man."

"Tilda's neighbor?" she asked. "What's he done?"

"More accurately, it's what he didn't do when he moved next door to Tilda and her two daughters."

The day was definitely clearing up. "He's a registrant?"

"Sexual assault on a child. Sarah found the warrant after she took over running the registered owners of vehicles from the canvass. Dickinson's got eyes on the house to make sure Vescent didn't leave until I had a search warrant signed and collected you," he said. "Would you like to meet me there, or ride over together so I can give you the details?"

The commanders were still standing by her car. She popped open his passenger door and slid in. "Tell me more."

* * *

Forty-seven-year-old Sebastian Vescent stood six foot four, weighed in at a svelte two hundred forty pounds, and was an alumnus of the Colorado Correctional System. Most recently, he'd attended the Buena Vista Correctional Complex for men, which despite its name did not, in fact, have a decent view.

Until seven months ago, Vescent had been diligent about checking in with his parole officer and registering his whereabouts with local law enforcement as required of a felon who'd been convicted of sexually assaulting his neighbor's twelve-year-old child.

Intel suggested Vescent was a typical bully, relying on his size and demeanor to intimidate others, but was quick to back down or flee when confronted by police. His unilateral decision to relocate to Echo Valley without giving his PO a forwarding address explained his current aversion to chatting with the local po-po. More importantly, his lapse of judgment gave law enforcement an opportunity to return him to the proverbial straight and narrow. Jo looked forward to a conversation with him that didn't involve a second-story window.

Squint drove in from the south and parked a block from the duplex shared by Vescent and Tilda. Officer Estes pulled his patrol car in behind them. Jo used her cell phone to alert dispatch and Dickinson that they'd arrived.

Property records identified the homeowner as ninety-two-year-old Amelia Thompson, a current resident of Evergreen Manor, the assisted living facility. According to Tilda, Glowering Guy was Amelia's nephew and had been there about three months.

The officers split up as they neared Tilda's townhouse. Jo rounded the back of the duplex and scrambled up the hillside. She concealed herself behind a big clump of bitterbrush that was aligned with the fence that divided the two backyards.

The incline gave Jo the tactical advantage, and the two-foot retaining wall on her side of the fence created what amounted to a steeplechase obstacle. If Vescent vaulted the six-foot barrier, he'd have to clear the narrow gully between the fence and the low masonry wall and then stick the landing on ground that was at a higher elevation than his takeoff. Jo placed the degree of difficulty firmly at a nine point seven. Far easier to go out the gate and straight into Dickinson's outstretched arms.

It was always a good idea to have a uniformed patrol officer during the initial contact, and Estes accompanied Squint to the front door.

Once everyone was in place, Estes knocked. "Echo Valley Police Department. Open the door."

The *or we'll break it down* was implied.

The next three raps had a metallic clunk to them indicating he'd switched to his flashlight. "Sebastian Vescent. We know you're in there. We have a search warrant." Knock, knock. "Open the door or we'll break it down."

Jo's heart rate picked up. If Vescent didn't open the door, the final knock would come from Squint, courtesy of the department's dynamic entry tool—a fancy name for a high-priced chunk of steel with a couple of handles that enable the wielder to get a good swing before smashing the door from its frame.

The vertical blinds fluttered, then Vescent flung open the rear sliding door.

Jo radioed, "He's coming out the back."

Vescent barreled across the patio. The side gate swung open and Vescent swerved toward the rear fence.

Keeping low, Jo sprinted a collision course. Vescent's hands grasped the top of the planks. Momentum propelled his head and body up, and he folded forward and swung his right leg onto the top of the fence. It was too easy. With both hands and one foot all on a single narrow plane, he had no stability. Jo rose to her full height, caught him by the shoulder and shoved. Gravity took over and he toppled backward. Jo jumped the fence after him, landing on the hardpack dirt beside his sprawled body.

Dickinson grabbed Vescent's hand, yanked the slack out of his arm, and flipped him over onto his belly into an arm bar control hold. Jo searched him for weapons. It was a bit like a team roping event, and she suppressed a whoop.

The other officers busted through the gate. Squint disappeared through the sliding door. Estes charged toward the melee. Jo closed the second handcuff and grabbed the key ring from her belt, double-locking the cuffs so they wouldn't tighten.

Vescent unleashed a misogynistic, profanity-laced tirade, which, when parsed, boiled down to his frustration about being flushed out of the town-house and unhappiness that his great escape was foiled by "a girl."

"Echo, David-three." Jo brought the mic as close as possible to her mouth to muffle Vescent's yelling in the background. "We're code-four, one in custody."

Jo and Dickinson each grabbed an arm and hauled Vescent to his feet.

"Is there anyone else inside?" Jo asked Vescent.

He swung his shoulders to break Dickinson's grip and lurched toward Jo. "You bitch. You wouldn't last a second in a fair fight."

"Station?" Dickinson asked.

Jo nodded. "You good? Squint—"

"Go," he answered.

She sprinted toward the patio door. Her partner was inside conducting a safety sweep of a felon's home by himself. No telling what or who he'd encounter.

"Stay the hell out of my house! Bitch, you need a warrant."

"She's got one," Estes said behind her.

Jo drew her gun and crossed the threshold.

The place was nearly empty.

"Squint?"

"Up here. Code-four."

By the time she reached the stairs, Squint was already descending. "Lena?" she asked.

"No one. And the upstairs is almost as empty as the first floor."

The tension she'd been holding in her shoulders released a fraction. She holstered. Since learning a sexual offender with a penchant for prepubescent girls lived next door to Tilda and her daughters, she'd imagined all kinds of horrors.

"If I didn't know better, I'd say it looks like he's been squatting," Squint continued. "There's a bedroll and a duffle bag upstairs in the smaller bedroom."

Jo nudged a light switch up with her elbow, and the pendant light in the foyer brightened. "Utilities are paid. And while the backyard isn't going to earn any awards, the front is at least mowed. What's in the garage?"

"Most everything that should be in the house." He pulled open the garage door and held it for her.

"Always the gentleman." She slipped inside and hit the light. Squint fell in behind her. It was as if they had stepped into the middle of a storage unit filled with furniture. "At least the search will be quick."

26

Squint's car always smelled better than hers. A combination of leather and tobacco, which mystified Jo as he neither smoked, nor had she ever found a saddle in the back seat. It left her with an unreasonable desire to visit the local tobacconist, buy a pouch of vanilla-scented pipeweed, and hide it under her seat.

He pulled onto the access road to Columbine Lake. The lot was still crowded with cars and equipment, but the command staff and media vans had left, and most of the searchers were in the field.

He idled next to her car. "You headed back to the station?"

"I am." She shut the door and leaned back through the window. "If you're looking for a way to develop rapport with Vescent when you talk to him, tell him what a pain in the ass I am to work with." She held up her finger and started laughing. "Don't. Even."

He lifted his hands off the steering wheel. "Never crossed my mind."

She tapped the sill twice. "See you back at the barn."

Heat wafted from her car when she opened the door and she stood outside a minute to let it air out.

The arrest had gone well. Vescent's choice to foot bail had saved them from breaking down a door, and his unceremonious tumble from the fence had forestalled a brawl. Now the trick was to get him to talk. Some paroles loved to blather on as a way of delaying the inevitable trip to the Graybar Hotel. Others were notoriously reticent. But if Vescent had seen anything out of the window he was so fond of glowering through, Squint would be the one to ferret it out of him. The way people rushed to confess to him during interviews, Jo'd swear he'd changed into a priest's collar and cassock before entering the room.

She cranked the A/C. At the end of the access road, she turned toward the station. Two curves later, she pulled off along the shoulder and jammed the car into park so suddenly the front end dipped.

Ten minutes, she told herself. No more.

Knee-high patches of rabbitbrush and yarrow crowded the far side of the guardrail and released a woodsy scent when Jo stepped into them. She bent over and selected an egg-sized stone from the rocky soil and closed her fingers around its warmth. Below her, the hill unfolded in a carpet of golds and browns and dusty greens that marked late summer in southwest Colorado and ended at the edge of Columbine Lake.

And somewhere below her, Lucero had hiked Sunday morning carrying a rucksack that may or may not have looked like Lena's. A hike he hadn't wanted to discuss with Jo, after a night he'd lied about.

She leaned against the guardrail, her back to her detective car parked with its blinking hazard lights, and tossed the stone between her hands.

Time thinned here. Jo could face any direction and see life and death caught between the geological upheaval that forged the San Juan Mountains to the north, and the Colorado Plateau with its basins and gullies and sandstone monuments that stretched south. Here, where one could feel the slow, steady pulse of the earth, she wasn't able to slow her own.

She clenched the rock.

When they hadn't found Lena with Vescent, her first emotion had been relief. Here, under the noon sky, there were no shadows to hide the uglier emotion she'd also felt. Disappointment. She bowed her head against the sun that burned her face. They hadn't found Lena. That was the acceptable reason for her dismay. But there was something else. Something darker. Something that swirled like a dust devil—formative from a distance, but when viewed from within dissolved into particles of grit too small to be seen, but that made her eyes tear.

She couldn't shake the feeling that the answer to Lena's disappearance was closer to home. The longer Lena remained missing, the more likely she'd been hurt. And although it was wrong of her, Jo would rather have found Lena hurt at the hands of a stranger than betrayed by someone she'd loved and trusted.

Tilda and Lucero. Tilda *or* Lucero. The names swirled around Jo, trapping her between them and strangling her with their secrets.

Had Lucero taken Lena?

Jo had responded to plenty of civil standby calls as a patrol officer to ensure estranged parents didn't do anything stupid during their custody exchanges. Her presence reduced the name calling and accusations children shouldn't hear. Occasionally, a parent was late to the exchange—either out of spite or to exert control. It was behavior meant to punish the other parent, not the child. But the cases most likely to end in tragedy were when a child was snatched by a parent the child feared.

And Marisa had suggested Lena had something to fear.

Jo unclenched her hand. The sharp edge of the stone had creased her palm.

Wherever the investigation leads.

"Shit." She pushed away from the guardrail, and hurled the stone as far as she could. It landed with a dull thud, lost in the weeds below.

* * *

Jo unlocked the armory door. It was the only bomb-rated room in the police building. The recording equipment for the interview rooms and the department's server took up the rear corner. She squeezed between a rack of shotguns and an industrial shelving unit crammed with footlockers of tactical equipment, and double-checked the recorder to make sure it was still capturing Squint's interview with Vescent. Unlike her interview with Lucero, Squint spoke with Vescent in the interview room adjacent to the department's two holding cells.

The room commanded less real estate than most pickup truck beds. Inside, a slab of metal jutted from the wall and served as a table between two plastic chairs. Squint sat with his back to the reinforced steel door, a folder on the table in front of him. Vescent sat across from him.

Vescent's transformation from foaming arrestee to compliant conversationalist had been startling. Jo had missed the very beginning of the interview, but when she first started monitoring the recording, Vescent's arms had been crossed and his fists jammed under his biceps to make the muscles appear bigger. As Squint spoke, Vescent shifted, first relaxing his fists, then drawing in his outstretched feet, and finally dropping his arms and leaning forward. Since then, Squint had been asking questions and taking notes.

Estes came up behind her in the armory and stood on his tiptoes to look over her shoulder at the small monitor. "Well?"

She held out her hand palm up. "Told you."

"Shit." He dug into his pocket and slapped a five-dollar bill into her hand. "Fucking felon whisperer."

Inside the interview room, Squint stood and shook Vescent's hand.

"That's my cue." Estes swung his key ring around his finger and left to collect Squint's booking paperwork and transport Vescent to jail.

Jo met Squint in the doorway of the armory. "Anything?"

"He really doesn't like you."

"Anything valuable?" she clarified.

Squint clicked his pen shut and stowed it in his shirt pocket. "As Amelia's favorite nephew and only relative—"

"Which makes the term 'favorite' somewhat misleading," she observed.

"—he's been taking care of the townhouse in her absence, and keeping it squared away in the event it needs to be sold to help pay for her assisted living and medical expenses."

"And in exchange?"

"Rent-free accommodation in a place unknown to his parole officer."

"Until now."

"There is that." He sidled past her and turned off the recording equipment. The machine resembled a high-tech VCR, only with dual DVD-ROM synchronous recording capabilities and automatic archiving to the department's server.

"And this is helpful how?" she asked.

"He's a paranoid insomniac with a guilty conscience. He sits by the front window—"

Pieretti shadowed the doorway. "Is Vescent still here?"

"Estes just left with him," Squint answered.

"Good. Whatever you've got going, put it on hold. We're going to Hank's."

Jo balked. "I've got—"

"Two minutes to meet me outside."

* * *

"He said what?" Squint's first forkful hovered in midair. A bit of gravy dripped onto his biscuit.

It wasn't noisy enough in Hank's Diner for Squint to have missed Pieretti's words, which meant he was as startled as Jo.

"That we were close to making an arrest," Pieretti repeated. "The media went ape-shit. Wanted names, timelines, motives."

The breakfast crowd had disappeared hours ago. Lunch was winding down too. Other than the couple at the counter nursing their bottomless cups of coffee, the three detectives were the only ones left in the restaurant.

"And does the chief have someone in mind?" Squint pressed.

"It's my impression he's leaving that to us." The sergeant slathered his blueberry pancakes with extra butter, then doused the stack with syrup. "I briefed him before the press conference that we'd identified a sex offender who'd violated parole living next door to Marquet. That you guys were en route with patrol to pick him up. During the Q and A, Cloud asked if the department had identified a person of interest."

Jo groaned. "And the chief said yes."

"Which is why we're having this little meeting. I need to know what's going on so I have something in hand by the 1800 debrief." He glanced at his watch. "Which gives us what, four hours?"

"Wait. When did the news conference air?" Jo pulled out her phone. "We've got to notify Tilda. Lucero too. They're going to assume the worst."

"Put your phone away," Pieretti said. "I already made the calls."

"You told them about Vescent?"

"Not by name. As you can imagine, neither party was very happy."

"Holy shit, Kip." Jo called her sergeant by his first name on average three times a year: once at Christmas, usually on his birthday, and when things went so incredibly sideways that rank went out the window. It had never occurred over afternoon pancakes.

Patsy approached the table and slid Jo's huevos rancheros in front of her. "Here you go, hon. Sorry about the delay."

"Always worth the wait."

Patsy topped off their coffee mugs. She'd been slinging hash since Jo had first sat at the counter with her dad. She still wore the same size jeans, although the odds of her putting her boot to someone's backside had increased exponentially over the years.

"Take your time." She dug their tickets out of her waist apron and dropped them on the side of the table. "Hank's about to shut down the grill so if you want anything else, speak now or forever hold your peace."

Pieretti raised his finger. "Do you have any more whipped cream?"

"You want a side of bacon with that to restore your manhood?"

"Thanks, no. Just the frou-frou stuff today."

After she stepped away from the table, Pieretti said, "What? Ever since Lisa got pregnant, I've been craving sweets."

Jo stabbed the fried egg on her plate to release the yolk. "Keep it up and you're going to gain more weight than she does—and she'll be the only one to have a baby to show for it."

They sat in the back of the diner with a clear view of the counter and the door. Jo shoveled in a huge bite. She hadn't eaten anything but a protein bar at the command post, and it looked like it'd be a while before she called it quits for the day.

"Talk to me about Vescent," Pieretti said. "Is he a suspect now?"

"There was nothing to suggest Lena had ever been inside Vescent's townhouse," Squint said.

"Shit." Pieretti took off his glasses and scrubbed his face. "Did he say anything in the interview?"

"He said he watches out the front window every morning, but he never saw Lena leave the house for the fairgrounds Sunday morning."

"Is he saying that to throw suspicion elsewhere?"

"He doesn't have a television or a computer. When I mentioned Lena was missing, he acted surprised. Asked if she was the young one. When I said yes, he mentioned they'd met once. She was really nice."

Jo picked up her mug. "That's not something I want to hear a sex offender say about a girl the same age as the one he assaulted."

"Funny you should say that. It concerned me too, and I brought it up. Even went so far as to mention his prior victim, Tracy Singleton, was the same age. After a long pause, he politely pointed out Tracy was a boy."

"A boy." Pieretti put his glasses back on. "And this wasn't in the arresting agency's reports?"

Patsy returned with a bowl of whipped cream and a side of bacon. She placed the bowl in front of Pieretti, and the bacon next to Jo. "Your eyes lit up when I mentioned bacon."

"You are a goddess."

"Remember that when you leave your tip." A splash of coffee later, she was gone.

Squint tipped creamer into his mug and stirred. "I made the decision to move on Vescent before the arrest reports were faxed over, in case Lena was inside the townhouse. I'd spoken to the parole agent. Got the background intel on drugs, weapons, reaction to police. Confirmed the sexual assault on a child charge. She read off the victim name and DOB. I made the assumption."

"A boy named Sue," Jo said.

"It actually worked to our advantage. I don't think he realized the severity of failing to register and was relieved not to be facing a new assault charge. He offered to let us search his truck and signed a consent waiver."

"Good, move on that." Pieretti pointed his fork at Jo. "And Lucero?"

"Still nothing on his whereabouts the night Lena went missing. Tilda dropped the name of a woman who works at the casino as someone Lucero's been dating. I'm hoping she can shed some light on what he was doing, but that's taken a back seat to me talking to Marisa. Guess it depends on who I can reach first."

"Because of her ditching Lena?"

"That and a concern I have regarding the paper delivery guy who took a smoke break at Tilda's driveway." She lowered her fork. "I didn't bring it up this morning but I think he may have hooked up with Marisa while Lena was alone in the pavilion. They left the fairgrounds together but they came back solo, and she looked a bit worse for wear. Tingler handed her a beer, so if nothing else I can talk to him under the pretext of contributing to the delinquency of a minor."

"If there was a problem wouldn't she have reported it?"

"And fess up to abandoning her sister the night before she went missing? No way."

"Great." Pieretti turned back to Squint. "Anything from the ranch?"

"I've set aside time this afternoon to go through the items," Squint said. "It's mostly school notebooks, some personal cards. But other than adding to her list of friends for us to follow up on, I'm not confident we're going to find anything new."

"No way to get to Lucero's computer?"

Jo shook her head. "Lena doesn't have an email account or play video games, so for now, his computer's off limits."

"That's too bad."

"Phone records may be more promising," Jo said. "We asked both parents to sign a release for their records. Tilda agreed—and in fact, she's already pulled her last couple of statements. She's cross-referencing the numbers so we know who's on the other end of the call or text. Lucero, not surprisingly, refused.

"But here's the thing," she continued. "Lena doesn't have a phone of her own. When she needs to communicate with anyone, she uses her parents' cell phones. I can write up a warrant request for Lucero's records as soon as I get back to the station. If you sign off on it before you go home, I'll track down a judge tonight and fax it to the carrier."

"Good." Pieretti mopped up the remaining syrup with his last bit of pancake. "Unless you get tied up on something, plan on attending the briefing. I'm hoping search and rescue saves the day."

"Before we go, I want to bring up one other thing," Jo said. "You may have heard a rumor the chief's offered to promote me." There were more important things to be thinking about right now, but she also knew she wanted her partner and sergeant to hear it from her. "It's true."

27

The gospel music in the thrift store should have been a clue.

A weak smile flickered across the clerk's face. "Everything happens for a reason."

The coffee Tilda had accepted at the last stop left her twitchy, and the current shopkeeper's faux concern pushed her a step closer to disregarding the *Do no harm* pledge she took in nursing school.

"Would you like to pray?" Betty's name tag had a sticker of a cat wearing a Santa hat batting at the name like it was a wayward ornament. It was August for chrissakes. During a heat wave.

"Not now," Tilda said. "But I'd be grateful if you put in a kind word for Lena." She knew she should smile, but her lips refused to obey. "I'd appreciate it even more if you'd place one of these fliers in your front window, maybe another by the register?"

A blast of hot air followed two older women into the store. They beelined past the shelves of sorry appliances and mismatched china toward the final reductions corner.

Here in the center of the room, racks of clothing pressed so close to each other they brushed both Tilda's arms. If she dropped to her knees she'd disappear through a scuffed linoleum floor and plunge into a depth of hell no prayer would reach. Christian charities thrift store or not, no one had that kind of pull.

"Of course." Despite her vigorous head nodding, Betty's Aqua-Net-shellacked hair didn't move. "Anything we can do." She reached out to pat Tilda's arm.

Tilda dodged the woman's hand and dug into her tote bag before the clerk could make contact. Everyone today felt entitled to touch her, and she was one awkward hug or patronizing pat away from a full-blown toddler-worthy meltdown. "Marisa, honey?"

"She's over by the designer consignments." A bit of the love-thy-neighbor tenor had disappeared from Betty's voice.

Designer in Echo Valley usually meant Patagonia or Marmot for the active crowd, or bedazzled jeans and sequined sweatshirts for those who weren't. Neither option offered the type of couture that would interest her eldest daughter. Even the valley's wealthy second-home owners embraced their inner cowpoke during their long weekends or ski holidays and left no trace of their more upscale tastes.

Tilda raised her voice. "Marisa, do you have any more fliers with you?"

"Just a minute. I think I found something."

Great. Marisa hadn't even wanted to come along. Now Tilda couldn't get her to leave. "If it's not your sister, leave it."

This was supposed to be a bonding experience. Already they'd wallpapered half the town and valley with fliers of Lena, and the hardest part had been tearing Marisa away from her phone. They'd spent all afternoon together and Tilda didn't feel any closer to her first daughter. But at least they'd been productive.

They'd started in their own neighborhood and worked their way downtown. One of the websites meant to help parents of missing children warned that a lot of municipalities didn't allow things to be stapled to utility poles, but if people could post fliers about their goddamn lost dogs, she was damn well going to post a flier of her missing daughter.

"I saw your news conference," Betty said. "I hope the police take a closer look at the father. It's usually someone close in situations like this."

"So I've learned." Two fliers. Two goddamn fliers. That's all she needed to end this conversation. She should have detoured to the car after their last stop to restock her tote and drop off the industrial staple gun that banged against her hip and weighed down the bag. Instead, she had to deal with yet another expert who'd learned everything they needed to know about life by watching true crime shows. "Marisa?"

"Is there a reward?" Betty asked.

"Reward?" Maybe it was fate—or considering the venue, predestination—that Tilda still had her tote bag. One swing and the staple gun could take out Betty *and* her fucking Santa-hat wearing kitty. Seriously, what kind of person needed a reward for helping return a child to her home?

"People will ask." Betty clutched the single strand of pearls around her neck, resting her hand on the neckline of her twinset. It was a thousand degrees outside. Who did that?

"Marisa?" Tilda called. "I just need a couple, honey. Then we should get going. We have a lot more places to visit." She had to get the hell out of here before she did something to get herself arrested. Or excommunicated.

Her daughter wove her way around the racks. "Look what I found on one of the regular racks. It's a Khaite." She held up the dress. "Catherine Holstein designs the line. She's out of New York."

"I never heard of her."

Marisa practically pranced. "That doesn't mean she isn't a thing. And check out the cut. Super cool."

"Put it back," Tilda said.

"But I don't have anything this nice. It's a crepe de chine. That's like a silk. Perfect for summer."

"I said put it back."

Betty retreated behind the glass case that separated customers from the register. Good riddance.

"I'll buy it my—"

"You do not need a goddamn black dress!" In the silence between songs, Tilda's voice rang across the store.

Marisa shrank against the clothes rack. The two hens in the corner stopped talking.

The burn of bile closed Tilda's throat and for a horrible moment, she thought she was going to throw up, right there in the store. Marisa's beautiful gray eyes slowly filled with tears. Because of her. There were a thousand things Tilda wanted to say. Should say. Didn't.

"I'm sorry, Momma," Marisa whispered. "I wasn't thinking." She removed a couple of fliers from her bag. Without looking up, she slid them across the glass case toward Betty. Then wove through the racks. Replaced the dress. "I'll be outside."

Betty returned bearing a piece of paper she held out to Tilda. "When my son and his wife divorced, she ran away with their children. Here's the number of someone who can help."

28

The only times Jo had been in the casino were when she'd popped in to use the bathroom or refill her water bottle while cycling through the small towns and tribal lands just north of the New Mexico border. At night, the resort complex dominated the landscape. Dramatic uplighting drew out the texture of rocky accent walls and highlighted copper-roofed porte cochères. Behind the resort the setting sun left broad brushstrokes of mauve and orange that colored the distant San Juans, while the massive marquee sign at the entrance electrified the roadway.

Jo followed a double-decker tour bus into the resort.

"Great," Dakota drawled from the seat beside her. "There goes all the slots."

"You realize the goal is to find Misty Trujillo, not gamble."

"*Your* goal is to find Misty. My goal is to hit a jackpot—which should be your goal, too. You're off duty. Live a little."

Southwest Colorado was a mishmash of federal, state, county, municipal, and tribal jurisdictions. All the Echo Valley police officers were cross-deputized by the Animas County sheriff, but Jo's police authority ended when she crossed onto the reservation.

Jo followed Dakota inside and exchanged the hot tranquility of the evening sky for the chaos of the flash and ching of slot machines, layers of conversation, music, and the occasional whoop.

"We need to get you a player's card," Dakota said.

"What if I don't want to play?"

Her friend arched her eyebrow. "You think you're just going to strike up a conversation with an employee without the pit boss intervening?"

"No?"

"Bless your heart."

Which coming from Dakota was neither a blessing nor heartfelt.

Ten minutes later and holding a bit of plastic the size of a credit card, they hit the floor.

Walkways divided the casino into sections and provided numerous opportunities to veer off course. The majority of the space was dedicated to slots, and a player occupied the seat in front of almost each one.

"See?" Dakota pointed at an aisle of slots where the gray-haired players wore identical pink *Slotty Queen: I'll pull your handle* T-shirts. "Tour bus groupies. Do not look them in the eyes. They'll cut you."

Cameras dotted the ceiling and strategically hung over each gaming table. The casino employees all wore maroon button-down shirts with credentials hanging from a lanyard around their necks. The pit bosses were equally easy to pick out in their suits and ties. The roaming plainclothes security were harder to spot.

"How do you know she's working?" Dakota asked.

"I have a friend who works for the hotel side of the house who knows her."

A woman walking the opposite direction passed them holding an umbrella drink.

Dakota knocked her shoulder into Jo's. "You know, since we're undercover, we should probably get a drink. Blend in better."

"We're not undercover."

"Doesn't change that I'm thirsty, and you look downright parched."

"Fine. Order me a Smithwick's if they have it." Jo pulled some cash out of her purse. "And whatever you're having if they don't. I'll be at the table games."

Dakota waved the money away. "Just give me half your winnings when you strike it rich."

The craps table had a raucous crowd, laughing and blowing on dice before sending them tumbling down the table. One employee wielded a stick to gather the dice, and three others managed the mayhem—one with a murderous look on his face as if he'd like to choke out the next person to say "baby needs new shoes."

Aside from the dice wrangler, the others worked from inside an area cordoned off by velvet ropes and shared by the other table dealers. Jo paused behind the first card table. The dealer dealt out cards with remarkable precision.

Beyond the other card tables was the roulette table. The woman working the wheel had her back to the pit. Another gaggle of pink T-shirts joked and jostled each other across the table from her. Jo approached just as the *I like big bets and I cannot lie* group decided to move on.

"*Maiku.*" Misty Trujillo greeted Jo with the Ute word for hello. "Welcome to the casino." She pushed the burnished mahogany roulette wheel one direction and, with a flick of her manicured finger, sent the steel ball rolling along the rim in the other direction. "Are you ready to play?"

"I'm afraid I don't know the rules," Jo said.

The woman barely reached Jo's chin, but the way she planted her feet and threw back her shoulders suggested she'd be the number one draft pick for a bar fight—manicure or not.

"We'll have to rectify that." Misty waved her hand over the table. The ball jumped around until it landed in a pocket.

"Fourteen, red, even." Misty placed a marker on the corresponding number on the felt table. "If you had placed a dollar bet on that number, I'd be adding thirty-five dollars to your initial investment."

"Makes me wish I'd bet a ten spot."

She removed the marker. "Place your bets."

Jo didn't move.

"Nothing?" Misty waved her hand over the table. "No more bets." She spun the wheel and again sent the ball spinning the opposite direction. The ball settled into a pocket. "Number ten, black, even."

"Is that good?" Jo asked.

"It would have been had you bet on it," she said with an enigmatic smile.

Jo flashed her player's club. "How do I use this?"

"Roulette one-oh-one. You need chips to bet, the card you have is for slots. You can buy chips from me or the cashier. There are twelve ways you can wager." She indicated the table. "And where you place your chip on the table tells me how you want to bet."

"Walk me through it." Jo dug out a twenty and slid it across the table.

For the next ten minutes, Misty explained how the markings on the felt corresponded to the game's various betting options. "The more specific the bet, the higher the payout."

"And the less likely you are to win," Jo pointed out.

"That's why it's called gambling." Misty laughed. "Ready?"

Jo put a white chip on the black square with the number seventeen and then hedged her bet by placing a second chip on the red diamond.

"An inside and an outside bet. Very nice." Misty waved her hand over the betting table. "No more bets."

The ball whirled around the rim in a blur before it lost momentum and ricocheted against diamond-shaped deflectors and bounced around the pockets. Just when Jo thought it was going to land in a red pocket it bounced into a black.

"Seventeen, black, odd!" Misty placed a marker over the number. "Congratulations! You won thirty-five dollars. While my marker is on the table, you don't want to touch any of your chips." She cleared the table of the losing chip, picked up her marker and placed the payout next to Jo's lonely white chip. "Now comes your next choice. Collect, divide it up, or let it ride."

"It's customary to tip the dealer, right? Jo asked.

"Tips are never expected, but happily accepted. Oh, and technically, I'm a croupier. You keep playing like that and you should at least know the lingo."

Jo pushed the entire pile of chips toward Misty. "For you."

Misty tilted her head while she sized up Jo. "Reporter or PI?" She took the chips and tapped the edges loudly against her tip box before dropping the chips through the opening.

"Neither." A pit boss wandered their way, and Jo put down another bet. "Appreciation for taking the time to teach me roulette."

Misty spun the wheel as Dakota came up to the table carrying a pint of red ale and a pink-tinged drink in a martini glass that made Jo glad the bar stocked her beer.

"Number two, black, even." Misty said. "Good thing you didn't let it ride."

"Beginner's luck only works once." Jo shifted some chips in front of her friend and nudged her. "Did you know my player's card was only good at slots?"

"Oh, gosh, really?" Her drawl was thicker than usual. "Does that mean I'll have to use it for you?" She clinked her martini glass against Jo's pint.

The pit boss paused behind Jo and sent some silent signal to Misty because she responded with a microscopic nod and an enthusiastic "Place your bets."

Jo chose *Odd.*

Dakota placed a chip on *Even.* "This way one of us will win."

The ball bounced. "Double zero. House wins." Misty placed the marker down and swept up the dollar chips. The pit boss moved on.

They had the table to themselves and played several rounds. The clink of chips was seductive, and the ornate roulette wheel almost made Jo wish she was wearing a dress and holding a martini glass. In Monte Carlo. Feeling cocky, she placed her bet on a row of three.

In a way, police work was little more than a game of chance. Sure, there were detectives who could count cards, skew the odds in their favor, but ultimately, they all bet that the people they interviewed would have something valuable to contribute to their investigations. Sometimes the payout was the equivalent of even money: enough to stay in the game but not the jackpot they'd hoped for. But every now and again the score was far bigger than the expectation. So much so that they all wanted to believe it really wasn't chance at all.

Dakota squealed next to her. Misty stacked chips next to her friend's bet and collected Jo's chips.

Jo slid two more red chips toward Misty. "For you."

Curiosity flickered behind Misty's eyes. "Thank you." She tapped the two chips twice against the box and deposited them. "Place your bets."

Jo placed a chip on the intersection of four numbers. "I'm betting you can tell me something about Lucero Flores."

The steel ball whipped around the rim. "You didn't answer my earlier question," Misty said.

Dakota glanced between the two women.

"I'm not a reporter or a PI, but I am trying to find his missing little girl. I'm Detective Jo Wyatt with EVPD."

"A bit out of your jurisdiction, aren't you?"

Jo held up her pint glass. "I'm off duty. Just having an interesting conversation with a nice croupier."

"Look at you, remembering the lingo." The ball settled and she placed her marker. "Thirty-four, red, even."

A herd of pink shirts headed their way. Time was running out. "Lena's young, she's—"

"Only eleven. I know." Misty collected the chips.

"I'm trying to nail down where Lucero was on Saturday night." Jo tidied her two remaining piles of chips.

"Are you asking if he was with me?" Misty's bar fight stance widened. "Who told you to contact me?"

"Does it matter?"

Misty spun the wheel one direction and flicked the ball the other. "Place your bets."

Jo divided her chips between black eleven and red fourteen. "Lena's birthday."

The pink-clad ladies approached and their chatter filled the space that stretched between the cop and the croupier.

Misty waved her hand over the felt. "No more bets."

* * *

"Now are we working undercover?" Dakota whispered.

"Nope. We're two friends having a quiet conversation in a parked car."

"'Cause it feels like undercover work."

Jo glanced at her friend. "And you know this how?"

The windows of the Explorer were rolled down, and sultry night air filled the interior of Jo's Explorer with the scent of hot earth and sage. When they'd pulled into the lot earlier in the evening, she'd intentionally chosen a spot that had a clear view of the back door and was far enough away from the closest light pole that their presence in the car would hopefully not draw undue attention.

"I watch TV. Any second now, we're either going to get made by the bad guys or end up in a foot pursuit."

"There are no bad guys," Jo said. "We're just waiting for Misty to end her shift."

Dakota propped her elbow on the sill and leaned the side of her head against her hand. "Why didn't you try to catch her at home? Then we wouldn't be sitting out here in the heat when we should be inside having another umbrella drink and pretending we're in Vegas."

"By the time I had a free minute, she'd already left for work. Besides, she lives on the reservation."

"Need I remind you she works on it, too?"

"But this particular spot is open to the public."

Dakota dropped her arm and looked at Jo. "What, you're going to ambush her on her way to the car?"

A pickup truck entered the lot, and Jo lowered her eyes to protect her night vision against the headlights that raked across her windshield. "I wouldn't characterize it as an ambush."

"She might."

"I don't think so." Or at least Jo hoped not. "She could have signaled the pit boss to remove us the second she thought there was something hinky going on. She didn't."

"Probably didn't want to blow the chance for another tip." Dakota resumed watching the lot.

"She didn't blink when I mentioned Lucero."

"Which means she could be warning him this very minute."

Jo shrugged. "So? It's not going to change how he thinks of me, and it may annoy him enough that he decides to talk to me."

"Or file a complaint."

"There is that," Jo said.

"Kiss your sergeant stripes goodbye."

"Funny you should mention that. I've decided to politely decline the promotion."

Dakota's head snapped around so fast she'd have made an owl jealous. "You will not! What the hell are you thinking?"

Jo shushed her with her hands. "I'm thinking of my future."

"No, you're not." Dakota spoke at the same volume. "You're worried about what people will say right now. So what? You'll be the topic of conversation until you prove yourself."

"And what if I don't?" The words came out sharp as a blade and she dulled them. "What if I can't?"

"It's natural to be scared."

Was that what she was feeling? Fear? She didn't think so, but she also couldn't put a better name to it. "It wouldn't be fair to anyone else who wants to test."

"If the last test had been fair, you'd already be a sergeant. You were passed over. You tested higher, you had more experience, and—"

"I wasn't selected. I know. I lived it, remember?" The debacle had almost ruined their friendship after Dakota had tipped off Everett Cloud.

"The new chief is trying to bring us into the twenty-first century. Let him. You're still the same woman you were then—and an even better cop." Dakota's drawl thickened. "Don't pass up a golden opportunity because someone's going to bitch about it. Someone always does. You've earned it and everyone knows it. This isn't a handout. It's a correction."

"A correction."

"Yes, so drop the *fuck me, I'll show them* attitude. You want to do some good for the department? Set the example. Prove that it's a welcoming place for other women. Take the pay raise, then prove you're worth it."

Jo straightened. "There she is."

"This conversation isn't over."

"Stay here, I don't want to freak her out."

Dakota slumped in the seat and crossed her arms. "You're probably a little late for that."

Jo stepped out and wove through the lanes of parking. Misty had her keys poking between her fingers.

Jo approached with her palms up. "Misty, can we talk for a minute?"

"I'm off the clock."

"I know. But I couldn't ask you these questions inside."

She stopped next to a Toyota Corolla. "Make it quick, or my babysitter will charge me extra."

"Were you with Lucero Saturday night?"

"No."

"Do you know where he was?" Jo asked.

"No."

She'd be the perfect court witness. Short, succinct answers that only addressed the question. Not at all what Jo needed. "Please, Misty. You said you've met Lena. This is for her."

Misty lowered her head. "I was sorry to see that she's missing. Lucero must be frantic."

Must be? "Don't you know?" Jo asked.

The barroom brawler reappeared. "We haven't been together for months. Not since I found him sexting some other woman."

"Do you know her name?"

"Didn't stick around long enough to learn it. When I said what the fuck, I got the *she's a friend* shit. If she was only a friend, how come he wouldn't come clean? He got really angry when I pushed. I got the impression she was married." She flashed her left hand. "He has a history."

"You said he got angry. Did he hurt you?"

She didn't seem surprised by the question. "He knew better than to try. He did take out a piece of drywall though. That was enough for me."

"Did you ever see him lose his temper with Lena?"

"He was different with Lena. He had a patience with her he didn't have with anyone else. Even his other daughter. Look, I really got to go."

"Thanks. I appreciate the info. One more question. Do you know anyone I might talk to who knows more about who this woman is?"

"You might try Lucero's ex. Supposedly, the bitches are friends."

29

It would be dawn soon. Jo pressed her thumb and index finger into the corner of her closed eyes and tried to knock off some of the sand plastered to the inside of her lids. She opened them again and blinked several times. No good. Still raspy.

Hours of staring at the screen had taken their toll. She shifted focus to the window. Other than the quad workout she got going up and down stairs every day, the best part of her office was the view. Main Street occupied the lowest elevation in the valley, and even though it was only a block off the main drag, the PD building commanded higher ground. From her second-floor window, she had an unobstructed view of Peregrines Peak, and its slow reveal at dawn was the reward for hitting the office early.

She had time before Squint would show up. Jo folded her arms and slid them across the desk, resting her head against her forearm.

She was trapped in a giant game of blind man's buff, blindfolded while all around her information swirled and tapped her shoulder but disappeared before she could grab it.

Vescent's disclosure. Had he really been watching out the window? Or was he intentionally trying to mislead investigators—either to protect himself or for sport? If he was telling the truth, that meant they had to consider three possibilities. One, Lena never made it home from the fairgrounds despite Marisa's statement and the footage that showed the two girls leaving together. Two, Lena made it home, but voluntarily left sometime between 2200 hours on Saturday and 0600 hours when Vescent was on his paranoia patrol. Or three, she was abducted from the home. The open window certainly supported the last possibility.

Then there was Misty, a woman who had about as much affection for Lucero's current flame as Tilda had for Misty.

"Why is it that even when I get here early, you're already here?" Squint's voice sounded entirely too chipper for the ungodly hour.

She rocked her head and peered through her hair. "I'm rethinking this whole detective gig."

"Got a better position lined up, do you?"

Jo raised her head and gave him her best stink-eye. "I should never have told you about being offered the sergeant's position."

"Didn't have to. I heard the chief when he offered it to you."

She should have known. Nothing got by her partner. But unlike Dakota, he'd wait for Jo to bring it up to discuss.

He placed his Stetson on the office coatrack and came over to the desks. "What's this?" He tapped the stack of printouts on her desk.

"Surveillance screenshots." She pushed the documents toward him. "Don't mix up the pages. It might look messy, but there's a method to my madness."

"There always is." He leafed through the documents. "What time did you get here?"

"Early."

"I'm here early," he said. "Which makes whenever you got here something else."

"I needed to know more about what happened this weekend before I talk to Marisa."

"Anything interesting?" He collected her mug and disappeared into the break room. A moment later the coffee maker started gurgling.

Jo raised her voice, too tired to follow him. "Over the course of three days, nineteen thousand three hundred and twenty-seven people visited the Echo Valley Fair, according to admission stats. And that's not counting the carnival workers, maintenance folks, cops, medics, and miscellaneous exhibitors, so let's call it an even nineteen-five." She recited the statistic with all the enthusiasm of a tenured math professor. "And based on what I saw in the surveillance videos, every single one of them entered the livestock pavilion at one time or another. Of those nineteen thousand five hundred people, five people caught my eye. Marisa, Lena, Aaron Tingler, Sebastian Vescent, the 4-H leader . . ."

"Chuck Ellison," Squint supplied from the break room.

"And finally, a man of mystery who turned out to be not very mysterious at all."

"That's six."

She grabbed an elastic from her drawer and raked her hair into a ponytail. "It's before breakfast and I can only deal with numbers when I've got a full stomach and am properly caffeinated."

He returned with two steaming mugs and placed one on her desk. "What's up with the mystery man?"

"He came out the rear of the pavilion while the fireworks were going off. Lena and Marisa came out the front a moment later." She blew on the coffee. "Neither looked particularly happy, and for a reason I've yet to figure out, Lena had Marisa's outer shirt wrapped around her waist."

"Does mystery man have a name?"

"Not yet. Turns out he's a carny who ran the High Striker on Saturday." She pulled one of the screenshots out of the stack. "Here's the best photo I've been able to find so far, but there's still a ton of footage to go through if you feel the need to locate a better one."

He took the page. "Leave him to me. Carnival employees tend to work the same booths. I'll run down the road boss or HR and see if I can get him ID'd." Squint's computer whirred and he sipped his coffee while he waited for it to boot up. "What did the others do to get themselves on your list?"

"Why's a twenty-one-year-old college kid sniffing around high school girls?" Jo asked.

"I'll assume that's rhetorical." Squint replied.

"Tingler spent all day with one gal, only to dump her after Marisa entered the picture. And after reviewing the footage again, I'm convinced he enjoyed their little rendezvous more than she did. Plus, he lied to me on the traffic stop."

Squint leaned back in his chair. "Which I suspect will be a topic of conversation at your next meeting."

"Undoubtedly. Vescent was a surprise. I expected someone who broke parole to keep a lower profile."

"And that got him on your list?"

"He's been on my list since he glared at you Sunday morning. No one gets to disrespect my partner."

"Present company excepted," he said.

"That goes without saying." The coffee he'd brewed was strong. She relished how the caffeine would soon race through her body. It gave her hope of making it through the day. "The 4-H leader landed on the list because of his access to the kids. There's nothing I can point to. Just that he was in and out of the pavilion a lot and I wonder if he's telling us everything he knows."

"So now what?" He pulled case files from his drawer and placed them on the corner of his desk.

"Interviews, mostly." Jo wrapped both hands around her mug and leaned back in her chair. "I called Tilda yesterday. Bottom line is she's okay with me talking to Marisa."

"Much negotiation?"

"A little. I've left a message for Marisa but haven't heard back yet. Judge Kline signed off on the warrant last night, so keep an eye out for the return on Lucero's phone records."

He hit a few keys on his computer and the printer whirred. "After I dig into the background of the carnival worker, I'll knock out some of the tip line leads. I also need to follow up on one of Tilda's neighbors who was going to send me a digital file from the game camera he's got set up in his yard."

It was too early. Jo couldn't see the connection. "How's that going to help?"

"He's right across the street from a whole patch of squaw apples and he's been filming the bears that come through at night. Passing cars set it off, too."

"That sounds promising."

"It's not time to bet the farm," Squint warned. "He's north of the townhouse. Most traffic comes in from the south."

"Speaking of bets, I spoke to Misty Trujillo last night at the casino."

"You're going to get sick if you don't sleep."

It was the same thing she told him when he put in long hours, and now probably wasn't the time to admit to a scratch in the back of her throat. "Despite Tilda's intel, Misty's no longer Lucero's girlfriend. Seems Misty caught him sexting another woman and the only thing she knows about the new girlfriend is that the woman is friends with Tilda."

"Doesn't sound like much of a friend."

"You up for checking that out with Tilda? You have a better relationship with her." She took another sip. Some people's liquid courage came from a liquor bottle. Jo's came from a coffee mug. "Why is that?"

"She was Maddie's nurse in the days before she died."

Squint's wife. Maddie's death had occurred before Jo and Squint had become partners. A tractor trailer had lost control of his rig on ice outside of town and clipped Maddie's car, sending it into a tree. She'd never regained consciousness in the days that followed. Due to the limit on visitors, Jo had only seen Squint and the boys when they rotated through the ICU waiting room. "I never knew that."

Squint had taken a leave of absence after they took Maddie off the ventilator. *So he and the boys could grieve proper,* he'd once said. Even now, years later, a softening overtook his expression whenever he mentioned his wife.

"I'd sure like us to find Tilda's daughter," he said.

Such simple words.

"Me too."

The morning gloam coaxed the crags of Peregrines Peak into view and now dawn painted the landscape with color and warmth. Jo rubbed her arms to banish a creeping chill she couldn't explain.

30

Glowing skin. Shiny hair. Trendy clothes. The occasional goofy expression hash-tagged #keepingitreal. Different locations for the fashion shots. A consistent background for makeup tutorials. Post after post, selfie after selfie of Marisa smiling at the camera, or staring pensively into the middle distance. A coy glance over her shoulder. Filtered, staged, and ruthlessly curated images of a life she wanted but didn't actually have. At least not here, in Echo Valley.

There was a vulnerability to Marisa that came out in the images that she lacked in person. The intimacy made Jo uncomfortable. Those eyes. Layers of gray flecked with promise: the illusion of a private conversation between her and the camera that anyone with an internet connection could follow.

Marisa held her audience in thrall, captivated by that inexplicable energy that encouraged them to keep scrolling, liking, and commenting on the color-saturated posts. The comments skewed overwhelmingly positive, even when tinged with envy. The criticisms, when they came, were disturbing. Observations about Marisa's body. Passive aggressive remarks cloaked as suggestions. Lewd invitations that reduced a fifteen-year-old child to little more than someone's wet dream.

Marisa had shared the news that her sister had disappeared. Since then, she'd continued to post every day. Haunting black and white images of herself in an empty playground. The poor grieving sister.

And that's where Jo found her, phone in the air, before the dramatic shadows of morning disappeared.

The park was only a few blocks from Marisa's home. Walking distance—even for a teen. Surrounded by trees and boulders large enough to climb, the park was nearly hidden from the street. A play area with sand as hard as concrete took up one corner. The rest of the park was open space. Jo parked along the roadway and walked across grass so dry it crunched.

Marisa sat on a swing. One of those A-frame swing sets made of metal that stung your hands in the winter and was impossible to hold onto in the rain. She held her phone, but a selfie stick peeked out of a leather tote on the edge of the grass. A mini-tripod sat atop a nearby rock.

Marisa lowered the phone when she noticed Jo approaching. "Did you find Lena?"

"No. I'm here to chat with you."

"Chat." Her voice was husky, as if she'd been crying, but her eyes were dry.

"You chose a nice place to find some quiet. You okay?" Jo asked.

Marisa toed the asphalt and twisted the swing until the chain touched.

Jo sat in the empty swing next to her. "I know a lot of people are probably asking you how you're doing right now, and you probably feel like you have to say yes." She rocked back and forth on her heel. "You don't."

"Could have fooled me."

"Want to talk about it?"

Marisa pocketed her phone. "You wouldn't understand."

"Try me."

"People are stupid."

"Some are," Jo agreed. "The rest are trying to do the best they can to get by."

"What makes people think that just because they bring food with them, they can come in and act like they own the place and stay as long as they want? Some even bring flowers. Lena's missing, not dead."

"Is that why you're hanging out in the park?" Jo asked.

"Sometimes I have to get away. I can't even grab a drink from the refrigerator without vultures picking at me. I don't even know who half the people are. It's awkward as hell." She twisted another loop in the chain. "And if I stay in my room, it's even worse, because mom feels like she has to constantly check on me."

"Have you told your mom that sometimes you need some quiet time in the park?"

"It's easier to tell her I'm going over to a friend's house. That way she doesn't think I'm alone. But even then, if I'm a minute late coming home or don't answer my phone on the first ring, she totally freaks out."

"All things considered, her worry is understandable."

"I know. But I'm almost sixteen. I'm not a child." She lifted her feet and the chain unwound. "She dragged me to church for a couple of hours the last few days, but I can't escape for five minutes without the world coming to an end. I told her this morning I'm not going anymore. It's not fair."

"I watched the news conference," Jo said. "You did really well."

"That's what we should be doing. Getting in front of cameras. Working social media. Not handing out stupid fliers that no one even looks at."

"Fliers are the social media of a different generation," Jo said.

"Right after it aired, a lot of people texted me and told me how good I did. I wasn't nervous at all." She gathered her hair and smoothed it over her shoulder. "But now I'm dealing with all the stupid questions people think they can ask me."

"Like what?"

"Oh, you know, shit like did Lena run away because of something I did? Or do I worry that whoever took my sister is going to come back for me? The zit-faced kid down the street asked if I thought Lena was being sexually abused. Like that was something I even wanted to think about."

"People can be unintentionally cruel," Jo said. "But it's normal if you're worried that what happened to your sister could happen to you. People touched by catastrophe often imagine it happening to them as well."

"Courtney sent me a text asking if I thought Lena was dead. I mean, best friend or not, WTF kind of question is that? That's when it hit me, I was the last one in my family to spend time with my sister."

Jo let the minute spin out.

"The last thing she said to me was turn off the light." Marisa laughed half-heartedly. "Words to treasure."

"What did you say to her?"

"Good night." She sighed. "Equally lame."

"I checked out your Facebook page." And a lot more, but it was best to start small.

"I hardly do anything on Facebook anymore. Wrong demographics. My Threads channel is really taking off, though."

"Threads?" She'd missed that one.

"It's like Instagram, only for fashion. Great for influencers."

"Walk me through being an influencer."

"It's not difficult. You just have to find a niche to make your own. Most people assumed I'd want to go all cowboy chic, but that market's been cornered. Besides, Ralph Lauren is more for people like you."

"Old?"

"No, not old, but for people who want to wear clothes, not create an outfit. And yes, there is a difference—even in places like Echo Valley."

She grabbed the chains above her shoulders and tiptoed backward. "Platforms are important, too. Demographics, finding an audience, content strategy that builds a community." The swing moved forward, and Marisa stretched out her legs. "You have to promote yourself, but be modest—or at least act like it." As she swung back, she pushed off the ground to get more momentum. "You have to put yourself out there. Be vulnerable. Authentic. A lot of influencers run everything through filters. I take photos and post them right away. People care about me, but only because I provide value. I give them a dream in real time that they can be just like me."

"What's your endgame?"

"What do you mean?" She straightened her arms and leaned back. Rose higher.

"Is it just to get vendors to send you stuff?"

Her hair fluttered around her face as she swung back. "That's definitely nice. Most of the stuff I get isn't something you'd ever find in the valley even if I wanted to—and could afford it. But no. That's not it."

Jo saw Lena in Marisa's moves. Leaning back and slicing the air. Then falling backward, knees bent, toes pointed. A pendulum constantly swinging between childhood simplicity and the complications of adulthood.

"So why do you do it?"

"Did you know they're going to replace the swings?" Marisa asked. "Monkey bars too. They say they're too dangerous." She let go with one hand and pointed to a cluster of four spring animals. "That duck was always Lena's favorite."

Even at a distance, the playground animals were a sorry lot. Dull colors, the paint on their saddles worn away. They stared at each other with vacant eyes from atop industrial springs bolted onto crabgrass-covered slabs.

"I never saw anyone ride the duck but Lena." She dragged her feet on the backswing to slow herself down. "Finally, one day I asked her why she never picked the horse or the elephant. Heck, even the stupid cow was more popular." She dragged her feet again and stopped. "She said because it was ugly."

Marisa stared at her shadow until a passing cloud blocked the sun. "Every time I walk past this park, I expect to see her. Last night I dreamed of her." Her eyebrows drew together. "Is that crazy?"

"No."

"In my dream I couldn't stop looking into her eyes. They're not pretty. Just brown. But there's always been something about them." Marisa stared at Jo. "When she listens to you, it's like she really cares. In the dream, it was like she was trying to tell me something, only I couldn't figure out what."

"Maybe you weren't meant to."

"I wish I'd been nicer to her."

The statement put Jo on alert. "What do you mean?"

Marisa slid off the swing and headed toward the spring animals as if she could walk away from the question. Jo followed.

They reached the quartet of animals before Marisa began speaking again. "Saturday night at the fair? I wasn't with Lena the whole time like I told your partner." She wrapped her arms around herself. "I went down to the river with . . . well, it doesn't matter who. But when I came back, there was a guy. A carny. He was bothering Lena. I lost my shit."

"What was the carnival guy doing?"

"Bothering her. It was like he had her trapped in the stall next to her cow. She'd move one way and he'd move as if to block her. She asked him to leave."

"Did he?"

"No." Marisa chose the horse and sat sideways on it. "He called Lena pretty. I don't remember the exact words. He likes them quiet or something. She started to cry." Marisa hung her head and tears dropped onto her skirt, darkening the blush-colored fabric. "She was so scared she wet her pants. Something inside of me broke." She raised her chin. "I grabbed a pitchfork."

A fierceness entered her eyes that dared Jo to tell her she'd done the wrong thing. To blame her for leaving her sister alone. It was a fuck you to all the adults who were going to line up to whisper this never would have happened to Lena if only . . .

"I thought he was going to hurt Lena. I grabbed her. Pulled her behind me. I wanted to stick the pitchfork right through his goddamn chest." She tucked her chin against her shoulder, refusing to make eye contact. "Are you going to have to arrest me?"

"For saving your sister? No."

Marisa closed her eyes and released her breath.

The news kicked Jo's legs out from under her and she sat on the elephant, as if by tacit agreement the duck was reserved. She wanted to tell Marisa that everything would be all right, but Jo wasn't sure it would be. Not in light of this. "What did the guy do when you faced off on him?"

"Just kind of held up his hands and backed away. Then he walked out of the pavilion."

"And what did you and Lena do?"

Her head flew up. "What do you think we did? We got the hell out of there and went home."

"Did you get any sense you were followed?"

"Lena kept stopping and turning around. Jumping at any little noise. I was so pissed and scared, I didn't hear anything. We stopped on the footbridge. I didn't see anyone on the path behind us."

Jo steadied her voice to bury any trace of accusation. "You gave Detective MacAllister a different statement on the phone on Saturday."

She remained quiet so long Jo thought she'd have to ask the question again more bluntly.

"We were driving home from shopping when I got the message. I didn't want to say anything in front of all my friends." Her chin quivered. "I never heard the carny following us. Lena's gone because of me. If I had stayed with her Saturday night, he wouldn't have caught her alone. Become obsessed with her. None of this would have happened."

"You can't blame yourself for someone else's actions."

Her chin dimpled right before she burst into tears. It was the long, sad release of a child. Jo sat quietly, wishing she had one of Squint's handkerchiefs.

"The other stuff's true." Marisa's breath stuttered and more tears cascaded down her cheeks. "I'm not a liar." She swiped her fingers under her eyes and dragged away mascara. "She and Dad have been arguing a ton lately."

Jo lowered the pitch of her voice. "I know it's difficult to talk about your father, but it's important I know what kind of problems they've been having. If they're bad enough your sister might have considered running away."

Marisa shrugged. "She wanted to move back home."

"Home." That didn't compute. Not for a country girl like Lena. Jo's mind jumped. There were plenty of reasons why children wanted to put distance between themselves and their parents. Spats and slights. Growing pains. Other reasons were more sinister. "Why did Lena want to move back in with you and your mom?"

Marisa raised her eyes. Only now, shadowed, the gray darkened. Two black holes that swallowed light and time. "It doesn't matter. Dad wouldn't allow it. The last time they argued was right before she stayed the weekend. She had a big red mark on her arm where he'd grabbed her."

"Did your father ever hurt you?"

Marisa gave that same half-laugh. "We were never that close."

31

Jo eyed the impressive array of vintage Underwoods and Coronas. Who knew the lion's den was full of typewriters?

"Detective Wyatt?" Everett Cloud buffed his glasses as if he couldn't believe she was standing in the foyer of the *Valley Courier* building. She could hardly believe it either.

"In the flesh," Jo replied.

"To what do we owe this unexpected pleasure?"

"I need a favor."

Cloud laughed, one of those barroom booms that exploded from people after they've had one drink too many. It was the loudest noise she'd ever heard him make. And it was infectious.

"Yeah," she said, smiling. "I can see the irony in that statement."

The paper was founded in 1901 and still occupied the original building. Outside, a sign that mimicked their masthead floated above a wood awning that shaded the sidewalk. The dark wood planks gave it the air of an Old West saloon. Or a brothel.

"Come on back to my desk."

A decorative wooden railing, the kind often found in courtrooms, separated the display of typewriters in the foyer from the inner sanctum of the paper. He held open the hip-high gate for her and escorted her through the newsroom—a short trip of about twenty paces.

The space was unexpectedly welcoming. Oak plank floors, cranberry-colored walls, a quad of sage cubicles in the center of the room. Two additional desks faced the rear wall, one holding a fax and copy machine, the other a commercial coffee pot.

He closed an open file and then swept a stack of papers off the wooden chair next to his desk. "Sorry, research for a story." The paper-strewn desk had little room, and he finally put the papers on the floor next to his own chair. "Please." He remained standing until she sat, and then pulled out his marginally more modern office chair so it faced her. "What can I do for you today?"

"I'm here to inquire about one of your employees."

"If it's an HR inquiry, you'll need to talk to Julie, but she's not here right now."

"How about someone in circulation?"

"That would be Julie, as well." He leaned back in his chair and crossed his hands in front of him. "Or you could talk to the editor."

"That would be great," she said.

"Except he's out with Julie. Late lunch."

"You're enjoying this, aren't you?"

"I'm sorry," he said, solemnly. "I am."

She rethought her approach. "Are the delivery guys employees of the paper, or do you outsource that?"

"We're not big enough to need to outsource it. We have six people who deliver for us."

"Do you know Aaron Tingler?"

A faint bell tinkled near Jo's feet, and she found a young gray and white cat staring up at her.

"That's Cat," Everett said. "She's our current security system."

"Cat." She leaned over and drew it onto her lap. "Words are your stock in trade and 'Cat' is the best you can do?"

"I'm waiting for someone to claim it. I found it the other day huddled under the dumpster in the alley."

Jo flipped the kitten onto her back and its legs curled. "Her. You've got yourself a little cutie." She rubbed Cat's belly. "Was she wearing the collar?"

"No, I got that for her," he said. "Self-preservation. She kept trying to climb my pants. At least now, I get a warning before she launches her attack."

"You big brute." Jo found a spot behind the kitten's ear. Cat made a production of gnawing on the side of Jo's hand before closing her eyes. "Don't worry, little one. Someone's going to come back for you."

"If not, I believe I'll be giving you a call."

"I wish." Cat's purrs rumbled against Jo's fingertips. When Jo had her own house, maybe she'd have a cat. As much as she'd love a dog, cats were more self-sufficient, less impacted by the occasional all-nighter and long hours that went along with being a detective. She glanced up. Cloud watched her, an unreadable expression on his face. She focused on Cat again. "Not at the moment, though."

"I heard you ran into one of our drivers the other morning." Everett leaned his elbow against his desk and drummed his fingers. "You left quite an impression on him."

Was the admission he knew Tingler his way of extending an olive branch? "Impressions come in two flavors, and I'm fairly certain the one I left wasn't a good one," she said.

"It left me wondering what you were doing." He drummed his fingers again. "Why you pulled him over."

Her eyebrows shot up. "Mr. Tingler left that part out?"

"Oh no. He recited a litany of infractions. But I'm not sure any of those reasons were the real reason you chose to have a conversation with him," Everett said.

"They were not."

"And here you are asking questions about him."

"I am."

"And what a coincidence that you were both in the same neighborhood the morning after Lena Flores disappeared from her mother's home. Curiouser and curiouser." There was a similarity between Cloud's voice and her partner's. Both were deep and rich. Soothing. The kind of voice that encouraged confidences. "I don't very often have a chance to talk with you, at least not where we actually converse." Mesmerizing, even. "May I ask you a question?"

The air conditioner wound up like a jet engine and the spell was broken.

"If it's about the investigation, I can't an—"

He waved away her objection. "Why did you become a police officer?"

It was a question she fielded every time she made a community presentation. Coming from a reporter, however, it made her wary. "Is this background for another story?"

"I heard you were offered a promotion, but no. I'll only cover that story if you choose to take the position."

Jesus, Mary, and Joseph. Did everyone in this town know? "The answer's complicated."

"Is it?" He seemed genuinely surprised.

"Some days it is."

"I don't mean why do you continue to serve, but what was it that made you realize you wanted to be an officer?"

Cat stretched, turned a circle, and went right back to sleep in Jo's lap. "The short answer is that I don't like bullies."

"And the longer answer?"

An image of Lucero came to her mind—not of who he was now, but of the boy she'd first met on the playground who'd spoken broken English. Then three Pratchett brothers surrounded him and shoved him back and forth between them. Called him ugly names. She'd slugged the closest brother. Crank. The biggest of the bunch who'd had the longest to ferment into the meanest. Lucero and Jo both had their asses handed to them, but in the aftermath they'd became friends. Not so much with the Pratchetts.

"The longer answer is something I save for second dates," she said.

"I can offer you coffee."

"You could but I'm sure you have a deadline, and I've still got a little girl I need to find. I'll call later to talk to Julie."

"Truth and facts are different," he said. "I got tired of people citing one fact and thinking it represents a broader truth. That's why I became a reporter. To do my best to uncover the truth. Celebrate victories. Hold people accountable when appropriate. In many ways it's a lot like police work. It's all about asking the right questions."

"Sometimes you don't know the right questions until you ask several that don't give you what you need." She stroked Cat. Reconsidered waiting for Julie. "What can you tell me about Aaron Tingler?"

"He doesn't work for us anymore."

"Is that a fact?" Jo said. "I tried to contact him at the address I have for him, but he no longer lives there."

"I run stadiums on my lunch hour a few times a week. He does the same from time to time. I'll tell him hello if I see him."

"No need. I'd rather stop by myself. Reconnect." It was too late today. Hopefully, he'd be there tomorrow. "I have some questions I want to ask him that I didn't get to broach during the traffic stop."

Picking up a sleeping kitten was like trying to wrangle Jell-O, but she finally succeeded and placed her on the floor. Cat drunk-stumbled over to Cloud's leg and reared up to climb it.

"Oh, no you don't, you little trickster." He picked the cat up and in a flash she was walking across his keyboard, her elevated status erasing all vestiges of sleep.

Maybe Cloud was more like her partner than she thought. She found herself wanting to confess. "People expect me to say I became a cop because my father was. The fact is my father was a cop. The truth is I wanted to impress him. It's a fact I dislike bullies. The truth is it took standing up to one to make me understand that I could make a difference in someone's life. A positive difference. That maybe I could right some of life's wrongs. Prevent others from happening. Find the truth behind facts that don't seem to make sense." She gave Cat one more tickle under the chin. "And now that I've made a fool of myself in front of a reporter, I'm going to go save the world. Or at least try."

He scooped up Cat and, in the process, shifted the folder, revealing his reporter notebook. Jo read two names.

Lucero Flores.

Sienna Castaneda.

Cloud replaced the folder. "By the way, my cousin said to tell you hello the next time I saw you."

"Do I know your cousin?"

"You left a good impression on her the other night at the casino."

32

The Romanos had lived on the block longer than anyone else in the neighborhood—even the Wyatts, who'd moved there before Jo had been born. Every time Jo walked past their house she smelled some combination of roasted garlic, tomato, and bread that left her hungry. It seemed like ages since she'd cooked a meal to share with her father. Occasionally he grilled up a burger or dog for her, but that was about the extent of his culinary expertise.

She'd dressed for a run, but the past several days had been a series of long hours and little sleep. About a mile in, she bonked. What she'd intended to be a four-mile run morphed into a two-mile walk that wound through the older part of town. It wasn't all bad. What she lost in distance, she gained in perspective.

Most of the homes had seen better days, but a sagging fence often surrounded a tended garden, and the occupants more often than not were the type to clear the snow from their neighbor's sidewalk in winter. It wasn't the near-new construction she and Cameron had lived in, but she'd grown up here. It was home.

She rounded the final corner. A big blue truck blocked the front of her father's new mailbox. Even without being able to see the logo on the side, she knew it was Lucero's.

In the shade of a large chestnut, she stopped and studied him. He sat on the porch swing, nearly hitting the porch railing with each rock. Even as a kid, he'd been an aggressive rocker, testing the worthiness of the eyebolts securing the chains. But he'd only chosen the swing when he was chewing on a problem, trying to make a decision. Otherwise Lucero would sprawl across the wicker loveseat on the other side of the patio, arms draped across the back, feet solidly on the ground.

Sweat prickled her scalp. Her father hadn't been home when she'd left, and she didn't have her cell phone with her if things went sideways. And recently, that's the only direction they'd gone when she and Lucero were together.

He abruptly stopped and hunched over, his forearms resting on his thighs, hands clasped. Jo watched until he crossed himself and sat up. She got to within two houses of her home before he noticed her and stood.

Jo stopped on the walkway. More escape routes than a railed porch if his intentions were less than friendly. It had taken a couple of years for Lucero to bulk up as a kid, but she remembered what the elder Pratchett brother's face looked like after Lucero called him out in high school.

"What are you doing here?" she asked.

"Your car was in the drive." Lucero held out his hands palms up, as if in supplication. "Can we talk? Please, it's important."

His shirt was untucked. No telltale bulge of a gun around his waistband, but it was impossible to tell if he'd stashed a weapon in his boots.

"I'm going to check if you're armed. Interlace your fingers behind your head."

He raised his hands in the air. "We were friends once, Jo."

"Turn around." She'd expected an argument. A compliant Lucero only increased her concern, especially considering the number of guns registered to him. She patted him down and stepped back, creating space between them.

"Can we go inside?" he asked.

"Out here's just fine."

"Please have a seat." He pointed to the porch swing where a manila envelope lay.

Even when he needed help, he had to be in control. The bossiness he'd displayed as a child had intensified as he aged. "This is my home, Lucero. Why are you here?" She remained standing.

He lowered himself onto the swing. “I got a notification from the phone company that my telephone records were subpoenaed by the Echo Valley Police Department. I assume that was you.”

So much for flying under the radar with the cellular search warrant.

“I thought I’d save you the trouble.” He extended the envelope.

Its flatness didn’t allay her wariness. “What’s this?”

“My phone statements for the last six months.”

This from the man who’d spit at her feet for asking where he’d been on Saturday? “Why the change of heart?”

“I highlighted the number you’re looking for.”

“How do you know what number I’m looking for?”

“You want my secrets? It’s all right there.”

Jo pinched open the brad of the envelope and peered inside. No powder. Slowly, she drew out the most recent statement. The page was slash after slash of yellow, but unlike Tilda, he hadn’t annotated his statement with names.

“I’m pretty sure I already know them,” Jo said.

A bit of his bravado from the other day surfaced. “I doubt that.”

The number on the page was the same one she’d found on Tilda’s statements after cross-referencing the name she’d read on Everett Cloud’s notebook. Here was her chance to confirm it. “Sienna Castaneda.”

His eyes widened, but he recovered quickly. “Yes. Sienna.”

“Were you with her Saturday night?”

“I was. All night.”

“Define all night.”

He pointed to the pages in her hand. “You can check the call record. The last one you see on Saturday was when I was on my way to her place. I stayed until about seven thirty, eight o’clock Sunday morning.”

“Why would you keep this secret? You had to know how it made you look.”

“I was trying to avoid a scandal.”

“By having an affair with your ex-wife’s best friend who just happens to be the wife of the representative from Colorado’s Third Congressional District? Or by covering it up? Because I’m confused.”

“I was trying to do the right thing.”

“The right thing?” She smacked the pages against her thigh. “Your daughter is missing!”

"I thought she'd run away."

"And why did you think that?" She narrowed her eyes. "What did you do?"

He hunched over again. "She asked me what I thought about her moving back with her mother." His head dropped. "I said no."

Marisa was right. Lena had wanted to move back.

"Don't make me pull this out of you, Lucero. What's going on?"

"Marisa's got this strange idea that she can just land in Los Angeles and become an overnight celebrity, or whatever it is that she does. She'd asked her mom, but Tilda wouldn't even consider the idea unless Lena moved with them. But once Marisa gets an idea in her head, she gnaws at it like a dog with a bone. Instead of working on her mother, for the past year she's been trying to convince Lena to move back."

"How did Lena react when you told her you wanted her to stay with you?"

"I thought she was relieved. I thought she considered this her home. With me. Then I thought maybe she was jealous of Sienna." He looked up again and there were tears in his eyes. "I've been gone a lot. I thought maybe she took matters into her own hands."

"And exactly where do you suppose she went, Lucero? It's not like she was going to scout out LA before they could all meet up in California."

"She didn't run away, Jo. I found her backpack in my barn. It wasn't there when your partner came by and searched."

Fatigue coursed through her arms. He was lying to her again. "Witnesses saw you with her backpack."

"I'm assuming you mean Clyde Dawson. I can't fault him for saying that, but I was carrying my own pack. Lena liked mine so much I got her one of her own. She carries it with her everywhere. That's why I'm here now."

"Why were you at Columbine Lake Sunday morning?"

"Sienna's husband was out of town for the weekend. I spent Saturday night at her house. Her property backs up against the woods above Butch's Fishcamp. I hiked to the house the night before so my truck wasn't sitting in her drive. Sunday morning, I hiked home. I don't carry my bag as much as Lena does hers, but I had my stuff in it when I went to Sienna's." The chains groaned when he started rocking again. "I'm telling you the truth, Jo."

"Do you know what that is?" She paced. Now would be a good time to run. Her body buzzed with all the energy she'd lacked earlier. "Think very hard before you answer this next question. What happened that summer? Between you and Tilda?"

He paused on his heel and then gently shifted his weight back to his toe and brought the swing to a stop. "That was a long time ago, Jo. Does it even matter anymore?"

"Depends on how much you want me to believe you."

A boy around Lena's age rode by on a bicycle and Lucero watched him until the boy was out of sight. "I hit Tilda. Threw her to the ground. Just like she told you."

"Why did she recant?"

He looked directly at Jo. "Because I told her to."

"All these years you let me believe I was at fault for turning you in. For you losing your scholarship." She shook the pages in his face. "You're a bastard, Lucero Flores."

"I was young."

"You weren't young when I told you your daughter was missing. You acted like a dick then too." She took a breath. Snapped back into cop mode. "Lena's backpack. Did you move it?"

"I flipped the flap open, but otherwise, no. It's in the same spot. Inside the doors, where the shelves are."

"Where your barn cat likes to hang out?"

"Yeah."

Already her mind was racing with things to do. Notify Pieretti, detain Lucero until they could process the barn—consent or not, they'd want a search warrant, expand the search parameters, collect the bag, lock down his truck. "When did you notice the backpack?"

"When I got home. Four thirty. I called the station and was told you weren't in. I took the chance you were here."

"When was the last time you were in the barn before you saw the pack?"

"This morning. I loaded up the truck and headed out around seven. Every Wednesday, I meet with the guys at Hank's for breakfast, then I started my rounds."

"Who knows you go to Hank's on Wednesdays?" she asked.

"Everyone. We've been meeting for a couple of years now."

"Any idea who left the backpack?"

The chains groaned again. "Not a clue," he said.

"Why not try to hide this too?" Jo asked.

The tempo of the rocking increased.

"Lena's backpack has blood on it."

33

"And you believe him?" Pieretti asked.

The sergeant, Squint, and Jo huddled around the computer monitor in the armory and watched in real time while Lucero paced in the small conference room.

Jo sidestepped the question. "We need to ask the DA to include Lucero's truck in the search warrant. Make sure he didn't transport the backpack from lord knows where and this whole thing is a setup."

But in her heart she did believe Lucero. She just refused to let what she believed blind her to what might actually be. Not again, anyway. If she was right, the next several hours would cost the city three detectives worth of overtime but provide exculpatory evidence to support Lucero's innocence. If she was wrong and they found traces of blood in his truck, well, all bets were off.

"Where's the truck now?" Squint asked.

They eyed the monitor again. Lucero sat down at the table and cradled his head in his hands. Was he acting for the camera or had the reality of the situation finally sunk in?

"In front of my dad's place," Jo answered. "He's keeping an eye on it until we can process it."

Pieretti turned his back to the monitor and addressed the two detectives. "Okay, I'll babysit Mr. Flores. Squint, I'll need you to write up the warrant." He glanced at his watch. "Contact the on-call deputy DA. See if we can make a run at more than just the barn and truck. It'd be nice to get out there before it's completely dark."

Squint retrieved his notebook from the computer stand. "I'll see if there's a deputy who can lock down the scene until I can get the paperwork in order."

"Good." Pieretti addressed Jo. "Find out what Mrs. Castaneda has to say about Saturday night."

"And if the congressman is at home?"

Pieretti pushed his glasses up his nose. "That is Mrs. Castaneda's problem, not ours."

Jo headed upstairs to grab her gear and verify Sienna's address. A new stack of messages sat next to her phone. Jo sifted through the slips of paper. Most were tip line messages, but one from Olivia Walsenberg caught Jo's eye. She had a warm spot for the teen. Daughter of the prior district attorney, her life had been upended last winter when tragedy had struck her family in a case Jo had investigated.

Jo placed it on top of the pile to follow up on tomorrow. She'd swapped her running gear for slacks and a blouse and now grabbed her spare blazer from the coatrack. At least she'd look respectable before asking the congressman's wife if she was sleeping with another man.

* * *

The log cabin belonging to the Castanedas was rustic only in the sense that it was, indeed, located in the country. Otherwise, the postcard-perfect, multistoried, lodgepole pine house had more in common with the luxury homes profiled in *Architectural Digest* and less with the abode of Abe Lincoln.

The house sat back from the road. In addition to the split rail fence that outlined the property, a second fence surrounded the residence. Low and decorative, it framed sodded green lawns and exuberant flower gardens too lush for the arid Southwest.

Jo parked by the ornate entry gate and crested a small footbridge that spanned a river rock stream bed.

Sienna tipped a galvanized watering can over a rose bush. "I was wondering when you'd get here." She doused another plant. "Do you know anything about roses?"

Everything Jo knew about flowers came from her mother. She'd nurtured a bed of hybrid tea roses with names such as "Peace" and "Silver Jubilee" along the east side of their house. "Enough to know it's better to water them in the morning." She pointed to a leaf that looked as if it had been dusted with gray talc. "It helps cut down on powdery mildew."

"I've heard that." Sienna continued sprinkling the blooms. "Bernard's a romantic. Loves to come out here and gather a bunch each week to give me. Cuts them himself. But I don't suppose you want to talk about roses."

"I need to ask you some questions regarding your relationship with Lucero Flores."

"My relationship." Sienna put down the watering can and wiped her hands against her shorts. "You already know our life histories."

Which wasn't exactly true. Sienna had been in Lucero's class, and all three of them had grown up in the same neighborhood. She'd been a quiet child, watchful. When Jo wasn't running wild with Aiden, she often found Sienna and Lucero together. Always at his home. Never once did Sienna invite them to hers. Jo complained about it to her mother, and then had to listen to a lecture on how some houses weren't really homes—which made absolutely zero sense at the time.

"It's been a long time since we've caught up," Jo said. "Is there somewhere we can sit down?"

"Not the short version, then." Sienna tucked a highlighted curl behind her ear. "It's cooled down a bit. How about the gazebo? That way, we won't disturb Bernard." Without waiting for an answer, she strolled along the flagstone path that led away from the house and the husband inside.

The gazebo was bigger than Jo's bedroom and was topped by a two-tier shingled roof with a weathervane. Decorated with cane outdoor furniture and tall hurricane lamps, it had the curated look of a space rarely used. Jo waited until Sienna chose the loveseat, and then Jo removed her jacket and settled into a thick-cushioned chair. Cooler or not, the mercury was still unseasonably high.

"When's the last time you talked to Lucero?" Jo asked.

"Based on how quick you got here, I'd say not too long before you did."

"And where were you?" Jo opened her notebook.

"Here. He called. Needed some advice."

"About?"

"Is this really necessary, Jo?"

She lowered her pen. "I'm sure you're aware his daughter is missing."

"I'm betting every person in this entire valley is aware of that," Sienna answered.

"Then you know my questions are important."

By the time they'd reached their teens, Sienna had developed a way of reading the room that sharpened with each birthday she celebrated. If someone laughed, she'd join in; if someone mentioned they liked a particular country song, she'd say it was her favorite. The only thing she had a definite opinion about was alcohol. She never drank—at least not then.

Sienna splayed her manicured hand across her upper chest, momentarily hiding the solitaire diamond that hung from a delicate chain around her neck. "Lucero and I are friends."

"Then I'm sure you want to provide any help you can so we can learn what happened to Lena," Jo said. "What did the two of you talk about today?"

"Him going to the police. Someone planted something of Lena's in his barn."

The word *planted* used in this context would make any investigator's spidey-sense tingle. It ranked right up there with *That's not mine*, *I don't have my ID on me*, and *I've only had two beers*. It might be the gospel truth, but it deserved further investigation.

Sienna leaned forward and rotated the small potted flower on the table in front of her. "He wanted my permission. Or blessing, or something."

"Why would he need that?"

She attacked the ornate tray next. Straightening items already perfectly posed. "Bernard doesn't know much about our friendship."

"What am I going to learn when I read the texts you sent each other?" Jo asked.

"More than Bernard knows." Sienna slumped back against the cushions. "Lucero's a gentleman. He doesn't want to make any trouble for me."

"How long have you and Lucero been in an intimate relationship?"

"Jesus, Jo." She raked her hand through her hair. "Not that it's any of your business, but we've been seeing each other about a year."

That's where she was wrong. It was Jo's concern. A lover's statement was far more likely to contain half-truths and omissions than a witness with nothing at stake. "Walk me through this past week."

Hands so animated a moment ago now fluttered weakly. "I got a call on Friday that Bernard needed to stay longer in Washington. I invited Lucero for dinner Saturday night, but he was supposed to stay over at the fairgrounds with Lena. He didn't want to change his plans."

Sienna picked at the hem of her shorts. "I kept after him until he changed his mind. Bernard . . . he's usually home on the weekends, which is when Lena goes to her mom's. This was an opportunity for us to spend some time together and I didn't want to waste it," she said. "No one could have possibly known what was going to happen to Lena," she added, quieter.

"What time did he come over Saturday?"

"Late afternoon some time," Sienna said. "We usually text, but he was driving, so he called. We talked until he got to the parking lot at Columbine Lake. Bernard's a congressman. Lucero's truck is pretty distinctive. I couldn't risk anyone seeing it, and there isn't even enough room in the garage for my car so that we could swap places. He hiked up from the lake."

"How long did he stay?"

Her features sharpened. "I made him breakfast, if that's what you're asking."

"I'm not trying to make this difficult for you, Sienna, and I'm not passing judgment. I was asking about the time."

"Just doing your job, right? Poking into other people's business. Why not come right out and ask if we screwed."

A hummingbird swooped through the gazebo arch, pirouetted around the potted plants, and zipped out.

Sienna swiped at her eyes, seemingly oblivious to the motion. "You'll be happy to know it's over."

Her rancor was startling. "Why would you think I'd be happy about that?"

"Come off of it, Jo. You always had to be at the center of every guy's attention. Aiden, Lucero. They never looked at anyone else when you were around. Well, Lucero's single. Now's your chance."

"Lucero and I were childhood friends, nothing more." Aiden's friendship; that was more. "When did you break up?"

"This afternoon. Lucero thought it best. Gentleman, remember?" Sienna pulled a wadded tissue from her pocket. "Just as well. Tilda's my best friend."

Jo circled back to her earlier question. "What time did Lucero leave the house Sunday morning?"

"Seven? It was going to take him about an hour to hike back to his truck. Even that early, I didn't want to risk driving him and outing ourselves."

"Was he with you throughout the night?" Jo asked.

"Yes."

"And are you a heavy sleeper?"

"If you're asking if Lucero left during the night the answer is no. His truck was too far away."

The glass sliding door at the back of the house opened. Congressman Castaneda stepped onto the patio and called across the lawn. "Can I get you two ladies anything to drink?"

Sienna deferred to Jo. "I could use a glass of chardonnay. You?"

"I'm on duty, but don't let me stop you."

Disappointment flitted across Sienna's face before she called back, "No thanks, Bunny. We're just gabbing."

Jo made a production of checking her notes. "Remind me again why Lucero parked by the lake?"

"I told you. We did everything we could to make sure Bernie wouldn't find out about Lucero." Sienna's bravado dissolved. "I guess that's too much to ask for now."

Jo closed her notebook. "You are Lucero's alibi. At some point that news will come out. Whether your husband learns about it from you or the media is ultimately your decision." Jo stood and handed Sienna a business card. "Thank you for your time this evening. I'll need you to set aside some time to come in to the station for a formal interview."

"Of course." Sienna pocketed the card. "I heard you and Cameron split. I'm sorry. Truly." She hesitated before adding, "Does it get easier?"

There was something behind Sienna's eyes that reminded Jo of a child looking for reassurance after their world had been turned topsy-turvy. The home, the clothes, the luxury car. None of it mattered if one's heart was breaking.

Jo gentled her response. "I don't know that easy is the word I'd use, but the pain fades."

"Bernard brings me a bouquet every week from the garden his first wife planted." Sienna played with her wedding ring. "Lucero knows I hate roses."

34

Jo slept a solid seven hours and awoke with renewed optimism that the clues from the previous day's developments would bring her closer to finding Lena.

That feeling was reinforced when, for the first time since standing up the command post, the morning briefing felt productive rather than perfunctory. Plus, the bagel shop had her favorite garden-veggie schmear, she was fully caffeinated, and eager to attack her lengthy to-do list with an eye to mining new possibilities.

All before zero eight hundred.

"Bagels are just as bad for you as donuts." Pieretti plunked down in the chair next to Squint's desk.

"Only when you order extra cream cheese." Jo dug into the bag and handed him a paper-wrapped cinnamon-sugar bagel. "Still eating for two, I see."

She reached around Pieretti and placed Squint's next to his phone. "Plain bagel. Plain cream cheese. Jalapeños on the side."

He stopped typing. "Thank you, ma'am."

Armed with a fresh cup of coffee, Jo sat at her desk, unwrapped her bagel, and studied her list. Most of the tasks were administrative. She had to type up Lucero's statement. The interview with Sienna. Phone Olivia and follow up on the tip line calls. At lunch, she'd head up to the college. Track down Tingler, ask if he noticed anything suspicious Sunday morning, and then politely suggest he leave Marisa alone. This afternoon, she'd review the evidence Squint had collected last night, familiarize herself with the photos. Regroup.

She kicked the backside of Squint's desk. "Hey, did anything come back yet on that guy's bear cam?"

"It caught three vehicles roughly a half hour after the fair closed. But the headlights washed out the actual image. There were two more light flashes during the night. The last light bobbed a bit, so I'm assuming that was the stop and start of the paper deliverer."

"Well, that's disappointing." She sipped her coffee while her computer booted up.

"The bear visited around zero three if that helps."

Young Sarah came into the office holding a report. "Your carnival guy is quite the gentleman." She handed the pages to Squint and headed back for the door. "Let me know if you need anything else."

Squint leafed through the printout. "Our carny is Mr. Brock Donaldson, also known as Donald Brock, Daniel Brock, Donald Brack, Dennis Donaldson, Brock Dennison, and Chuck Lansing. It appears as if he's worn out his welcome in several states—most recently, Colorado."

Pieretti ate his bagel like a sandwich, and cream cheese squished out from between the two halves when he took a bite. "History?" he asked.

"Drug problems. Some weapons charges. Stole a car in Arizona." He handed the page he'd just read across the desks to Jo.

She scanned the face page. "Holy cow, the man has a lot of tats. The typical snakes, skulls, and naked women nonsense, plus a Thor's Hammer, a couple of iron crosses, and some runes." She slapped the page onto her desk. "And before you wonder if he's merely a neo-pagan, the SS bolts tattoo takes that off the table."

"Any sex crimes?" The sergeant rewrapped the remaining half of his bagel.

"No," Squint answered. "Although he does have a couple of domestics."

"Domestics." Jo rocked back in her chair. "It would be interesting to find out if the victim had children around Lena's age."

Squint ripped the top square off the cube of paper by his phone. "I'll follow up with the arresting agency," he said, making a note.

Pieretti wiped his mouth. "What's the consensus on the carny versus Lucero matchup?"

Jo slid the bagel off her portfolio and opened it to the notes she'd taken during her interview with Sienna. "Between the surveillance footage showing the carny enter and leave the pavilion and Marisa's statement about finding him pestering Lena, it's a safe bet that Donaldson did in fact contact Lena. If Sienna and Lucero are to be believed, he wasn't anywhere but in Mrs. Castaneda's bed."

"If?" Pieretti let the question hang.

"Lucero's truck is a higher profile vehicle than my PD car, but from where I parked I couldn't see the road. So the concern about Lucero parking on the property baffles me a bit."

"Overabundance of caution?" Squint asked. "I doubt either Tilda or the congressman are going to be too pleased once the news gets out."

"And it could be as simple as that," Jo acknowledged. "It was definitely a different Lucero who came to talk to me yesterday. If I had to base it solely on that, I'd hazard he was telling me the truth. That you didn't find any trace evidence in his truck bolsters that. I'd be leaning toward the carny."

Pieretti removed his eyeglasses and used his dirty napkin to clean the lenses. He smeared cream cheese all over them before he noticed and grabbed a fresh napkin. "If that's the case, who left the backpack in Lucero's barn?"

A question Jo had asked herself repeatedly since Lucero first dropped the bombshell that it had appeared. "I'll defer to my esteemed partner to explain that." She batted her eyelashes with dramatic abandon. "Squint?"

"I'm still chewing on that myself. I think we'll learn the who only after we figure out why it suddenly cropped up."

"Do we know for certain it's hers?" Jo asked.

"It had a dictionary inside. I haven't run the photo past Tilda yet, but she'd mentioned Lena didn't go anywhere without it."

Pieretti's desk phone rang. He jammed the glasses back on his face and hopped up to answer it.

Jo opened up the records program on her computer. "Do you know where the carny is now, or did finding Donaldson just move to the top of our to-do list?"

"The road manager identified him for me, but the minute I started asking about Donaldson's whereabouts, the manager developed amnesia. Directed me to contact HR." Squint separated his bagel and tamped jalapeño slices into the cream cheese. "I put in a call yesterday but haven't heard back. I'll call them again shortly."

"If you have evidence that still needs processing, I can flesh out the background," Jo offered.

"Much appreciated. We might need to plan a road trip. The carnival's currently in Pueblo through Sunday."

"Say the word."

Pieretti stepped out of his office with his hands thrust deep in his pockets, his lips a tight line. Jo's stomach knotted.

Before he'd been promoted to sergeant, Jo had become friends with Pieretti in the quiet intimacy that only graveyard officers experienced. The darkness encouraged officers to share bits of their souls. In some ways, officers knew each other better than the spouses they went home to. It forged a bond that allowed officers to face danger together. To fight harder for each other than even for themselves. A fissure opened in Jo's chest. She knew Kip Pieretti—and the draw of his face warned her of the news to come.

"Where did they find her?" she asked.

"In a cave off the Mercy Creek Trail," Pieretti replied.

All she could do was nod.

Squint rubbed his forehead. "Who called it in?"

"A couple of guys—teenage hikers—stumbled across the opening. Thought it was an abandoned mine and went inside." He cleared his throat. "Deputies are on their way out. The chief offered to assume the investigation since the missing case originated with us. The sheriff politely declined. We need to stay above the politics and tread lightly from here on out," Pieretti warned.

"I'll see who caught the case and respond." The fissure in Jo's chest widened as her eyes rested on her partner. "Tilda?"

"When you are absolutely certain. Call me." Sorrow creased his face. "She should hear it from me."

35

The road shimmered with heat as Jo passed the massive entry gate of Johansen's ranch and approached the junction with the upper fork of Mercy Creek. She slowed for the ninety-degree turn and started climbing. A short distance beyond the first culvert, pavement gave way to dirt. She slowed. A cloud of dust rose in her rearview mirror.

Below the road in a section dubbed the Playground, the terrain fell away in a patchwork of stone. It reminded Jo of a quilt, the rocks stitched together with white fir and Gambel oak that blanketed nearly a square mile.

Any other day, she'd park in one of the pullouts, grab her climbing gear and hike between rock walls that leaned so close and rose so high that they squeezed the path, hiding the sun that glared from the sky.

Reluctantly, she drew her eyes back to the road.

The chief had wanted Jo to contact the two teens prior to responding to the scene, so she'd detoured to the sheriff's office. She'd watched on a monitor while a sheriff's office investigator spoke to first one, then the other nineteen-year-old man in an interview room. It was the SO's case now. Jo's missing person had been found. A murder had occurred in the county's jurisdiction. One person, two linked cases, but the sheriff was going to take credit for finding the child.

All because her chief wanted to hog the spotlight and had failed to mention that the majority of resources he took credit for directing were only possible under the county sheriff's office auspices. There'd been a reason the sheriff didn't show at the press conference. He hadn't been invited.

Any investigator would agree. The jurisdictional squabbles on television had it backward. Cops didn't fight over who got to keep a case, they fought over who had to take it. At least until politics entered the equation and made the expense of a homicide investigation worth the hit to the budget.

Now Jo found herself caught in the middle of a pissing contest between department leaders. The rank and file would do what they always did, watch each other's back—even if they ribbed each other about working for the wrong agency. Investigators cooperated on cases all the time. Politics be damned. The sheriff's office would be privy to every bit of information she could provide. She was still working for Lena.

The scattered collection of Animas sheriff vehicles narrowed the roadway to a single lane, and Jo found a spot behind the mobile forensics van.

Deputy Harper's patrol car blocked the trailhead, and he'd strung yellow crime scene tape between two trees that flanked either side of the path.

Harper rolled down his window as she approached. "Hey, Jo." Cold clung to the metal clipboard he handed her. His car idled, the A/C running full tilt. "Acevado said to send you in when you got here. They may be still processing the trail, so stay in the grass along the left side as much as possible."

She logged in and returned the clipboard. "Thanks."

The trail climbed gently, paralleling the road until a gnarled juniper marked the junction where hikers faced a choice. The main path continued around the hillside and skirted one of Johansen's meadows and beyond that eventually linked with yet another trail system. The offshoot trail rose sharply in a series of switchbacks that rewarded hardy hikers with a breathtaking view of the Playground and Sycamore Reservoir at the bottom of the canyon.

Jo followed the offshoot. A mechanical growl from portable generators grew louder as she neared the cave. Evidence flags sprouted like flowers, drawing attention to shoe impressions, a discarded water bottle, items to be photographed, collected, or cast. Every step she took potentially contaminated the sheriff's crime scene. She kept as far off the path as possible.

The southwest was dotted with abandoned mines. Leftover dangers from a time when disillusioned Civil War soldiers had struck out in search of buried treasure. Profitable mines had names. The others, with their rotted infrastructures—or no buttresses at all—were often little more than caves, forgotten until, like today, drought-wizened foliage slipped enough to attract a curious eye.

Cleared of the vegetation that had hid its presence, the mouth of the cave gaped dark.

An unreasonable desire to turn away gripped her. As an investigator, she knew the physiological processes and predatory damage that accompanied death. Lena might be unrecognizable. She'd braced for this moment. But, confronted with its reality, she wanted nothing more than to put as much distance between her and this goddamn cave as she could.

At the entrance, Jo slipped surgical booties over her work boots. Donned gloves. Rock ringed the edges of the opening, forcing her to stoop as she entered the maw.

Still keeping left, she picked her way across rock and rubble. Klieg lights blazed throughout the cave but couldn't chase away the chill. Only a few yards in, the rubble lessened and the tunnel opened up. Jo straightened to her full height. The air carried a stale scent of decay—earth, vegetation, but something more.

This wasn't her crime scene, but she couldn't help but examine the sandy dirt beneath her feet. Evidence placards drew her attention to fresh boot impressions. Those heading deeper into the cave were partially obscured by the same heavy tread that marked the hikers' departure. And underneath it all were the telltale wavy lines of something being dragged to sweep away earlier tracks.

The voices of investigators bounced against stone, and their shadows danced. She came across their collection of tackle boxes, camera cases, evidence collection bags, vials, and tins stowed alongside a depression in the wall. The cave narrowed, and Jo stopped at the point the space flared into a final chamber. Only the sheriff's office investigators and the coroner would enter that area until they released the scene.

Jesse Acevado sketched an outline of the room on his pad. Beyond him, Beth Barnhill wielded her camera, capturing an overall image and then zooming closer and closer until it was time to move on. Jo steeled herself and lowered her eyes to the shell that was once a vibrant little girl. She was partially covered with a blanket as if merely sleeping.

Jo focused on the living again. "Hey, guys. Thanks for allowing me access."

Jesse lowered his pad. His bald head imparted a fierce air, but the façade masked an inordinate amount of compassion: he was a cross between a cage fighter and Gandhi. "You're always welcome."

"I know it goes without saying, but I'll say it anyway. You'll get every scrap of info I have."

"Never thought otherwise," he said. "The beef's between the bosses, not us."

Jo bobbed her head. "So what do you have?"

"Blunt force trauma to the side of her head," Beth said. "Far enough back that she was probably struck from behind. I haven't found spatter, so I'm guessing one strong blow. A bit of pooling behind her ear."

"The blanket?"

"Still tucked on one side. Someone took the time to roll her over. You can probably see from where you're standing that her hair was arranged neatly over one shoulder."

Jo's face grew hot with shame. Professional or not, she was glad this wasn't her crime scene. Glad she didn't have to replace the image she held of Lena wearing denim overalls and an inquisitive expression on her face.

Jesse jumped in. "It's possible she's been here since Sunday. It's cold enough in here, but I'm not seeing any of the typical markers that would suggest that time frame. It's going to be interesting to hear what Doc Ingersleben has to say."

"Have you called him out yet?" Jo asked.

"He's en route. You sticking around?"

"No. I wanted to see if I could get a probable ID." From the threshold, she was close enough to note the resemblances between her missing child and the child on the ground, but she still had to ask. "Do you think this is Galena Flores?"

"Afraid so," Beth said. "Or at least she's got the gap between her teeth like the BOLO listed, and what looks like a small scar on her forehead."

"Are you okay with us doing the notifications? Squint knows the mother. I know the father. Nothing is going to make it good news, but there might be some comfort hearing it from a friend. And I'd like to stay ahead of the media."

"I'd be grateful," Jesse said.

The walls of the cave closed in around Jo, and she longed to feel the sun on her face. "Who's lead, so I can make sure the info is passed along to the parents?"

"I am," Jesse answered.

"I'll work on getting the rest of the supplementals done so you can pull them up sometime tomorrow. When you have a chance to take a breath, we'll schedule a meeting to review the evidence we have. We've focused on two possible suspects, the father who initially gave us the runaround about where he was Saturday night, and a carnival worker with an extensive history. Dad gave up a witness yesterday and I spoke with her last night, but heads up, his alibi is being corroborated by Congressman Castaneda's wife."

"Well, isn't that ducky," Beth said.

"This is a hard case for me to give up. If I can help with anything, I'm just a phone call away. Day or night," Jo said.

"I'll keep you updated as soon as we know anything," Jesse said. "Promise."

"Thank you."

She retraced her steps. Each time she passed a light, the shadow moved, sometimes leading, other times following, for brief moments in perfect step.

The sun hit the mouth of the cave at an oblique angle, highlighting the crags in the ceiling and walls with color, while throwing the ridges and depressions in the dirt in stark gray relief. It was oddly beautiful, this liminal space.

In the brightness of the entry, the shadow stood next to her. Jo removed her glove and the shadow reached out in time as she placed her palm against a wall etched and scarred by millennia.

"Go in peace, Galena Flores."

36

Jo slid the final item back into the pantry—a Campbell's tomato soup can rescued from the depths of obscurity and now in a new place at the front of the shelf where her father would see it. Finished with the canned goods, she opened the spice cabinet. The Morton salt canister fell into her hands and she placed it on the counter. A discolored tin of Ehlers cream of tartar joined the collection of expired items on the kitchen table.

The phone in her pocket rang and she let it go to voice mail.

She'd cleared Mercy Creek about an hour ago. By the time she'd returned to the station, the admin staff had already left for the day. Pieretti waited for her in his office.

"Go home." He'd held up his hand. "I'm waiting to tell Squint the same thing, so don't argue. Everything will still be waiting for us in the morning."

Her phone rang again. She dug it out and put it to her ear without looking at the screen.

"Wyatt."

"Are you okay?" The connection sputtered, but Aiden's voice cut through the noise.

She'd sidestep the question with a lot of people, but not Aiden. "No, not really."

"I'm so sorry, Jo-elle."

Only two people had ever called her that, and he'd been the first. "Me too." She bit the inside of her lip so she wouldn't cry. "How'd you hear?"

"The *Courier* posted a blurb on their website about hikers finding a body. I connected the dots."

"That didn't take long." The kitchen chair screeched as she dragged it away from the table. "Where are you?"

"Can't say."

She nodded even though he couldn't see her. Wherever he was, it sounded breezy. "I'm looking forward to the next time you pass through."

"It's going to be a bit longer than I thought," he said.

"You know that's not how to cheer me up, right?"

"I miss you too," he said.

Each of his deployments stretched longer than the one before, or at least it seemed that way to Jo. Working for the DEA came with its perks, but agents could be assigned to offices anywhere across the nation, plus a host of foreign countries.

"I know the timing sucks, but the camera in the kitchen shows I have a water leak. Do you think you can get over to the house and check it out?"

"Is this a tomorrow leak, or should I take my sleeping bag and a wrench?" But she was already pulling a trash bag from under the sink to clean up the expired stuff she'd purged from the cabinets in her father's kitchen. Anything to keep her mind busy.

"You know the minute I left for college, Ma redecorated my room for you, right?"

"She always did like me better." Jo missed Aiden's mother almost as much as she missed her own. "Give me an hour before you call for an update. In the meantime, try to stay out of trouble."

"I really am sorry, Jo-elle."

"I miss you too."

* * *

Lupine Ledge Ranch often felt more like home than the house she'd grown up in. It wasn't that her childhood lacked for love. It hadn't. But at the Teague ranch, she came face to face with herself in a way she couldn't anywhere else. These fifty acres had borne witness to everything.

Through it all, there'd been Aiden. As kids they'd run wild, learned what snakes you could chase and which ones would strike back, tested how bad you could get scraped up before Mrs. Teague broke out the iodine, developed profound respect for the power of water after getting trapped in an irrigation headgate. Together they were a murmuration of two. Starlings that twisted and swirled in flight, so closely aligned that it was impossible to determine who altered course and who followed.

The screen door slammed behind Jo with a level of volume that would have earned a tongue lashing from Mrs. Teague. She left the inner door open. A breeze had picked up for the first time in days. The house would need airing.

A flick of the switch held back the gathering twilight, and Jo cut through the house toward the kitchen. Mrs. Teague never met a person she didn't want to feed, and even now the scent of food permeated the house.

The pipes sang as a faucet deep in the house opened and then shut. Jo froze. No one else was supposed to be here. She lowered her backpack and unzipped the compartment that held her Glock, then tucked the extra magazine into her left pocket. A metallic clang rang out. Definitely the kitchen.

Armed, she crept forward.

"Put your gun away and wash your hands. Dinner's almost ready," Aiden called from the kitchen.

Jo stormed through the saloon doors into the kitchen. "Just how many times in your life do you want me to shoot you?"

His lopsided grin was on full display. "Once was enough. Your aim's improved since we were kids, and that isn't a BB gun you're holding." He raised his eyebrow and glanced at the gun now down at her side. "Still holding, I might add."

"I'm deciding whether or not to shoot you." But he'd racked up enough scars along the way without her adding another.

He sidled around the butcher block table that took up the center of the room. "How about a hug instead?"

She stowed her gun on the counter by the phone.

Aiden leaned over and caught her up in a bone-crushing embrace that lifted her off her feet. "You should have seen your face," he said.

Feet firmly on the ground again, she smacked his broad chest. "Ass. What are you doing here? I mean, how . . . ?" She touched his bare cheek with her fingertips. "Your beard." But she was glad it was gone. He had the kind of face that shouldn't be hidden behind a beard—or at least not the bushy mess he'd had for his last assignment.

"I wanted to meet you at the door, but I didn't want to make you cry the minute you entered the house." He captured her hand and placed a light kiss on her knuckles. "I really am sorry, Jo-elle."

The concern in his eyes was too intense and she had to look away. "Me too." Disappointment had a taste: bitter and burning, deep in the back of her throat. "I feel responsible."

"We investigate crimes, Jo. We don't cause them." He pulled her into another hug. Gentle this time, and just held her.

"I know." And intellectually, she did. Convincing her heart was another thing entirely. She ached for the family Lena left behind. No parent should lose their child. And Marisa. That day at the playground, Jo had told Marisa she couldn't blame herself for someone else's actions. But Jo suspected Marisa would always wonder if Lena would have been murdered if Marisa had stayed with her like she was supposed to. Jo understood the guilt. The loop in her own brain kept asking what she had missed, what she could have done differently, why she hadn't found Lena, where she had gone wrong. "It just hurts."

He stroked the back of her hair. "That's what makes you a good cop."

The loop continued. What had she missed; what could she have done; where had she gone wrong? She stepped away from him. "I wish I could have done more."

He reached over a plate of steaks on the butcher block and picked up an open bottle of red wine. "Are you on call tonight?"

"No."

"Good." He poured two glasses and handed her one. "To Lena. May her memory always be a comfort to those she left behind." He tipped his glass lightly against hers.

"To Lena." She took a small sip.

"I know it's getting late, but I'm betting you didn't eat much today." He turned to the stove and lit the flame under his mom's cast iron skillet. "So while I'm making dinner. Tell me, what did you organize?"

"Dad's pantry." She set down her wine and washed her hands, then tore off a couple of paper towels and blotted the steaks dry.

"Did it help?"

"Not a bit. But you saved me from cleaning out the spice cabinet."

"You really need to find your own place. Or move in here. There's plenty of room and I'm hardly ever here."

Move here. After that first kiss, she'd dreamed of a life with Aiden, but the truth was she was scared. Scared that if they ever fell out of love she'd lose her friend as well. Sometimes, when the darkness refused to allow her to hide from herself, she wondered if that's why she married Cameron. To remove the temptation of Aiden.

"Why are you here?" she asked.

"I needed to burn some time off and I thought I'd surprise you. Then I saw the news."

It had been months since they'd shared a kitchen, but they fell back into a comfortable routine.

Jo pulled a stick of butter from the fridge and set it out to soften. "Back in a sec." She grabbed the kitchen shears from the knife block and slipped through the back doors.

Mrs. Teague had always maintained an herb and kitchen garden, and Jo had continued to tend it in Aiden's absence. The basil had gone to flower and was leggy, but she snipped several sprigs of thyme. Under the shaded part of the back porch, she unwound a garlic head from the braid that had been drying since she had harvested the bulbs in July.

Through the screen door, she heard the sizzle of the steaks when Aiden placed them into the skillet.

The ranch had been in the family for generations. Over the years the property had been whittled down. But it backed up to a state wildlife area. From the back porch, the view of the day's last rays hitting the peaks behind the house gave Jo a hint of what Lupine Ledge Ranch must have looked like in its glory days. She'd never own the acreage of the ranch, but someday she hoped to own a place that imparted the same level of peace as filled her here.

* * *

Aiden's leg stretched over the side of the hammock, and his gentle rocking made it difficult to keep her eyes open as they studied the night sky.

"What are you going to tell the chief?" he asked.

They spoke softly as if their voices would somehow disturb the frogs or insects humming by the irrigation ditch that cut across the property.

Tomorrow was the deadline. Her chief needed to know whether she was going to be the next Echo Valley police sergeant. The first woman ever promoted to the rank. "That I appreciate his confidence," she murmured.

He poked her ribs. "But."

She twitched her body away, but her head never left the cleft of his shoulder. "What do you mean, *but*?"

The breeze freshened. Strong and hot enough to chase away the mosquitoes and suck the last bit of moisture from the already parched landscape.

"That you appreciate his confidence is a preamble, not an answer."

She'd waffled for days. Made a pro/con list. Calculated how much more house she could buy with her raise. "What do you think?"

"It doesn't matter what I think." He pointed. "There."

The Perseid meteor shower had peaked a couple of weeks ago, but there were still stragglers and one made a break for it across the sky.

"Dad says I'm nuts if I do. Dakota says I'm crazy if I don't."

"It doesn't matter what they think, either." His rocking stopped. "What's your gut tell you?"

It had been such a long week. Her gut had been taken up with more important things. Things she'd failed to solve, at least in time. "I should become a fed."

He chuckled, low and close to her ear. "I've already told you that."

"Then why won't you weigh in on the promotion?"

He drew her closer. "Because I knew you'd never leave the valley and become a fed."

"I hate you." She yawned and rolled into him, her leg crossing his hips. The hammock bobbled, and he steadied it with his foot.

"No, you don't," he said.

"No, I don't," she agreed.

37

Jo waited in the hallway outside the chief's office and blew her nose. It wasn't the first time she'd caught a cold right after a big investigation. Her body had answered the call. Carried her through the preceding days on adrenaline and determination. Now it needed a break. *She* needed a break. After her meeting with the chief, she'd finish her reports, send them over to Detective Acevado, and with any luck, start the weekend with Aiden an hour or two early.

At 0900 hours, she knocked.

"Come in." The chief stood as she entered, his uniform impeccable. "First lesson. If you're not ten minutes early as a sergeant, you're late."

Perhaps she should have blown her nose louder.

He waved for her to sit. Two buffed leather chairs were angled in front of his desk. She perched on the edge of the closest, careful not to scuff the finish with her equipment belt.

It was the first time she'd been in the office since William Prather had been sworn in as chief. The dimensions remained the same and the built-in bookshelves still lined an entire wall, but the chief's predecessor had been erased, replaced by a person who preferred a beachier vibe that matched his tan.

"I appreciate your confidence in my abilities, Chief." Somewhere Aiden was laughing.

He held up his hands. "Stop right there, because it sounds like you're about to say no to the opportunity of a lifetime. That would be a mistake."

Mounted on the wall behind the chief's chair was a photo of several hundred officers in class-A uniforms lining the steps of an ornate building. The brass plate embedded in the matting identified it as his prior department. A curious choice considering his position in an agency that had a fraction of the personnel.

"Well, I hope it isn't my only chance," she said.

"I'm a bit of a visionary." He leaned back in his executive office chair. "When I moved here, I put a stake in the ground. I assured the city manager that I intended to build a legacy. One that includes promoting the first woman in this agency."

Heaven forbid he suggest she was more than her anatomical attributes.

"Your promotion would be a quick win," he added.

There it was. This wasn't about her. This was all about him. The script she'd intended to follow evaporated. "For whom?"

"Who?" He scowled. "What do you mean, 'for who?'"

"There's a process for promotions. Straying from it would create a perception of favoritism and set a precedent that would be detrimental to the department. So I am curious. How could this possibly be a win for anyone?"

His whole face tightened. "I assumed since you tested for the job in the last go-around you wanted the position."

"I do want the position, it's the timing I've reconsidered. You see—"

"I'll note you've declined the offer. Perhaps Officer Asher would be more inclined."

Jo didn't bother to tell him that Pam was fixing to file her retirement papers at the end of the year. "Perhaps she would."

"You're dismissed, Detective."

If this is how he dealt with someone expressing their opinions, the department was in for a bumpy ride. The radio on her belt scraped the flared side of the chair as she stood. "Thank you, sir."

The door snicked shut behind her. The walk between the chief's office and her own wasn't particularly long, but the path reminded her of the labyrinth in the garden at All Saints in the Valley Episcopal Church. Each turn drew progressively sharper until just when she was close enough to touch her goal, the path veered away once more.

She ascended the staircase to the detective bureau. A few years ago, this had been her goal—a goal she'd worked hard to attain. As Lena proved, happily-ever-afters didn't always happen, but it didn't negate the importance of Jo's job. She wanted to do better.

Squint glanced up when she came through the door. "And?"

"Let's just say it's a good thing I like being a detective."

"Are you okay?"

"I've got a cold." She sat at her desk. It wasn't a gravel circle in the center of a labyrinth, but she'd reached the culmination of a different journey. One that made her gut pretty happy. "But, yeah. I am."

"Can't say I'm sorry." He shuffled through his files and pulled one out of the stack. "I'd hate to have to break in a new partner."

Her eyes watered. Damn summer colds.

"How is Tilda?" she asked.

Yesterday, they'd timed it to deliver the death notifications simultaneously so one parent wasn't informed before the other. Jo had responded to Lucero's with a deputy in tow. Squint drove over to Tilda's with Pam, in case Tilda wanted help from the school resource officer while talking with Marisa.

It was impossible to predict how an individual would react to the news that a loved one was dead. Some cried, others raged, a few needed medical attention after hearing the news.

Lucero had refused her request to come inside, forcing her to deliver the news on his doorstep. Then he'd quietly closed the door.

"About as good as you'd expect," Squint answered. "As an ER nurse she sees more death than most, but this was beyond her. I left after Father Meehan arrived."

Tilda had converted to Catholicism for Lucero, but until Marisa mentioned her mother going to church, Jo hadn't known if Tilda had remained faithful. "I hope she finds comfort."

Sergeant Pieretti came out of his office and walked past their desks. "I'll be downstairs with the chief for a bit if you need me."

"Sorry," Jo said. "I owe you one."

"Yes, you do." He spoke over his shoulder. "Glad you're staying."

Squint leaned forward. "By the way, while you were shirking your duties in the chief's office, I cleared the carny."

"What? How?"

"I checked with all the counties between here and Pueblo to see if he'd become a resident of one of their jail facilities."

"No way," Jo said.

"He never made it out of our county," Squint said. "Shortly after he left the livestock pavilion, he'd also left the fairgrounds—much to the delight of a state trooper who arrested him for DUI and booked him in the county jail."

"It's hard to beat that for an alibi. Does Jesse know?" she asked.

"I already sent him an email."

It was equally important to eliminate suspects as to develop them, but without the carny, who? Lucero? Or was there someone out there who wasn't even on their radar?

Jo opened her notebook and reviewed the notes she'd jotted after her interview with Marisa at the playground. Lucero's bombshell about Lena's backpack had taken precedent, and Marisa's contact was one of the last reports Jo needed to write up.

"Have you heard of the social media platform Threads?" Jo asked as she typed the word into her browser.

Squint swiveled his chair and slid his copy of the Colorado Revised Statutes into the bookcase beside his desk. "I've been on it since its inception. What do you want to know?"

She leaned around her monitor. "You're so full of it."

He chuckled. "Ask a stupid question . . ."

He wasn't one to laugh often, and the very sound of it was often enough to make her join in. It somehow signaled that remaining a detective was exactly the right choice.

The login box on Threads prompted her to create a new account, and she entered an email address specifically designated for poking around social media sites. When she was in, she searched for Marisa's name. The nice thing about looking for an influencer was they made their profiles easy to find.

"Wow." Jo scrolled through the account. "Marisa posts a lot of content."

As expected, there was nothing from today, but yesterday she'd been busy. Evidently, the moratorium on cowboy chic had expired. She looked like she'd walked straight out of a Sundance catalogue. Five posts, three outfits. Leather, fringe, conch belts, turquoise jewelry, sloppy braid in one, flowing locks in another, an off-the-shoulder black dress trimmed in bright embroidered flowers.

Hats, boots, and a pretty girl; it was a winning combination. Marisa had an eye for scouting locations too. Each photo had a different background. A barn door, a wooden corral fence, a hay shed, and an old tractor. The most artistic image had a narrow depth of field so she was in focus, but the barn with its cupola and wind vane behind her was blurred. No doubt about it, she'd hit all the notes.

Jo copied the website and Marisa's user name to add to her report and started typing. When she was finished, she opened a new supplemental report for the SO that documented Jo's presence at Lena's crime scene. She stared at the screen a moment, then closed it. That could wait a little longer.

Instead, she attacked the stack of messages. First up, Olivia Walsenberg.

It rang three times and Jo was bracing for it to go to voice mail when Olivia's cheerful voice came over the line. "Hey there, Detective Wyatt."

"Hey there, yourself." For a couple of minutes, the two caught up, then Jo brought it back around. "I'm returning your message. What's up?"

"I'm friends with Jake Gembrowski." There was the slightest hesitation as if the teen were rethinking her options. "Anyway, he's dating Marisa. Or at least he used to be dating her. This could totally be nothing, but everyone knows Marisa hooked up with this other guy at the fair. Since then she's totally ghosted Jake."

Ah, the angst of high school. "Olivia, I can't—"

"He's not trying to get back with her. I wouldn't bother you with boyfriend-girlfriend drama, but he's worried that something happened that night. Something bad."

Tingler.

"I'll give him a call. Can I tell him we spoke, or do you want me to keep you out of it?"

"He knows I called you. He's a good guy, and I hate to see him all worked up over someone like Marisa."

Someone like Marisa. "It doesn't sound like you're a fan."

"Jake's better off without her. But I don't know her well enough to tell you why. Just a gut feeling."

"I'm a big fan of gut feelings," Jo said. "What's his number?"

Olivia rattled it off. Jake must really be important to her. Hardly anyone under the age of twenty could recite a phone number anymore.

Jo repeated it back. "I've got an appointment over lunch. I'll give him a call this afternoon."

After they said their goodbyes, Jo held her breath and dialed another number.

"Hello?"

"Tilda, it's Jo. I know Squint expressed our condolences last night, but I wanted to tell you personally how very sorry I am about Lena."

"What happened to you working for my daughter?"

It was a valid question. "I still am," Jo answered. But it was a woefully inadequate response to offer a mother whose child was dead.

"Can I have her photo back?"

The little girl with a heart-shaped face and a curious look in her eyes. No one should have to stare at an empty frame. "I'll bring it by after lunch."

"Make it this evening," Tilda said. "I'm visiting my mother this afternoon. And I want to ask you something."

"Of course."

Tilda hung up.

Jo tapped her pen against her blotter several times, then threw it down. "I'm going to try to track down Aaron Tingler at the college."

38

"Sorry, I don't know anyone named Marisa."

Jo's impression of Aaron Tingler hadn't improved since contacting him on the traffic stop. This time, however, they were on his turf. Or at least the turf of the Echo Valley College stadium. "Didn't your probation officer tell you that you shouldn't lie to a police officer?"

He made a production of rubbing his chin. "Wait, is that the local hottie who's all over social media?"

"If you mean this young woman, yes." She held up her phone and flashed one of Marisa's G-rated posts.

"Never met her but I'd like to." He smacked his lips.

Eww. "Let me refresh your memory. She's the one you took down to the river and drank beer with."

"Sorry, you got the wrong guy. I like my beer too much to share."

"I've got you on tape, so I'm just going to pretend you stipulated to that and move on. Did you know she's fifteen?"

"What do you mean she's fifteen?"

If he kept this up, a ten-minute contact was going to take an entire semester. "I'm not quite sure what part of that you're having trouble with," she said.

"That she's fifteen." He wrapped his hands around the rail that divided the stands from the field and stretched his right leg out behind him. "She said she couldn't wait to start taking classes up on the hill."

"In another three years, maybe," Jo said. "You on the football team?"

"Yup."

"What would your coach say if he knew you contributed to the delinquency of a minor."

Tingler abandoned his stretch. "You really are the queen of chicken shit."

She preferred to think of it as using all her resources—especially since it gave her the authority she needed to contact him. "Here's the thing. I've got a lot of options. You, not so much. You see, under state law, contributing is a felony—low-grade, but a felony nonetheless. If I charge you under the municipal code, that section is a misdemeanor, which allows me some discretion." She counted off her arguments. "One, I could arrest you. Two, write you a notice to appear. Or three, if I think the case warrants it, simply issue you a warning to stay away from fifteen-year-old girls. Honestly, if I were in your shoes, it's that last option I'd focus on."

"She put you up to this?"

"I'm here on my own after seeing you dig a cold one out of your backpack and hand it to her behind the livestock pavilion. I also saw the condition she came back in. So this is me offering you some friendly advice."

The age of consent in Colorado was sixteen. However, if a fifteen-year-old wanted to have sex with someone who was less than ten years older, it wasn't a crime—as long as the encounter was consensual. Jo had broached the subject with Marisa at the park. The teen had admitted the hookup, but then became evasive. Granted, there could be a whole slew of reasons she wouldn't want to discuss such a sensitive subject with a cop, but Marisa's body language had made Jo question how consensual their river rendezvous really was.

"How was I to know she was fifteen?" He leaned into a new stretch. "She's got her own car."

"No, she doesn't."

He looked up. "She does. I've seen her driving."

An image of the car in Tilda's garage flashed in Jo's brain. "When?" she asked.

"I'm not a stalker. It's not like I keep track of shit like that."

Interesting choice of words considering where she'd first seen him. "What's your best recollection?"

"Saturday, maybe?"

"This past Saturday?" she asked. A prickling sensation raced across her hairline.

He nodded. "Actually, it was Sunday morning. I was delivering papers."

What the hell was Marisa doing driving around the night her sister disappeared? "What kind of car?"

He pushed away from the rail. "How did this go from her age to her car? Who gives a shit?"

"Humor me."

He was silent for a long moment and then his eyes took on a calculating squint. "This isn't about me any longer, is it? This is about Marisa's sister. That dead girl."

Maybe he was shrewder than she gave him credit for. Or maybe he knew more than he was letting on. "What can you tell me about her?"

"Nothing. Never met her."

"Ever see her when you were taking one of your smoke breaks in their driveway?"

"There's no law that says I have to talk to you, right?" he asked.

She'd hit upon a sensitive subject. "That's correct."

"You interrupted my workout." He flexed his pecs and his singlet jumped up and down. Did men really think women found bouncing man boobs alluring? "But I like you."

Oh, goody.

"Tell you what. I'm going to run my stadiums. If you think you can keep up with me, I'll answer your stupid questions. Do you need to stretch?" he added solicitously.

If he was a receiver, she was screwed. But he carried enough bulk to be a tackle. All beef, little speed. Or so she hoped, anyway.

"I probably should. Being old and all." She brought her left heel back, grabbed her boot around the ankle, and got a handful of fabric along with it. Cargo pants and boots weren't optimum running attire, but at least her vest would act like a sports bra and it certainly wasn't the first time she'd had to run with a gun belt. She pulled her foot toward her tailbone. "What position do you play?"

He bounced up and down on his toes, stretching his neck side to side. "Tight end."

Damn. She stretched out her other leg. Thank goodness Echo Valley College football was a Division II team. On the plus side, she was about to get her first workout in nearly a week, and she desperately needed an outlet for the grief and anger that had been her constant companion since Lena's murder.

"You still look tired. Are you sure you're up to it?" he asked.

"Just fighting a cold."

Ambrose Stadium was built right after the first educational building was opened in 1936 and was named after its most prominent benefactor, Olivia Ambrose—namesake of the teen she'd spoken to earlier this morning. Its size was to accommodate a boom that never quite materialized. But Echo Valley was a town that loved its football, so while the stadium had never sold out, it was always crowded.

Jo leaned against the railing and stretched her calves.

"Stalling?" He grinned.

It was wrong to hope he tripped, but there it was. "No cutting it short when you get tired. Every section, all the way to the end."

His grin grew. "I'm not waiting for you when I finish."

She straightened and swept her arm out. "After you."

They walked to the end of the railing and climbed the few steps from the field to the stands. Aaron shook his head, laughed, and took off like the college football player that he was.

Jo took off after him. Her boots had thicker soles than her running shoes and she nearly face-planted twice before learning to pick her feet up higher. Karma.

There was a rhythm to doing stadiums. Up the bleachers. Down the steps. Move to the next section of seats. Burn. Recover. Repeat until all the sections of the stadium were done.

Tingler ran—hopping noisily from bleacher to bleacher like a three-hundred-pound dragonfly over metal lily pads. He dusted her on his way up the first set of bleachers. Her gun belt bounced against her hipbones as she gave chase. She'd have bruises in the morning.

On his way down the aisle of concrete steps, he winked at her. He wasn't even breathing hard. Bastard.

Tingler held the lead, but he hadn't extended it. And that was critical. There were faster women in her age class, but she'd learned that speed rarely won a foot pursuit. Strategy did—and she was playing the long game.

Most people fleeing from the cops ran an all-out panicky sprint. Arms flailing. Heart pumping. Limbic system in overdrive. It was a hard pace to maintain. More than once, Jo had merely dogged someone until they stumbled to a stop and flung up their arms in surrender.

Tingler wasn't panicked, but he'd probably started off too fast in an effort to impress her. His dragonfly energy had flagged. Now he ran with bumblebee determination—legs pumping to keep his heavy body in motion.

Slowly, she regained the ground she'd lost to his quick start. Thank God he smoked.

Her quads recovered a bit on each descent, but the minute she hit the bleachers again, her muscles burst into flame. Tingler suffered too. His toe slammed against the metal bleacher with the force of a hammer and he stutter-stepped forward, catching himself with his arms on the next bench. The recovery was quick, but he was getting clumsy. Good.

She drew even with him. If she'd truly been in a foot pursuit, this would be the most dangerous phase, when suspects made their decision to fight or give up. She kept far enough away to react in case Tingler juked toward her.

"What kind of car?" She tried to cover how winded she was, but the words still came out as a gasp.

"What?"

He'd heard her. He just wanted her to waste her breath when she had precious little to squander.

"Marisa." Her belt creaked with each stride.

He put on a short-lived burst of speed.

She caught him a second time. "What kind of car she drive?" No points for grammar.

"Sedan."

Well, that narrowed things down. "Color."

"Dunno."

That pissed her off. This knucklehead could hold the key to what happened to Lena and he was playing games. She waited until they were on the straightaway between sections and sacrificed a lung to sprint out in front of him. "I can do this all day." She'd leave on a gurney, but damned if she'd let him know that.

They descended the stairs in tandem, separated by a metal railing that kept them in their own lanes. At the bottom he held up one hand. "Okay.

It's a draw." He interlaced his fingers behind his head to open up his chest and paced back and forth in front of the lowest bleacher. She bent over and put her hands on her thighs, making sure this wasn't a ruse for him to sprint away into the sunset.

Everett Cloud descended the next set of bleachers. He acknowledged her but didn't stop.

Tingler spit. Not at her. Just to get air. "Damn, woman." He coughed and spit again. "I've changed my mind. I don't want to talk to you."

"And I'm thinking it's a good day to make a felony arrest." She drew a big breath so her voice sounded strong and nearly coughed up her other lung. "Let's start over." Her heart still raced, but she no longer thought she was going to die. "Would you please describe the car Marisa was driving?"

He flopped down on the bleacher. "Since you said please." Leaning forward, he planted his elbows on his knees and let his hands hang free. "It's one of those piece of shit gas guzzlers like my granddad drove."

Only in this case it was a grandmother. Marisa's to be exact. "Two or four-door?"

"Four-door sedan."

She wiped the sweat from her eyes. "What about the color?"

He bumped his shoulders. "I never saw it during the day. When she pulled into the garage, there wasn't a light. Blue maybe? Something dark."

"Was anyone with her?"

"Not that got out while the garage door was up."

"Was she carrying anything?"

He leaned against the bench behind him. "Is this going to square us?"

"As long as you don't do anything stupid moving forward? Yeah, we're good. This might even earn you some brownie points."

That seemed to satisfy him. "She had two bags."

"Two," she said. "Like grocery bags or what?"

"One was the stupid-ass giant purse she had with her at the fair. The other was a backpack."

She pictured the neighborhood at four in the morning. "You said it was dark. How could you tell?"

"She opened the door when she came around to the passenger side. The interior light came on."

A part of her didn't want to learn the answer to her next question. Didn't want to contemplate what new horrors this would rain down on Tilda and Lucero. "What can you tell me about the backpack?"

"I don't know. It was a backpack. Like something you'd pick up at an army surplus store or something."

39

A bead of sweat trickled down the back of Tilda's neck. The A/C needed Freon. Another task that could wait. This couldn't. She cracked the car window, but the air outside was as heavy with heat as the air trapped inside her mother's Crown Victoria. It had been stupid driving it today, but she'd given in to a momentary bit of nostalgia. One that would probably go unnoticed despite having nabbed a parking spot visible from her mother's room. Plus, it kept the battery from going dead.

She ran through her speech one more time. Dispassionate. Just the facts. She stared at the odometer reading, distracted by the numbers that were higher than they should be. She turned the key and they disappeared. A secret.

Within minutes, the heat pushed her out of the car and drew her toward the doors. She pressed the doorbell and faced the camera.

The intercom buzzed. "Welcome to Evergreen Manor. How can I help you?"

Laura or Callie? The static made it impossible to tell.

"It's Tilda Marquet, here to see Chantel Marquet. Room fourteen."

"Oh, hey there, Tilda. Come on in."

The buzzer coincided with a metallic click and Tilda entered the foyer of the facility. After the stifling heat of the car, the blast of air-conditioning hit her like a storm front and she shivered. No wonder her mother always complained of being cold. Maybe this Christmas Tilda would finally find the perfect sweater for her. So far, she was zero for two. Four, if she counted the ones she'd bought for Marisa to give her. At least Lena had never given her grandmother a sweater. She always made her gifts.

Tilda scuffed the rubber sole of her shoe across the tile floor and flung her arms wide to regain her balance. Since Lena's death, every thought triggered a memory and each one crashed with a wave of fresh pain, but even more frightening was a future where those memories would fade and at some point whole days would pass without thinking of her daughter, and oh God! What was wrong with her? How could she possibly ever forget her daughter? She pressed her back against the wall and struggled to catch her breath. What had Lena given her last year? Steel bands tightened around her chest. Relentlessly constricting. The foyer faded to sepia.

Paper. Last year, Lena had learned how to make paper. Had turned the kitchen into a pulpy mess. Tilda drew a breath. Pictured her daughter shredding the prior year's Christmas cards in the blender while Marisa teased her about making paper smoothies. Tilda focused on the memory. Drew another, deeper breath.

Once Lena had spread the goop in the frame, she'd oh so carefully embedded pressed flowers into the pulp to create designs. Bored, Marisa retreated upstairs but not before telling Lena that next year she should just buy something. The finished pages were beautiful, but Lena never made another. Now she never would.

A stab of anger surprised Tilda. Anger at Marisa's ability to diminish Lena with a few cutting words.

She swiped her sweaty hair off her forehead, then pushed away from the wall and veered toward the large reception desk to check in.

Callie sat behind a monitor and held out a pen. "Great timing. Your mother's having a good day."

Tilda scrawled her name on the first empty line in the register. When had her handwriting become so shaky? "Is she still trying to trick you into thinking she swallowed her pills?"

Callie laughed but quickly stifled it. So she knew. But of course, everyone knew.

"She's adopted a new tactic," Callie said. "Now as soon as the meds are in her hand, she tries to prescribe them to other people."

Figured. Her mother was notorious for trying to fix things—especially her daughter. "She always claimed being a nurse was the best job in the world."

"She's elevated herself to physician," Callie added. "She's Dr. Marquet now, if you please."

Tilda did not. Buying into delusions didn't make them real. Wishing didn't do much, either. She'd tried that enough times over the past twenty-four hours to know. "Is she in the community center?" She peered through an arched doorway but didn't see her mother seated at any of the tables within view.

"No, she's back in her room. She recently checked out some library books and now she's researching how to prevent brain freezes."

Tilda's attention snapped back to Callie. Was her mother aware of her own decline? "Cognitive or physical?"

"We bought a bunch of Palisade peaches and made ice cream."

"That'll do it." Tilda rested the pen on the register, not sure if she was disappointed or relieved.

"We're all hopeful she succeeds," Callie said. "It will certainly make margaritas more enjoyable."

Sometimes she forgot how young Callie was. They'd run into each other one time at Valhalla, the biker bar at the north end of town. The pickings had been slim that night and they'd commiserated over margaritas. Since then, Callie presumed a level of chumminess that Tilda didn't share and wanted even less. What she did want was to be able to discuss her mother's health care with a professional she could hold accountable, not someone who knew she occasionally drank too much tequila and liked men who didn't ask questions.

"Tilda?" Callie's voice had lost its perkiness. "I heard about Lena. I'm so sorry."

Following the margarita crack, she didn't know what to say and hated the pity she saw in the girl's eyes. "I'll be closing the door behind me today."

"I'll make certain no one bothers you."

Tilda bobbed her head. The path to her mother's door required three hallways and two turns. She'd traveled the distance more times than she'd wanted, passing strategically placed chairs with easy-to-clean slipcovers, the crash carts stowed in closets with the cleaning supplies. The smell of lemon-scented bleach permeated the facility. It was the same scent she encountered at the hospital, and she found it oddly comforting.

The door to her mother's room was open. Chantel Marquet sat at her desk, and while there was an open book in front of her, she stared out the window toward the Crown Vic. Her hair, once impeccably styled, was clean, but now too short to require anything but a towel. Tilda had insisted on the pixie cut. After the stylist had finished, she'd declared her mother the spitting image of Audrey Hepburn. Her mother said nothing, merely stared in the mirror, her fingertips brushing the back of her shaved neck. But she never got rid of the ornate silver comb that once anchored her hair.

"Hello, Momma."

Her mother rose, and with a grace Tilda had never possessed, glided toward the door, her hand outstretched, a broad smile on her face. Tilda's heart clenched.

"It's so good to see you, child." She squeezed Tilda's hand.

The last time Tilda had visited, her mother hadn't even glanced at her. But here she stood, erect and bright-eyed. Something in Tilda's chest fractured with a pain so acute she yanked free of her mother's grasp and pressed both her hands tight against her belly to hold everything in. It was cowardly, but she'd counted on delivering the news to a woman incapable of understanding.

Her mother focused on Tilda's face. "Sit. Please. Tell me what's wrong." She tugged out the desk chair for Tilda, and then perched on the edge of her midnight blue bergère chair.

Tilda didn't dare move. Even a blink threatened to undo her.

Concern clouded her mother's face and she gently prodded. "I can't help unless I know what's troubling you, little one."

Little one. Tilda hadn't heard her mother speak those two words in years, and it gutted her. "Oh, Momma." She crumpled into a heap at the base of the bergère and pressed her head against her mother's thigh. Held her breath so she wouldn't cry.

Her mother stroked Tilda's hair. "Shhh. Nothing can be so bad."

But it was. "I'm so sorry."

"Shush. Tell me what has you so upset."

The words she'd practiced in the car jammed in her throat. Here at her mother's lap, she wanted to be a child again. Free of responsibility, free of the guilt of failing her own child. She started with the county fair and soon the words tumbled against one another. Whole sentences out of order as she tried to recount events she never wanted to think about again. Each word cut until she was drained of life. By the end, she could barely move. Her mother had listened without interruption, her hand never faltering. Her mother. The woman who made things right.

"I think Marisa had something to do with Lena's disappearance," Tilda confessed. "Maybe her death."

The hand on her head stilled. "Why would you think that?"

With the accusation in the open, it was easier to voice her misgivings. "I lost a key. To the car. Your car. Only I don't think I lost it. I think Marisa took it." So many secrets. But then, her mother had always been a master of secrecy. "I started tracking the odometer." Her fingernail scraped across the brocade cushion. "There's only been one time I've been out of the house that Marisa wasn't with me. There's no way anyone could open the garage door and sneak out in the car. Not since that first night." The horror of it washed over her and it became impossible to breathe again and she dug her nails deep into the fabric, and oh, God.

"What did you discover?"

That was her mother. Cut to the chase. It came from a background of quick decisions and stealth.

"Someone drove the car." Tilda's voice was barely above a whisper.

"And you believe that someone was Marisa."

She couldn't bring herself to agree.

"What now?" her mother asked.

Tilda had once been asked to describe her mother with a single word and had settled on discreet. Chantel Marquet had been raised to believe gossip was something for the tabloids. Each word she spoke was carefully selected. People confided in her. Trusted her. It made her a good nurse, but it also made her remote.

"I've already lost one daughter, Momma. I can't," she clenched her fists, "I won't lose them both." But heaven help her. What dark monster hid in her eldest child's breast, and would it turn on Tilda too?

"It sounds like you have a secret, little one."

Tilda could only nod. She'd never truly developed the ability to keep a secret. In high school, she'd chased the adrenaline rush of ferreting out seemingly inconsequential tidbits from people unaware of the value of their knowledge. Secrets were currency. The more secrets she knew, the more powerful and popular she became. After all, the first to tell the story was often the one who shaped the narrative. Unlike her mother, Tilda knew it was worthless to bury secrets. Secrets only became powerful when they were revealed. Shock. Attention. Excitement. Lucero. Jo. Tilda.

"Tell me. What is your name?"

Tilda disengaged herself from her mother's lap. "What?"

"Your name." Chantel stood and went to her desk. "I'm prescribing you something to help calm you down, little one."

"Tilda." She used the chair to push herself upright.

"Oh, that's a lovely name."

"Momma. Look at me. Please. I don't know what to do. Everything has fallen apart."

"Don't you worry." She scribbled on the memo pad. "This should alleviate some of your anxiety. Make sure you take it with food. And get some rest. You look absolutely spent."

"Please, Momma. Come back to me. I need you. I'm so alone." Tilda moved closer to her mother. "I love you, Momma."

"Why, what a nice thing to say." A bird flew past the window and captured her mother's attention. It landed on the side mirror of the Crown Victoria parked outside. "I used to have a car like that." A small sigh escaped her lips, then she was all business again. She grasped her daughter's hand and led Tilda toward the door.

At the dresser, Tilda paused. Next to the silver comb sat a modest wooden frame that displayed bits of pressed flowers arranged decoratively on a piece of handmade paper. She wanted to snatch it and take it home. Care for it, so nothing bad would happen to it.

Her mother tugged Tilda into motion again. "Now don't you worry," she said. "This will be just between us."

Tilda bit back a sob and tasted blood.

A beatific smile bloomed across her mother's face. "Doctor confidentiality."

40

Jo practically skidded into her office. "We've been looking at the wrong person."

Sergeant Pieretti came out of his office. "Why are you talking like you swallowed a frog?"

"You look flushed," Squint said. He stood next to the printer while pages collected in the tray. "Are you okay?"

"I ran stadiums at lunch." She ducked into the break room and came back with a Dr Pepper from the fridge. It might not have electrolytes, but it had a healthy dose of sugar—which, after her little jaunt, she considered almost as good.

"In uniform?" Pieretti asked.

"It's ninety degrees outside," Squint added.

Her head swiveled like she was following a tennis match. "Focus, guys. Geez." She took a long pull of soda and then moved to the whiteboard that hung next to Pieretti's office. "We need to take another look at Marisa."

The printer spat out the last page into Squint's hand. "What did you learn from Mr. Tingler?"

"Not only is he faster than he looks, but he saw Marisa driving in the wee hours of Sunday morning." She uncapped a marker. "And get this, she had a backpack that looked like it came from the army surplus store."

"Need I remind you that we've been down that particular road before?" Pieretti said. "I'm beginning to wonder if the entire family has matching backpacks."

"Or maybe," Jo held up her index finger, "we should be concerned about the girl who has now lied to the police twice about what she was doing on the night her sister disappeared." She pointed the marker at Squint. "What time did the headlights come through on the bear cam? Was it close to the newspaper delivery?"

Squint referred to his notes. "Almost back-to-back, timewise."

"Marisa." She wrote the name across the top of the board and then printed the letters M, M, O down the side. "Put aside for a moment that Marisa doesn't strike me as the type of person who knows much about the surrounding trail systems and think about what she did have going for her. Her mom worked twelve-hour shifts and was gone the night Lena disappeared. Marisa had access to a car. That ticks off opportunity." She scribbled *car, Tilda at work* next to the O. "What about means?"

Pieretti stared at the board as if a little Ouija triangle was going to spell out the answer. "Blunt trauma, right?"

"I left before Doc Ingersleben arrived, but yes," Jo said. "There was damage to the side of her head."

"That could be anything," Squint said. "We'll have to wait for the autopsy results for guidance on the type of instrument used." He ran his finger under his chin. "They were in a cave and it was night, so they could have been carrying all kinds of gear, but definitely a flashlight. Marisa's physically fit. Depending on the weapon, I'd speculate she'd have the strength to deliver a killing blow."

Jo wrote *blunt trauma* next to the first M. "That leaves motive."

"What did Marisa want?" Pieretti asked.

Means, motive, and opportunity were often spoken in the same breath by those outside the criminal justice system, but the words didn't carry the same weight in the courtroom. Not all crimes required proving the accused's intent. But motive revealed the *why* behind a crime. It was human nature to want to know the full story. Motive helped people make sense of horrific deeds and convince themselves such violence would never be visited upon them. The absence of that insight left lingering questions.

"Fame, I would imagine," Squint replied. "She's a self-proclaimed influencer. That in itself suggests a need for attention. Celebrity."

"She already has that," Pieretti said.

"She wants it on a larger scale." Jo wrote *Fame + CA* on the board. "Lucero said Marisa wanted to move to Los Angeles, but Tilda wouldn't even consider it while Lena lived with him. Marisa had been trying to convince Lena to move back. What if she got tired of waiting?"

"It's a good hypothesis," Pieretti said. "And I'm sure the sheriff's office will be happy to follow up on the information and see where it leads. But starting Monday—or earlier if we get a call-out—we're back on regular programming. Plan your caseloads accordingly." He returned to his office.

Nine words, three initials, and some punctuation didn't come close to the elaborate boards that were always in the background on television cop shows. This was a pathetic representation of something that tickled her belly with the feeling of truth. She slid the marker back onto its metal tray.

"It is a good hypothesis," Squint said.

"It's a damn good hypothesis." Jo returned to her desk. "I hope for Tilda's sake I'm wrong." She took another long drink of her Dr Pepper, reached for the phone, and called Jesse Acevado.

* * *

Jo pulled the last tissue from the box and blew her nose. Her ears popped. "What do you make of the backpack showing up at Lucero's? Do you suppose Marisa was angry enough at her dad to try to frame him for the murder?"

"If she's willing to kill a sibling, it's not much of a stretch to think she'd frame her father."

"But how?" She hadn't been able to reconcile this part of the puzzle yet. "Tilda isn't pulling shifts at the hospital right now. So it's not like Marisa could sneak the car out of the garage. And if she didn't have wheels, there'd be no way she could get there and back without assistance."

A blotter calendar covered the top of Squint's desk, and he drew a line through the date. "You do realize this isn't your case anymore."

Squint had a ritual at the end of every day: double-check his calendar to make sure he'd done what he'd planned or rescheduled it; gather any loose notes and append them to the proper file; place said files in their appropriate place; lock his credenza; turn off his computer; and at the very end, place his pen carefully in the little rut every desk drawer had and close the drawer. It exhausted Jo to watch.

"Some cases never end. You told me that." She picked up her empty Dr Pepper bottle for the third time, annoyed that it didn't contain a last swallow. "I have one more phone call to make. Then I'm going to head over to Tilda's. She wanted Lena's photo back."

"I can drop it off. You sound horrible."

"Thanks, but she wanted to ask me something too."

"Would you like me to go with you? Marisa's public enemy number one, now."

"She won't know that until tomorrow when the sheriff's office arrives to impound the car." Jo shook her head. "I'm going to use my cold as an excuse not to go inside. With any luck I won't be there any longer than five minutes."

"Call me when you leave. Let me know how Tilda is holding up."

"I will. Have a good weekend."

He gathered his hat off the rack. "Get some rest and feel better."

She waited until he was down the steps and then dialed Jake Gembrowski's number. It went to voice mail. She left Olivia's friend a message and told him she'd call again on Monday. If he needed to speak to her before then, he could contact dispatch. They'd know how to get hold of her.

A coughing fit took hold of her. She took her coffee mug into the break room and filled it with tap water. After downing half of the contents, she refilled it and carried the cup back to her desk. The chair bobbled when she flopped down, and the edge of her mug glanced against the desk, sloshing water across the tip line messages she'd already returned.

"Goddammit." She dashed back into the break room for some paper towels and blotted at the spill. Somewhere between blotting and separating the messages to dry, the import of her blasphemy hit her.

Marisa had complained that Tilda was dragging her to church each afternoon, but she'd put her foot down and wasn't going anymore. That was Wednesday. The day Lena's backpack showed up on Lucero's property. The day Marisa went cowboy chic.

She pulled up Marisa's Threads account. Checked out the photos she'd posted and printed each one. Then she called up the photos Squint had taken at Lucero's house during the original search warrant.

There it was. The weather vane. In a valley full of deer, ducks, and high-stepping horses, Lucero had a cupola topped by a heron. It was blurred in Marisa's close-up, but the image of Marisa on the tractor had a different depth of field. The barn, cupola, and heron were all clearly visible in the background.

Jo dialed her partner's number.

"Hey, remember when I said I didn't want you to go with me? I've changed my mind. I found photos that put Marisa at Lucero's place the day Lena's backpack showed up."

"Give me twenty," he said.

"See you there."

41

Marisa

Another knock on the front door. Didn't people realize it was after seven and they should give it a rest?

"What do you want?" her mother demanded.

That got her attention.

"Can I come in?" Her father's voice.

Any minute the argument would start. No, thank you. She popped in her ear pods and turned up the music, glad she was upstairs.

Twenty minutes later and in the middle of her favorite song, he knocked on Marisa's bedroom door. Her mother always tapped five times, a friendly rhythm. Even wearing her noise-canceling ear pods, this knock demanded Marisa's attention on a day she just wanted to be left alone.

Sure enough, her father stood on the other side of the door. He hadn't shaved. Probably hadn't slept since getting the news about Lena.

"Marisa. I wanted to talk. May I come in?"

She wasn't used to him asking permission.

"Sure." She stepped aside and waved him in.

He took a step and his mouth dropped open. It was like whenever she invited a friend over for the first time. Whoever it was had a moment where they practically turned green staring at all the stuff vendors sent her before letting out a squeal of jealousy. But her father didn't squeal. He shook his head. But he was a guy. What did he know?

She flounced onto the bed, leaving the pink chair at her makeup table for him. He perched on the edge of the tufted seat. There was something she enjoyed about seeing him so uncomfortable surrounded by so much of her life that he'd never noticed before. He was always too busy with Lena. She lowered her head. She shouldn't think such a thing. Especially today.

"You can't imagine my joy the day you were born. The first time I held you, my heart was so full, I thought it would burst."

She tilted her head. He was acting weird.

"Talk to me about Saturday. What happened that night?" he asked.

Like everyone else, he only wanted to talk about her sister. No one cared how she felt. Marisa drew a big breath. "I wish I'd known when we went to the fairgrounds it was going to be the last night I'd spend with my sister." She blinked several times. "I'd like to think I'd have done some things differently. Maybe I'd have been nicer. Maybe I wouldn't have ditched her."

But she had.

"Was the boy worth it?"

How many people had seen the damn videos from the fairgrounds? Did everyone know about Aaron?

"No, he wasn't." But she hadn't known that then. What she had known was that Courtney was being a bitch. Gloating that she'd scored a college football player. It had been pure poetry to watch Courtney's face while Marisa whispered in Aaron's ear that she wasn't wearing any underwear. Fifteen minutes later he didn't even remember Courtney's name.

"Do you think so little of yourself?" her father asked.

The question surprised Marisa. "No." On the contrary. It had been such a powerful moment. Confirmation, really, of her power to make people believe what she wanted them to think. But she had miscalculated her control of the situation. She and Aaron had cut behind the fairgrounds and sat on the bank of the Animas River drinking beer he'd snuck through the fairgrounds. Before it was even possible, they'd killed the six pack.

"Every day, every photo, you give a little bit of yourself away," her father said. "For what?"

"To be seen." The words came out without thinking and she wished she could take them back. Yet another thing she'd do differently if she had a chance.

Aaron had grabbed her wrists in one hand and rolled on top of her. The uneven ground dug into her back as he pressed his knee between her legs, opening her in a way that scared and thrilled her. He'd released her wrists long enough to unzip his pants and push up her skirt. Shoved aside the thin lace she'd said she wasn't wearing so it cut into the crease of her thigh.

Her father shook her shoulder. "Are you listening to me, *mija*?"

"Yes, Papi. I was thinking about Lena." Her eyes filled and she turned the conversation. "What do you miss most?"

He lowered his head. "She never lied to me." He went on, but Marisa was back at the fairgrounds with Aaron.

The first thrust had hurt. Not at all like romance novels made it out to be. Icy stars slid back and forth across the sky, matching his rhythm until she closed her eyes and tried to hear the river that was inches from her feet.

It's funny what she remembered from that night. How his body had arched, the grunt he made right before he collapsed. The sharp edge of a rock that bit into her shoulder. Finally he'd rolled off her and she could take a full breath. It tasted of mud.

Her father sat next to her on the bed and put his arm around her shoulder, drew her close. "I wish things had turned out different."

"So do I."

Marisa didn't know how long she'd sat with the river rolling past. It was the fireworks that got her moving. Reminded her she had to find Lena. She'd dipped her hands in the river and splashed water on her face, carefully wiping away any smeared mascara. She used her panties to wash away the stickiness between her legs, and then tossed them into the river. The lace lapped against the shore a couple times before the current dragged them into deeper water and they disappeared into the darkness.

No surprise she found Lena with her steer. The carny was a different story. The stuff he was saying to her sister broke something inside of Marisa, and she wanted to bury the pitchfork deep into his chest. Make him pay for something she couldn't pin down yet.

After the carny left, Lena clung to Marisa, shaking. Ashamed she'd wet herself. Her baby sister. Tiny and insignificant. How could this—*she*—be all that stood between Marisa and the life she was so obviously supposed to have?

"What really happened, *mija*?"

His eyes drooped in a way she'd never seen before. He hadn't called her *mija* since she'd been Lena's age. For a fraction of a second she thought he understood. Before her parents split, their arguments had been epic. He'd warned her mom that she'd regret unleashing the monster.

The divorce had trapped him in the valley, too. The minute he'd agreed to split custody, he gave away his right to leave. He was as much tied to this godawful place as she was. But his droopy eyes weren't for his daughter—or at least not the one in front of him.

"What happened when you and your sister left the fairgrounds?"

"We walked home along the river." They'd stopped on the footbridge. The water pulled stuff from upriver across the spillway and dumped it against the tiny island in the center of the river. From the bridge, Marisa saw her panties, snagged in the weeds along the island's edge. Her own inner monster howled and clawed until she couldn't breathe pine-scented air a second longer.

Her father shifted, and the energy in the room changed. "You were always a fussy baby. You grew into a fussy girl. Everything had to be about you. Whenever we celebrated your sister's birthday, your mother and I had to give you a toy of your own or you'd take Lena's. Your sister, she was different. Lena always made you something special so you wouldn't feel left out."

Something crafty and stupid.

He moved back to the tufted chair, scooting it closer to the bed. Leaning forward, he captured both her hands between his as if they were praying together. "Where are the keys to your grandmother's car?"

"Hanging on the hook downstairs, why?"

"I mean the other set, *mija*."

He kept his voice low, but something about it now made her want to go downstairs. Be with her mother.

"They've been missing for a while." She tried to pull her hands back, but he squeezed his palms together tighter.

"I know that. I just had this conversation with your mother. So let me ask again." Sadness crossed his face. "Where is the other set of keys?"

He was a sucker for her smile and she gave him her best. "Papi, I don't—"

He slapped her. Hard across her face. Her head whiplashed to the side.

"What the hell, Dad?" Shock flamed into anger.

He struck her again. "Do not disrespect me, Marisa. I will not tolerate it. Where are the keys?"

Pain radiated down her neck, and she held her hand to her burning cheek. His face twisted, darkened. And she saw the monster he'd warned her mother about.

"I will only ask one more time. Do not lie to me."

Her cell phone lit up on the nightstand with an incoming call. She crabbed backward on the bed, her heels digging into the duvet. "I won't, Dad. I'm sorry."

He rounded the bed and swiped her phone onto the floor before she could answer. Brought the heel of his boot down with a crunch.

The path to the door was clear. She sprang from the bed. "Mom! Call the police."

He grabbed her. Hugged her to his chest. Held her while he cried. "I'm sorry, so, so sorry."

"Please let me go, Dad. You're scaring me."

His hands bit into her shoulders as he held her away slightly. "Don't be scared. I promise I'm not going to hurt you. Just tell me why, Marisa. Why did you kill your sister?"

All the heat drained from her body and she caught her reflection in his eyes. Not her physical face, but who she was at the core. Where she'd got it from. Everyone thought Lena was her father's daughter, but she wasn't like him at all. Marisa was. His demons got passed down to her alone.

"I snapped, Dad. I didn't plan to kill her." Lena had believed Marisa when she'd told her there was a hurt fawn that her friend had found hiking. If Lena had just said no, none of this would have happened. "How did you know?"

"Every photo gives a bit of you away. You should have kept the backpack."

She should have left the den window alone, too. But at the time, she didn't think anyone would believe Lena had run away.

He pressed her against his chest again. "Was this about California?"

"You knew?"

"Of course I did," he said.

"Then you understand. I have to leave this place. I'm meant for greater things." Her head pounded and she was crying. Not the fake tears that made her eyes bright. The kind that would ruin her makeup. "I'm so sorry. Something inside of me just—"

"Snapped." He smoothed her hair off her forehead. "I understand, Marisa. We are so much alike, you and I. Why didn't I see it before now?" He petted her like one of his animal patients. "Shhhh. It's going to be okay."

She sniffled and burrowed her head into the crook of his shoulder. She couldn't believe it. They understood each other. Her pulse slowed. It was going to be okay. Now nothing stood in her way.

In the cave, Marisa had removed Lena's backpack and wiped the heavy metal flashlight against it to clean the blood off. It was stupid but she hadn't really been thinking. She rolled Lena over. The headlamp Lena wore cast light on the ceiling of the cave and caught the glint of some mineral in the rock that sparkled like glitter. Marisa removed the headlamp and her shirt she'd let Lena tie around her waist to hide that she'd wet her pants. Marisa had used the same shirt to wipe away their tracks. Before she left, Marisa covered Lena with the blanket her sister had brought for a fawn that never existed. It was cold, after all.

Lena had beautiful hair and Marisa slid the elastic off the bottom of her sister's braid. Why she always tied it back made no sense. Loose, the silky strands remained crimped, reminding Marisa of the river, flowing through her fingers as she arranged it over Lena's shoulder in a way that hid the blood that trickled from her ear. The smell of rosemary and mint shampoo briefly overpowered the damp, dirty smell of the cave.

That was then. Now that everything was in the open, she could move forward. Plan for California. She'd prove to both her parents that sure, the price was steep, but when she hit it big, it would all be worth it. She'd take care of them. They'd care about her for once.

A wasp stung her bicep. Sharp and deep. She flinched, saw the hypodermic needle. It didn't compute. His grip tightened like a boa.

A roar built inside of her. Loud and all-consuming. "How dare—" Her whole body burned. "Mom!"

His arms squeezed tighter.

Her face was mashed against his shoulder. She bit down as hard as she could. Stomped, strained, kicked. Fought to break his grip.

The syringe dropped to the floor. His strong arms kept her still. "Shhh, daughter. Don't fight it."

"What did you do?"

The burn faded, replaced by a warmth that took over her body. Bit by bit her muscles refused to obey her commands. Then she didn't care. She'd killed her sister. He'd killed his daughter. Both their monsters were loose.

"I love you, Marisa."

He did understand. It made it somehow better.

Her eyelids weighed a ton and she let them close. The last words she ever spoke to Lena were not what she'd told that female cop, but they were still lame. *I think the fawn is around this bend* or something equally stupid. She wished she'd told Lena she loved her, or apologized, or even *Don't worry, I'm right behind you*. But that would have made Lena turn around.

And if Lena had, those eyes of hers would have settled on Marisa and she would have guessed what was about to happen.

But she knew Lena—she was her sister. She would have understood. That made it somehow better, too.

42

It wasn't even dark yet and already the radio chatter was picking up. Dispatch sent Estes to a collision on Mission. Siegel was handling a counterfeit twenty at the Conoco station. Sergeant Begay was downtown making traffic stops. Typical summertime Friday night.

Jo parked down the block from Tilda's place and waited for her partner. Ten minutes and half a box of tissues beyond their meetup time, she called Squint's cell for an updated ETA. No answer.

Estes radioed for another unit for field sobriety tests and a supervisor. A knot tightened in her belly. Estes had a drunk. There were a lot of reasons to request a supervisor, but one was when an officer was involved in the collision. Jo tried Squint's cell again and then tried to raise him on the radio. Dispatch answered and asked her to call in.

Lori answered. "Squint's okay, but he was involved in the collision on Mission. Guy ran a red and broadsided him. You probably heard Estes. Sounds like he's got a DUI. Do you need another unit on your follow-up?"

"Who's left?"

"Currently, no one. As soon as Larson clears, he'll go to the collision."

"Disregard the cover unit. Show me on-scene at Tilda's. I shouldn't be longer than twenty minutes. Tops."

"I'll give you a code-four check at fifteen."

"Thanks," Jo said. "You're sure Squint's okay?"

"The guy who called it in said both drivers were out of their cars. Squint was directing traffic."

"Of course he was," Jo said. "When I clear here, I'll head over to the crash as well."

Tilda's Pathfinder was parked in front of the mailbox. Jo crossed the street and approached the door. The porch light flickered, its sensor befuddled by the alcove and the deepening twilight. Jo knocked three separate times. She'd turned to leave when the door opened. Lucero's frame filled the doorway.

Jo hid her surprise. "I didn't realize you'd be here tonight. Tilda asked me to stop by."

The light guttered like flames across his face. "Can't this wait until tomorrow? Tilda and I are in the middle of making funeral arrangements."

"I'm truly so very sorry for your loss. This shouldn't take but a moment."

He took the photo out of her hand. "I'll give this to her. Goodnight, Jo."

The door swung to close, but she stuck her foot in the jamb. "If Tilda doesn't want to speak to me, that's fine, but she needs to tell me that herself. I'm here for her, not you."

"You never did take no for an answer." He sighed. "Come in. She's in the back."

A muffled scream echoed through the hallway. Jo stepped back. Dropped her hand to her gun. Before she could draw, Lucero clamped her hand, trapping it against her side. He yanked her across the threshold. Kicked the door shut.

Jo grabbed the mic attached to her shirt and keyed her radio, stepping on another officer's transmission. "Echo, David-three. Code—"

Lucero tore the mic out of her hand. He threaded her right arm behind her back, twisting the slack from her wrist. "I'm sorry, Jo."

Dispatch responded, "Units covering. Patrol-four, standby. Other unit?"

She tried to breathe past the adrenaline racing through her body. He had the advantage. His weight. Strength. Unless she could redirect his focus, she was screwed.

"Listen to me, Lucero. I know you didn't kill Lena."

"No, I didn't." He propelled her down the hallway. "Marisa did."

Pain throbbed through Jo's right arm and into her shoulder. "Let me do this the right way."

"I'm sorry—"

Jo raked the heel of her boot down Lucero's shin and spun to the right to break contact. He tightened his grip, increasing the pressure on her wrist until she thought it would break. She gasped and instinctively slapped her thigh as if tapping out in training. Her hand hit metal.

He laughed, but it was full of regret. "State wrestling champ, remember?"

She thumbed open the blade of her pocketknife and slammed it into his thigh.

Lucero bellowed. Raking his free hand through her hair, he grabbed a fistful at the crown and pounded her forehead into a picture frame. The explosion of pain stunned her. He yanked her back and the smashed frame fell to the floor. He pushed her several inches down the wall.

She raised the knife again. Turned her face as far as his grip in her hair allowed. Desperate to disperse the force. Closed her eyes.

Her cheek hit the stud with a deafening crack.

* * *

Jo tasted blood.

She wanted to hide from the pain, but it pulsed relentlessly, prodding her back into consciousness.

Someone sobbed. It sounded far away. Tilda or Marisa? Too far away to tell. Where was Lucero?

Jo's cheek rested on the cold tile. Her hands were pinned behind her back and her shoulders ached. She flexed slightly. Handcuffs bit into her wrists.

The sobbing subsided. Music from Vescent's neighboring townhome traveled through the floorboards and thrummed angrily through her body. She had no idea how much time had passed. The clock was ticking for Lucero. If they hadn't already done so, dispatch would radio her to ensure she was okay. Send officers to figure out why she hadn't answered.

Without moving her head, she ran her tongue along the inside of her teeth, surprised to find them intact.

Someone descended the stairs, their tread awkward. Heavy enough to belong to Lucero. She risked a peek through slitted eyes. Only one opened.

Lucero hit the landing with Marisa hanging limp in his arms. He nudged the door to the garage open with his foot, and then disappeared.

Jo lifted her head. A stabbing pain shot through her shoulder. With her one good eye, she scanned as much of the room as she could.

Tilda sat bound to a chair. Mascara ran from her closed eyes to the top of the duct tape across her mouth. Her chest rose and fell with muffled sobs.

A car door slammed in the garage and then the interior door reopened. Lucero limped toward the living room. A makeshift bandage encircled his thigh. He veered into the kitchen and out of sight. Items clunked and clattered against the kitchen counter as he looked for something. Jo's fingers touched her trouser belt. The roar of realization muffled all thoughts but one: her gun belt was gone.

He turned his attention to the living room again and Jo closed her eyes. Every sound he made brought him closer. Until he made no sound at all and she imagined him towering over her.

He toed her injured cheek. Jo gasped and her eyes sprang open.

"Time to go." He hauled her into a seated position. The room swirled and the volume of the neighbor's music sounded louder.

She focused on a syringe that appeared to have rolled off the kitchen counter and had landed on the floor. One piece of the puzzle fell into place. "What have you done to Marisa?" Her voice sounded raspy.

"She's waiting in the car."

"Waiting." The spikes of pain in her head intensified. "Drugged or dead?"

Out of her periphery, she caught a slight movement. Tilda was following their conversation.

Lucero knelt in front of Jo. A Glock pistol similar to her duty weapon was holstered on his hip.

"Where were you when my baby needed you?" Tears flooded his eyes. "Lena was the only good one among us. She didn't deserve to die alone in the dark."

"No, she didn't." Jo shook her head and instantly regretted the movement. "Don't make this worse, Lucero. This isn't what Lena would have wanted."

"You have no idea what Lena would have wanted." He held Jo's pocketknife. "Have you ever seen a rabid animal, Detective?" He opened the blade and continued. "The sad thing is, by the time you know they're rabid, it's too late to save them. The only thing you can do is put them down."

He raised the knife and stabbed Jo's thigh.

She screamed and the edges of her vision darkened; everything but her thigh blurred.

"Now we're even."

Tilda wailed through the duct tape, fresh tears escaping past her screwed shut lids.

Lucero wiped the blade against his sleeve. "Shut up, Tilda."

Blood soaked Jo's pants. It wasn't pulsing. Maybe that meant something. Maybe not.

"Where's your cell phone?" Lucero asked.

She had trouble looking away from her wound.

"Your cell phone." He shook her shoulder, prompting a new assault of pain. "There's no time for games. Where is it?"

"No cell." Her words had an underwater quality, crashing and receding. "Didn't bring one."

He found the phone in her front cargo pocket and wagged it in her face. "Everyone deserves to be found."

He dragged Jo to her feet, then drove his shoulder into her belly and hoisted her into the air.

Lucero carried Jo past the kitchen island. Her equipment was in a blurred heap on the counter. He paused to pick up her gun. He already had her knife. Where was her radio?

In the hallway, he turned a one-eighty. His body shifted as he raised his right arm.

"No!" Jo bucked.

The retort filled the narrow hallway. Lucero swung his arm back and tossed the gun. *Her* gun. Even through the echo in her ears, Jo heard the metallic clank as it slid across the tile.

Lucero continued toward the garage. Jo craned to see into the living room. The gun was at Tilda's feet and her eyes were wide: with surprise, then fear, then nothing at all. The red stain on her blouse grew.

Gunshots in the county rarely raised an eyebrow. Inside city limits was a different story. The music stopped.

She pictured Glowering Guy next door. Cell phone in hand. Silently begged him to call dispatch.

The music resumed. Louder.

"She was rabid, Jo. All three of us. We've always been rabid."

43

Despite his wounded leg, Lucero carried Jo into the garage as if she was no heavier than a piece of cottonwood fluff and scooted down the narrow path toward the rear door of the old Crown Vic. He turned sideways and Jo's leg smacked the side mirror. She bit the inside of her cheek. She was done giving him the satisfaction of her pain.

Marisa stretched across the back seat, but Jo couldn't see if she was tied.

Jo bluffed. "I thought you said she was alive."

"Dosing a human with a horse tranq is an inexact science. She went down pretty hard." He fumbled with the keys and moved closer to the trunk.

Panic rose like bile.

"Put me next to Marisa. I'll make sure she keeps an open airway. Don't do this. We can work something out. Think of your family. Your future."

He found the proper key and the lid of the trunk rose. Jo drew a breath to scream.

"You'll wish you hadn't."

Lucero dipped his shoulder and dropped her into the trunk. The landing nearly dislocated her shoulder and she whimpered.

He reached into the car and tore off a length of duct tape. "Should have muzzled you from the start." He pressed the strip across her mouth, then slammed the trunk lid.

The darkness pressed against her. Suffocating. She pushed against the duct tape with her tongue, scraped her face against the carpet. Couldn't breathe.

The garage door opener whirred to life. Lucero started the engine.

In the dark of night, Jo sometimes still heard the screams of the girl she'd rescued from a murderer's trunk years ago on patrol. It always sparked other memories. The kick of her gun. The brawl that followed. The terror painted across the face of a girl bound and struggling to breathe in the space no bigger than a coffin. Jo had cut the girl's binding, dragged her from the car. They'd both fallen to the ground, where Jo had hugged the girl while she screamed. This was the hell that girl had endured.

Jo tasted a fear so bitter she started to hyperventilate. She kicked the side of the car. But damn if she'd scream.

"Settle down, Jo."

The radio came on and a rapid succession of talking heads raced up and down the dial until he hit upon a classical music station. An unfamiliar opera seeped into her prison like a requiem. She'd forgotten about this passion of his. She'd once likened him to the operas he favored, by turns pompous and brooding. It brought her back from the edge. He was just a man.

The car backed out of the driveway. The decongestant she'd taken for her cold was wearing off. Her sinus cavity neared capacity. She blew her nose like a horse, not caring where the snot landed.

Fear was a gift meant to keep people safe. It was the quiet voice that whispered stop. Something's wrong. As a cop, she'd learned to listen to her gut, acknowledged her fear. Now she needed to push beyond it. She forced herself to remain still. The darkness and motion disoriented her, and she swallowed against her rising vomit. She flared her nostrils. Struggled for air. All her life she'd been afraid of drowning. How naïve to think it had to be in water.

Sweat trickled down the side of her face. The car was too old to have an interior trunk release. She had to find the tire iron to brain Lucero.

Her leg throbbed, but the blood seeping from the wound seemed to have clotted. She drew her legs up as close to her chest as possible. Ignoring the pain in her shoulder, she pushed her arms down and arched her back. The back of her hands skimmed her butt. She froze, then wriggled her fingers into her rear pocket. Tears leaked out of her eyes and ran across the bridge of her nose, into her ear. Lucero had taken her key ring—she'd seen it on the counter. He hadn't found the small key Aiden had given her that she carried in her back pocket.

Never give up.

She pulled the key from her pocket. Her fingertips explored the base of the cuff until she identified which side had the keyhole and maneuvered the tip of the cuff key toward the indentation.

The car hit a large bump. Jo's head cracked against the underside of the lid. She inhaled sharply, sucking at the duct tape. The key slid from her grasp. She flattened her hands and frantically patted the carpet. A decade passed before her fingers touched the tiny key. It took a good deal longer to jimmy the tip back into the key slot. Finally, the handcuff arm sprang open and she worked her wrist from the confine.

Jo ripped the duct tape from her mouth. She drew in huge lungfuls and set to work on the second cuff.

With both hands free, she started a systematic search of her cell. The spare tire would be the logical place to locate a weapon, but other than the rubber and the rim, there wasn't anything she could pry off to use. Even without being able to smell, she knew the lidless box on the driver side held several road flares, their waxy feel and caps a dead giveaway. But she couldn't think of a way to use them that didn't include burning herself. The only other finds included a piece of crumpled paper and her strip of duct tape.

That left the cuffs.

She placed the loops side by side and grasped the cuffs by the double strand edges, making certain the two teethed strands remained open and forming something similar to the claw end of a hammer. Its effectiveness remained to be seen, but she had surprise on her side.

Jo's shoulders ached from being forced behind her and she rolled them as much as she could in the cramped space.

For this to work, she'd have to think like him. He was expecting a fearful woman, cuffed and helpless in the trunk of his car. She had to capitalize on that brief moment before he realized his error.

She found the duct tape and pressed it to her upper lip, careful not to block her airflow.

They must have passed under a street light. Thick red light oozed through the colored lens of the tail lamps and then faded. She stared at the corner of the trunk and a nascent hope bloomed.

When her dad worked patrol, the fleet was comprised of Crown Vics. Thieves had discovered that by breaking the taillight of the car, they could snake their hand through the opening, pull the interior latch release, and get into a cop's trunk—a quick and easy way to steal rifles and other police equipment. The department had to install metal backplates behind the lights to correct the issue. This car didn't have a latch pull, but based on the murky glow, it didn't have that backplate either. If she broke it, she could signal someone.

She inched her head as close to the driver's side of the trunk as she could, bending her neck to give her more room. With a quick prayer, she arranged the handcuffs over her fist like brass knuckles and waited for an intense operatic moment. As the music swelled, she punched forward with all the force she could muster. The lens shattered and night air swooshed into the trunk.

She peered through the hole. They'd left the city streets behind and were climbing, which put them on the highway to Peregrines Roost Resort, but she didn't see any landmarks to help pinpoint her location. There weren't any headlights behind them, either.

Stress distorted time, but she guessed they'd been traveling for twenty minutes. The combination of the windy road, confinement, and pain made her nauseous. She swallowed several times to keep from being sick.

The car slowed and made a left turn. Through the broken lens, the massive entry gate of Johansen's ranch receded from sight.

Mercy Creek.

Time was not her friend. The twisting road climbed, but he'd be stopping soon. Once past the lower fork of the creek, the pavement turned to dirt and switchbacks hid the road from the world.

Lucero hadn't brought her all this way to open the trunk and shoot her. He could have done that at Tilda's place. No, he had something special planned for her. Something she wasn't going to find very special at all.

She peered out her peephole. The car lurched and the asphalt gave way to packed dirt. Sweat beaded along her hairline despite the chill that had settled in her body. Her whole body trembled.

Never give up.

The handcuffs were her salvation. She threaded her hand through the metal. Grasped the cuffs in a pistol grip. Made sure the tape was over her mouth and placed her hands behind her back. She'd have to be quick.

The tires chewed up the dirt road and coasted to a stop. The engine died with a slight shudder.

Jo closed her eyes against the dark and listened. Lucero opened the driver door. It creaked, and the car rocked slightly as he got out. His footsteps crunched against the stray bits of rock in the roadway and stopped at the back of the trunk. The light inside the car dimmed as he examined the tail lens.

Each ridge of the key clacked as it slid into the trunk lock. Tight bands squeezed Jo's chest, making it impossible to draw a deep breath. The worn hinges protested as he lifted the trunk lid, the sound ominous against the quiet fabric of the backcountry.

The scent of sage and pinion washed over Jo and cut through her congestion. It made her want more—to feel Aiden's arms around her, to make sure Squint really wasn't hurt, to share a beer and a joke with Dakota. Maybe even run stadiums with Everett Cloud. Lucero wanted to take all those moments away from her.

No fucking way.

44

Jo aimed for Lucero's eye, raking the sharp edge of the handcuffs across his face. He reared back, striking his head on the underside of the trunk lid, his hand clutching the torn flesh of his cheek.

"You bitch!"

Adrenaline fueled her body. She drew her legs to her chest and kicked him away from the car before he could slam the lid and trap her again.

On her feet, Jo punched his face, the metal acting like brass knuckles.

His hand dropped to his holster. She aimed a roundhouse at his wrist with her injured leg, but with one eye swollen shut, she misjudged the distance and kicked his forearm.

His fingers tightened around the grip. She charged on instinct. Drove her shoulder into his gut. He stumbled backward but recovered quickly, fumbled for the holster.

She ran.

The dirt road bisected the hillside. She plunged off the side of the embankment and crashed into the chaparral, the tangle of thorny shrubs slowing her progress. She had no light, no path, only a frantic need to increase the distance from her attacker.

Chaparral or boulders?

Lucero plowed through the scrub behind her, his trail easier without having to break through the dead branches of Gambel oak and mountain mahogany. Two bullets sliced through the canopy of pinyon between her and the boulders. Was he trying to herd her away from their safety or did he think she was already there? She would be easier to see against the lighter stone, but harder to hear, and the nooks and crannies of the rocks would conceal her. Buy her time.

And she desperately needed some of that.

Blood seeped from her injured thigh. She drew a deep breath. Released it slowly. She couldn't afford to lose any more blood. Once she got to the boulders, she'd tend it. Now she had to keep moving, stay beyond the reach of his flashlight. Beyond the reach of his bullets. He had fourteen left—unless he'd grabbed her extra magazines.

Snaps and cracks marked her progress as she charged through the brush. A branch poked her face, narrowly missing her good eye. She slowed.

A half-moon emerged from behind wispy clouds and cast its dingy light across the landscape. A game path cut across the ridgeline to her right. She kept low and crept along the narrow trail, tightening her grip on the handcuffs, afraid to lose her only weapon.

The brush thinned between her and the boulders. She held her breath, straining to hear anything over the rising wind to indicate Lucero's location.

Quiet. Too quiet.

She inched closer to the boulders.

By now, someone would have checked on her. Found her car. Forced entry after seeing Tilda through the window and discovered the crime scene. Squint would know—know Jo hadn't shot Tilda even though it was her service weapon at the woman's feet.

Then the manhunt would begin.

But what of Marisa?

Jo's head hurt as she contemplated her options. She could hide in the boulder field and wait for help. But that meant certain doom for Marisa.

A new plan developed in Jo's mind. One that would draw Lucero farther down the hill while she doubled back to the car.

A wave of vertigo crashed over Jo and she stumbled. It receded but left her shaking and unsteady. She couldn't wait to get to the boulders. She stripped off her trouser belt and wound it around her thigh. Pulled it tight over the wound. Pinching her eyes tight against the pain.

She repositioned the handcuffs around her knuckles and set off. The night air dried the sheen of sweat from her face.

A match strike, only louder, drew her gaze up the hillside. Lucero stood at the edge of the embankment holding a road flare.

Jo tasted fear. The Southwest had been in a multiyear drought so severe that even last winter's snowfall hadn't lessened the threat of wildfire. She snapped a twig on the shrub next to her. A decade of dried fuel covered this hillside. It would burn.

The red flame of the flare painted Lucero's ruined face with a demonic glow. He used one flare to light another, and in the light, Jo saw several more sticks at his feet.

"Come out now and I'll make it quick," he shouted into the darkness.

Jo remained silent.

"I thought as much." He heaved a flare down. It somersaulted through the air like a festive pink pinwheel and landed downhill south of her location. It smoldered for a few seconds, and then ignited the duff on the ground. Like a campfire, the tinder flamed and soon the entire bush was alight.

Jo edged away from the flames. Lucero lit another flare and tossed it closer to her position.

He lit another, and Jo knew that before long, all his flares would spread their death on the hillside. If she went lower, she might be able to escape the flames. Like water, fire traveled the path of least resistance. Unlike water, fire climbed uphill. Lucero meant to trap her between the flames and the road. Flush her into the open.

Lucero had a holster on his hip, but even now, she didn't see the outline of her police radio on his belt. She hoped it was in the car. If she had any chance of getting help for Marisa, Jo needed to get to that radio.

Provided she didn't pass out first.

Spot fires swelled. Sparks carried on the wind like fireflies, lighting new blazes, their flames brightening the slope. She had to leave her hiding place before the growing brightness revealed her. She stumbled along the game trail, the noise of her progress muffled by the crackle and pops of burning brush. With only one eye, her depth perception played tricks on her mind and she tripped and splayed out on the ground.

The adrenaline subsided, leaving only pain in its wake. Her leg throbbed, her head ached, she couldn't see. Here, on the ground the air was fresher. She should rest.

No. Marisa was in the car.

Jo struggled to her feet. The distance was still as far, but the prospect of Lucero getting the better of her spurred her forward. She paralleled the road until she was about twenty yards beyond the front of the Crown Vic. The scrub gave way to sheets of slickrock—a canted wall of stone that lacked a boulder's crevices and cracks.

Reluctantly, she tucked the handcuffs into the back of her pants. Hugging the rock, she worked her fingers into the shallow ripples and smudged her toes against the wrinkles. Keeping three points of contact, she climbed toward the road. The pale yellow stone contrasted with her clothing. But like looking past a campfire, she existed beyond sight, hidden by the very flames Lucero fanned to expose her.

Clawing her way to the top of the embankment, she crested at the apex of a switchback. Every instinct told her to flee. Instead, she sprinted as fast as her injured leg allowed and dove under the canopy of scrub on the far side of the road. Now she had a firebreak between her and the flames. But the flames were growing. Filling the air with the acrid smoke of a hundred campfires. She had to get to the car.

* * *

The hillside below the car burned.

Lucero remained a dark shadow against the light, the outline of his stocky body tense and watchful. He had a pattern. Stare down the burning hillside. Scan the dirt road in front of the car. Glance down the road behind it. Only once had he peered at the hillside beside the car, and for a moment Jo thought he looked right at her, but then he resumed his vigil.

She crawled as close to the car as she dared. The keys still dangled from the trunk lock like shiny bait.

The roar of the fire and scream of the wind negated the need for stealth, but even so, every snap, each crack she made echoed like a rifle shot in her ear. She waited for him to repeat his pattern of looking down, right, and left, then abandoned the concealment of the hillside and crept to the trunk.

Her hands shook as she reached for the keys and drew them from the lock. She peeked over the trunk. He still faced the flames. Good. She clutched the keys so they wouldn't jangle and retreated to the rear quarter panel.

Her wounded thigh screamed but she duckwalked to the passenger door and lay flat on the ground, watching his feet. He'd left the driver door open. But through the pain in her head, she couldn't remember if the car had automatic locks. She fumbled for the door key. Tried to hold the keys with her right hand, but her fingers couldn't close around the metal. Lack of depth perception and her left hand foiled her attempts to unlock the door. Precious time ticked by. She pushed herself into a crouch to get a better angle.

Finally, the key ratcheted past the pins of the lock.

The muzzle of a gun pressed against her temple. Lucero's left hand snaked around her shoulder.

"I was hoping—"

She didn't think. Training guided her. She swept the muzzle away from her face with her right hand. Reached across her body and inserted her left hand behind the slide of the handgun. She sprang to her feet and bent over, away from him. The thrust of her hips created space. Negated the difference in their size. She stripped the gun from his hand and delivered two rapid elbow strikes to his gut. Another to his face. Bone on bone contact reverberated through her body. She drew up her leg. Kicked backward with all the strength her wounded body had left.

He stumbled.

Jo spun and racked the slide to ensure a round in the chamber. Pointed the weapon at Lucero.

Redirect. Control. Attack. It had taken mere seconds.

"Get down on the ground." Her voice sounded hoarse.

Blood poured from Lucero's nose and he held his side as if to brace a broken rib. "No."

Oh dear God.

"I will shoot you." Jo sighted on his chest. Center mass.

He smiled and the boyish expression she knew so well fell across his face. "I'm counting on it."

"Get down on the ground, Lucero."

"Lena didn't deserve to die. Marisa doesn't deserve to live."

"You're right. Lena didn't deserve to die. But what happens to Marisa isn't up to us."

"I'm her father. Who better than me?" He held his hands in the air. "Shoot me, Jo. After all I've done? You know you want to pull the trigger."

Her finger tensed against the curved metal, removed the slack.

"It would be so very easy," he said, as if reading her mind.

"Seven and a half pounds of trigger pull. Now get on the ground. You're under arrest."

He took a step forward.

Jo retreated a step. "You only get one of those. Get on the ground."

"You're just like me."

"I'm nothing like you."

He laughed. "You will be when you shoot."

He took another step. The gun bucked in her hand, but she didn't hear a thing over the thumping of her heart. The roaring of the flames. A blood stain grew on the right side of his chest.

"Get down on the fucking ground."

He clutched his chest but stayed upright. "I told you."

He took another step toward Jo and she fired again. She wanted to empty the magazine. Make sure he never got up. Kill the bastard. He swayed and crumpled onto his haunches.

Jo trained the sights on his chest, but the barrel shook. "Put your hands on your head." Smoke made her cough.

"There's no one watching you, Jo." Blood soaked the front of his shirt. "I loved you, once." He pulled at the cuff of his pants and Jo shot a final time. He tipped over, a round hole in his forehead.

The gun slipped from Jo's hand and she left it in the dirt. A pool of blood puddled around Lucero's head. She rolled him onto his stomach and cuffed his hands behind his back. Policy.

She was forgetting something. Her thoughts refused to focus.

The gun in the dirt reminded her. Search. She ran her hands down his body, removed the pea-shooter from his ankle holster.

The ebb and flow of adrenaline left her exhausted. The belt around her thigh appeared to be soaked, but she couldn't figure out with what. The ground shifted under her, and she fell against the car. Nerves cramped her stomach and she doubled over, gasping for breath.

So tired.

A metal glint drew her good eye to the key dangling from the door lock. Jo tugged the handle. Nearly fell backward when the heavy door opened. She unlocked the rear door. Felt for a pulse in Marisa's neck. Left her tied and closed the door.

Jo collapsed into the front seat. The bench seat beckoned. She stretched out and her hand brushed over her cell phone wedged in the seat crack. She stared at it. There was something important she still needed to do.

The roar of the flames filled her ears. They licked the road.

Hungry.

45

She breathed in his cologne. That combination of sandalwood and soap that always wrapped around her like a blanket. Assured her she was safe.

Stubble scuffed her cheek. A deep voice. His voice. Soft as a breeze by her ear.

Jo-elle.

Calling to her with words that made no sense but drew her back.

Gave her courage.

A kiss on her forehead. A softer kiss on her lips. The wet taste of salt.

Aiden.

But he was gone.

* * *

Jo roused. The room came into focus slowly and seemed to be on a slightly wobbly axis. An alarm sounded behind the bed. She didn't care.

Motion behind her. She still didn't care.

Squint moved into her field of vision and checked the oxygen clip on her fingertip.

"Tilda?" Her mouth seemed out of sync with her brain and the word formed slowly.

"You're awake."

"You should be a detective."

He smiled, a rare expression that meant only one thing. She was going to die. "Why do I taste soot?"

"How are you feeling?"

Too many bandages seemed to be wrapped around bits of her body. She'd have to take inventory.

Later.

* * *

The next time Jo woke, light from the nurses' station sliced through the door. The ward outside was quiet. Nighttime, but how late, she couldn't tell.

She craned her neck to find a clock. Pain erupted in her head, erasing the fuzziness and leaving her queasy. Gingerly, she began to take stock of her situation and wiggled the fingers on her left hand. Good. Her right arm was in a sling, and a splint immobilized the fingers on her right hand. She lifted her arm to determine the damage and a searing pain shot across her shoulder. At least the hand was only splinted, not cast. Still, even in the half-light, the discoloration of her fingertips was obvious. Sweat broke out on her upper lip, but she rotated her wrist anyway. Stupid move.

Steeling herself, she contemplated her legs. She didn't bother to move her left leg. She remembered the sickening feel of the blade piercing her thigh. She'd just found the courage to move her right leg when her father walked in carrying a magazine and a cup of coffee.

"You're awake."

"I am." Her voice sounded scratchy and she couldn't draw a deep breath.

"We had a bet who'd be with you when you finally came out of it."

"Guess you won."

"Aiden got called back to work, or no doubt it would have been him. He never left your side. But true to form, you waited until you were alone. Out cold for twenty-seven hours and you wait for me to grab coffee."

Aiden gone. Over a day. Lost.

Her father dropped his magazine between two floral arrangements on the overbed table. "Squint claimed he won, but you didn't stick around long enough for it to count. How are you feeling?"

"Like I got run over by a truck."

"Sounds about right, since you got run over by a truck. Literally."

The fuzziness returned. "I don't remember that."

"Doc says you may not remember a lot of what happened."

What had happened? She closed her eyes to think.

* * *

Jo knew it was sunny before she opened her eyes. The room had the cloying scent of a florist shop—better than smoke, but not by much. She heard a muted musical fanfare and cracked her eyes to find Dakota folded in the bedside chair, engrossed in a game of Angry Birds on her iPhone.

"You're awake," Dakota said.

"Why does everyone lead with that?"

Dakota's brow scrunched. "Is this a riddle?" She stowed the phone in her pocket. "How do you feel?"

"Like I'm stuck in *Groundhog Day*."

Dakota leaned closer and placed her hand on Jo's forehead. "Do you want me to call the nurse?"

"I'm going to sleep now."

* * *

The smell of bacon woke her up. The searing pain in her shoulder had dulled to a nagging ache. She opened her eyes. Her vision seemed different. It took a moment to realize she had sight in both eyes again.

Squint stood next to her overbed table eating the bacon off her breakfast plate.

Before he could say anything, she blurted, "I'm awake. I feel like shit, and I'm hungry."

"I'm sacrificing myself for you. This stuff will kill you."

"I'm pretty sure it's turkey bacon. This is a hospital."

"That explains the taste." He dropped what was left of the strip onto the plate. "You just missed Pieretti, again. This time he was here with the chief, so maybe it's a good thing you were out cold."

"Squint, what happened?"

He wiped his hands on a napkin and watched Jo's face as he spoke. "Lucero's dead."

She was on the hillside again, the hot flames licking the roadway, the acrid smell filling her lungs. The gun kicked in her hand—three times.

"I'm tired," she whispered.

Squint squeezed her good hand. "Go to sleep. I'll be here when you wake."

* * *

Dr. Dibyendu scanned the updates on Jo's chart and a vertical line formed between her brows. "You're not eating."

Jo had an unreasonable desire to please her and held her tongue about the appeal of turkey bacon.

Dr. Dibyendu plucked a foot-shaped cookie from the basket with an assortment of goodies and handed it to Jo. "Perhaps this is better?"

Jo accepted it with her left hand.

"Can you read it?" the doctor asked.

Clumsy cursive writing covered the front of the cookie. "Hope you're on your feet soon."

"Any double vision?"

Jo shook her head and immediately wished she hadn't. "No."

The doctor scribbled notes.

"So how bad is it?" Jo asked.

"I haven't decided if you are brave, lucky, or stupid." Dr. Dibyendu peered over the top of her glasses. "But I know for certain you are very, very tough." She hung the chart at the foot of the bed and leaned over Jo. "You were unconscious when the medics brought you in. You had lost a lot of blood, mostly from the knife wound. Fortunately, there was no tendon or ligament damage. It's going to hurt for a while," she smiled kindly, "but something tells me that's not going to slow you down."

"And my face?"

"Based on the swelling and the location of the injury, the concern was a zygomatic fracture, but the CT results were negative."

Squint sauntered into the room. "Might have something to do with the thickness of her skull."

The doctor raised an eyebrow. "I'm sorry, we are discussing medical information."

Jo raised her good hand. "It's okay. He's family."

"As you wish. Your clavicle is broken—hence the sling—and you have a distal radial fracture in your wrist. An orthopedist will want to see a CT scan to better access the pattern of the injury, but based on X-rays, I'm fairly confident it's going to require surgery. As with any wound or injury, infection is the largest concern." Dr. Dibyendu patted Jo's forearm, careful to avoid the IV line. "The best thing you can do right now is rest and let your body heal. I'll be back in a couple of hours to check in on you again."

"Thank you."

Alone with Squint, she didn't know what to say. Silence filled the space, creeping into the crevices and around the flowers that littered the room. An arrangement of white lilies reminded her of a funeral arrangement. She shuddered. She'd come so close.

Squint noticed when her eyes went to the nightstand. A dog-eared *Fire Department Equipment and Vehicle Identification Manual* sat atop a stack of magazines. "That's from Station Two. They figured if you knew what their rigs looked like, maybe you wouldn't jump in front of one as it was responding to a fire."

"Is that what hit me?"

"In their defense, they tried to stop."

"I don't remember that part." There was so much she still didn't remember. "Tilda?"

"Alive. Vescent called nine-one-one. Officers were already en route to check on you. Otherwise, she would have bled out."

"They must have just missed us."

"I imagine so." He cleared his throat. "Marisa's at the juvenile facility. Lucero sedated her with ketamine, but she's okay now. Considering Lucero's destination, I'm sure you saved her life." He paused. "You may be interested to know that a young Mr. Jake Gembrowski called me after he heard what happened to you. The short story is he'd found the cave in June. The only person he showed it to was—"

"Marisa," Jo whispered. "The window was a ruse, wasn't it?"

"It was. Marisa thought it would confuse the investigation." Squint placed his hat on the manual. "When you're ready, you'll need to give an official statement."

She closed her eyes against the manual, against the flowers, against Squint.

"Will you ever forgive me, Jo?"

Her eyes flew open. Anguish reddened her partner's eyes, but he didn't flinch from her gaze.

"I should have been there," he said.

"Squint. None of this is your fault. None of it."

"You almost . . ."

"But I didn't." She clasped his hand and held it against her cheek for a long moment. Her stomach growled.

"How long since you actually ate anything?" he asked.

"How long have I been here?"

He dug through the care package basket. "Soup?"

"When there are more cookies?"

Squint opened a bag of Oreos—had to have been from Dakota—and handed her a cookie, took one for himself, and placed the bag next to her on the bed. "Off the record? Nice head shot."

Jo held the cookie with swollen fingers and twisted the Oreo apart with her good hand. "Not really, I was aiming center mass."

46

Two Months Later

The outfit Jo had chosen was simple. A black turtleneck, gray wool pants, a pair of low-heeled boots. She wore pearl earrings that had once belonged to her mother. Underneath the sweater, the tiny handcuff key that Aiden had given her hung above her heart on a chain that looked more delicate than it was. Once she received the clearance to return to full duty, it would again be placed in her pocket.

Risk was something police officers accepted. Jo had never been one to think she was immortal, or that because she wore a badge and carried a gun she couldn't be hurt. Having it proven, though, left scars every bit as deep as the ones on her body. They just weren't as visible.

Here, on the knoll, she was ringed by towering blue spruces. Artfully placed linden and maple trees added a celebration of golds, oranges, and reds. The breeze lifted her hair and she tucked a strand behind her ear. The sun set earlier now. Dusk had arrived.

Jo had missed Lena's funeral. Today was something different. Something private between a detective and the child she'd hoped to save. Even knowing Lena had been killed before she'd been reported missing didn't alleviate the ache that accompanied her ending.

Every investigation had a moment when everything Jo thought she knew turned on itself to reveal a deeper truth. Like Everett Cloud's view that a single fact wasn't emblematic of a larger whole. One piece, in isolation, did not reveal a puzzle. It was the same with life. Every time she thought she had it figured out, something unexpected came along.

But that was okay. It kept things interesting.

“It’s getting dark,” Aiden said. “They’re waiting on you to close the gate.” He wrapped his arm around her and she leaned against him, taking the weight off her injured leg. Physical therapy had been brutal this week.

Maybe it was odd to want to hold tight to the memory of a little girl she’d never met. Perhaps, in truth, Lena was merely a piece of a greater puzzle and Jo had to turn over more pieces before she’d understand what motherhood meant to her. What measures she’d take if someday she had her own child to protect.

Other memories she wanted to forget. The sound of a trunk closing still jerked her from sleep. More often, she’d feel Lucero’s presence while awake. He’d been wrong about many things, but he was right about one; she’d wanted to pull the trigger that night. She hadn’t thought of justice, revenge, or what he was trying to do to his daughter, only that she wanted to live.

She stepped out of Aiden’s embrace and placed the bouquet in front of the small stone that bore Lena’s name. The sage green ribbon wrapped around the stems had small teeth marks in it—courtesy of the kitten formerly known as “Cat.”

Lena would like that.

Acknowledgments

The bones for this book were conceived prior to the pandemic, but the story itself was written in the Year That Shall Not Be Named and the labor was difficult. Some authors found quarantine to be an opportunity to increase their word count. I did not. For long stretches of time, the words simply weren't there—and that turned out to be a good thing. I sat with this story, got to know it better, and when the time came, I was able to tell it properly. Now it's in your hands and I want to thank you and all the readers, librarians, and booksellers who have chosen this book.

From start to finish, a lot of people contribute to the creation and publication of a book. I'm grateful to all the smart, talented, and supportive people who shared their time, expertise, and Zoom links with me. Of course, any mistakes are mine alone.

My thanks to Daniel L. Bender for sharing his wonderful photographs of "Echo Valley."

To Russ Walkowich for his knowledge of all things IT, his wry wit, and the occasional smile.

My understanding of medicine is limited to air goes in and out, blood goes round and round, and any deviation from this is a bad thing. Thankfully, Dr. Deidre Anastas cheerfully shares what to do about the bad things I cook up for my characters.

Thanks also to Lon Davis—your southernisms crack me up, your support is enormously appreciated, and I really do hope you figure out a way to get my books into the hands of Drew Barrymore.

My gratitude to the inspirational troublemakers I'm proud to call friends: Norma Hansen, Autumn Blum, Laura Oles, Sue Duffy Schwall, and Janean Acevedo Daniels.

A heartfelt thank you to my agent, Helen Breitwieser—your guidance has been indispensable and I can't wait to see what our future holds.

To my editor, Faith Black Ross: thank you for believing in my stories. My appreciation also to the entire team at Crooked Lane Books, with a special shoutout to Madeline Rathle and Melissa Rechter for keeping everything on the rails, and to Nicole Lecht for her covers.

My deepest appreciation to my critique partner and dear friend, Mandy Mikulencak. I can't imagine being on this journey without you.

The writing community is populated with incredibly generous people. As a member of Sisters in Crime, Mystery Writers of America, and International Thriller Writers, I've encountered countless people who have made my path a little (or a lot) smoother. You know who you are—and I can't wait to see you again at the next in-person writers conference!

I come from a very small family, but I married into a close-knit clan of Coloradans and I love you all.

To my dearest David: there is no one else I could have quarantined with who wouldn't have driven me to practicing criminal activity instead of writing about it. I love you dearly.